Life Between the Lines

Diane Greenwood Muir

Cover Design Photography: Maxim M. Muir

CONTENTS

ACKNOWLEDGMENTS

Last spring, a friend posted pictures of a donkey at church for Palm Sunday. I asked questions and discovered Lusco Farms Rescue in Malvern, Iowa. My friend told me I should introduce donkeys into the Sycamore House family and the more I watched what Lusco Farms did for the animals, the more I knew she was right. There are a lot of great rescues out there, but I love seeing what this group does for donkeys ... and goats, ponies, mules, dogs and cats and whatever else shows up. They're awesome and have been very helpful when I asked crazy questions – like what does a donkey's ears feel like? (Soft and fuzzy).

Vikki O'Hara pointed me to the donkeys and is also a Master Gardener. Last summer, she gave me a wonderful information on what could happen in a garden the size of Polly's. I owe her a great deal of thanks.

A very special thank you to Rebecca Bauman, Tracy Kesterson Simpson, Linda Watson, Nancy Quist, Carol Greenwood, Alice Stewart, Edna Fleming, Fran Neff and Max Muir for continuing to help me tell my stories. I am always surprised at the care they give to my books when they proofread and edit and I have the best time reading their comments and asides, knowing that they want things to be written well. Without them, this would be impossible..

CHAPTER ONE

The low growl coming from her dog woke Polly out of a sound sleep. Obiwan's ears were straight up and he was poised, ready to jump. Both cats were perched on the edge of her bed, fully alert and facing the front room of the apartment.

"What is it?" she whispered. Then she heard an insistent rapping at the front door. She checked the time. Three-eighteen.

"Who wants what at this hour?" she asked and sat up. Bearing responsibility for the needs of demanding guests was annoying sometimes. When she moved, the cats jumped to the floor and slowly crept into the living room. Obiwan continued to growl as she grabbed her robe from the foot of the bed and swung around to plant her feet on the floor.

She wrapped the robe around her, covering the shorts and tank top she usually wore to bed, then dropped her phone into the robe's pocket. Obiwan followed as she flipped on lights and went into the entryway.

"Who's there?" she asked.

A faint "Polly" was the response. Whoever was out there didn't sound threatening and she unlocked the door.

"Oh no!" she cried out, dropping to her knees. "What happened?"

Thomas Zeller lay on the floor, clutching his midsection. The blood covering his hands had soaked through his shirt and jacket, seeping down into his pants.

"Thomas!" she cried.

He reached out and when she took his hand, felt him press something into hers. "Take this. For you. No one else. Find him."

"Find who? Who did this to you?" With her other hand, she fumbled in her pocket for the cell phone.

He squeezed the hand he held. It was barely noticeable. He had no strength left. "In there."

His hand relaxed and fell away and his body slumped. Whatever he'd given her, she slipped into the pocket of her robe so both hands were free.

"Thomas!" she cried again. "Thomas!"

She leaned in when he didn't respond. There was a faint scent of alcohol, but it wasn't overpowering. She heard no breathing, so she checked for signs of a pulse. This just couldn't be happening.

With a deep breath, she slid to the floor and leaned against the doorsill. Obiwan attempted to step over her to sniff the man, but she pushed him back. "No. Sit. Stay," and she created a barricade with her legs.

"He's not going to believe this," she said to her dog, scrolling through her contacts. "I don't want to make this call."

She dialed the phone and a sleepy Sheriff Merritt answered with, "Polly? It's three in the morning. Is this what I think it is?"

"Aaron, I'm really sorry about the hour, I really am. But I don't know who else to call."

"If this is another body, I'm buying you a grim reaper costume for Halloween."

"Oh Aaron, Thomas Zeller just died outside my apartment. There's blood all over him. I think he's been stabbed."

She heard his wife's voice in the background and then heard him say to her, "Go back to sleep, Lydia. You can take care of Polly in the morning. I'll take care of her tonight."

He returned to the conversation. "I'll call the squad. Stu Decker and I will be there as soon as possible."

"Thank you Aaron. I'm so sorry. Is Sarah on duty tonight? She knows how to get up here and I'll have the front doors unlocked."

"I'll let them know," he said. "We'll be there soon."

Polly opened the app on her phone that controlled the locks at Sycamore House and unlocked the main doors. She turned the downstairs lights on and with one more press of a button, lit the upstairs hallway. With all the lights on, she saw a trail of blood coming from the middle bedroom where Thomas Zeller had been staying for the last month.

"What happened, Thomas?" Polly asked the man on the floor.

They'd had lunch yesterday and he hadn't seemed worried or stressed. In fact, he told her he was nearly finished with his novel and would be staying one more week. It was time for him to return to reality. There was a movie deal in the offing and he needed to spend time hammering out the contract. He was looking forward to the financial freedom it would offer and was a little giddy at the opportunity to hob-knob with celebrities. Those had been his words. After all that had happened in his life, he told her it was as if all his dreams had finally come true.

Obiwan settled his head on Polly's thigh and she stroked him as they waited for people to arrive. He came alert before she heard the snick of the front door opening. She stood up, kept her hand on his collar and gave a weak wave when Sarah and another young man came up the last steps.

"You need an elevator, Polly," Sarah laughed. "I don't like carrying bodies down this many stairs."

The young woman knelt beside Thomas, checked his pulse and looked up, "You did it again, didn't you?"

Polly bit her lips and breathed loudly through her nose. "They just keep finding me. Maybe the world knows that the sheriff's wife is my friend and I'll call him for help."

"It's nice to know the universe needs you," Sarah said, "even if it's so that you keep Aaron and the rest of us employed."

"My job is safe without this girl bringing me extra bodies,

Sarah," Aaron said as he strode across the floor of the upstairs hallway. He looked down at the scene. "Oh Polly, what have you gotten yourself into this time?"

"I don't know, Aaron, He's been staying in the room across the hall for the last month. I've enjoyed getting to know him." Polly's eyes filled with tears. "This time, he's a friend."

"I'm sorry, Polly. Would you like me to call Lydia?"

"No, that's fine. I'll talk to her tomorrow."

"She wanted to come. She's desperate to hear from you."

Lydia, Beryl Watson and Andy Saner had met Polly and Thomas for lunch at the local diner one afternoon last week and he'd entertained them with tales of his travels and all the interesting people he had met while searching for his stories. This would be difficult for everyone.

"I'll give her a call. I promise," Polly assured him.

Stu Decker came up the steps, "Sorry, boss. I was caught on a domestic. What do we have here?" He quickly took in the scene, "Why don't I call in the team for you and we'll get started. Anything I should know?"

"That was his room," Aaron pointed across the hall. "Right, Polly?"

She nodded and looked down at the dog. "Let me get Obiwan inside." She walked back into her apartment, tugging his collar. "I'm sorry. You can't play with people tonight." She quickly ran to the kitchen and washed the blood off her hands.

When she got back out to the hallway Stu was standing in front of Thomas's room. "Can you open this, Polly?"

"Sure," she swiped the app to unlock the door.

"How much information does that app have on the doors around here?" Aaron pointed to her phone. "Can it tell us who opened which doors and when?"

"I suppose so," she said. "I've never used the tracking feature. It will be easier to access it on a computer, though. I can do it from my laptop or we can go downstairs."

"Let's go on in to your apartment. Do you mind?"

"I guess not."

"You know, you could make me get a search warrant for this information," he said quietly.

"I'm not going to do that, Aaron. I trust that you'll do the right thing and tonight, the right thing is finding out what happened to Thomas."

Aaron followed her into the apartment.

"I'll bring it to the dining room table," she said. He sat down to wait while she retrieved the laptop from her bedroom. She and Henry had been on video chat the night before. He was in Michigan delivering furniture he had refinished for his sister. It was nice being able to talk with him before she went to sleep, even when he was far away. He had asked her to go along, but she didn't feel like she could leave Sycamore House. Jeff Lindsay, her assistant, and Sylvie Donovan, one of her best friends and Sycamore House's chef were planning their big first anniversary Halloween Ball. It was happening in just two weeks and being gone for four days was more than Polly thought she could handle.

She sat down at the table and waited for the laptop to power up. "Do you want some coffee?" she asked. "I'm so sorry I woke you in the middle of the night."

Aaron rolled his neck and shoulders. "I'm fine and quit apologizing. It's my job."

"Here's the program," Polly said. "I'm not sure what I'm looking for."

"Why don't I make coffee and you figure this out," Aaron stood up and walked into the kitchen. "Where's the coffee?"

"You'll see it in the jar right behind the pot." She turned back to the program and began clicking through menus. "Stupid thing, when I need you to be intuitive, you escape me."

"Take your time, Polly. If it's there, you'll find it."

"Here it is. I found it."

Aaron flipped on the coffee pot and sat back down. "Okay, tell me what's what."

"These are the individual rooms." Polly pointed at the screen. "Here is the front door and the side door. This is the kitchen door and the door to the garage. And here is the main door of the new addition and its back door."

"It looks as if these are all the times when those doors were accessed. Can you tell who was using their keys?"

Polly pulled up another screen. "Uh huh. Here are the access codes for the keys each person has. This one is different because we had to program a card for it. The guy in the front room of the addition doesn't own a smart phone."

"I'm going to want a copy of this data. Can you do that?"

"If I can't, I'll call the company in the morning and have them help me," she said.

The two of them compared key usage and saw that the evening had actually been quite busy. Thomas had returned to Sycamore House about one fifteen in the morning. He'd accessed the front door and gone straight to his room. Then he accessed his room again twenty minutes later. Polly assumed it was a bathroom run. The guests on either side of them had accessed their rooms several times between ten thirty and midnight and the three guests over in the addition had been in and out until midnight as well.

"You have house full of night owls," Aaron remarked.

"I know," she said. "None of them are ever interested in breakfast until after nine o'clock."

"You know we're going to have to wake your guests on this floor, don't you?" Aaron asked.

"I suspect they're already awake," she said. "There's no way they could sleep through this much activity."

"Sheriff?" Stu Decker stuck his head in the door. "The team is here and they've started working the scene. There's a lot of blood in his room, so that's where the poor guy was hurt. Sarah says that with that gut wound, she's surprised he made it across the hallway to your apartment, Polly."

"Anything that gives us a clue as to who or why?" Aaron asked.

"'Nothing yet, but we're just getting started. Do you want me to wake people up?"

"We're going to have to. Polly can you tell us the names of people up here?"

"Grey Linder, a poet, is in the back room and Lila Fletcher is in the front room. Do you want me to knock on their doors or anything for you?"

"You're really not dressed for company, Polly," Aaron chuckled. He walked over to the coffee pot and poured a cup, then handed it to her. "Lydia would have my head if she knew you were out and about dressed like that."

Polly gasped when she realized the robe had come open at the top. She was dressed underneath it, but not in much. "Whoops!" she said. "Sorry. Let's not tell Lydia, okay?" She drew the lapels back together and tightened the belt around her waist. "Do you want coffee, Stu?"

"Maybe later. Could I use the conference room?" he asked.

"Of course. Let me change clothes and I'll run downstairs and start the coffee in the office."

"Thanks."

Polly set her mug on the table and trotted into the bedroom. In a flash, she changed into jeans and a sweatshirt. When she opened the door to the hallway again, she was shocked at the transformation. Sycamore House looked like a television crime show. A photographer was shooting pictures of Thomas Zeller's body while the EMTs waited to load it for transport. One person was dusting for prints and another was shooting pictures in the room across the hall. She excused herself and ran downstairs.

She flipped the switch for the coffee pot and then went into the kitchen, chuckling at herself. There was a crime scene and she felt the need to put snacks out.

Sylvie always had something in the refrigerator. There was a bowl of fresh fruit on the counter and containers of chocolate chip cookies in the freezer. Polly had a flash of a memory from her childhood. An older couple lived down the road from her home and when she was very young, before her mother died, she would ride her bike down to spend time with Mrs. Elmwood. Marie ... that was it. Marie loved making cookies and stored them in coffee cans in her deep freeze on the back porch. Whenever Polly showed up, they shared cookies and milk, and Marie usually sent a can of cookies home with her. She still loved frozen chocolate chip cookies and that memory reminded her why.

Polly arranged the cookies on a plate and carried it, along with the fruit bowl, to the conference room.

When she went back up the steps, Sarah and her young male counterpart ... Polly hadn't ever gotten his name ... were loading the body onto the stretcher. "I'm begging you, Polly. An elevator. Please," Sarah said.

"I would just as soon you never had to worry about doing this again. Maybe that's a better deal," Polly pointed to Thomas's body. "Take care of him, okay?"

"We will. You know we will," Sarah nodded. "Don't worry. Aaron doesn't like not knowing why people die in his territory."

Stu was talking to a bleary-eyed Grey Linder, who was nodding and trying to peek into the middle bedroom. She heard Stu say, "Do you understand what I'm asking you, sir?"

Grey looked back at the deputy, "What? Oh, I've been in all night. I didn't hear a thing."

"Why don't you come downstairs with me," Stu said. "Polly said she'd make coffee. Do you need to put on some shoes?"

"Shoes?" Grey asked. "Oh, that's probably a good idea. I should put those on. It might be cold outside. Just a minute."

Stu followed as the man stumbled back into his room and Polly heard a thud.

"What was that?" she asked Aaron.

"The man is drunk as a skunk. But, if he tells us he heard nothing, he's likely telling the truth. He was probably passed completely out. I'd love to watch Stu handle this, though. He's always so polite."

In a few moments, Stu Decker came out, holding Grey Linder's arm. "Are you sure you didn't hurt yourself, sir?"

"I'm fine. The rug tripped me."

"Yes sir, they have a tendency to do that sometimes. They're a menace."

Stu steered him around and over the blood trail. "Thanks for the coffee, Polly. I think we'll need it." He led the man down the steps and she shook her head.

"What about Lila Fletcher?" she asked.

"She isn't answering the door. I'll try once more and then I'll ask you to open it for me."

She followed Aaron across the hall and waited while he knocked. "Miss Fletcher? It's Sheriff Aaron Merritt. We've had an incident and I'd like to speak with you. Would you please come to the door?" He listened and waited, then motioned to Polly.

She swiped her phone and the door unlocked. Aaron opened it and flipped on the light to find no one there.

"Didn't the log say she came in just after midnight?" he asked.

"Yes," Polly replied, "but the program doesn't register when someone leaves. It only sees the key being used to enter the room."

"That makes sense," he said. "Is it normal for her to be out late?"

"I really don't know," Polly said. "It never occurred to me to pay attention."

Aaron nodded and turned the light off, then pulled the door shut. "If you see her, would you call? We need to speak with her."

"Sure," she said. "Anything else?"

"We'll be here for a while. Can you go back to sleep with all of this going on?"

Polly smiled, "I doubt it. Will I have to clean up all this blood? And how bad are things in Thomas's room?"

"Not tonight, Polly. You don't want to look at it tonight. Why don't you go back to your apartment and try to rest. Watch television or something to drown us out."

Polly lifted the left side of her upper lip and tried to growl.

"Polly, there is nothing you can do and you'll just be in the way. Thank you for helping us tonight, but you need to go away and let us work."

"I don't like that. The man died on my doorstep."

"I know. But go now, okay?"

She turned back to her apartment. "I'm going to tell Lydia you were mean to me," she said.

"I'm fine with that," he laughed. "Good night."

CHAPTER TWO

Her body ached and there was something heavy pressing on her. It took Polly a few attempts to just get her eyes fully open because she was so exhausted. Her confusion continued when she woke and discovered that Obiwan was asleep on top of her. Why was she on the couch? What time was it?

Then it hit her. She'd fallen asleep even with all of the activity in the hallway. When the sheriff ordered her back to her apartment, she had sat down and relaxed, and that brought on a flow of tears and she'd curled into a ball at the end of her sofa. Sometimes things were just more than she could handle.

Her eyes began to fill again and she sat up, pushing the dog to the floor. Leaning forward, her elbows on her knees, her head in her hands, she let the tears fall. She felt so alone.

What time was it? The phone lay on the coffee table and she swiped it open. Seven o'clock.

"I'm going to be late. Last night was crazy," she texted to Eliseo.

"Don't worry about it. It's Saturday morning and I have both Jason and Rachel here to help," he texted back immediately.

"Thanks." Polly dropped the phone back onto the coffee table

and looked at her dog. "I know you want to go out. You're going to have to be patient."

Her phone buzzed with another text. "What now?" she complained.

It was Sylvie. *"I have Andrew downstairs with me. Can he come up?"* There was a huge wedding this afternoon and Sylvie was in early to prepare the food.

"Crap," she said out loud. "I love him, but I don't want to deal with anyone right now."

Polly took a breath and sighed, then typed, *"Would he mind taking Obiwan for a walk while I shower? I hate to ask."* Before she sent the text, she cleared it and typed, *"Sure. That's fine,"* and sent it.

"Come on, bud. I'll put my shoes on and we'll go walk. It will be good for me."

"Polly? Are you still up here? Why aren't you out at the barn?" Andrew Donovan called out as he ran up her back steps. Andrew was Sylvie's nine year old son. He loved Polly's animals as much as she did and his older brother, Jason, spent every possible moment in the barn with the four Percheron horses she had rescued earlier in the year.

"It was a rough night, Andrew. I just woke up."

"Mom was worried about you," he said, coming into the living room. "Are you all right?"

"I'm fine. I just didn't get much sleep."

"Do you want me to take Obiwan out? I still have my coat on."

The tears that had been building in her eyes flowed again. "Thank you, Andrew, that would be wonderful." She hugged him close and held on while she cried, then let go when she realized the poor little boy had no idea what was happening.

"Sorry about that," she chuckled. "Really sorry. Yes, thank you. The leash is downstairs."

Andrew stopped for a moment, looked at her and then called Obiwan, who followed him through the bedroom and down the steps. Polly heard the back door close and she sat on the couch. She was going to need another nap and a long shower if there was to be any hope of getting through this day. At least a shower.

"Polly?" Sylvie's voice came up from below. "Can I come up?"

"Tattletale," Polly muttered to herself, then said out loud. "Sure. Come on up."

She waited while Sylvie made her way up the stairs, through the bedroom and into the living room.

"Andrew told me you look awful and cried all over him." Sylvie sat down beside Polly, reached over and took her hand.

"You won't believe it. Thomas Zeller died in my doorway last night. Someone killed him." Saying it out loud made it seem less horrific, but Sylvie's face registered the shock Polly had been feeling since the night before.

"He what? Here? How? Polly! No wonder you're a wreck."

"I called Aaron in the middle of the night. Thomas was stabbed in his room. Somehow he made it across the hall and then died right in front of me. Sylvie, how does this keep happening to me?"

"You really liked him, didn't you," Sylvie said, squeezing Polly's hand.

"I did. Who would do something like this? I don't even know if there are still people in my hallway or what I have to clean up."

"Let me look," Sylvie went to the front door and opened it. After closing it, she returned to Polly's side. "There's some clean up to do. A deputy is sitting in a chair on the other side of the hall and the door to the room has a seal on it. I'm sorry, Polly."

"Is there blood on the floor?"

"It looks like they tried to wipe it up, but it will need to be mopped. I'll let Eliseo know."

"I don't know what to do," Polly said. "The last time there were dead bodies here, they kicked me out. I don't want to have to leave again."

"They aren't going to make you leave," Sylvie patted her on the back. "I tell you what. You get more sleep. I'll keep Andrew downstairs and run interference for you. How long would you need?"

"Lydia is going to be in a panic if I don't call her," Polly said.

"Let me take care of Lydia. You need to sleep this off."

"Mom? Polly? Can I come up?" Andrew called from the back steps.

"Let me do this for you and text me when you're awake," Sylvie said. She stood up and went into the bedroom. "Andrew, let Obiwan come up. You are going to hang out in your nook this morning, okay?"

"Okay," he said.

Obiwan came dashing in to the living room.

"You. Sleep," Sylvie pointed at Polly. "Turn your phone off. You can deal with it in a couple of hours."

"Thank you so much. I really appreciate it." After Sylvie left, Polly went into the kitchen to pour out food for the animals. Looking out her front window, she saw cars filling the parking lot and a couple of Sheriff's vehicles already there. Surely they could do without her for a while. Polly checked her phone, turned it to silent and went into the bedroom. She flopped down on the unmade bed, pulled the blankets up over her shoulders and lay there.

There weren't many times in her life when she questioned the decision to do something as crazy as Sycamore House, but this morning she wondered what it would be like to live a simple life. To work a normal job, be married with kids, go home at night and watch television until she went to bed, then start the same day over again each morning. Maybe she wasn't cut out to be the person she was. It was emotionally exhausting.

As she nestled into her pillow, she mentally berated herself for throwing a pity party. One messy night did not equate emotional exhaustion. More sleep and a shower and things would return to normal.

One of the cats padded across the bed and curled up on the pillow at the back of Polly's head and Obiwan jumped up. She opened her eyes again and watched as Luke tucked himself into the crook of her legs, then closed them and went to sleep.

When Polly's eyes popped open again, she smiled. Much better. How long had she slept? It was nine thirty. Perfect.

Her phone was flashing an alert and she swiped to unlock it.

Texts and emails, but no missed calls.

Text from Lydia, *"Sylvie told me you were sleeping. Call when you get a chance. Love you."* Sylvie was awesome.

A text from Eliseo, *"Aaron said I could clean the hallway. It's taken care of. No worries."* Best employees and friends ever.

A text from Jeff, *"You did it again. I had no idea when I took this job. See me later."* Brat.

A text from Henry, *"Sylvie called and told me what happened. Call me."*

And finally, one from Aaron Merritt, *"You can't have the room for a while. No sign of Lila Fletcher yet. Call if you see her."*

That was enough. Emails and phone calls could happen after a shower and fresh clothes.

"I'm ready to grab the day," she said to her animals after she pulled a sweater on over her head. "You all be good."

Obiwan thumped his tail on the bed and rolled over on his back. "I know, I know," she said. "Never enough tummy rubs." She snuggled him for a few minutes, then slid her phone into the back pocket of her jeans and went downstairs.

Her first stop was at Andrew's desk. Henry had cut out a nook for him under the stairway earlier in the summer. It was a perfect place for a boy to read and write his stories.

"Hey Andrew," she said. He was sitting in his favorite place, which was under his desk with the lamp beside him.

"Hey Polly. Are you better?"

"I'm sorry I fell apart on you."

"That's okay. Mom told me you had a guy die in front of you. I would have cried too. Was it Mr. Zeller?"

"It was."

"Do you know why he died?"

"Someone killed him. That's why the police are here."

"My friends aren't going to believe me. They thought I was lying when I told them I was there when you found old lady Rothenfuss in the field this summer."

"Maybe you should quit hanging out with me," she chuckled.

"Heck no! This is awesome!"

"Not so much this time."

"I know. When someone dies, that means someone else is sad. But, if I have to hear about people dying, it's pretty cool that you're there."

Polly brushed her hand over the top of his head. "I'll see you later. And I really am sorry that I cried on you this morning."

"Mom says I should learn how to take care of girls when they do that because it will make them like me better. That's more scary than finding dead bodies."

"I suppose it is," she chuckled as she walked into the kitchen.

"Thank you, Sylvie," she said, catching Sylvie's eye. The woman was perched on a stool, wrapping bacon around something green ... beans or asparagus, Polly wasn't sure.

"For what?" Sylvie asked.

"For making everyone leave me alone. I feel human now."

"I hope you don't mind that I called Henry. I didn't want him to worry when he couldn't reach you."

"No, everything you did was perfect. Thank you. I have phone calls to return, but at least I got some rest." Polly hugged her friend.

"That looks like it's going to be awesome," Polly said, pointing to the asparagus (*it was asparagus*) Sylvie was wrapping. "But, it seems like a lot of work."

"It will be awesome. Hannah will be here soon to help and Rachel is coming in as well. I like having her around."

"Me too," Polly said. Rachel Devins was dating Billy Endicott, one of the two young men renting the apartment above Polly's garage. "Have you seen Jeff?" she asked Sylvie.

"He was here about a half hour ago, begging for some of that chai spiced coffee." Sylvie pointed to a pot on the main counter. "It's there if you want some."

"Oh I do. I really do," Polly gushed. "I'll be back later. Andrew can go upstairs any time now. He's a good kid." She poured a cup of coffee and walked through the main foyer to the offices.

"Good morning," she called as she walked in. Jeff was in his office. He came out to stand in his doorway when he heard her voice.

"You really are a magnet, aren't you?" he laughed.

"Don't start with me. I feel better than I did, but I could still get all growly and mean." Polly went into her office and sat down. "Is there anything I need to know?"

"Leo Evans and Myron Biller were in this morning worrying that we had a crazed killer stalking Sycamore House. They wondered if they were still safe here. The Sheriff can't find Lila Fletcher and Grey Linder is probably still asleep."

Jeff took a breath. "There's a deputy hanging out in the hallway upstairs, just in case Miss Fletcher shows up. They're bringing back another team to go over the middle bedroom again and I've made sure they have access to the key card program down in Boone. The Sheriff thinks we ought to install a video monitoring system ..."

"He what?" Polly gasped. "No. Freakin'. Way!"

"Well, it might make sense," Jeff said.

"It makes no sense at all. This is Bellingwood, not Des Moines or Ames, not even Boone or Webster City. I'm not putting video cameras up. People come here to get away from the insanity of things. I'm not monitoring their every move. No way. Big Brother doesn't live at Sycamore House. I don't ever want to hear you suggest that again."

"Umm, whoa! Okay, I didn't. It was the Sheriff."

"Aaron Merritt would feel better if I had armed guards around here all the time. It's bad enough that because I have a cool piece of technology with the keys, people's movements can be tracked at all."

Jeff put his hands up in defense. "I'm not pushing it. I'll just leave this hot button issue alone now."

"Okay. Good idea. So ... Eliseo was able to clean the floor upstairs?"

"Yeah. I called Aaron first. Eliseo is working in the auditorium right now and I think Jason is helping him." Jeff smiled when he said that. "They're good for each other."

"You're right. They really are. I'm glad there's someone in

Jason's life that just lets him be a boy."

Jeff turned to leave her office, "You should call Lydia Merritt. When we spoke this morning, she told me not to let you get too busy before you phoned her."

Polly rolled her eyes. "Sometimes friends are a little overwhelming. I'll call. I promise. But I'm calling Henry first."

"Smart girl," Jeff laughed. "Oh, and I told the guests that they were safe. I made something up and told them the murder was personal, not random. Here's hoping it wasn't a lie."

Polly brought her computer to life after he left, then dialed her cell phone. It went to Henry's voice mail, so she told him she would call later and dialed Lydia Merritt.

"Hi, Lydia. I hear you're looking for me," Polly laughed.

"I know I drive you crazy, but I worry about you."

"Did you have to sic Jeff on me too?"

"Is that what he said? That brat. I called him about Halloween decorations. I wanted to make sure that we were on the same page for Beggar's Night."

She was planning to decorate the foyer for the kids. Since Lydia lived on the edge of town they never had kids show up and she'd always wanted to do a haunted house. She coerced Beryl Watson to help and they were bringing ghosts and witches to Sycamore House.

Polly chuckled, "He made it sound as if you were circling the wagons."

"No. I might have asked if you had come downstairs yet, but I knew you'd call when you could. I'm sorry you had to deal with last night alone."

"Lydia, that's probably the most difficult thing about it all. When I finally relaxed, I really did feel alone. I knew that Aaron and his team were out in the foyer, but I was all by myself."

"I wish I would have come over with him. He wouldn't let me, but I could have forced my way into the car."

"It's fine now. I was just being a cry baby."

"You had a man die on you. I don't think you reacted inappropriately."

17

"Thanks for that. What time did Aaron come home?"

"He hasn't been home yet. I'm headed down to Boone with his lunch and a change of clothes. He has a long day ahead of him. Would you come over for supper tonight? Henry isn't back until tomorrow, right?"

"Actually, he won't be back until Monday. He's doing something with his sister tomorrow afternoon."

"Have you talked to him yet?"

"I called, but had to leave a voice mail."

"Come over tonight. Just come hang out with me."

Polly paused and thought about it. "Let me text you later, okay? I don't know what the rest of the day is going to bring."

"That's fine, dear. I'd love to have you, though."

"I know. Thank you."

"I'll let you go. I love you, Polly. Take care of yourself today."

"I love you too, Lydia."

They hung up and Polly opened her browser and clicked on the email tab that popped up. She smiled as she saw one from Sal Kahane. They had been roommates and best friends in college and in one short trip to Iowa, Sal managed to fall for the local veterinarian. Mark Ogden had fallen just as hard for Sal and the two of them were trying to figure out if they could ever make their relationship work. Sal lived in Boston and Mark wasn't planning to leave Iowa. He'd gone out in September to spend time with her and when he got back, told Polly he could never live in in that city. There were way too many people confined in a small space.

Sal intended to surprise him in just a couple of weeks. Sycamore House's Anniversary Ball was set for the Saturday after Beggar's Night and this year the theme was a Black Masque. Invitations had been sent over a month ago so people could begin gathering costumes and masks and Polly could hardly wait.

"Hey, girl. I'm all set to fly out. I've shipped my costume to you, so hold on to it for me, will you? I've got the rental car scheduled and I will just drive up that afternoon. I can't wait to see you again. Who knew I'd be spending this much time in Iowa! Do you have a room for me yet?"

She had planned to put Sal in the middle room after Thomas Zeller vacated it. If they had to do a lot of work in there to get it back into shape, she wasn't sure it would be ready.

"Jeff?" she called.

She heard him sigh loudly and then footsteps as he crossed over to her office. "Why do you do this to me?" he asked. "Come see me. Don't yell at me."

"Why not?" she laughed. "You always respond."

"My mom never let us get away with yelling up and down the stairs. If she caught us, there was punishment."

"Well, I didn't have any sisters or brothers, so it was never a problem at my house. It looks as if you are going to have to re-train me. Good luck with that."

"Whatever. What did you need?"

"I was going to put Sal in Thomas Zeller's room, but now I don't know if it's going to be ready. Do you have any ideas?"

"Something in the addition will be open if that room isn't ready. No worries. I've got your back."

"What would I do without you?" Polly winked at him.

"Yell at an empty office."

He spun around and walked out.

"Jeff?" she called again.

"What now?" He poked his head back in her office.

"Thank you."

CHAPTER THREE

After the day she'd had, Polly wanted nothing more than to stay home and spent time on video chat with her boyfriend. Boyfriend. It still sounded odd.

Henry Sturtz had gone from being Polly's contractor, to friend and then boyfriend in the course of the last year. When she looked forward to doing this rather than spending the evening with anyone else, she knew she'd been hooked.

He was in Ann Arbor, and when they had talked earlier, he was frustrated because Lonnie was dragging him to some of her favorite antique stores. He couldn't say no to the girl and this time she had him measuring her kitchen because she had a bright idea for new ... well ... old cupboards. They scoured the shops for cupboard doors, knobs and hinges. Lonnie wanted nothing to match exactly and planned to paint cupboard doors as long as Henry built the carcasses. Polly had laughed at his frustration, which caused him to growl back at her.

Then Polly had called Lydia and begged off spending the evening at her house. After she and Henry finally said good night, she wanted nothing more than to go to sleep. She was looking forward to Sunday morning in the barn with the promise of an early trail ride.

The familiar trill of the video ring tone had Polly scrambling to bring up the chat window. She clicked the button to share video and in just a few moments, saw Henry's face smiling at her.

"Hi there, hot stuff," she said, winking at him.

"Hi there yourself. How are you?"

"I'm fine. How was your day?"

He laughed. "Let me show you my day. Care to take a walk?"

Polly considered herself a child of the technology age, but she still couldn't believe how cool some of it really was. Henry walked outside to his truck.

"Look," he said, "Look at this crap I'm bringing back with me." He panned the phone over the bed of his truck.

"What in the world do you have in there?"

"I have the strangest conglomeration of cabinet doors and drawer faces you could imagine. I'm supposed to make something cohesive out of all of this."

"You didn't say no again, did you?" Polly grinned.

"You know I don't do that very well."

"I'm never going to commiserate with you if your biggest problem is saying no to your sister. She knows you will do whatever she asks, so she keeps asking."

"No pity?"

"None."

He dropped his eyes, "I can't say no. This will be attractive when we're finished, but it's going to be a pain in the butt."

"Well, when you figure out how to say no, I'll figure out how to feel sorry for you."

"I thought you were supposed to be on my side."

"Hah. I'll always be there, but I can't guarantee that I won't be laughing at you, too."

"That seems fair," he sighed. "How are you? I can't believe that I'm out of town again when your life turns upside down."

"I'm doing fine. It all seems really surreal."

"Does Aaron have any leads yet?"

"None at all." Polly said. "And I seem to be missing a guest. Her stuff is here, but she's gone. The guy on the other side of Thomas was passed out drunk in his room last night. Aaron was hoping that my key card system might tell him who went in and out, but it isn't enough information. The killer could have come in with anyone and we'd never know."

"Can you upgrade your system to give you more information?"

"I'm not monitoring Sycamore House just because this happened, Henry. I can't let paranoia turn us into Orwell's 1984."

"Okay, okay. That makes sense, but at the same time, wouldn't it be safer if you had a record of things happening there?"

"No! I'm not doing it."

"Got it. No excessive monitoring at Sycamore House. So … back to surreal. Polly, you had a man die in your house last night. How are you doing with that?"

She shook her head. "It was awful. Henry, I've never felt so helpless. At first I didn't know what was happening and then I realized I couldn't do anything to help him. Even before I had my wits about me, he died. Then there were people everywhere and then Aaron sent me in to my apartment and then I fell apart."

"I'm sorry I wasn't there."

"I wanted you to be here. I felt so alone."

"Polly, you're killing me!"

"I'm sorry. I don't mean to make you feel bad about this. That's not it at all. I missed you. I hate to admit that when things fall apart, you're the first person I want to talk to."

"You could have called me."

"I wasn't going to wake you up just to cry all over you. I managed to get through it."

"You can always call me."

"I know, but it was stupid early in the morning and I didn't want to wake you up."

Henry actually growled. "How would you feel if I didn't call you when something awful happened around me?"

"I'd be mad at you," she said, a bit petulantly. "I'm sorry. I should have called you. That was silly of me."

"It really was. I thought we were past all of this. I'm not just a fair-weather friend. I'm here through all of it. Even if it is stupid early and you have your ugly crying face on."

"I'm ugly when I cry?"

"Well, you aren't as pretty as you are right now. You can work up a good set of red eyes and snotty nose."

She threw a cat toy at the screen, then realized the camera was on top of the screen.

"That wasn't very effective, now was it?" he laughed.

"Leave me alone."

"So, what can you tell me about Thomas Zeller? What does Aaron have to say about this?"

"Aaron hasn't talked to me yet. He asked a few questions, but I don't know what might have led to Thomas's murder. At least I don't think I do."

"You really can't think of anything?" he pressed.

"I really can't. We talked about a million things this last month. He told me a little about his life before and after all of the drugs." She stopped and looked at Henry. "He was going to Hollywood next month. I can't believe he doesn't get to go now. He was looking forward to it. He couldn't wait to be a celebrity, talking to reporters and sitting through casting calls. He had so much life ahead of him." Polly sighed and slumped, then yawned.

"Am I boring you?" Henry asked.

"No, I don't think I completely made up for the sleep I lost last night. Would you mind if I walked away for a moment and got changed for bed? I'll take you in there with me and when we're finished talking I can fall asleep."

"That's the sweetest offer I've had today," he said. "I'll do the same thing. Meet me back here in five minutes?"

"You have a lot of confidence that it doesn't take me long to get ready for bed."

"You're my efficient, pretty Polly. Do you need ten?"

"No," she giggled, "Five will do it."

Polly left the laptop on the coffee table and went in to her bedroom to change into a fresh pair of pajama bottoms and a sloppy t-shirt. She slipped her arms into her robe and tied it around her waist.

"I'm picking you up? Are you back yet?" she called out as she walked to the computer. There wasn't any answer, so she assumed she had moved faster than Henry in getting ready for bed. When she picked the laptop up, his grinning face greeted her.

"I'm here, are you?" he asked.

"I was just picking you up so I could take you to bed."

"That sounds promising."

"Stop it," she scolded. "Just stop it."

Polly settled into the bed with the laptop on her lap. Obiwan jumped up and got comfortable beside her. She yawned once and then again.

"You stop that," Henry said, "You're making me tired."

"I know, but I can't stop!" The laptop moved on her lap when Luke jumped up and tried to settle himself between her stomach and the computer.

"What's this?" she asked as she felt something hard and sharp in her pocket, then she said, "OH!"

"What's oh?" Henry asked.

"Oh is this!" Polly pulled a small USB flash drive out of the pocket of her robe. "Thomas gave this to me last night just before he died. I completely forgot about it."

"What's on it?"

"I have no idea, but he told me that it was only for me. Henry, I feel so stupid. How could I have forgotten about it?"

"You were thinking of a million other things this morning and you were probably in shock too. What's on it?"

"I don't know. Let me plug it in." Polly inserted the USB drive into her computer and waited for it to load. She giggled.

"What's so funny?"

"Oh, I had this thought that all of a sudden my screen would explode in light and sound like it did in the Whoopi Goldberg movie, *Jumpin' Jack Flash* when she finally figured out the key so she could have a conversation with a spy. It was silly then and it would be even sillier now."

"I suppose ..."

"Tell me you've seen the movie," she laughed.

"No. I can't say I ever have."

"We're fixing that when you come home. It's one of my favorites! I'm a little black woman in a big silver box." Polly started to cackle.

"What?"

"I can't repeat lines from movies to save my life, but that's just one of my favorites." She continued to laugh, and then she drew in a breath. "Wow. There are a lot of folders on here. I'm never going to be able to dig through all of this."

"What are you seeing?"

"Tons of folders and there are more folders inside of those. There are manuscripts and jpegs and PDF files." She looked into the camera at the top of her screen. "Henry, I'm never going to get through all of this. And before he died, he told me to 'find him.'"

"Who is him?" Henry asked.

"I don't know. I figured it was his killer, but it could be anyone. Was he looking for someone? I don't have any context for this massive amount of information!"

Polly's voice got higher as she started to panic.

"Polly. Slow down. You don't have to figure this out tonight. You can take your time with it."

"But, what if he was killed because of this information? Should I give it to Aaron?"

"What exactly did Thomas say to you when he gave you the drive?"

"I hardly remember. I was watching this poor man bleed to death in front of me and trying to stop Obiwan from getting into it and making a mess and trying to call someone for help and oh, Henry, I don't remember!"

"Breathe. Calm down. Shut your eyes."

Polly closed her eyes and took a couple of deep breaths.

"Now what did he say to you?" Henry asked.

"He told me that it was for me. It wasn't for anyone else and I was supposed to find him. That's all he said, Henry."

"Do you have space on your laptop?"

"Sure. I have a ton of space on here."

"Copy the data to the hard drive, then tomorrow morning, put it on your drive downstairs. You don't want this to be the only copy. I don't know what he has given you, but I'm not comfortable with you being its keeper. Please call Aaron in the morning and tell him. Let him have the drive."

"Aaron's going to think I held this back on purpose."

"Oh, come on. No he's not. He knows you better than that. He also knows what you went through this morning. You don't want to call him tonight, do you?"

Polly checked the time. It was ten fifteen. "No, I don't want to wake him, especially since there are no dead bodies this time."

Henry chuckled. "You know, someday I'm going to be there when the ..." he stopped talking and began laughing.

"What's so funny?" Polly asked.

"You won't even believe it."

"What?"

"I owe you dinner."

"Okay. Awesome, but why?"

"Because I won the latest pool at the Elevator."

"You what?"

"It was a whim. I said that one of your guests would die at your front door. Polly, I'm so sorry!"

"How much did you win?"

"It's not much. Only fifty bucks, but it will take us to Davey's." He continued to laugh. "I know this isn't funny. It's horrible, but I can't believe I won the pool."

"Well, I'm certainly glad you were in Michigan. At least you have an alibi! I'd hate for someone to accuse you of murder just so you could win the pool."

"I am never going to live this down. You're my girlfriend. I shouldn't be setting you up to find dead bodies."

"That's right. This is your fault. I'm going to blame you."

"That's fine. I deserve it. I'm so sorry, though, Polly. I hate that you keep facing these things when I'm unavailable. I was going to say that someday I would be there when you found a dead body, but I would certainly like for this to be the last time it happened."

"So would I. I can't believe that it has happened again. Andrew thinks it is going to be cool to tell his buddies and my friends all just think I'm a wackadoo dead body magnet."

"No one thinks you are wackadoo. We don't get it, but we don't think you are a crazy person."

"Thanks. I'm not sure if I believe you, but thanks."

"Will you be able to sleep tonight?"

"I think so. I'm exhausted. Eliseo is taking us on a trail ride in the morning. He told me I should spend time with Demi."

"He's probably right. Those horses do wonders for your soul."

"I'll copy this to my laptop and then go to sleep. Thanks for spending time with me tonight, Henry."

"Thank you, my pretty girl. Do me a favor? Call me in the morning before you head for the barn?"

"It's going to be early."

"That's okay, I'll be up. Will you do me one more favor?"

"What's that?"

"If you wake up all freaked out tonight, will you call and let me calm you down?"

"Really?"

"Really. I want to hear from you."

"Thank you, Henry. I love you."

"I love you too, pretty girl. Now get some sleep. I'll talk to you in the morning."

Polly hung up, dragged the folders from the flash drive onto her laptop, then watched as they finished copying. She thought about starting through them, but her eyes were drooping and all she wanted to do was sleep. She powered the laptop down, pulled the USB drive out and dropped it into the drawer in her bedside table. She'd deal with it later. Tonight, she slept.

CHAPTER FOUR

There was something wonderful about a good night's sleep. Polly felt much better when she woke up at five thirty. After getting dressed, she put a new hat on, one that Eliseo had given her for her birthday in September. It was a perfect fit and she felt pretty country in it. Her work boots were at the barn, so she slipped into her tennis shoes.

"Come on Obiwan, Eliseo says we won't be gone long today since it's Sunday. You can tag along."

She went down the main steps and ducked into her office to offload the flash drive to her desktop computer before calling Aaron. While she waited for it to copy, she checked email and social networks to see if anything interesting was going on. When she leaned back in her chair, something caught her eye in the window and she turned around to see what it was.

There was something on the window. That was strange.

"Come on, Obiwan. Let's check this out." He followed her back through the office to the front door.

She pulled the door open and was shocked to see yellow paint splattered all over it.

"What in the hell?"

A quick glance to her left and right told her there was paint splattered everywhere. They'd hit the door with yellow and then splashed other colors up the walls and across the windows.

"What's going on?" she asked and dropped to her haunches. She held Obiwan as she crouched and looked up at the horrible mess. "Who would do this and how do I fix it?"

Eliseo, Jason and Rachel weren't due to be at the barn until six thirty and she didn't want to wake Aaron up. The last thing she needed was for him to think she'd found another body, but this was more than she knew how to handle. She was damned tired of dealing with these things by herself.

Well, he had told her to call when she woke up. She pulled the phone out of her back pocket and dialed Henry.

"Good morning!" he said. "You called. I didn't think you would."

"Henry?" was all she could get out before she began to cry.

"Polly, what's wrong?"

"Henry, someone threw paint all over the front of Sycamore House. It's a horrible mess and I don't know what to do."

"They did what? Is it spray paint or paint paint?"

"It's like they flung buckets of the stuff. They got the door, it's on the windows and the bricks. It's all over the sidewalk."

"Is it still wet?"

"What?"

"Is it still wet?" he repeated.

"I don't know."

Very patiently, he said, "Would you mind touching it? Has it been on the building all night or did it just happen?"

"Oh!" She walked back to the front door and swiped her index finger through the paint. "Still wet."

"If there is one time of the night when they might get away with this, it would be between three and four thirty."

"Maybe that's what woke me up," she said to herself.

"What?"

"Well, I was surprised when I woke up so early, but I assumed it was because I'd had plenty of sleep." She tried to avoid it, but couldn't get past the catch in her throat.

"I can't believe this." Henry sounded furious.

"I can't either." She cried again.

"I also can't believe I'm not there to help you. I'm cancelling my plans with Lonnie and I'll be home later today."

"No. Don't do that. I have plenty of people here to help me."

"You need to call Ken Wallers."

"I'm not going to wake him up."

"Call the police station. They'll send someone. Do that first and then we'll start dealing with the next steps."

"I will in a minute. Obiwan needs to go."

"I'll get the phone number while you walk with him. Don't hang up on me."

"I won't. Henry, this looks awful. My beautiful home!"

She heard him clicking away in the background as she walked toward the north side of the building. Obiwan followed, bouncing into the grass. When they got near the row of Sycamore trees, he dashed off to make sure they'd all been properly marked. She followed him to the creek and waited while he pranced in and out of the trees.

"Polly?" Henry said.

"Yes?"

"I have the number. Call the station and tell them what's happened. After you hang up, go back around front and take pictures. I want to see what has happened, so email those to me."

"Okay." They ended the call and she quickly dialed the number he gave her before it was forgotten. A woman's voice on the other end asked what she could do to help.

"This is Polly Giller over at Sycamore House," Polly said. "Someone has flung paint all over the front of my building and I need to file a report."

"Yes, Miss Giller. I'll call Ken. He'll be over in a little bit."

"I didn't mean to wake him up," Polly protested.

"That's fine, Miss Giller. He's on call this morning and I think he'll be relieved to hear that you don't have a body for him."

Polly couldn't help it. She laughed out loud. "Oh, thank you. That made me feel better. I'm glad I don't have one for him, too."

"He'll be over soon and I'm sorry this has happened to you."

"Thank you." Polly hung up and said, "Come on, Obiwan. It's time to head back inside."

She called Henry. "I'm sorry I messed with your morning."

"Don't be sorry. I feel terrible that I'm not there."

"I've called the police. Ken Wallers is coming over. I'll take Obiwan upstairs and feed him before I take pictures for you."

"When Eliseo gets there, ask him to call me. I have some ideas on how to clean it up. Don't worry, okay?"

"I won't. I'll send the pictures over and talk to you a little later."

"I love you, Polly. Does that help?"

She smiled. "It does right now and I love you too."

"Talk to you later."

"Bye, Henry."

She opened the garage door and went inside to the back stairs. Obiwan followed her up the steps and into the apartment. The cats were already moving toward the kitchen for breakfast. Polly filled their dishes and made sure water was available. She took her hat off and put it on the table in the entry way, saying "I'm not going to need you today, am I?"

When she got back outside, her heart sank at the mess. She walked far enough out into the parking lot to take an all-encompassing photo, then moved closer and took more pictures, emailing each to Henry. She turned around as she heard a car pull onto the gravel in the parking lot. She was expecting Ken Wallers and was surprised to see Lila Fletcher get out of the passenger side of the car that pulled up in front of the building.

"What happened?" the woman asked.

"I don't know," Polly said. "It's been a crazy weekend here."

"It has? I was gone. What was the excitement?"

"Well, this," Polly pointed to the front of Sycamore House, "and there was an incident Saturday morning with Thomas Zeller."

The woman stopped in her tracks and demanded, "What happened?"

Polly explained that he had been killed and that the Sheriff wished to speak with her. Lila said nothing more and went inside.

"Well, that was odd," Polly muttered to herself.

Ken Wallers drove in next. He got out of his car and came over to stand beside her, looking up at the front of the building. "What in the hell?" he asked.

"Those were my words," she commented. "Hi there."

"Do you have any idea who might be angry enough to do this?"

Polly thought about it. "Angry with me? I don't have a clue."

"Have you had any other vandalism around here lately?"

"Other than the murder the other night?"

"Yes. Other than that."

"No, I haven't."

"You're going to want to make sure things are locked up tight and put away for a few days. This isn't an accident and if someone has gotten it in their head to hurt you, they might try other things.

"Do you want to come inside?" she asked. "I can turn on the coffee pot in the office."

"That would be great. I need to start a report and then I'll be out later with my camera. Are you cleaning this up today?"

"As soon as I can. I hate the idea that everyone will see this."

"You could always put a 'Pardon the Mess' sign out front," he chuckled.

"Aren't you helpful," she grinned. "I talked to Henry and he and Eliseo will come up with a plan for cleanup." She flipped the coffee pot on in the outer office and followed him into her office.

"You're up awfully early this morning." He pulled a notepad out of his jacket pocket.

"I slept so badly the other night that I went to bed early."

Ken scratched notes and asked about her insurance.

Polly heard the coffee pot end its cycle and said, "Excuse me," then left the room. She poured two cups and brought them back into her office, setting one in front of him. He was pondering something he'd written and automatically picked the cup up, blowing on it as he thought.

"What are you thinking about?" she asked.

"We haven't had any vandalism in town for quite a while. I'm just thinking about who my regular offenders are."

"Do you think this was done by a regular offender?"

"It won't hurt to check them out."

"Polly?" Eliseo came in the door to the office. "Oh, I'm sorry. I don't mean to interrupt."

"That's all right," Ken said. "I need to get the report finished and come back with a camera. Come on in."

"You two have met, haven't you?" Polly asked. "Oh, sure," she said. "What was I thinking?"

Earlier that spring, Eliseo had been living in her barn as he looked for a former army mate who had stolen a priceless vase and large amount of cash when they were stationed in Iraq. Two others from their unit were also looking for the vase and money and had killed Harry Bern, who had just begun working as the custodian at Sycamore House. When Polly discovered the vase in the hay loft, Eliseo had come to her rescue when the two former soldiers tried to steal it from her. Just as she and Eliseo were getting the two men under control, Ken Wallers and his team arrived on the scene and ensured everyone was safely dealt with.

The two men shook hands and Ken asked, "How is that old place coming along? Are you getting it fixed up?"

"I'm nearly finished," Eliseo said. "Henry asked his friend, Len Specek, to help me with the cupboards in the kitchen. Once those go in, that room will be done."

Eliseo was living in the house Harry Bern had been renting. The landlord had agreed to let him live there rent free for a year. In return, Eliseo provided the labor to renovate the home which had been torn to pieces by the two men who were searching for the vase and cash. To Polly, the mess seemed daunting, but Eliseo had dug in and was creating a nice home for himself.

"It's good to see you," Ken said and left the office.

Eliseo took the vacated seat and turned worried eyes toward Polly. "What's going on?"

"I don't know. I found it when I came down this morning." She shook her head. "You haven't seen any other signs of vandalism around here, have you?"

"No." He thought for a moment and then repeated himself, "No. I haven't seen anything. When can I clean it up?"

"Ken is returning with a camera and then we can do whatever we want. I've already talked to Henry. He wants you to call him before you start."

"The kids are going to be here in a little bit. Do you still want to go out riding?"

"I hate to take that away from them and I'd hate for Demi to be left home because I'm feeling sorry for myself." She looked down at the desk and then back up at him. "The vandals won't come back during the day, will they?"

"Polly, anyone who does something like this relies on the cover of darkness. They're cowards. If you want to go riding with us, you should. Let Demi carry you for a while. This has been a tough couple of days for you."

"I didn't get to the barn yesterday."

"That's okay, but those beasts have a lot to give you when things are falling apart. Come on. Let's head down."

"You're right. Ken doesn't need me." She stood up and took a deep breath, releasing it through her nose. "I'm ready."

They walked through the building and out the side door into the covered walkway. There were only two guests in this addition, but it felt good to have the rooms used. Polly couldn't believe she was really an innkeeper. All of those years she'd spent in college and working as a librarian in Boston had prepared her for quite a bit, but not for this.

She put her hand on Eliseo's back. "I don't tell you thank you enough for all you do here. I really appreciate you."

"I appreciate the work, Polly."

She stopped him and pulled him into a hug. "No, really. I'm so glad you are here."

He stiffened and then hugged her back. "I am too. You've given me a pretty wonderful life."

She released him and they left the covered walkway and headed for the barn. "I've given you a job. You've made a life here.

I don't know how you get everything done. Lydia told me a couple of weeks ago that Mrs. Mulberry said you cleaned out her pond and then you promised to clean her gutters before winter."

"She's a nice lady. She feeds me pie. Each time I see her, she has pie for me. I have to work like this or I wouldn't be able to walk!"

They were laughing as they opened the doors to the barn.

"Good morning, everyone," Polly called. She heard movement and watched as the horses came to life. Nan's head was first out of the stall and Eliseo strode over to greet her. He murmured at her and stroked her head, then moved to Nat, who shook himself before putting his head out.

"Polly!" Jason and Rachel both ran into the barn and pulled up short when they saw Polly and Eliseo.

"Did you see it?" Rachel asked.

"Yes, and the police have already been here," Polly said.

Rachel was moving toward Daisy's stall and Jason stepped up to Nat. Both of these young people had bonded with the four horses, but had chosen their own favorite to care for. When they all rode together, they knew who was most comfortable on which horse.

"Come on, guys. Let's feed them breakfast and we'll saddle up after cleaning out the stalls. No time to waste!" Eliseo said and hefted a bucket to Jason. He tossed a second at Rachel and Polly caught up to him before he tossed another.

The horses were soon eating and the humans made quick work of clean up. Jason hauled the last of the waste out to be dumped while Rachel and Polly followed Eliseo into the tack room. There wasn't a day that went by when Polly wasn't grateful for the months she'd put in hauling hay bales and cleaning these stalls by herself. She was in better shape than she'd ever been and the thought of lifting a saddle up on to Demi's back no longer frightened her. She could tell he looked forward to their rides together and this morning she could hardly wait to feel his muscles move underneath her. She was still in awe that she got to be part of their lives.

CHAPTER FIVE

Demi's strength and calm demeanor was the perfect remedy. Eliseo was right. Other than a few words of guidance as they rode, these early morning rides were quiet. Rachel and Jason were still trying to wake up, Eliseo never had much to say, and this morning Polly was fine with silence. She had a lot to think about.

When they returned to the barn, they brushed down their horses and Eliseo stepped out to take a phone call. "Henry thinks that pressure washers will clean up most of the paint," he said, walking back in. "He's a little worried about the front doors, but told me that we should do as much as we can and he will look at it when he gets back."

"Okay, so we need to line up pressure washers and ladders," Polly said. "Did he say anything about where to get that stuff?"

"No, but he told me that you should call him when you're free."

"Thanks. I'll finish in here and head up to the office."

"You go. The kids and I can do this. I'll stop in to find out what's next."

"I'm sorry about this, Eliseo. I know today is usually your day off."

"Don't even think about it. I'd rather be outside cleaning than stuck in my kitchen working on tile. That job will be there this winter when it's cold and miserable."

She smiled at him. "Thank you. I'll make it up to you."

"You already have, several times over. Don't worry about it."

Polly dialed her phone as she left the barn.

"Henry? Hi," she said.

"Hi there, pretty girl. How are you doing? Did the ride help bring you back to normal?"

"It did, but now I'm stressing about how to get my hands on the equipment to clean this up."

"I'm already on it. Jimmy Rio knows where mine is in the shop and he said his dad has one he could borrow. I called Doug and Billy and Doug is pretty sure his dad has one, too. They'll be coming downstairs any minute to talk to you."

Polly listened as he gave her instructions and then said, "Where are you? What am I hearing in the background?"

"I'm on the other side of Kalamazoo, heading your way."

"I thought you were going to some lecture this afternoon with your sister. It was some guy she wanted you to meet."

"I'll meet him later. I woke her up and told her what happened and she asked why I was still in her house. She kicked me out and I let her."

"Henry," Polly whined, "I didn't want you to do this. I could have handled it." Then she stopped and chuckled. "Well, at least with you on the other end of the phone. You seem to be handling it for me even long distance."

"I'm coming home. I'll be there late this afternoon and you better have some good food to feed me because the only stops I'm making are for gas. Snacks are gonna get me to you."

"I'll cook whatever you'd like. I promise. I can't believe you're doing this for me. You're a nut."

"I have to tell you, Polly, I can't take any more of this."

"Any more of what?"

"Any more of you having terrible things happen when I'm nowhere near."

"You can't hover around me all the time."

"I can give it my best shot. But, I promise you this, I'm not leaving town for an extended period of time unless you're with me. And that's all I have to say about that!"

She chuckled, "I love you too, Henry."

Doug and Billy came around the corner and into her office.

"Henry, can I call you back in a bit? Doug and Billy are here."

"Sure. I love you. Talk to you later."

"I love you too."

The two young men were roommates, living in the apartment above her garage. Polly felt like they were her two younger brothers. She'd met them last fall when renovation had started on Sycamore House. They worked for an electrical contractor and had ended up as part of her family.

"Hey Polly, was that Henry?" Doug asked.

"I certainly hope so," she laughed. "Who else would I be telling that I loved them?"

"You say it all the time to everybody," Billy deadpanned.

Doug nodded in agreement. "We're going over to Dad's to get his power washer. We'll be back."

"Thank you. Eliseo will organize this, but I appreciate you."

"If we borrow your truck, we could bring back a ladder."

"Uh," she hesitated.

"It's only across town," Doug laughed. "I'm a good driver. I promise."

Polly tossed him a key. "You hurt it, I'll mess you up," she said. "Deal."

They walked out of the office and she heard Billy say, "Dude! She doesn't trust you. Maybe I should drive!"

Polly almost stopped them. She stood up from her chair, then sat back down. "If I trust them in my house, I trust them with my truck," she muttered. She loved her truck, but only because it had belonged to her dad. It had gone into storage after he died and was one of those things that made her think of him every time she drove it. She wasn't sure how she would ever let it go, so she did her best to take care of it.

She looked down at the flash drive on her desk. "Crap," she said and looked at the time. She knew Aaron went to ten thirty church with his wife. Polly had time to call him. She didn't want to explain why she hadn't done so yesterday, but figured she might as well face the music.

"Polly?" Aaron's deep voice was a little hesitant when he answered her call.

"No more bodies. I think one is enough for this week, don't you?"

"Well, that's good news. What's up this morning?"

"First of all, Lila Fletcher came back early this morning. She said she'd been gone."

"I'll have one of my boys stop up and talk to her. What else?"

"Did you hear about the vandalism here?"

"I heard it on the scanner. Talked to Ken. It sounds like he'll do what he can. Did you need me to do something with that?"

"No, we've got it. But, I've done something bad, even though it was totally unintentional. I'm afraid you're going to be mad at me."

"I've been mad at you before. It doesn't do me any good. What did you do?"

"I kind of forgot to tell you about a flash drive that Thomas Zeller gave to me just before he died."

"You what?" Aaron sounded more irritated than usual.

"I totally forgot about it until late last night when I was talking to Henry on the phone. I dropped it into the pocket of my robe and I found it there when I put it on last night."

"Why did he give this to you?"

"I don't know, Aaron. He told me that it was only for me and that I was supposed to find him."

"Find who?"

"I don't know that either. I haven't had time to go through the files."

"You're just going to give it to me? No argument?"

Polly was shocked. "Why would I argue with you? I want you to find out who killed him."

"You're sure you don't want to figure it out?" he teased her.

"If I do figure it out, that would be pretty cool, wouldn't it?"

"Not the way you do things. Your luck, the murderer will show up and try to hurt you and I'll have to rescue you. I'd like to tell you to just let me do my job and keep your nose out of things, but I'd be making noise into the wind, wouldn't I?"

"Maybe?" she laughed.

"Polly, you give me a headache."

"I don't do it on purpose. It's not like I ask these people to die around me. I keep insisting that it's not my fault and no one seems to listen."

"Lydia and I will stop by after church. With this vandalism episode, she isn't going to rest until she's wrapped her arms around you at least once."

"We're washing down the front of the building this morning. Hopefully it will be clean by the time you get here."

"What does Henry have to say about all of this?" Aaron asked.

"Excuse me?" she said.

"Lydia would probably swat me for that question, wouldn't she? I'll ask again in a different way. Is Henry helping you clean this up?"

"Not exactly," Polly laughed. "He's still in Michigan."

"That's right. That has to be frustrating for him."

"I think it is. But not in that 'caveman gotta protect his woman' way, though."

"Oh. No. He would never act like that," Aaron laughed.

"Not if he wants to live through the next week," she responded. "He's smart and doesn't treat me like I'm going to break just because I'm a girl."

"He is smart," Aaron replied. "And one of the smartest things he did was corral you. You're good for him, Polly."

"Thanks, Aaron." This was the longest conversation she'd ever had with Aaron about something other than a dead body. His wife was one of her best friends, but Aaron usually let the two of them chatter while he remained quiet, observing and rarely commenting.

"I'll see you later. If you still need help with cleanup, you know I'll be there."

"I think we'll be fine, but thanks." She watched as Jimmy Rio and Sam Terhune drove into the parking lot. Jimmy parked his truck and they got out.

"Good-bye, Polly."

"Bye, Aaron. Hug your wife for me."

She hung up and when she got outside, said, "Hi guys. Thanks for helping today."

"This is really something!" Jimmy said, "When Henry called, I couldn't believe it. Who would do this to you?"

"I've got nothing." Polly shook her head and rolled her eyes.

Eliseo came around the corner of the building.

"Hi Jimmy. Hi Sam," he said.

"We've got two power washers and some hose here. Where do you want us to hook up?"

"Follow me," He strode toward the garage and they followed him, the end of a hose trailing behind them. Doug drove in with Polly's truck and parked. He and Billy jumped out, unloaded a ladder, then went back to pull more hose and another washer out of the bed of the truck.

"Do you think your water pressure can handle this?" Doug asked.

Polly shrugged. She had no idea. "Ask Eliseo," she said.

He was coming back, carrying one end of a ladder. "We'll be fine. We're going to run one from the kitchen and then one from the other side of the building."

"But," Polly interrupted.

"No, I've got it," he said. "Don't worry."

"Okay. What can I do?"

"Really?" he asked.

"Really. I need to do something or I'll go out of my mind."

"You're going to get wet."

"Then I'll get wet. It's going to be 82 degrees today. I think I'll live through it."

"When the paint and water comes down to the sidewalk, you

need to sweep it into the gravel. We'll wash it down again after the walls are clean, but I don't want it to stain the concrete."

"Brooms in the shed?" she asked.

"They are. Let me get these hoses hooked up and water running. Guys, we're going to begin up high and wash it down. Jimmy, you work on the doors. Henry and I are most worried about those. The windows and brick should clean right up."

As they were setting up, cars were slowing down on the highway in front of the parking lot and several drove through. The first person to pull in was a couple Polly had met several times with Henry. She could not believe that she didn't remember their name.

"What happened, Polly?" the husband asked.

"Paint. All over everything."

"Do you know who did it?"

"I don't have a clue. Ken Wallers was here earlier. That's all I could do, I guess."

"Wow, that's too bad. I hope it cleans up for you."

"So do I. But, Henry seems to think this will do the trick and I figure if anyone knows, he does."

"He's a good man, that Henry is," the man said. "Well, good luck!" They drove on out and before she took two steps toward the shed, another car pulled in. This time it was Lisa Bradford, Polly's mail-person.

"Wow, Polly, this looks awful! Who did it?"

Polly shook her head. "I have no idea. It's disgusting, isn't it?"

"Have you called the police?"

"Yep, Ken was here earlier. Now we just have to get it cleaned up."

"If you need anything from the store, we'll be up there after one o'clock. I'm sure Paul has some stuff that would help."

"Thanks, Lisa. If I need him, I'll let you know."

"If we don't hear from you, I'll see you tomorrow." She waved and drove off. Paul Bradford ran the hardware store in town. Polly hoped that by the time he opened his store, everything would be clean and his assistance would be unnecessary.

She continued to the shed behind her garage, ignoring other cars that drove through to peer at the damage.

Polly hated being the subject of conversation, even though she knew there would always be some level of interest in her because she'd bought and renovated the old high school. Between the bodies she kept finding and the Percherons and now this, people had plenty to talk about. She sneered as she grabbed a couple of brooms, and thought, "Well, this ought to keep the lips of all the church biddies in town flapping. I'm sure they're praying for my soul now. Next thing you know, they'll tell me that if I'd been in church this would never have happened."

"Hey, Polly?"

She turned around, relieved that someone would distract her from her nasty thoughts. Rachel and Jason were coming up from the barn.

"Yeah, Jason. What's up?"

"Mom says I can stay if you need me."

"I think we're fine. You can go to church."

"Please?" he begged.

"Nah. It's probably bad enough I don't go on a regular basis. You need to go."

"Rats," he said. "I finally get a good reason not to and you won't let me get away with it."

"Is it really that bad?" Polly asked.

"No. It's fine. I just thought I could hang out here."

"Call your mom and tell her Rachel is bringing you home. Okay Rachel?"

"Sure. Whatever," Rachel shrugged. "I gotta go, too." She looked up as Billy came out of the building. "Hey, Billy," she said.

"Hi Rachel. Did you ride this morning?"

"Yes, we did. Jason and I were just polishing tack. I'm going to take him home. So, you aren't going to church today?"

"No, I'm helping with this. Are you mad?"

Polly stifled a giggle. Kids were awesome.

Rachel said, "No problem. You're probably needed here."

"Okay." He turned around and opened the front door again to

go inside without saying anything else.

Rachel stood there looking at his back and watched the door close. She took a short breath and let it out, then said, "Come on, Jason. We'd better go."

"Rachel?" Polly stopped her.

"Yeah?"

"Don't let it freak you out. Boys can be terrible communicators sometimes."

"I know. He does pretty good, but sometimes I want to kill him."

"I'm guessing that might be a pattern," Polly laughed.

"Mom says I need to tell him how to talk to me. Doesn't that seem like something *his* mother should have taught him?"

"Like he'd listen to her?" Polly asked.

"I suppose you're right." Rachel gave a quick shudder. "I don't want to have to tell him how to be nice."

"Here's the deal," Polly said conspiratorially, "You either talk to him when you guys aren't mad at each other or you will be telling him when you're having a huge fight."

"We don't fight," Rachel responded.

"You will. Trust me. If you are frustrated with him now, you'll fight with him later."

"Yuck," Rachel spat. "I hate talking about that stuff. And I know he hates it. He'd much rather talk about his computers or games or movies."

"Rachel! We gotta go!" Jason called from the passenger door of her car.

"I gotta go," Rachel said. "Thanks, though."

"Have fun!"

Rachel waved and ran to her car. They drove out of the parking lot and Polly turned around to see Doug on the ladder, beginning to wash down the brick wall. She was relieved to see paint coming off the brick. They might get through this after all.

CHAPTER SIX

Returning the casserole dish to the oven, Polly checked the time. Henry was stopping at his house before coming over. He wanted to unpack his things first. They planned to eat at six o'clock and she hoped he meant what he said when he told her he was hungry. She'd cooked hearty and she'd cooked plenty.

Everyone had worked until about two o'clock cleaning down the front of Sycamore House and she was fairly pleased with the result. Her beautiful front doors didn't clean up quite as much as she'd hoped, and she was afraid that meant Henry was going to have to strip them down and refinish them. What a terrible time of year for that to happen, but at least they were no longer covered with bright yellow paint.

Her friends had stopped by after church with lunch. Lydia and Andy, Sylvie and Beryl had gone to the grocery store and picked up food to make quick sandwiches. When Polly had given Thomas Zeller's flash drive to Aaron, he glanced through the files on her computer and agreed there was an awful lot of information. None of it seemed to have a flashing red light over it that said, "Here's the murderer, read me.," though.

Eliseo had finally pulled Polly back into the parking lot and asked her to look up at the building. "I think we've done it, Polly. It looks good."

She had thanked the others and was frustrated when they wouldn't accept any money.

"It's what we do, Polly," Jimmy Rio had assured her. "This was a bad thing that happened to you. We like being able to help out."

"At least let me send you guys to Davey's for supper."

The boys had all looked at each other and grinned. "We'll take some of that action. Tonight's prime rib!"

"I'll make the call. Dinner with everything you want ... even dessert ... is on me."

The four had walked away, making decisions about what time to meet up for dinner.

"Billy?" Polly had called out.

"Yes ma'am," he said with a laugh, knowing how much she hated that term.

"Well, I was going to tell you that you could take Rachel, but maybe I shouldn't be that nice to you."

"I'm sorry," he dramatically said and stuck out his lower lip. "I'll be good."

"Call her and if any of you other guys have figured out how to ask a girl on a date, feel free to invite them out tonight. You've been amazing today and I owe you."

She watched Billy punch Doug in the shoulder and both of them laughed. Sam Terhune and Jimmy Rio looked at her and she said, "What? I wasn't kidding. Invite your girlfriends. That's good with me."

"Thanks, Miss Giller," Sam said. "Thanks a lot!"

"The horses won't need much tonight, Polly," Eliseo said. "We did good work this morning. Jason and I will get them in and fed. Henry's coming home, isn't he?"

"Yes. Thank you, Eliseo. I'll see you tomorrow."

When Polly got up to her apartment, she pulled chicken out of the freezer and set it in a warm water bath in the kitchen sink, then ran down the back steps with Obiwan. They wandered through her back yard, and down along the creek. When they got to the fence for the pasture, they wove in and out of the trees until they came to where Nan and Nat were standing.

"Hi there," Polly said, reaching out to rub Nan's muzzle. Obiwan yapped at the two of them, then pulled the leash to keep moving. Polly felt Nat graze the top of her head with his lips. "I love you too, but it looks as if Obiwan is in a hurry. I'll see you in the morning." They continued down between the fence and the trees and the two horses followed.

"We have a parade," she laughed. They followed the fence around the pasture to the highway and then she picked up the pace and they jogged back to Sycamore House.

"Can you believe those big guys live with us, Obiwan? How crazy is that?" They went in the front door and up the steps to her apartment.

"Okay, everyone," she said. "We're on a mission. We have two and a half hours to get a good meal on the table, the apartment cleaned and I need a shower. Who's up for helping me get this done?"

Since she was standing in the kitchen when she made her grand announcement, all eyes were watching her. "I know, I know," she said. "Treats it is." She tossed a fresh rawhide bone into the living room for Obiwan and opened the bag of dental treats for the cats, giving them a few. "If you aren't going to help me, the least you can do is leave me alone while I work like a crazy woman."

Promptly at six o'clock, her front doorbell rang and she flung the door open.

"I missed you!" she said, ready to pull him into her arms, but then saw that his hands were full. He had a small bunch of mums in one hand and a plastic grocery bag in the other.

"I missed you, too." He leaned forward to kiss her and she put her hands on his cheeks and held him until he wrapped his arms around her and squeezed. When she finally let him go, he said, "I always like coming back to that."

Henry had only been gone since Wednesday and they'd talked

on video chat every night, but having him here was exactly what Polly needed.

"Come on in," she said, but Henry stopped and gestured with his head across the hall. "Didn't think I'd ever see another police seal at Sycamore House."

"Oh Henry, I'm glad you're here. I'm so tired of handling this without you around."

"I'm glad I'm here, too." He kissed her again and looked down at Obiwan, who had been sitting patiently beside Polly. "I'm even glad to see you, big guy."

Polly closed the door and followed Henry inside. He held out the flowers and said, "It's not much. They're from my back yard."

"They're perfect. I have a vase in the kitchen."

Then he held out the bag. "I brought ice cream treats."

She chuckled. "Those might have to wait until later. I made a pie."

"You what?"

"It's just an apple pie, but it will be warm and I have ice cream."

"These can go in the trash. Homemade apple pie?" he asked, astounded.

"I make great pie," she laughed. "I just never do it. Mary used to let me help her all the time and she was one of the best pie makers I've ever known."

"Do I have to wait until after dinner?"

"Dinner is going to be pretty good, too. I hope you weren't kidding when you said you'd be hungry."

"I'm starving. What are we having?"

"Come on in and get comfortable. Take off your shoes if you want and I'll get it on the table."

Henry looked around and his eyes got big. "What have you done here?"

"What do you mean?" Polly was a little offended.

"This place is so clean. What did you do?"

"The cats helped me. They wanted more treats." Polly had spent a lot of time cleaning the apartment that afternoon. The table was set for dinner, candles were lit, and serving dishes were waiting on the kitchen counter. All she needed to do was serve it."

"The place looks really nice, Polly and the table looks fantastic."

"Maybe I wanted you to know how much I missed you. When you left last winter to go to your parent's house in Arizona, I told you I wasn't going to let you go away like that again. You snuck this one in on me and I hated it. I'm going with you next time."

"The trip would have been much more fun if you'd been there. That drive today nearly killed me."

"You shouldn't have come back early. We took care of it. I know you helped me figure it all out, but you could have come back at a normal pace tomorrow."

"I couldn't have stood myself if I'd waited until tomorrow. I had to see you today."

Polly put the ice cream treats in the freezer and pulled a vase out from under the sink. When it was filled with water and the mums were arranged, she placed it on the table.

"What did you think of the front door?" she asked. He grabbed her when she tried to return to the kitchen and pulled her onto his lap.

"Just a minute. I need to do one more thing before I think about that door."

"What's that?" she innocently asked.

"This." He kissed her and she felt herself swooning as they prolonged the kiss.

"Are you in a hurry to think about the front door?" she asked.

"Nope," and he kissed her again. "I'm just about ready to think about it, but I wanted you to know how much I really did miss you."

"Uh huh," she breathed. "I think I've forgotten. Can you remind me?"

Henry chuckled and gave her a quick kiss, then pushed her up. "Feed me, woman. I'm dying here."

"So really, what do you think about the front doors?" she asked, walking into the kitchen.

"They're all right if you don't mind a yellow hue."

"I hate it."

"Then, I need to take them down and back to the shop. We'll sand them and put a new finish on them."

"How long am I going to be without doors?"

"I know. That's the problem. I need to think about this. We won't do anything until I'm sure you're safe with them down."

Polly put a basket of hot rolls and a dish of cheese encrusted asparagus on the table, then went back for the main dish.

"What's this?" Henry asked.

"It's a recipe I made up."

"It smells amazing."

"Anything that has bacon in it smells amazing. It's a country chicken recipe I learned from Mary. This should have everything you need to stay alive for one more night," she laughed.

She sat down and they began to eat. Henry smiled and nodded as he took a few bites. "You can cook for me anytime," he laughed. "This is great."

When they finished supper, he helped Polly take their dishes into the kitchen.

"While you serve up pie and ice cream, I need to run downstairs to my truck to get something. I'll be right back."

Before she could respond, he put his shoes on and went out the front door.

"I wonder what that was about." She walked to the kitchen window and watched as he opened the passenger door of his truck and pulled out a large package.

"What has he done now?" She cut the warm pie and dropped scoops of ice cream onto the slices she'd placed on plates. They were on the table when he came back in.

"I know you will think I'm crazy," Henry said, handing her the package, "but I had to do this."

"What did you do?"

"Just open it."

The package was simply wrapped in brown kraft paper and she tore it off, then laughed. "This is cool! I love it!"

"It isn't every day that you have a First Anniversary Celebration and I thought we should commemorate it. I was going to give it to you the night of the ball, but I thought maybe today would be better. I like to see you smile."

Polly kissed him. "Oh, this makes me smile!"

Henry had framed the full page advertisement for the masquerade ball. She couldn't wait to hang in the outer office downstairs, where everyone could see it.

SYCAMORE HOUSE
FIRST ANNIVERSARY

When *dark* and *bleak*, the night takes hold,
Those *faint of heart* leave to the bold,
To make their way through *shadows* deep
And draw them *nigh* unto the keep.

A *black masque* ball, please do attend
Two days beyond *October's end*.
The dress – *Victorian*; a *mask's* a must,
No entrance allowed, if you've not *fussed*.

Steampunk and *vampires, gothic* and ghosts,
Two *prizes* awarded by *friendly* hosts.
At *Sycamore House*, be there by eight,
Unless *dark* shadows make you *late*.

A quick *response* to be on the list
An evening, *we promise*, must not be missed.
When *dark* and *bleak*, the night takes hold,
Our *lights* will *welcome* you into the fold.

Polly had spent time one Sunday afternoon dreaming up the text and was proud of the invitation. Jeff's eyes lit with possibilities when he saw it. He was friends with one of the costume designers at Iowa State and planned to ask for her help in rounding up costumes for the event. Some people in town had pooh-poohed the idea and others had jumped on board and begun planning their outfits right away.

The gown Polly had found online was gorgeous. She wasn't too sure about the corset and petticoat, but for one night, it would be fine.

"Thank you for this, Henry," she said. "I would never have thought to do something like it and you're right, it should be commemorated." She set it up in a chair and looked at it. "It's been a whole year, Henry. A year!"

"It's been a good year."

"Do you remember putting this floor in for me? I wasn't even in town when you brought all of my furniture up from downstairs."

"That was a fun night. We were all so glad you were safe. That's the night you got Obiwan, too."

The dog heard his name and padded over to sit between them. Polly reached down and scratched his head. "When Lydia came in my front door with Beryl and Andy, I couldn't begin to comprehend the changes that were about to happen in my life. It's not as if I had a big plan, but somehow Lydia knew that I was supposed to be her friend and she made it okay for me to be part of the community."

"She's a pretty big presence in town."

"You warned me," Polly laughed. "You told me that things weren't ever going to be quiet once I became friends with them."

"I was right, wasn't I!" he said.

"It's been a year," she said again, taking a bite of pie. "Wow. So, when did you decide to ask me out?"

"I was getting close when Joey showed up and made a mess of everything. Then, you were so busy with finishing the renovation and then Jeff showed up and you made all these Christmas party plans." He took a breath. "I finally just figured I had to do it or I'd never get the opportunity."

"Can we go back to that same restaurant to celebrate our first year?" she asked.

Henry reached out and took her hand. "Of course we can. That was a great night. I knew I was in love with you then."

Polly pulled her hand out and laid it on top of his, squeezing it. "It took me a long time to admit it, but I knew that I wanted something with you." She sat back and took another bite of pie, watching as he ate. "Do you ever think about how many things had to align for us to find each other? Do you believe in fate?" she asked.

"I believe that if we pay attention, good things have a tendency to show up. You showed up and I paid attention and I wasn't going to let that blasted Mark Ogden get a chance at you."

Polly had been a bit smitten with her veterinarian's extraordinary good looks. After spending a wonderful evening with him learning to dance last winter, she'd realized, though, that she really wasn't interested in him. It had always been Henry.

"You never had anything to worry about, you know."

"I didn't know. But I did know that for the first time in my life I wasn't going to be the nice guy and let someone else push me out. I was in love and I wasn't about to let you go."

"Thank you," Polly said. "I really do love you and I'm awfully glad you're back in town."

"I love you too, but I have to tell you that I've eaten way too much this evening. I hurt," he laughed.

"Well, come over to the couch and stretch out. That will help."

"If I fall asleep, will you cover me up? I didn't sleep very well last night because I was so worried about you and your phone call this morning sent my adrenaline into overdrive."

"Do you want to go home?" she asked.

"No, I'm not ready to do that yet. I want to be with you for a while. Is that okay?"

Polly blew out the candles, shut off the lights in the kitchen and they walked across to the living room. She sat down and patted the sofa beside her. He joined her and leaned back into her arms.

"This is exactly where I want to be right now," he said.

CHAPTER SEVEN

Using her dad's letter opener to reach a book on a top shelf in her office, Polly jumped when Henry spoke.

"What are you doing?" he asked.

She looked at him a little sheepishly, "Trying to reach a book?"

"Why did you put those things up so high and why are you using a deadly weapon?"

The letter opener was made of heavy steel and the blade was pretty sharp. Polly grinned and got out of the way while Henry reached up to pull the book down. "*A Universe of Star Wars Collectibles*? What do you want with this?"

"Nothing." She grabbed it and stuck it in a drawer.

"What?"

"Nothing, okay?" she laughed.

"It's something. Tell me."

"Fine. I was messing around on an auction site and wanted to see what a piece was worth."

He gazed around her office. "You don't have enough already?"

"We're not talking about it. Got it?"

"Got it," he said. "So, it looks like you made it through a night without a crisis."

"I'm going to assume it's because you're back in town." Polly winked at him. "They knew you had come riding in on your white horse ready to defend my honor and destroy any who set out to harm me," she laughed. "So what are you doing here today?"

"I'm still on vacation. I didn't schedule anything because I thought I'd be driving back from Michigan, so ... " he looked around her office, "I have nothing to do. Will you entertain me?"

"I'd love to, but Lydia and Beryl are coming at ten o'clock. They're in charge of Halloween here next Thursday night. Then I am having lunch with Joss Mikkels and this afternoon Jeff and I were going to go over decorating plans for the Black Masque."

He pouted at her. "I drove all the way home so I can take care of you and you're too busy for me?"

Polly hadn't been paying attention to his face, distracted by an email that she was reading and snapped her head up to look at him. "I'm sorry!" she said. "I can probably try to rearrange things with everyone and I'll bet Joss could call Nate. Maybe you both could join us for lunch."

"I'm kidding you, Polly. I came back because I love you. You don't have to feel any other obligation."

"Whew," she said, dropping her head into her hands. "I thought you'd totally lost your mind, but if I needed to feel guilty, I was going to at least try to muster some up."

"That's my girl," he laughed. "Actually, I came over to look at your doors in the broad daylight. I really don't want to pull them off and leave you exposed, especially when things are a bit strange around here."

"I'm not really comfortable with that either. The yellow hue isn't all that awful, is it?"

"It's not awful. I won't to make any decisions about it today. We'll leave them alone until I can come up with a good plan."

"Thanks." She picked up her coffee cup to take a drink and it was empty. "Do you want some coffee? I'm a little low here."

"No, I'm good. I think I'll take off. Len Specek had asked me last week to come over and look at some old furniture in his basement. He wants to know what kind of wood it is and if he should spend time refinishing it."

"He's not asking you to do the work?"

"I hope not," Henry said. "The man has more free time than I do and infinitely more patience than me when it comes to that. As much as I love antiques, I prefer building furniture from scratch."

"What kind of furniture does he want you to look at?"

"I don't know. He's being kind of cagey about the whole thing. I can't tell if he's doing something for Andy or what."

"That's what I wondered," Polly said. "They're so cute together."

"Both of them would strangle you if they heard you say that."

Polly watched Jeff Lyndsay run into Sycamore House from the parking lot. He dashed past her inside window and ran into the office, coming to a stop in her doorway.

"I'm sorry I'm late this morning! I got caught up at Iowa State's costume shop. They've got great stuff and have already heard from some people in Bellingwood. Isn't that awesome?"

"It's great, Jeff. I didn't expect to see you until later. Isn't it supposed to be your morning off?" Polly asked.

"There's so much to do to get ready for the Black Masque that I didn't want to sit around my house twiddling my thumbs. That thing is less than two weeks away!"

He took a breath, then said, "Do you know anything more about who might have murdered Thomas Zeller? And how long until we're able to get in there and clean that room?"

"I don't know anything more," Polly said. "And I don't know when we can get in there." She frowned. "I guess I don't know much of anything."

"Well, I got a good lead on masks. I figure we need to have extras here that evening. By the way, did you get the email I sent with the gorgeous mask for a horse? Wouldn't it be smashing to have you and Demi out front, welcoming people to the Ball?"

"I got it. I haven't talked to Eliseo about it, but I'll ask."

"At least I didn't send you the image of a black horse with a skeleton painted in white on it."

"At least you didn't," she acknowledged.

He left her office and Henry laughed. "He loves a party, doesn't he?"

"I'm so glad he does. I'd just stick food in front of people and let things be boring after they ate."

"No you wouldn't. Lydia and her crew would never hear of that. As long as they're around, you'll have great parties."

"I suppose. I think Lydia and Beryl have huge plans for Beggar's Night here. She's talking about transforming the foyer into a haunted house."

Henry cocked his head and looked at her in surprise. "Lydia? Lydia who runs all of the church events and is the Sheriff's wife? Sweet Lydia?"

Polly snorted with laughter. "Oh, she'd hate you for labeling her that way. Yes. Sweet Lydia. I gave them a budget, figuring we could just begin with a little bit of decorating to give the kids something fun and she's managed to come up with some great ideas. Has she talked to you yet?"

"Nope," he said, shifting his eyes back and forth. "What should I be expecting?"

"I think you're going to build a coffin for the vampire ..."

"Oh, that's easy. In fact, that would be fun."

"You should stick around for this meeting. They'll be here in a bit."

Henry's entire body shivered. "Do I have to?"

"No, you don't have to." Polly laughed out loud. "But, I can't promise they won't assign extra tasks to you."

"You won't protect me?"

"I can try. Would you believe she talked Aaron into being Frankenstein's monster?"

Henry had started to stand up again and sat back down, a look of incredulity on his face. "I actually don't believe that. How in the world did she make that happen?"

"Feminine wiles, I suppose. She asked Eliseo to bring Nan up and be the headless horseman. Jason is going to be draped over Nat as the horseman's latest victim."

"Who are you going to be?"

"Well, Aaron keeps telling me I should be the Grim Reaper. I don't know if I'm that courageous, but it will be dark and spooky. Maybe I'll be a vampire. You could build the coffin for me!"

"You're doing all of this on Thursday night and then you're having the Black Masque Ball on Saturday?"

"What's wrong with that?" she asked.

"That's a lot of planning. How are you going to get everything together for each event?"

Polly was confused. "It's not that big of a deal. They're in two different parts of the building and two different groups are planning them. We'll be fine."

"Okay," he drew out. It didn't seem like he was buying it.

"It will be great. Just wait and see."

"I'll do anything I can to help. I promise. Now. I'm gone before those ladies show up and rope me into a meeting."

Polly looked at the time on her computer. "Better hurry."

Henry's eyes grew big and he bolted out the door of the office.

Jeff came around the corner from his office and said, "I meant to ask you. What's with all the paint in the gravel out front?"

Through gritted teeth, Polly said, "We had some vandalism early Sunday morning."

"What?"

"Someone flung paint on the front of Sycamore House. The only things we weren't able to fully clean were the doors."

"How did you get it cleaned up?"

"Fortunately they used latex paint and we used power washers.

"So, no idea who did it?"

"None at all. I filed a report with Ken Wallers. I hope that's the last of it, but he doesn't seem to think it's over, because it was too brazen. You haven't made anyone angry, have you?"

Rather than look shocked, Jeff took a moment to think about it. "No, I don't think so. There was the guy who was staying here last month who thought he shouldn't have to pay us for the week he spent out at the river getting high and taking pictures. But, we worked that out. He wouldn't have been angry enough to come back and retaliate. And besides, he lives in Idaho."

"Well, if you do know someone from around here who might have a reason to hurt us, let me or Ken know. I hate to think about what they might do next."

"Hello!" Lydia called from the front door. She came into the main office with Beryl and Andy and pointed at the conference room. "Can we use your projector? We have great ideas."

Polly stood up and grabbed her nearly empty mug. Three cups wasn't a record, but she didn't feel as if she was finished yet. "Sure," she said. "Come on in. I'm getting excited about this."

"We are too," Andy laughed. "Did you talk to Henry about building the coffin? Len said he'd help."

"Henry's on it. I invited him to stay for this meeting, but he ran over to Len's house for something or other." Polly nearly bit her tongue when she finished speaking.

"Really? What for?" Andy asked.

"I don't know. He wanted to ask Len about a project they were working on."

"Oh," she said. "I'm glad Henry asks for his help. Len enjoys working with him."

Polly nodded and turned back to the coffee pot, which was just starting a new cycle.

Lydia had grabbed Jeff, who was helping her sync her laptop to the projector system. "Do you want to stay while we show Polly what we're planning?" she asked him.

He looked at Polly, who shook her head in the negative, then shrugged her shoulders. "No, if you don't mind. I've got some things to take care of for the Ball. I also have a meeting with the ministerial association this morning."

"What's that about?" Lydia asked.

"The food pantry can't handle all of the food that gets distributed before Thanksgiving, so we're going to open up that Sunday through Wednesday for collection and distribution."

"That's terrific," Andy said. "They've used the elementary school in the past, but with all of the school budget cuts, it's probably easier if they don't have to keep the building open."

Jeff went into his office and Polly waited for the coffee pot to finish brewing, then poured herself a cup. "Fresh coffee if you want it." She went into the conference room and sat down and didn't have to wait long for the others to join her. Lydia clicked onto the first page and they looked at the screen.

She had found strobe lights and black lights, a fog machine and netting to create the ambience of a haunted house. The women weren't using blood and gore for the children, but according to Beryl, shock and surprise was always good for the heart.

The littlest children could get their candy at the front door and leave, but anyone who wanted to brave the short path through and around the foyer would have a good time. A ghost made from white netting would float down from above, hung by dark fishing line and lit by black lights. They had ordered haunted house soundtracks and Beryl was going to dress as a horrible clown who would jump out as strobe lights flashed in the guest's faces. That would be the worst fright they'd have this year. Tombstones and gargoyles would round out the decorations.

"Who is cleaning up the floor when those little kids wet themselves?" Beryl asked.

Polly grinned at her. "What do you mean?"

"I mean, I'm going to be the creepiest clown ever. All of their nightmares are going to be real when they see me."

"So, you don't think that a vampire coming out of the coffin or a ghost floating above them or a real, live stomping Frankenstein's monster will scare them?"

Beryl slid Lydia's laptop over in front of her and clicked through, then pointed at a clown, with huge red lips and blood smearing its face. One arm was missing and the costume was aged and horrific. "That's what I'm planning to look like. Still think your pale-faced vampire is worse?"

Polly shuddered. "I hate clowns. More than I hate snakes, I hate clowns."

"I know!" Beryl laughed. "That's why it's such a great idea. I've always wanted to horrify kids. I still don't understand why Ronald McDonald gets away with it. He's awful looking."

"Because he gives kids great-tasting fries," Polly said. "His priorities are in the right place. And besides, McDonald's has had fifty years to make kids believe he won't eat them in their dreams."

"You did a nice job cleaning the front of the building, dear," Lydia said, interrupting them. "The doors don't look too bad today. I was worried about those."

"We all were, but I'm going to leave it to Henry now."

"Did you welcome him back last night?" Beryl asked coyly.

"I'm not sure what you mean by that," Polly said, "but I cooked him a really nice meal and I even made an apple pie."

"They say the way to a man's heart is through his stomach, I guess," Andy said.

"Is that why you keep inviting Len over for dinner?" Beryl laughed. "Are you trying to get to his heart?"

"I think I've already found it, thank you very much," Andy retorted. "We're having a very nice time together. So there." She stuck her tongue out and made a raspberry sound.

Beryl wiped the front of her blouse. "You're sloppy," she said.

Andy just groaned.

"Do you have a wedding this weekend?" Lydia asked Polly.

"I'm sure we do. I don't think there are any open weekends until next March. Why?"

"Can we begin construction on Sunday afternoon? I want to make sure things are coming together."

Polly stood and walked to Jeff's office. He looked up. "Can they get in on Sunday to build the set for Halloween? Do you have anything scheduled that would be affected by that next week?"

"There are things going on in the classrooms. Just tell them to leave a path for people to walk," he said, a little distractedly.

"Is everything okay?" Polly asked.

"I don't know," he said and continued to look at his screen.

"What does that mean?"

Jeff looked up at her. "Okay, what do you make of this?" He turned the monitor on his desk so she could see it.

"What am I looking at?"

"Read the email."

Polly bent over and looked at the email. *"Tell pretty girl it's going to cost her."*

"Pretty girl?" she said. "That's what Henry calls me."

"I know. I've heard him. Everybody's heard him. What do you think this means?"

"Call Ken Wallers. I'll call Aaron. I don't know if this is about the vandalism or the murder, or if it's something else, but they should know about this. It sounds like a threat."

"You should check your own email. This just came in."

Polly stepped back into the conference room. "Jeff says that Sunday is cool."

"What's wrong, Polly. You look like something scared you to death."

"I don't know," Polly said. "I think someone just threatened me in Jeff's email. I need to go check mine and then I'm calling Aaron." She didn't say anything more and walked into her office. She opened her email in the browser and sure enough there was one to her from the same email address

"You will pay for what you did or things will get worse."

Great. She had no idea what was going on. Polly picked up her phone and dialed Aaron.

"Polly? Why are you calling me?"

"No body. I promise. But, I just got a strange email and so did Jeff. Someone is threatening me. It sounds like they want money, but I don't know what for. Jeff is talking to Ken Wallers, just in case it's about the vandalism."

"Why don't you just marry Henry so I can quit worrying about you being there by yourself," Aaron asked.

That was enough to make her chuckle, "He hasn't asked me yet and don't you dare tell him that he has to so that he can keep me safe. You know how I feel about that."

"Yeah, yeah, yeah. You're a strong woman and can take care of yourself."

"And don't you forget it."

"I'm sending my tech goddess up to you about two o'clock.

She'll see if there's anything she can do to track down who sent that email. Her name is Anita Banks. You'll like her. She thinks men are useless appendages, too."

"That's not what I said," Polly protested.

"I know. I'm teasing. But, I think you'll like her."

"Thanks, Aaron."

They hung up and she looked at the time. She needed to head up to the diner to have lunch with Joss, but she couldn't take her eyes off the screen. Why would someone threaten her?

She looked up to see Lydia, Beryl and Andy standing in her doorway. Lydia stepped in, "Are you okay?"

"I think so. Aaron is sending some girl up to look at my email."

"Oh, that's Anita. She's fantastic. Talk about a bright girl."

"I have to meet Joss for lunch at the diner, but I'm a little weirded out by this," Polly said.

"Go have a tenderloin," Beryl said. "You know that's what you need. Some grease and some carbs. It will make you feel much more normal."

"I can't forget to let Obiwan out when I get back," she muttered to herself.

"Use your note app to send yourself a reminder," Andy quietly said.

Polly chuckled. "I'm training all of you, aren't I!"

"Yes you are. Now go on. Your friend is waiting."

"Thanks," Polly said. She walked out of the office with them and then hugged each in turn. "I love you all."

"We love you too, dear," Lydia patted Polly's arm as they left. "Be safe today."

Polly went through the kitchen to her garage and got into her truck. They were right. A tenderloin would help.

CHAPTER EIGHT

Nothing was better than lunch with a friend, and Polly had something new to think about. Joss wanted Obiwan to come to the library as a reading therapy dog. She had done the research and found training in Des Moines. Polly could begin immediately and finish before Thanksgiving. It would be a terrific opportunity for her to spend more time with books and kids. She didn't miss her job at the Boston Public Library, but when things got to be too much, she looked back on those days as simple and quiet.

She pulled into the garage and ran upstairs to get Obiwan. He was sitting at the top of the steps waiting for her. "Come on," she said. "Let's go for a walk."

He followed her back down and they went outside. "We were talking about you today. How would you like to spend time at the library letting kids read to you? Do you think that would be fun?"

He wagged his tail and they walked toward the creek. She was so fortunate to own this property. The sycamore trees growing on either side of the creek bed had been there for years and offered wonderful shade in the summer. The leaves were beginning to turn now and she knew they would soon fill her yard.

When they went in the front door, she started for the stairs until she heard noise coming from the offices. She and Obiwan went in and a woman was practically screaming at Jeff.

"But, I have to get into his room. His computer is in there and he told me the manuscript was finished. Do you understand how important this is now that he is dead? I have to get it now!"

"What's going on?" Polly asked.

"Are you the owner? Let me into Thomas Zeller's room! I must be allowed access to his things. Open that door!"

The woman was in her late thirties with closely cropped dirty blonde hair. She wore no makeup and her eyes were red-rimmed, behind a pair of glasses that were much too large for her face. She had thin lips that kept pressing together as she spoke.

Finally Polly had enough. "Whoa. Stop. Who are you?"

Jeff began to speak, but the woman interrupted him. "I do not understand why this is so difficult for you. I can't help it that Tommy hid in the boondocks, but surely someone understands the importance of time. I've been traveling this hell hole of a state and isn't there someone with some intelligence?"

"I'm sorry you are upset," Polly said, "but please stop yelling."

"If you would get me what I need, yelling would be unnecessary, but until I'm allowed access, I am your worst nightmare. Do you understand? Now fix this, you stupid, stupid people!" The woman ramped up to a shriek and Polly backed up.

She took a deep breath, closed her eyes and gathered herself, knowing that what she was about to do could make things worse. "I'm going to ask you to sit down in the conference room and when you have finished ranting and raving, we will be glad to help you. Until then, neither I nor my assistant have time for you."

Polly pointed to the conference room and put her hand on Obiwan's collar. The dog sat beside her, completely alert.

"I will not be spoken to this way," the woman shrieked, making no move toward the conference room.

"I'm perfectly willing to call for help to escort you off my property," Polly said. "Or you can settle down. Your choice. Now go. If you'd like coffee, I'm glad to bring some to you."

When the woman remained standing, Polly chuckled. "I actually insist." She took the woman's arm and guided her toward the conference room. "I'm going to shut the door. When you're ready to be human, come find us."

She gave the woman a little push into the room and pulled the door shut, then looked at Jeff. "Who did I just insult?" she asked.

He laughed, then took a breath and laughed again, a deep, throaty laugh. "What did you do?"

"I was tired of listening to her. Who is she?"

"From what I understand, she's Thomas Zeller's agent."

"That surprises me. He was so normal. I can't imagine he would work with someone like her."

"I doubt that they spent a lot of time together. She's scary," Jeff glanced toward the closed door. "But Polly, you are scarier than she is and that's saying something."

"I'm so tired of things happening around me without having any control, I snapped. I'm taking Obiwan upstairs. If she comes out before I'm back, don't let her get away with anything."

"I'm not sure how I'll stop her, but I'll do my best," he laughed.

Polly said, "Come on, Obiwan. Let's go. I appreciate you having my back when I get confrontational." The dog followed her out of the office after giving the conference room door a quick glance. Once they hit the stairway, he trotted up beside her. She unlocked the door and let him in. "I'll be back later. You guys be good."

Glancing across the hallway, she saw the police seal on the middle room. She'd have to call Aaron to see how long they were going to keep her out. If she needed to replace things, she wanted to do it as quickly as possible.

Polly walked slowly down the steps thinking about the fragility and resilience of life. Two days after he died, life for the living was still going on. She would remember Thomas, but other things immediately began taking the place of the time she normally spent with him. Other crises would take over her thoughts and other people would fill her days. Life was for the living, but death always hovered at the edge of it.

Jeff was in his office when she got back and the conference door was still closed.

"Nothing?" she asked him.

"Nope. Not a peep."

"Did you get her name?"

"It was Natalie something. That was all I was able to get from her before she lost control."

"Okay, I'll go deal with Natalie something. We'll see if we can figure this out."

"Thanks. I'm going to hide in here if you don't mind."

Polly smiled at him, "Chicken," she said and turned back to the conference room. She took a deep breath and opened the door.

Natalie-something was slumped over, her head cradled in her arms and her shoulders shaking. Polly sat down beside her.

"I'm sorry," Natalie sobbed, "I'm so sorry. All I could think about was that everything was over for me. I don't know what I'm going to do."

Polly rolled her chair over to a counter and picked up a box of tissues, then rolled back to Natalie and set them in front of her. The woman began pulling them out one by one until Polly stopped her by placing a hand on top of her hand.

"I don't know what I'm doing." Natalie began sobbing again.

Polly pulled out her phone and texted Jeff, *"Could you bring in a bottle of water and a small plate of those chocolate chip cookies?"* She didn't say a word, just let the woman cry.

Jeff was back quickly and lightly knocked at the door. He handed Polly the plate and the bottle, then rolled his eyes and backed out of the room, shutting the door.

"Here," Polly said. "You should take a drink."

"I'm not thirsty."

"I wasn't asking if you were thirsty. I was telling you to take a drink." Polly twisted the top off and handed the bottle to Natalie. "Drink," she said.

"You're very pushy," Natalie complained.

"I know I am. It's one of my best things."

Natalie took a gulp of the water and then another one. When

she set the bottle down on the table, Polly handed her a cookie.

"Everyone likes chocolate chip and I'll bet you haven't eaten anything today. Your blood sugar is probably low. I choose to believe that's why you've been so out of control. Eat a cookie."

"You won't let me not eat this, will you?" Natalie asked.

"Not unless you tell me you are allergic to chocolate."

"You should live on the east coast. You'd rule that world with this attitude," Natalie said through bites of cookie.

"I lived there once. I like it better here."

"Are you going to let me into Thomas's room?"

"I can't do that. It's sealed by the police. Until they release the room, we can't get in."

That sent the woman into another crying jag. "How will I take care of his things? I need to get that manuscript. His books are going to fly to the top of all of the sales lists now that he's dead."

"I suspect you can take a breath and wait. He's only been dead a couple of days. All of this hysteria over his manuscript seems really out of place. Especially since a good man was just killed."

Those words caused more sobbing and Polly had to take the cookie out of the woman's hand before it was a crumbly mess. She was so out of control that Polly was becoming a little concerned.

"You must stop the hysterics," Polly said calmly. "Right. Now."

"But he's dead," Natalie wailed. "He's dead!"

"Honey, I know he's dead. He died in front of me. You aren't doing anyone any good with this wailing."

The woman looked at Polly. "I'm sorry I insulted you. I got lost. I've been all over the state, and then I ended up in another little town with streets named after poets and authors." Natalie wrinkled her forehead. "Where was I?"

"That was Stratford. It's a cool idea for a town though, isn't it? Do you have a place to stay tonight?"

"No. I figured there would be a hotel in town."

"We don't have a hotel. If that's what you want, you'll have to go to Boone or Ames."

Natalie looked at her in panic. "I'll never find my way. I don't drive very often. That's the best part of living in Brooklyn. I always take a cab or the subway."

"Sit here. Let me ask a quick question," Polly said. She left the conference room, walked into Jeff's office, and shut his door.

"What's up? Is she coherent yet?" he asked.

Polly screwed up her face and looked at him.

"What?" he asked, then he stopped, "You're going to ask me something, aren't you, and I'm not going to like it."

"Don't we have a room in the addition that's still open?"

"Well, yes."

"Can she stay for a few days? She isn't going anywhere until she can get Thomas's manuscript and computer."

"Will she be hysterical every time I run into her?" he asked.

"I won't guarantee anything," Polly laughed. "Can this work?"

"Sure. You get to take her up though. Put her on the second floor toward the front."

"Thanks, Jeff."

Polly went back into the conference room and found Natalie eating a third cookie. At least that was a good sign.

"We have an open room." Polly sat back down. "It has internet access and you can do all of the work you need to do. As soon the sheriff releases Thomas's things, I'll let you know."

"Thank you," the woman's shoulders sagged and then she continued in an overly dramatic fashion, "I just couldn't get back in that car and drive. I would be lost the minute I left town."

"Let me show you to your room," Polly said.

"Do you have anything to eat or can I get someone to deliver?"

"I'm sure we have something. There are also a couple places that will deliver pizza or sandwiches. There is coffee in the kitchen and water in the refrigerator. Feel free to help yourself."

"Thank you. I do apologize for being so awful. It's just that ..."

Polly put her hand up. "It's fine." She hated apologies that turned into justifications for people's bad behavior. She was just beginning to tolerate this woman and didn't want to have to be angry again. "Come on, I'll show you where your room is."

As they left the office, another young woman came in the front door. The girl was in her mid-twenties and had bouncy brunette hair that hung to her shoulders. It was held back with a bright green headband that matched her belt. Black pants and a striking pink and green blouse which seemed to reflect the girl's demeanor were finished off by a pair of hot pink flats.

She waved to them as they crossed in the outer office. Polly stopped. "Are you Anita?"

"Yes, are you Polly?"

"I am. That's Jeff Lindsay in there. I'm just going to show Natalie ..." She paused, not knowing the woman's last name.

"Dormand," Natalie said.

"Natalie Dormand to her room. Jeff can get you started. My office is fine. I'll be back in a bit."

Polly was glad the addition, which had been designed for those with special needs, was available. They took the elevator to the second floor and Polly unlocked the first door.

The front of the building mimicked the look of a barn and the garage on the other side of Sycamore house, but the side looking out on the horse's pasture was filled with windows. Lydia had worked her magic in these rooms, ensuring that each was unique and comfortable. She'd chosen deep burgundy and a rich green as the colors for this room, accenting the rustic pine furniture. Henry had consulted her, building cabinets and closets to match as closely as possible. Polly was thrilled with the work they'd done.

"This is very nice," Natalie said. "Thank you."

Polly picked up the tablet on the desk. "Here is everything you might want to know about Bellingwood. If you want food delivered, just call them. They know where we are and all you need to do is tell them you are on the top floor of the addition and they'll find you. I hope you are comfortable here."

She explained the lock system and emailed a key to the woman's phone, then left her to unpack and settle in. While waiting for the elevator, she rolled her head on her shoulders. "Thomas, you didn't tell me she was so high maintenance. What were you thinking?" Polly asked, looking up at the ceiling. "You owe me now, you know."

CHAPTER NINE

Knowing that Anita Banks was waiting, Polly hurried back into the office and found her tapping away at the computer keyboard.

"Have you found anything?" Polly asked.

"You have a rockin' system here. I don't see power like this very often," the girl laughed, not looking up from the screen. "But really, only one screen? This baby could support a bunch of them and with your sci fi stuff, it would only be the right thing to do."

Polly loved geeks. "Honestly, I just haven't gotten around to looking for another one."

"You can buy them online. You should buy yourself two or three that match. Really make this place awesome."

"I'll think about it," Polly responded. "So, ummm, anything?"

Anita looked up. "You aren't going to like it."

"What's that?"

"Whoever sent that email used your own wireless server. How far out does it reach?"

"We've got repeaters boosting the signal down to the barn and throughout the buildings here. There's enough bandwidth coming in so anyone could use the signal."

"Well, it's either one of your guests, an employee or someone who got close enough to use it."

"That's just fabulous. I'm positive it isn't an employee and I'm fairly confident I don't have a guest who is angry with me. There are only four of them here and Aaron is already investigating them. This information doesn't help me at all, does it?"

"Have you considered surveillance cameras? That would be a pretty cool use of the extra monitors - like a never-ending movie."

Polly shook her head. "No. I'm not doing that. I don't want to intrude on my guest's privacy."

"What if you were to look at it as if you were offering them better security? A safer place to stay."

"This is Bellingwood. I think that's pretty safe as it is."

"It's just a thought. With the system you have in place, it wouldn't be that difficult to get them hooked up."

"Everyone is trying to get me to do this," Polly quietly complained. "I'm not going to."

Anita shrugged, "Not my deal. It was just a thought." She looked at Polly, "Aaron says you're having some big Victorian era masquerade ball in a couple of weeks. Steampunk costumes too?"

"Absolutely. Are you interested?"

"I am. I've been to a few events with the Iowa Steampunk Group in Des Moines and Iowa City. They came up to ride the Chinese Steam Engine in Boone last winter. That was a blast."

"That's cool. I can hardly wait for the ball," Polly replied. "There is so much that can be done with the Victorian era, from Steampunk to Victorian elegance to vampires and nearly anything else. We only ask that you do something and that wear a mask. It's going to be fun. Do you have a character name?" Polly had read enough Steampunk novels and done enough research into the phenomena that she was absolutely fascinated by it.

Anita giggled a little and shrugged her shoulders. "I'm Claire Astlebury. She was my mother's grandmother and came from England in the late eighteen hundreds. My Claire travels in her father's grand, lighter-than-air dirigible. She loves to fly and is building her own contraption so she can cross the Atlantic alone."

"That sounds awesome," Polly said. "Do you read a lot of these novels?"

"I don't have as much time to read as I used to. I kind of got myself wrapped up in a couple of online computer games and between that and work, I don't read like I should."

Polly's mind began to race and then she made herself stop thinking about it. She wasn't about to play cupid for a couple of kids. But, all she could think was that this girl would be perfect for Doug Randall. She was a few years older than him, but still. It would be perfect. She let out a giggle and then stopped herself.

"What?" Anita asked.

"Nothing. I just told myself to stop something before I started." The girl looked at her, perplexed.

"I would only get myself into trouble," Polly sighed, but she couldn't help herself. "Are you dating anyone, Anita?"

"Do I need a date to come to the ball?"

"Oh, no, that's not it," Polly assured her. "I was thinking that I should introduce you to a friend of mine. You two would hit it off and even if there was no love at first sight, you'd make great friends. I adore him and I ..." she paused. "I'm really sticking my nose where it doesn't belong and I'm not going to do that to you. I'm sorry. Forget I said anything."

Anita pushed her bangs back on her forehead. "I wouldn't hate meeting someone. Why do you think we'd be friends?"

"He's a total computer geek and a gamer ..."

"What games does he play?" Anita interrupted.

"I'm not sure of all of them. I know he plays Sword Lords with my friend's sons. I've seen Diablo and Spore and I'm sure he plays World of Warcraft. And he's a total Star Wars nut."

Anita smiled. "He sounds kind of perfect. I can't believe someone hasn't grabbed him."

Polly laughed deeply and heartily. "Oh, sweetheart, you're wonderful. You do know that most girls aren't quite as impressed with that as you think. They like their men to be interested in cars and sports." Polly did a quick self-check and groaned internally. Just like she was attracted to a man who liked those things.

"I'd like to meet him," Anita said quietly. "It sounds like fun."

"Really?"

"Yeah. Why not. It isn't like interesting boys come dropping out of the sky. I shouldn't turn this down, even if it doesn't work out."

"Give me your number and I'll see what I can do to set up a meet before the Ball. Unless you want to meet him for the first time with a mask on and in full regalia."

"That sounds kind of romantic, don't you think?"

"Not really, but I've had enough surprises in my life," Polly said.

"That's right. I've heard stories about you."

"I'm sure you have. I'm glad that I know who to call when dead bodies show up, but it is starting to get a little weird."

"No kidding! The Giller file is red-flagged down at the office. We just wait to see what will happen next."

"You're joking, right?"

Anita giggled, "Maybe a little. It's gotten to be quite the thing. We'd laugh if it weren't so sad that people die around you."

"Oh, that sounds horrible! It makes me seem dangerous or something. None of these have been my fault!"

"We know that. You just end up being in the right place at the wrong time. But then, that's what they all say." Anita winked at Polly and stood up. "I should be getting back to the office. Ask your friend if he wants a mysterious date for the Ball. If he does, tell him that Lady Claire will be dressed as an aviatrix."

"I will." Polly walked with Anita as she left the office. "Thanks for coming up and you'll tell Aaron what you found?"

Anita grinned, "I have to fill out a report. I'll make sure it's on his desk ... with the Giller red flag."

Polly went back into her office. The boys should be here by now. She spun around in her chair and looked out the window in time to see Jason and Andrew cross the parking lot. She turned back around as they came in the front door of the building, past her office window and into the main office.

Andrew dropped his backpack and hopped into a chair. "We're late because Jason got in trouble," he announced.

"Shut up, runt," Jason sat down in the other chair.

"What happened?" Polly asked. This was the last thing she expected and she didn't want to be the one to tell their mother.

Andrew started to speak, then caught his brother glaring at him. He shut his mouth and slumped down in his chair.

"Jason?" Polly asked again.

"It was no big deal," he said.

Andrew spoke up, "You have detention tomorrow."

This time Polly glared at the little boy. "It's not your story to tell, Andrew. Let Jason do it."

Andrew, chagrined, seemed to slump a little lower.

"Jason?" she asked.

"Mom is going to kill me. She has to sign a note and call the principal tomorrow." Jason sighed. "I'm going to so die. You don't think she'll stop me from helping out in the barn, do you?"

"What did you do to get detention?" Polly asked. Andrew opened his mouth, thought better of it and slammed it shut.

"I got in a fight."

"You what?" Polly was shocked. Jason was pretty even tempered. Even when his younger brother pushed him to the edge, he didn't get physical. "With who?"

Poor Andrew was dying to speak, but she held her finger up to keep him quiet.

"It wasn't a big deal. I don't want to talk about it."

"You don't have to tell me about it," Polly said. "The two of you should go upstairs and do your homework. Eliseo will be ready for you in about forty-five minutes. I'll come up before you go out to the barn. Do you have a lot of homework tonight, Andrew?"

"I just have spelling words and a math worksheet," Andrew said. "I'll be done in a jiffy."

Polly giggled, "A jiffy? Where did you hear that word?"

"Oh, some book I was reading. Can I go back to my desk and do my homework? I want to look at my globe. We're studying the United States and I'm going to draw a map of Iowa."

"Go on upstairs first and do your homework. When Jason goes out to the barn, you can go down to your desk."

She watched Andrew move through protest, to acquiescence and finally acceptance. "I'll do it. Come on Jason. I'll race you."

"You already win, runt. I'm not racing. I'll be up in a minute."

Andrew grabbed his backpack and took off up the steps. Jason stayed seated. "Polly, I heard some seventh graders talk about beating Andrew up. When I told them that I was going to report them, three of them came at me and I had to punch the first kid to get him off. He's bigger than me, but the other two started screaming when the teacher showed up."

"Did you tell anyone what happened?"

"No. I didn't want Andrew to know. I think they'll leave him alone. But, he's kind of a dork and his friends aren't much better."

"I don't care whether kids think he is a dork or not. That's no reason for anyone to get beat up. Will you tell your mom?"

"Yeah. I hope she believes me. I'm really scared she'll ground me and won't let me help with the horses."

"Don't worry too much about that. Since you have to be here every afternoon anyway, I'll talk to her. We'll see what we can work out. Did you hurt the kid you punched?"

"His nose was bloody. The nurse said he'd be fine, but he was really mad. I hope he doesn't get me in more trouble."

"Did he get detention, too?"

"No, his buddies told the teacher that I just came unglued on him because he was being mouthy."

"Okay. Deal with your detention and tell your mom everything. It's not fair sometimes, but it's what you get."

"I know. Promise you won't tell Andrew?"

"I won't say anything. I promise."

Jason hitched his backpack on his shoulder and went out and up the stairs. Polly couldn't imagine how difficult it must be for him to feel responsible for taking care of his younger brother without a dad around to give him support. Sylvie wasn't going to like it and the school probably hadn't heard the last of this episode. That was one mama bear who protected her kids.

Her cell phone rang and caller ID told her that it was her friend, Sal Kahane.

"Hey there, gorgeous," Polly sang out as she answered.

"Hi sweetie, I miss you!" Sal said.

"What's up?" Polly asked.

"Are you getting my room ready?"

"We're working on it."

"I told Mark I couldn't come since I'm planning to be there for Christmas."

"Wait. What? You're coming for Christmas too?"

"Didn't I tell you that?" Sal asked coyly.

"No, you never tell me anything. Especially since you got hooked up with that hot veterinarian. You talk to him and not me. I'm a little jealous, you know."

"You have your wonderful boyfriend, you can't be jealous of me with Mark."

"No, silly. I'm jealous of him. I want more of your time and you're much too busy getting all googly-eyed over Dr. Hottie."

"Well, tough tiddlywinks. Live with it," Sal laughed. "I can hardly wait to surprise him."

Polly was absolutely certain this had the potential to be a bad idea. Mark was head over heels for Sal, but she didn't know if he was planning to come by himself to the ball. "Are you sure you want to go ahead with this surprise?"

"He told me that he was going by himself, if that's what you're worried about. So, do I get my favorite room?"

"If the mattress shows up, you can have the room across the hall. Otherwise, you get my couch."

"What mattress are you talking about?"

"Oh, crap. I haven't talked to you and told you what happened here. One of my guests was killed Saturday morning."

"Polly!" Sal cried out. "What happened?"

"He was stabbed in the middle bedroom. I haven't been in there, because the Sheriff has the room sealed, but it sounds like the mattress needs to be replaced and I think some furniture is broken. It was Thomas Zeller. I told you about him, didn't I?"

"The author? Yeah. I've read his books."

"He managed to get to my apartment and died in front of me."

"Polly, no! Not again."

"Don't you start with me," Polly warned.

"But how are you handling this?"

"Well, I don't have time to do anything but handle it. Things keep happening around here and I just deal with them."

"I'm so sorry. You should have called me."

"Oh Sal, you're right. But I was a mess and then someone threw paint all over the front of Sycamore House and Henry came home early from Michigan and then Thomas's agent showed up today and someone is sending me threatening emails."

"Stop it. All of this happened in the last couple of days? Maybe you should hop on a plane and spend time with me instead."

"To be honest, there was a moment when I thought that my life was quieter and simpler when I lived in Boston. I know it doesn't make any sense, but sometimes my head starts to spin."

"I guess so. Is Henry being a good boyfriend?"

"He is. He was in Michigan visiting his sister and rushed back yesterday. He hates it when he's gone and bad things happen."

"Well, I hate it too. What did your trusty Sheriff say this time?"

"Not much. It was three in the morning and I woke him up."

Then Polly chuckled.

"What are you laughing at?"

"Would you believe that Henry won the pool at the local elevator? He put money on one of my guests dying."

"That is really funny, in a sick and twisted way. Are you really doing okay?"

"I don't have a choice. Eliseo made me take a ride yesterday morning and that was good, but then we had to come back and clean up the front of the building and I cooked a big dinner for Henry and oh, Sal ... I'm really glad you are coming to Iowa. I could use a friend who remembers what I used to be like before bodies started piling up in my life."

"Well, I will sleep on your couch or on an air mattress or wherever you find room for me."

"Hopefully we'll get the room opened up before you're here. That would be the best option."

"I've made my reservation and rented my car. I'll see you soon and don't tell Mark, okay?"

"Mum's the word. I promise."

"I love you sweetie. Call me if you get overwhelmed."

"I will. See you soon."

Polly hung up. It was going to be fun watching Mark's reaction at the ball.

She looked up and saw Natalie Dormand in the doorway. "Can I help you with something, Natalie?"

"I told the delivery guy to come in the main door. I wanted to check out your place here. Thomas would have loved it."

"We enjoyed having him here. He was really an interesting man," Polly said. "Let me show you to the kitchen. Follow me."

She led Natalie to the kitchen and offered her a cup of coffee.

"Thank you." Natalie peered out the window into the foyer. "I think my food is here. Thanks again for your hospitality."

"No problem," Polly said. Natalie left as Sylvie came in the back door.

"Hey there," Polly said. "I'm glad you're here."

"Where's Jason? We need to talk. I got a message from school that he is in detention for hitting someone." Sylvie was furious.

"He told me about it. I think he did the right thing, but it was misinterpreted," Polly said.

"This is one of the things I absolutely hate about being out of reach," Sylvie growled. "I barely feel like I'm parenting my kids any more. You're here for them more than I am."

Polly didn't say anything.

"I shouldn't be upset that he told you. I should be glad that he's got someone else in his life he can trust." Sylvie slammed her bag on the prep table. "But, damn it. He's in trouble, I'm busy, and you're the one who knows what's going on."

"I'm sorry," Polly said and crossed the room to hug her friend. "I can't imagine how difficult this is for you."

Sylvie looked at her and said, "Grrr." She patted Polly's hand and then said, "Okay, tell me what he told you."

"He overheard some kids talking about beating Andrew up.

When he threatened to tell an adult, the three of them came at him. He punched one to get him to back off and a teacher walked in. The other two accused Jason of attacking for no reason."

"Did he at least defend himself from the accusation?"

"I think he tried," Polly said. "He has detention and you have to sign some letter."

"Well, I'm not going to class tomorrow morning. If my boy has been set up, I'm going to fix it. I'll sit in that principal's office all morning if that's what it takes, but they aren't going to get away with this. And threatening Andrew? Why would anyone do that?"

"Jason says he's a bit of a nerd and they're bullies. Andrew is lucky to have his brother there paying attention."

"I know he's smart, but we try to make sure he dresses like the other kids and he's really social and outgoing."

"And he's nice to other kids who aren't as social and outgoing and he has never pretended to be cool."

Sylvie sat down on a stool. "I knew these years weren't going to be easy." She looked at Polly. "And I'm sorry. I couldn't ask for a better friend to help me. The boys love you and so do I."

"I get it. You have a lot going on right now. I'm not upset," Polly assured her. "Don't worry. You have two really great kids."

"Thank you. You're sure Jason didn't do something awful?"

"I'm pretty sure. He's terrified you won't let him help Eliseo with the horses. That worried him more than anything."

"Oh, I'd never do that to him. He lives for those hours in the barn," Sylvie thought for a moment, then took a deep breath. "Oh, I don't know what to do. If I step in and make a huge scene, Jason loses all credibility. He's trying so hard. And that's another reason I'll never stop him from spending time with the horses. It's the one time that he can be a kid." She sighed. "I'll call the principal and find out what's going on and what I need to do to make sure this is fixed. Jason can do his time in detention. It won't kill him."

"That's probably the right thing to do," Polly agreed.

"Sometimes being a parent is the worst job ever," Sylvie said. "It's such a fine line between protecting them and letting them grow up on their own. I'm never sure if I'm doing it right."

"Anyone who knows your boys very well knows you are doing it right."

This time Sylvie reached out and hugged Polly, "Thanks for letting me fall apart and letting me figure it all out. I love you."

Polly squeezed her tight, "I love you too and I love that you trust me with Jason and Andrew. They mean the world to me. You know that, don't you?"

By now, there were tears in both women's eyes. "I know they do," Sylvie said, "and you are so important to all of us. We're lucky you moved into town. So lucky."

They heard Andrew's feet running down the back stairs and were watching for him when he dashed into the kitchen.

"Mom, did you hear that Jason got detention?" he asked when he saw her.

"I did. And did you hear that it's not nice for little brothers to tattle on their older brothers? You are supposed to have his back."

Andrew looked down at the floor. "But mom!"

"No buts. The world is always going to look for ways to pit the two of you against each other, but I'm going to love both of you and your job is to take care of me and each other. Always. Get it?"

"Got it," he said. "Are you going to ground him from the horses? Because that would be bad."

"I'm not going to do that to him," she said. "Now, have you taken Obiwan outside for a walk?"

Polly grinned.

"No, do I have time?" Andrew asked.

"You do. Make it quick, but make sure he is done with everything, okay? Scoot." Sylvie said.

Andrew turned around and ran back for the doorway to Polly's apartment. They heard Obiwan come down the steps and then the garage door slam shut.

"Like I said," Sylvie said. "I never know whether I'm doing it right or not."

"You're fine, Sylvie Donovan. Just fine." Polly replied.

CHAPTER TEN

Eager to be done for the day working with the hundreds of files on Thomas Zeller's flash drive, Polly was glad to see Jason and Andrew arrive the next afternoon. So far, nothing made sense and she wasn't sure whether or not to involve Natalie Dormand. Thomas had been insistent that Polly was the only person he wanted to see the information and she'd already betrayed that request when she gave the original drive to Aaron Merritt.

She'd looked for a copy of his current book, but hadn't found it yet. Thomas had named his folders with strange titles and so far all she could do was dig into them one by one. She hadn't gotten very far at all, since she was afraid that if she didn't read a document closely enough, she'd miss something. She ended up reading through long, involved research notes he'd taken and at this point, Polly felt like a complete numbskull.

Jason seemed to have survived his in-school suspension. He was no worse for wear, but was a little more subdued than usual. They walked upstairs to her apartment together.

"How'd your day go?" she asked.

"It was really boring, but it was okay. I had to sit in one room by myself all day long. I got my homework done, so that was good, but I didn't like it."

"I don't suppose it would be a lot of fun," Polly acknowledged. "They probably don't want kids choosing to do that."

"Can I take Obiwan out for a walk while Andrew does his homework? I'm tired of sitting on my ..." he looked up at her and gave a small smile. "I'm tired of sitting."

"Sure. You two haven't been out for a while. He'll be glad to spend time with you." She opened the door to the apartment and glanced across the hall. Just as she turned to go inside, she caught a glimpse of Grey Linder peeking out his door at her. He caught her eye, pulled back quickly and shut the door.

"That was weird," she said.

"What was?" Jason asked.

"Nothing. Go on and take Obiwan." Jason walked through the living room into her bedroom and calling the dog, then left by the back steps to go outside.

"I don't have very much homework," Andrew said. "Can I play a video game first?"

"You know the deal," she reminded him. "Do your work and then your time is free. I'm going to make pumpkin bars. How does that sound?"

"Can I lick the frosting bowl?" he asked.

"Sure. You get busy and maybe we'll finish at the same time."

Andrew set his backpack on the dining room table and took out several workbooks. Soon the apartment was quiet except for the sound of the mixer. Polly looked out the window at the front parking lot, thinking about the person who had sent the email the other morning. Things had been quiet since then and she was grateful. There hadn't been any other signs of vandalism and she was hoping that maybe the problem would resolve itself.

She sprayed the jelly roll pan and poured the pumpkin mix in, then put it in the oven to bake. This was her favorite fall recipe. There was nothing better than the scent of cinnamon and pumpkin to get her ready for crisp leaves on the ground and a brisk chill in the air.

Jason and Obiwan were running in and out of the sycamore trees lining her driveway and Polly smiled at their energy. A school bus passed by on the highway and cheerleaders were hanging out the windows, yelling and cheering. Tuesday night - JV football. What wonderful memories these kids would make. Friday night football had been one of her favorite high school events. The band had so much fun together. The colder it got, the more layers she put on under her band uniform. As it got to late October and early November, blankets filled the bleachers so the kids could huddle together after the pre-game show and before half-time. Those were great times.

Jason had found Obiwan's tennis ball and was throwing it to him. Obiwan was just figuring out how to play fetch. It took some doing to get him to bring the ball back to be thrown again, but he was learning.

"How are you doing there, Andrew?" she asked.

"Look at these words, Polly."

She bent over to look at his paper. "What about them?"

"Illustrate and illuminate. Did you know they sound kind of alike? At least the beginning of the words do. We talked about that today."

"What did you decide?" she asked.

"They came from the same place."

"That's probably right. Do you understand why?"

"I suppose," he said, nonchalantly.

"Here, let me show you." Polly went to the coffee table and picked up her laptop, triggering it on while she walked back to the dining room table. They waited while it booted up and she typed in 'illustrate etymology.'

"What's etymology?" he asked, slowly sounding out the word.

"It means the study of where words came from."

"Etymology," he said again. "So you're looking up the etymology of the word illustrate."

"I am and look at this," she pointed to the screen. "See how both of the words come from the same Latin word?"

"They do! That's what my teacher said."

"They both come from a word that means light."

"That's so cool! Can I look up more words?"

"Are you finished with your homework?"

"I have my spelling done. I did my math in class today. Mrs. Walker gave a quiz and I finished it early."

"How did you do on it?"

"I don't know. I think okay."

"No science or social studies?"

"Not really."

"What does 'not really' mean?" Polly grinned down at him. She wasn't going to make it easy.

"I don't have anything due tomorrow."

"Are you sure or will I be in trouble for letting you be a slacker?"

"I'm not a slacker!"

"Okay, then. Type in any word you think of, then type the word etymology after it and this information will show up."

"Will you write the word down in case I forget how to spell it?"

"Sure. But, shut your eyes and think about the word. Can you see it on the screen?"

"Yes."

"How do you spell it?"

"E t y m o ..." he spelled through the first letters slowly, then spun through the last letters, "l o g y." Is that like biology or zoology?"

"Of course it is, you bright boy," she laughed. "ology is the study of something."

"Zoology is the study of animals, then."

"Yep and Biology ..."

"Is the study of bio ... I don't know."

"Bio means life. You keep looking things up. Words are fun." Polly's heart was aflutter with excitement. She loved watching someone fall in love with words. Andrew was soon clicking through pages on the screen.

Jason came in through the bedroom. "Obiwan is getting good at fetch," he said.

"I saw you guys out there. Thanks for doing that. He needs all the practice he can get."

"It would be cool to use a Frisbee sometime. We have a bunch at home. I'll bring them over."

"That would be great."

The timer on her phone rang out and she opened the oven door to pull the pan out. It smelled wonderful.

"What are those?" Jason asked.

"Pumpkin bars. When you get back from the barn, they will be cooled and frosted."

"Can I go down early? I know Eliseo won't be there yet, but I'd like to hang out with Nat."

"Of course," she said. "Would you do me a favor and snuggle Demi a little for me?"

"Thanks, Polly. I will." Jason bent over and hugged Obiwan around the neck and ran for the front door. It slammed behind him and he was gone.

Andrew looked up from the laptop. "I know what he did, Polly. Everybody is talking about it at school."

"What do you mean?" she asked.

"Some seventh graders were going to beat me and my friends up and Jason told them not to. They've been bragging about how they got him in trouble with the principal."

"How do you feel about that?"

"I don't know why they want to beat me up. It's not like I ever did anything to them."

"Sometimes kids are bullies. There's nothing we can do. You're pretty lucky to have Jason around."

"I'm going to hate it when he goes to the high school next year. He won't even be in the same town."

Bellingwood had lost its high school in the nineties. In fact, she was living in the old high school building. The kids were bussed to Boone now. It was going to be difficult for both boys. Even when they didn't get along, they were still each other's best friend.

"Don't think about it too hard right now, Andrew. You have practically a whole year before that happens."

"I know. But, I'm not going to like it."

"I probably won't either. Maybe we'll go down and get him every once in a while so we don't have to wait for the bus to drop him off. If we have time, we'll go to the bookstore. How's that?"

Andrew loved Boone's bookstore and its long shelves of used books. They were becoming regulars and Polly's bookshelves were overflowing again.

"That would be awesome!" he said. "Thanks."

She held her hand over the top of the pan of bars to see if they'd cooled enough. Not yet, but she could start the frosting. She measured cream cheese and butter into the mixer and let it whip. A teaspoon of vanilla and she turned it to the lowest speed before adding powdered sugar. A little milk and the texture was perfect.

"Can I taste it?" Andrew asked.

"I thought the deal was that you got to clean the bowl."

"But you'll scrape it clean. You won't leave much," he complained, but not too exuberantly.

"I'll leave you enough," she laughed. "If you're done with homework, you should pack up your things."

She slathered cream cheese frosting across the top of the bars and scraped the excess off the whip and the edges of the bowl. With a smirk, she handed the nearly empty bowl to Andrew.

"I knew it," he said, dejectedly.

Polly ran the spatula across the pan of bars, filling it with some of the excess and handed it to Andrew. "I'm not that mean."

There was a knock at her front door and Sylvie walked in. "How's my boy today?" She saw Andrew licking the spatula. "What are you doing?" she asked.

He looked shocked. "It's not very much. Polly cleaned the bowl."

"Let me see that." Sylvie strode over and took the spatula from hand, then over his head, she winked at Polly and licked it clean.

"Hey!" he cried.

She ruffled the top of his head, "Hey, what?"

Andrew's shoulders drooped and he said, "I didn't get any extra frosting. That's not fair."

Sylvie had watched Polly run a spoon across the bars and nodded at her.

"You know we love you. Right, Andrew?" Polly asked.

"No," he moaned.

"Then you don't want this?" she pushed it in front of him.

"Thanks!" he brightened up and clutching the spoon close to his body, slipped past his mother. "I'm eating at the other end of the table," he announced.

"Pumpkin bars," Polly said, to explain what she'd baked.

"Cool. Is Jason down at the barn?"

"Yes. He said he spent all day in detention."

"I called the principal this morning. They were fully aware of what really happened, which is why that's all he had to deal with. They aren't putting it on his record, but had to do something since the other kids wouldn't back off their story. That behavior makes me so angry. It doesn't seem fair that my boy should have to be punished when everyone knows he did nothing."

"He could have made a big deal about it if he wanted to, but he didn't. He sucked it up and learned a good lesson," Polly said.

"That bullies get their way?"

"Andrew says everyone in school is talking about it. I'm guessing they won't be quite as popular. The kids know that Jason stood up for his brother and got messed up. Jason's a popular kid. This is going to work itself out."

"I hope so. It makes me mad that I can't fix it."

"Me too, but I'm guessing some time with Nat and Eliseo will help. Oh, that reminds me, just a second."

Polly took her phone out and typed a text to Eliseo, *"Have you been in Lila Fletcher or Grey Linder's room lately?"*

In a moment she had a response, *"I was in Grey Linder's room yesterday. He left for a while and I did a quick clean and fresh sheets. I haven't been in Fletcher's room since Friday. Is everything okay?"*

"It's fine. I just wanted to make sure that things were normal."

"As far as I know."

"Thanks. A lot."

Polly sliced some pumpkin bars and put one on a plate. She

handed it to Sylvie and poured milk into a glass. They put those in front of Andrew and then she cut more.

"Living room?" she asked. "Coffee? Milk?"

"I'd like milk, what about you?" Sylvie asked back.

"Milk."

"I'll pour, you go."

Sylvie soon followed and they sat down on opposite ends of the sofa. Obiwan tried to jump up between them, but Polly caught him with her leg and pushed him back to the floor. "Stay," she said and he put his head between his front paws. "Oh, stop with the drama. You haven't been beaten."

The cats hovered on the back of the sofa, sniffing at the glasses.

"No," Polly said sternly. "Back off." When Luke got pushy with Sylvie, Polly brushed him away and he leapt to the floor. She stared Leia down and then picked her up and set her on the floor as well. "It doesn't take much, but sometimes you have to insist with those cats."

"Have you heard anything more about Thomas Zeller?" Sylvie asked.

"Nothing. I don't know if they're doing anything and just not telling me or if they are stymied. I wish I knew."

"And nothing about the vandalism?"

"I told you about Anita Banks, didn't I?"

"Yeah. But nothing since then?"

"It's been really quiet. I like it, but I don't trust it. Every night I dread going to sleep because I'm scared I will wake up to something horrific the next morning."

"I'd be nervous all the time being by myself in this big place."

"I'm not by myself very often," Polly said.

"But you don't know and trust these people. Any one of them could be an axe murderer."

"Yeah, thanks. That's going to help me sleep tonight. Doug and Billy are right there, though," Polly pointed to the roof of the garage apartment outside her window.

"I suppose. But I saw what kind of insulation they put in there. Those boys would never hear if you screamed."

Polly's eyes grew wide, "I don't intend to ever have to scream," she said. "You're just mean."

They talked about Sylvie's classes and Andrew went downstairs to his nook to read. It wasn't long until Jason came in. He saw his mom sitting on the sofa. "I'm really sorry, mom."

"I know, honey," she said and stood to meet him. "It's okay. We know what happened and you lived through the day, right?"

"Yes," he said, "I don't want to do that again, though. It was so boring. No one talked to me and I had to sit there all alone."

"Do you want some milk and a pumpkin bar?" Sylvie asked.

"No, can we just go home?" Jason sounded exhausted. Polly bet he hadn't slept well the night before.

"How about I put some bars into a plastic container and you all can have them for dessert tonight," she said.

Jason nodded and Sylvie smiled. Polly filled a container, then handed it to Sylvie.

"Thanks, Polly. I'll be here tomorrow afternoon. I have deliveries coming in and a meeting with a bride and her mother."

"See you later, then." Polly rubbed her hand across Jason's shoulders. "Things will be better tomorrow and then better the day after that. I promise."

"I know. I'm just tired and want to go home."

Sylvie scooted him out through Polly's bedroom and down the back steps to get Andrew pried out of his nook. Polly looked at the clock. Henry was coming up in a little bit. They hadn't decided on what to do for dinner, so she sat down at her laptop and opened her recipe file. The browser tab for her email told her she had three new things to read and she clicked over. The message from Sal with her flight plans was sent to Polly's note application. Her daily word was epicurious. Fine. Delete.

The third email was from a person who named themselves igotyou. It was sent just a short while ago. The person was here in broad daylight. How bold!

"I haven't forgotten. Have you? Don't ever relax."

Now what should she do? If she told Henry, he'd insist on staying or making her go to his house. If she told Aaron, he'd make Doug and Billy stay up all night to protect her. She was just going to have to live through whatever came at her.

She heard Henry open the door and call up, "Are you there?"

Polly ran to the bedroom, "Come on up." She walked back into the living room and sat down on the sofa.

"Hey," he said when he saw her. "What's up?"

"Why? What do you mean?"

"Well you usually come kiss me when I get here. I didn't expect to have to come find you."

"It's been a long day and I didn't get much done. I don't feel like cooking, but I can."

"You sound like the world sucked all your happy away."

"No, I'm fine. Sorry."

"It's okay. What can I do to make you smile again?"

He sat down and picked up her feet, turning her so they were resting on his lap. He slipped one shoe off and then the other and began rubbing the sole of her left foot.

She smiled at him, "That's kind of nice. That makes me smile."

"Are you going to tell me what upset you?"

"No. It's nothing."

"Hmm. This is going to be a long night of foot massage, isn't it?"

"What do you mean?"

"You're not getting off the couch until you tell me what's bugging you."

Polly realized she hadn't told him about the earlier emails either. He was going to kill her. The foot massage felt so good, and she knew it was going to end when he heard what she had to say. She leaned back in the couch and said, "Can we talk about this later? Right now I am way too content."

"I walked into that one, didn't I?" he laughed. "You have until nine o'clock tonight to tell me what's going on. And I'm going to have to stop at some point because my hands will cramp up."

Polly shut her eyes and enjoyed the feeling of blood rushing through her feet. "Nine o'clock," she said. "I can work with that."

CHAPTER ELEVEN

"No! Why did you let me fall asleep?" she cried out.

"I figured you needed it." Henry waved a piece of pizza back and forth in front of her face. "It's about time, though. I thought I was going to have eat the entire thing by myself."

"But I'm never going to be able to go back to sleep tonight. What time is it?"

"Calm down. You weren't asleep that long."

"But I feel like I slept for hours!"

"It was only forty-five minutes. It's seven o'clock."

She stretched out her arms and snatched the piece of pizza from his hand and took a bite. "Waking up to pizza isn't nearly as good as you kissing me, but it comes in a pretty close second!"

Polly swung her feet to the floor and stood up, following Henry to the dining room. He'd managed to get the table set and pizza delivered while she slept.

"Why didn't I wake up when it was delivered?" she asked.

"I know the kid, he texted me and I opened the door."

She swallowed and wrapped her arms around him. "You're too good to me, I don't deserve you."

"Got that right, pretty girl," he said and held out her chair, waiting for her to sit down.

"Crap," she said and sat in the chair.

"What? I'm sorry." He sat down beside her.

"No, I'm the one who is sorry. I have to tell you something and I'd better not wait until nine o'clock. Don't move." She got up and went to the other end of the table and opened her laptop. She swiped the touch pad to wake it and set it down in between them.

"Something interesting online?" he asked.

"No, it's in my email. You're going to be mad at me."

"Is there someone else?" he asked quietly.

Polly looked at him in shock. "No! Nothing like that!" Then her eyes filled. "I'm sorry, Henry. It's nothing like that. I promise."

She opened the tab for her email and clicked on the first message. Henry read it and slumped in his seat.

"Who wrote this?"

"I don't know. But there's another one." She opened the email she had received before his arrival earlier that evening.

Henry reached over and put his hand on her forearm, "Polly. This is scary stuff."

"I know. But, I have to tell you something else about it."

He pulled his hand away and sat back in the chair, waiting.

"Aaron's tech-goddess came up yesterday and tracked back to the origin of the email. It came from my own server. It's either someone here or someone who piggy-backed my Wi-Fi."

"You don't have it password protected?"

"No, how could I? It's available for our guests and for all of the employees. Doug and Billy use it and when they have gaming parties, everyone accesses it."

"I suppose."

"Henry, it's not like this is the big city. It's Bellingwood. If someone wants to steal my Wi-Fi every once in a while, what do I care?"

"Well, you should care if this is happening."

"Don't start with me," Polly warned.

"I know, I know. But this is bad. Have you told Aaron?"

"What am I going to say? There's nothing they can do unless they catch the person in the act."

"It has to be someone who knows us. They know that I call you pretty girl," he said.

"That kind of creeps me out. But, that's what makes me think it isn't a guest. They aren't around us that much." She looked at him, "Do you think someone is mad at you and taking it out on me? Why would they reference you in Jeff's email?"

"It's really strange to try to think back on your life and figure out who hates you enough to threaten people you love," he commented. "I can't wrap my head around this."

"I'm with you," Polly agreed. "I've only lived here for a year and I can't imagine I've angered anyone so much that they would do this to me. Well ... to us."

They sat in silence for a while, contemplating their friends and enemies. Finally Polly spoke, "I'm sorry I didn't tell you earlier, but I thought maybe you might force me to do something stupid."

"Like what?"

"Like move into your house or let you move in here. I'm so tired of people thinking that I'm not strong enough to handle things." As soon as the words were out of her mouth, she regretted them. She knew what Henry could say, that every time a crisis happened, she enlisted the help of her friends to get her out of it. She hadn't cleaned up the front of Sycamore House alone; she had help. "I'm sorry," she said. "I seem to be saying that a lot tonight. I know that I need people and I know that I need you."

"We don't give you enough credit, Polly. You're right. But, it's difficult to watch these things happen to you and not want to protect you. It's because I love you, you know."

Polly chuckled, "You were trying to protect me before you loved me and for that matter, what's Aaron's excuse?"

"Well, I think he cares for you a lot, just like a father would. As for me loving you, will you laugh if I told you I fell in love with you the day we met to discuss renovating Sycamore House?"

"What?"

"You walked into the diner and I knew that someday you and I would be together. I had to do whatever it took to make that happen."

Polly smiled as she remembered some of the crazy moments they'd had. "You might have bitten off a bit more than you expected," she laughed.

"You are a bit ferocious and I suppose if I were smart, I'd realize that is a good indication that you can take care of yourself. But it still doesn't stop me from wanting to keep you safe."

She sighed, "It's never going to get any easier with you, is it?"

"I could say the same thing, you know." He picked up their plates and took them into the kitchen. Polly closed the pizza box and took it to the refrigerator, looking for a place it would fit. She finally jammed it on top of some cans on the lower shelf.

"I made pumpkin bars," she said, lifting the tin foil from the pan. "They're fresh. Want one?"

"Maybe three. Are they any good?"

"The best you'll ever eat. I got the recipe from my old church cookbook. These are so moist you won't want to stop." She took a plate down from the cupboard and put several on the plate. "Do you want milk or something a little harder to drink?"

Henry looked at the clock. It was eight thirty. "Milk is good. I'm a lightweight. Anything too hard and I'll fall asleep."

"Me too, then," she said and took down two glasses. "Here, you pour." She backed up so he could get to the refrigerator and held the glasses while he poured. She took them to the living room and he followed with the plate of pumpkin bars.

"A movie?" Polly asked. There were still a lot of films she wanted to share with him.

"That sounds great. Will you be able to stay awake?"

"I had a nice nap. I'll bet you fall asleep before I do." She walked over to the bookshelf and looked for the movie she wanted to watch. "Have you ever seen *Labyrinth*?" she asked.

"No, have I missed something important?"

"I didn't expect you had. It's with David Bowie. It's kind of old, but still one of my favorites." She put the DVD in the player and sat down beside him with the remote. Obiwan jumped up on the other end of the sofa and when she got comfortable, tucked in beside her.

"We're going to have to let him out at some point tonight," Polly said. "But not now." She started the movie and picked up a glass of milk and a pumpkin bar. "This is living," she giggled. "Good heavens, we're old."

"What do you mean by that?" Henry was offended.

"We don't go out on dates, we stay in, eat pizza and watch old movies. We might as well be married."

"Well ..." he began.

"Don't start with me. Not tonight," she laughed.

"So tomorrow night?"

Polly elbowed him in the belly and said, "Shhh. It's beginning."

At one point, Henry whispered to her, "Are these muppets?"

"Yes. They're made by Henson. Now watch."

They'd finished the pumpkin bars and milk and she had snuggled onto his lap. He reached over her to the back of the sofa and pulled the blanket down to cover them and the dog. Just as they were both relaxing, Obiwan sat straight up and growled, struggling to get out from under the blanket.

Polly tried to figure out what was happening and paused the movie.

They both heard glass breaking. Once, then again.

"What in the hell?" she said, jumping up. Obiwan was right beside her.

The dog started for the back stairs.

"Where did that sound come from?" she asked Henry, who was already tying his shoes.

"I think it came from the back. Maybe the kitchen. You stay here. I'll go check."

Polly scowled at him. "I'm coming. And so is Obiwan. Don't even think that we're not." She slipped into a pair of clogs in her room and followed Henry down the steps. Using the app on her phone, she turned on all the lights on the lower level, as well as the outdoor lights and the lamps along the lane.

"That ought to surprise whoever is out there," she said.

Henry opened up the door at the bottom of the steps and Polly grabbed Obiwan's leash, just in case. They went into the kitchen and looked up. Three of the glass panes had been broken in the eight-foot windows, all of them above her head. She reached down and caught Obiwan's collar to stop him from walking forward into the broken glass on the floor.

"Better call the police," Henry said. "I'm going outside."

"I'm coming with you," she said as he opened the door.

"Please, Polly. Just call the police and let me do this?" he pleaded.

"Fine. But I don't like it."

Fortunately, the back yard was brightly lit and she didn't see anyone out there. Henry went on out and she watched as he turned the corner around the garage. She dialed the phone.

"Bellingwood Police Department," said a now familiar voice. Polly wasn't sure if that was a good thing or not.

"Hi, this is Polly Giller over at Sycamore House and I need to report more vandalism."

"What happened, Polly?"

"Someone just threw rocks through the windows in my kitchen and broke the glass."

"Anything else?"

"That's all I know for now. We were upstairs and heard the glass break and came down. Henry Sturtz is outside checking the rest of the building."

"I'm sending someone over."

"Thanks. I'll meet them out front."

She hung up. In her wildest dreams, she never imagined having a relationship with both a Sheriff's department and a local police department. But she was becoming friends with people in both. Somehow in Bellingwood, that didn't seem odd at all. Polly locked the back door. Henry had access to all the doors at Sycamore House, so she wasn't worried about him getting back in.

She opened the front door and stepped outside. Obiwan stood beside her and she looked to the left and to the right. In the light, she saw Henry walking back from the barn. He waved at her and veered off to the other side of the building. She went back inside, closed the door and sat down on a bench.

"You're a good boy, Obiwan," she said, scratching his head. "You've got pretty good ears." He looked up at her and then set his chin on her knee. "Tomorrow night we're going down to Des Moines for therapy training. Are you going to be good there too?" she asked.

His tail thumped on the floor. Even if he didn't understand all that she said, he certainly knew when she was talking to him.

Polly saw flashing lights through the window and went back to the front door to open it. Henry was coming up the sidewalk.

"Hi, Bert," he said to the young man getting out of the car. "Night shift this week, eh?"

"Hi Henry. I hear you had some trouble here tonight."

Polly took a deep breath. She gritted her teeth. Henry took one look at her and smiled, a coy look crossing his face.

"I did have trouble," he said, "but that has nothing to do with why you're here. Have you met the owner of Sycamore House?"

The young man looked up and had the decency to blush, "No, I haven't. I've heard a lot about you, though, Miss Giller."

"Great," she said. "My infamy precedes me?"

"What?" he asked. "Oh no! Not from the station, though I've heard that, too. My aunt and uncle own the hardware store. She's your mailman, Lisa Bradford?"

"Come on in," Polly said. "The kitchen is back here."

"I was here for the barn raising last January," he said. "That was quite a day."

"It was a lot of fun," she agreed. Henry winked at her behind the young man's back."

Obiwan followed them and when she told him to sit and stay in the corner of the kitchen, he stopped and watched while they picked their way through the glass.

"Here's one of the rocks," Bert said, leaning over to pick it up.

"Fingerprints?" Polly asked, essentially stopping him.

"I suppose so." He dug in his pocket and pulled out a glove and a plastic bag.

"Here is another one," Henry pointed under the prep table."

"And I have the third one," Polly stopped beside the sink.

The young officer picked them up and scrawled on the bag before dropping it into his pocket. "I'll fill out a report, but I don't think there's much we can do. May I sit here and write?" He pointed to the trestle table.

"That's fine. Would you like something to drink?"

"No thank you, ma'am. I'll just finish this and let you get back to your evening. Do you have a way to cover those holes?"

Polly looked at Henry, who said, "I'll take care of it. If you'll be here for a few minutes, I'll go home and get some wood. We'll close them up until the glass company replaces them."

"I'll wait," Bert nodded.

"Guys, I'll be fine. I don't need a babysitter." Polly protested.

The young policeman looked to Henry for help.

"We're not babysitting," Henry said. "I promise. But, I'll be back soon and I'll take Obiwan with me. He can use my backyard while I get what I need. Then you don't have to walk him." He took the leash from her and walked over to Obiwan and snapped it on.

Polly followed him. "I know what you're doing."

"What's that?"

"You don't want me walking around the property tonight. You're making me stay inside."

"I'm trying to be as efficient as possible. That's all."

"Whatever."

"You sweep up the glass. I'll be back."

She heard him chuckling as he led Obiwan to his truck.

"He is such a brat," she muttered and took the broom with her back into the kitchen.

"Can I help you with that," Bert asked.

"No, I'm fine. By the way, what's your last name?"

"It's Bradford, too. My dad and Paul are brothers."

"Did you want to come back to Bellingwood to work in the department?"

"Yes ma'am. It's a good place to live."

Polly had about had it with being ma'amed. She knew he was

just being polite, but enough was enough. She sat down across the table from him, still holding the broom.

"Officer Bradford?" she said.

"Yes, ma'am."

"About that ma'am thing. You really should try to control it."

"What do you mean, ma'am? We're taught to be polite."

"Most young women don't like to be ma'amed. I've been known to pour coffee down a guy's front for it."

He blanched a little, and then asked, "What would you prefer?"

"You can call me Miss Giller if you need to be formal. Now that you've met me, Polly works just fine, too."

"Am I offending every woman when I say that?" Both his face and his voice were quite sincere. He was so young.

"Probably not. Older women ..." she stopped and giggled, "much older women are probably fine with it, but if you think they're under forty, you might want to be careful using it too often." She winked at him and stood back up. She'd seen a glint of light on a piece of glass and wanted to make sure she'd completely swept the room clean.

"Yes, ma ... Miss Giller," he corrected himself. His face was bright red and he went back to his report.

"Your father would have your head for being so mean," Polly said quietly to herself and laughed out loud.

Bert looked up. "Ma' ... Miss Giller?"

"Yes?"

"Oh, I didn't know if you needed something."

"No. I was just thinking about my dad. It made me laugh."

He stood up and brought the paperwork to her. "If you could just sign this here and here," he pointed to the form. "I'll get it filed. I'm sorry we can't do any more for you tonight."

"I suppose it would have been too much to ask for the ground to be wet so you could take casts of footprints."

He laughed at her. "Yes. Probably. Chief Wallers will come out tomorrow." He sat back down at the table and slowly went through the motions of putting things away.

"You're waiting for Henry to get back, aren't you?"

The poor young man looked up at her, obviously unsure of what to say or do.

"Do you men have some kind of code where you know that the other one is asking you to protect the poor female?"

"No?" Then he sighed. "I can't leave. He'd kill me."

She laughed. "I'll make it easy on you and let you stay. I have some pumpkin bars upstairs. Would you like something?"

"Really, I'm fine. Mindy brought chocolate chip cookies to the office. I've already had too many."

Polly dumped the glass into the trash and returned the broom to the storage room. She hoped she had everything, but since she was the only one who ever wandered around Sycamore House in bare feet, she wasn't too worried.

The front door opened and both she and Bert Bradford jumped up. She heard footsteps going up the stairs and said, "Must be Lila Fletcher coming back in for the night."

"Lila Fletcher?"

"One of my guests upstairs."

"Oh."

They heard another door and footsteps approached the kitchen. Natalie Dormand looked in and saw him and her eyes grew wide. "Is everything okay?" she asked.

"We had a little vandalism," Polly replied. "Nothing to worry about. Officer Bradford is just finishing up and about to be on his way. Can I get something for you?"

"I'm having trouble settling down, so I thought I'd see what there was to eat in here."

"Come on in. I think Sylvie has chocolate chip cookies in the freezer. How does that sound?"

"Amazing! I never get home cooked food, especially baked goods."

Polly strode over to the freezer and took out a container filled with cookies. She filled the plate and handed it to Natalie, saying, "If this doesn't do, come back for more."

"Thank you," Natalie replied. "I've been working all day and this will be perfect while I read. Good night."

"Pretty busy around here tonight," Bert Bradford observed.

"I suppose it is. The guests know they can wander around all they'd like. They know how to reach me if they need anything. Are you sure you don't want a cookie while I have them out?" she asked, holding out the container to him.

"No. I've had too many already."

Obiwan came in just after Polly heard the back door open. She put the container back in the freezer and said, "You guys weren't gone very long. Are you good for the night?"

"He's good," Henry said, coming in. "He took care of everything."

Bert stood up, "Well, I'll be off. Call if you need anything more."

"Thanks Bert," Henry reached out to shake his hand.

"Miss Giller," Bert Bradford said, shaking her hand as he walked past.

"Good night, Officer," she called out as he left, then she turned on Henry. "You are a brat."

"I know. I'm terribly ashamed. I'm going to get the ladder and I'll think about my bad behavior while I'm working."

He boarded up the windows and when they headed back upstairs, he picked up an overnight bag he had dropped on Andrew's desk under the stairs.

"What's that?" Polly asked.

"I'm sleeping on your couch," he replied.

She simply laughed and opened the door to go upstairs. "It won't do me any good to argue with you, will it?"

"Nope. Live with it, pretty girl." He kissed her cheek, then patted her bottom as she went up the steps first.

"Stop it," she said, swatting at his hand.

"Never."

CHAPTER TWELVE

Polly emerged from her room. "I think I finally know what to do with it." Henry had gotten up earlier, was showered and dressed and drinking a cup of coffee at her dining room table. She wrapped a robe around herself, and the animals followed as she headed for the coffee pot.

"Do with what?" he asked.

"I think I know what the key is to Thomas's flash drive."

"There's a key?"

"I think so. That's why nothing has made any sense. It doesn't seem to have any organization to it. But I think it does."

"When did this come to you?"

"When all crazy things come to me. You know that time between being asleep and really waking up? I let my mind relax and that's when I realized there was a key to unlock the pattern."

"What's the key, then?"

Polly poured a cup of coffee and sat down beside him. She pulled her laptop over and swiped to turn it on.

"I'm not sure what it is exactly, but one day Thomas and I were sitting at the Joe's Diner talking about books and authors and other weird things. He told me that he had a special affinity for Edgar Allan Poe."

Henry nodded and took a drink from his mug.

"I think it's because of his youth," she said.

"What are you talking about?"

"Thomas lost himself in the drug culture in San Francisco in the sixties. He was a talented author, but couldn't get it together. His family had some money and he was an only child, so he went to Berkeley and managed to graduate. He even published some early mysteries. They're kind of fun. But then everything went to hell."

"Wasn't Poe some kind of drug addict?"

"He wrote a lot about it, but I think he had more trouble with alcohol," she replied. "Anyway, one of the reasons Poe fell apart was because people he loved died and he couldn't get past it. Thomas lost the love of his life while he was living in San Francisco and it destroyed him. He'd already gotten himself pretty messed up, but when she was gone, he lost everything. He would pull it together to write a novel and then he would fall apart again. Up and down he went with each novel.

"Well, it was his fiftieth birthday party that did it for him. He went to the party and there was hardly anyone there. People had gotten so tired of his lifestyle, they just quit showing up. He'd lost everyone in his life that mattered and it was his own fault. So, he decided he didn't want to live the rest of his life like that. It took two years. He was in and out of rehab. His agent literally hauled him out of a gutter one night and he went back into the clinic and committed to stay there for six months. He said that he still fought that demon and it's been thirteen years since he quit drinking."

"Wow. I had no idea."

"Have you ever read any of his mysteries?" she asked.

"I don't think so. How did he find himself in Bellingwood?"

"He said that he heard about Sycamore House and thought it would be a good place to finish his next novel. But I don't think that's all he did. He was always doing research and spent a lot of time driving around."

"So, tell me about the key you figured out."

Polly quickly typed into her browser. "I'm going to have to spend some time with this today. We talked about a lot of Poe's stories. Thomas taught several classes at CUNY on Poe's work. He really knew his stuff. One of the stories was about a cipher, but I can't imagine how Thomas would have used it."

"I'm sure you'll figure it out," Henry said and went back to the coffee pot. "So what's up for you today?"

"We're close to having things ready for the Black Masque and Lydia and her crew are nearly ready for Halloween. Sylvie will be here this afternoon and then I'm in Des Moines this evening."

"What are you doing in Des Moines?"

Polly laughed. "I really don't tell you anything, do I? I'm sorry."

"You're bad that way. So what's in Des Moines?"

"Obiwan and I have a few weeks of training. He is going to be a reading therapy dog at the library."

"So, Obiwan is learning to read? I know he's smart, but wow."

"No, you nut," she laughed. "Little kids will read out loud to him. Talk about no judgment. He'll just be glad to have attention."

"So how long does this training last?" he asked.

"Are you asking me how long I'll be gone tonight or how many weeks we're doing this?"

"Well, both ... but mostly, when will you be back tonight?"

"We'll be gone for a few hours each week for the next few weeks. There's a certification test mid- November."

"That's pretty cool, Polly. I'm proud of you. There isn't much you aren't willing to take on, is there?"

"I figure this will be fun for both of us and it will get me busy in a library again."

"Okay, I'd better go. You have to feed the beasts and I'm building cabinets for the Millers' kitchen remodel." He bent down and kissed her. "I'm glad nothing else happened last night."

"Oh, that's right!" she exclaimed. "Who should I call about replacing the glass in those windows?"

"I'll make the call and then let you know when they're coming."

Polly stood and followed him through her bedroom to the top of the steps. "Thank you for taking care of things last night, and thanks for staying. I know my couch isn't that comfortable."

"It's better than my couch." He kissed her and left.

"He's pretty good to me, Obiwan," she said to the dog who was focused on the missed opportunity to go outside.

She pulled on jeans and a sweatshirt, glanced in a mirror and moaned. "Well, at least he didn't run away because of my morning hair," she said to no one in particular. Grabbing a ball cap, she pulled it over the mess on top of her head and went into the living room. Both cats were on the kitchen counter, looking at her with pitiful eyes.

"I'll be back. Stay calm," she said. "Come on, Obiwan. We'd better get this morning started before they panic."

She met Eliseo in the barn. "Good morning," he said. "I saw Henry leave. Is everything okay?"

"Someone broke windows out in the kitchen last night. He covered them and is calling the glass company."

"What's going on around here?" Eliseo asked.

"I wish I knew. It scares me. Henry was worried last night, too, so he stayed on my couch."

"You can't think of anyone who would do this?"

"I've only lived here for a little more than a year. I can't believe I had enough time to really make someone so angry."

"That's really strange. It's not one of your guests?"

"They're too involved in their own business to spend time thinking about how to vandalize my building."

They went to work mucking out stalls. Demi was feeling especially playful with Polly and when she turned her back on him to pick up a large mass of muck, he nosed her in the butt, nearly sending her face down into the bedding.

"Hey!" she said. "Stop that." She felt like he was laughing at her and opened the door so he could go outside. If he was finished eating, he could get out of her way. He started through the door, then stopped and shook himself from head to tail. "Sheesh," she muttered, "I didn't need the breeze."

When they were finished with chores, she and Obiwan went back to the apartment. The cats had given up and were curled up on the sofa. As soon as she set foot in the door and walked to the kitchen, they came fully alert and ran to follow her.

Luke stretched out across the path in front of her. "You're going to be the death of me. I'm getting your food, let me walk!" Leia parked herself in front of her food dish. When Polly attempted to fill it, Leia rubbed against the container, just as she did every morning. The cats were always a good distraction from the world.

After a shower, Polly got dressed and headed back to the kitchen. She was still hungry, so she pulled out a loaf of bread, sliced two pieces off and dropped them in the toaster. While the bread was toasting, she poured herself another cup of coffee and set it down on the dining room table, and then went to her bookshelves and pulled out her *Complete Tales and Poems of Edgar Allan Poe*. She wasn't sure what Thomas had done, but she was sure that she would find it in this book.

One evening he had been in her apartment, browsing through her bookshelves. She was astounded at how well-read he was. Writing took up so much of his time, she couldn't believe he had time to read and that he enjoyed reading the classics.

The toast popped up and she dropped the book on the table as she went past. The thud caught the attention of her animals, but they went right back to their food. Back at her laptop, she opened the folder containing Thomas Zeller's files. If she could figure out the puzzle and the order these things were meant to be in, she knew she could get closer to what it was he wanted her to know.

Her phone buzzed with a text from Lydia.

"Can you do lunch at Davey's today? Sylvie is going to be back in town, Andy isn't at the library, and we all should bond. Yes?"

Polly smiled. Trust Lydia to make good use of a time when they would all be free. *"I'll be there. What time?"*

"One o'clock. Will that work?"

"Perfect. Thanks."

"I love you, dear!" came the response.

The thing was, Lydia really did love her. Polly didn't know what she would do without her friends. These women had gone out of their way to welcome her to Bellingwood. She'd never known anyone quite like Lydia Merritt. She was always busy, but had plenty of time when people needed her. She was a wonderful mother to her kids, a terrific cook, a great wife to her husband, she organized a million things at church, she was head of the Bellingwood welcoming committee and managed to make it all look easy. Polly hoped that she would be half as capable someday.

Before she could get back to the puzzle in front of her, her phone buzzed with another text. *"The glass company will be there tomorrow afternoon. I love you, pretty girl!"*

That made her feel warm inside. Henry had seen her at her worst that morning and he still called her pretty girl. She wasn't quite sure what to do with his confession that he'd fallen in love with her before they'd begun remodeling Sycamore House. At that point, she was still coming off the rawness of a terrible relationship and hadn't been ready for another one. But Henry never pushed. He just stuck around. When she got scared, he kept sticking around and waited while she figured it out.

She insisted that she wasn't ready to be married and he never argued. Every once in a while, though, a flicker of something more crossed her mind. Polly sat back in her chair and raised the mug of coffee to her lips. Was she really thinking about being married to Henry? What would that even look like?

She had no desire to live anywhere other than Sycamore House, so how would they make that work? They couldn't live in this small apartment. It was big enough for her and three animals, but there wasn't room for another person. She didn't want to live in his house. He refused to move into the master bedroom because it was too strange to sleep where his parents had slept and he hadn't changed anything after his parents moved south. But his shop was right there and it was a wonderful house. She loved his front porch. They'd spent some wonderful evenings sitting in the porch swing during the summer, watching the world go by.

They had talked around some of the issues in their relationship, but Henry was insistent that they didn't have to play by anyone else's rules and that they weren't in any hurry. She had never been able to corner him on what he wanted for his future. It wasn't his fault. She knew he was trying to keep her from being terrified at the prospect of making a long-term commitment. But what if she was ready? How would she tell him that? Was she going to have to go down on a knee and propose?

Polly laughed out loud, startling the animals. While she'd been quietly sipping coffee and thinking about her future with Henry, Obiwan had curled up beside her on the floor and the cats had settled in on the table beside her laptop.

"Sorry guys," she said. "I thought about proposing to Henry and it made me laugh. He'd kill me. As much as he says that we can do things our own way, he's still pretty traditional."

The animals listened as she spoke and she leaned forward to scratch Luke's ears. Leia had curled up beside him and reached out a paw. Polly took it in her hand, feeling the warmth radiate from it. She released it and rubbed her hand down Leia's back, swirling her tail around before sitting back again.

"What's my problem?" she asked them. "I don't think I'm ready to settle down. It's not like I'm looking for anyone else, but I'm not finished being Polly Giller yet. I like waking up in the morning alone with you guys. Sure, there are times I'd like to have Henry here and I think I'd like to snuggle with him in the mornings, but not all the time. I'm not ready to give that up. Am I being selfish?"

The cats blinked at her and then curled back in on themselves.

"You are absolutely no help," she scolded. "And I don't know who else to talk to about this. The girls all think I should be married. I know that Aaron and Henry would like to have me married because they think I'd be safe that way. Stupid men."

Her phone buzzed again, *"Hey. You there?"* It was Henry.

She looked at the list of texts. Whoops. She'd forgotten to respond. *"Sorry. Got caught up in something. I love you too. Doing lunch with the girls today. You weren't planning on going with me tonight, were you?"*

"Nope. Not tonight. If I don't talk to you before, drive safe and text me when you're there and when you're leaving."

"I will. I promise. Love you."

"Love you too."

She opened her video chat program and dialed Jeff's computer. He was sitting at his desk. "What's up, Polly?"

"I'm working upstairs this morning and then I have lunch with the girls at Davey's. Are you okay without me?"

"I'm fine. There are a couple of meetings going on, but nothing catastrophic. What's up in the kitchen?"

She chuckled. "We had a little vandalism again last night. Did you get another email?"

"Oh, I just got in, I haven't looked yet. Just a second."

She watched him peering at his computer screen, then he said. "Yeah. I got another one. It says, *'Pretty rocks for a pretty girl.'* That sounds creepy, Polly."

"I know," she said. "He threw three rocks through the glass panes. I have no idea what's going on."

"Do you want me to call Ken?"

"I called last night. They sent someone over and there's nothing they can do. We don't have enough information."

"Should I call about the glass?"

"Henry already did. They'll be here tomorrow."

"Well thanks, I feel totally helpless right now. I don't like that."

"Neither do I, but what can we do?"

"What are you working on?" he asked, "See, I changed the subject. Did that help?"

"It did," she said. "I have an idea about these files that Thomas gave me, but if I don't get working on them, I'm going to run out of time. I've already wasted too much time this morning being a girl."

"Being a girl?" he asked.

"Yeah. Worrying about silly stuff. Now I'm going to get to work. If you need me, holler."

"Cool. See you later."

He clicked off and his image left the screen. Polly pulled the book closer to her and did a quick search for Edgar Allan Poe online. When the amount of information overwhelmed her, she opened up the book. This was going to take a while.

CHAPTER THIRTEEN

One more story or poem by Poe and Polly was going to moan. She was tired of this. She'd read *Tamerlane* and *The Gold Bug*, some of his poems, and had gotten lost in a few of her favorite stories, but she couldn't make sense of how to associate these files with what she was reading.

She had been interrupted several times. Sheriff Merritt released the crime scene and she had to wait for a cleanup crew to deal with the room. He'd found nothing to incriminate anyone on Thomas's laptop, so Polly let Natalie Dormand know that the it was coming back. The woman seemed glad to hear it, but looked wan and weary. She asked Polly if there was a possibility of her staying for several more days so Polly sent her to Jeff.

Her first look at the middle bedroom had been when she'd opened the door for the cleanup crew. Her heart fell. She knew the mattress would need to be replaced, but the beautiful writing desk had been smashed in the struggle and there was blood spattered on the rug and the floor. The crew leader assured her that the floor would be fully cleaned up and asked how she wanted to deal with the rug. She told him that everything could be replaced and to simply get rid of it, hoping that would make his job easier. They had donned their protective suits and gone to work. She went back to her apartment and collapsed on the sofa.

"It has to be easier than this, Obiwan," she said, stroking his head. He was lying beside her, his head in her lap, his tail wagging. "You want to go outside, don't you."

He jumped off the couch and ran for the bedroom, so she followed and they went outside. Obiwan took off for the tree line. It was one of his favorite places to explore. Polly followed more slowly, her mind still trying to figure out Thomas's puzzle. He should have given her some clue. She stopped and shut her eyes, thinking back to one of their conversations.

He'd come down to the horse pen, watching Polly exercise Daisy. Eliseo had gone to Boone for supplies and she was glad for the company. Thomas didn't seem to want anything, he was just watching the horse. When she released Daisy into the pasture, she came back to stand beside him.

"Do you ever want children, Polly?" he'd asked her.

"I don't know. Why do you ask?"

"I was watching the time you take with your horses. You have to really exert control over them or they'd take over. Do you suppose it's that way with kids, too?"

She had laughed. That was one of the things that scared her about being responsible for a child. Polly knew she had a strong personality and was terrified of trying to find the balance between being too harsh and being too lenient. She didn't figure a child would have a chance in her crazy life.

"Why do you laugh?" he'd asked.

"Raising a kid scares me to death. When I see what Sylvie has done with her boys, I'm so proud of her I can't stand it. But she worries over them all the time and I'm not ready for that."

"You'd be great at it," he said.

"I don't know. It just seems overwhelming. What about you?"

He'd gone quiet, then said, "Polly, I was such a mess that I would have devastated children. My Nelly? Any child would be lucky to have her for a mother."

"Have you ever searched for her?"

Thomas didn't respond. He just looked off into the pasture and watched Nat and Demi bouncing around, nipping at each other. Polly let out a whistle, one that Eliseo had taught her, and caught their attention. They stopped what they were doing and wandered to the pile of hay.

"See, you'd make a great mother," he said to her.

"They're horses. I won't have to pay for therapy when they get older."

He'd gotten quiet and they walked back up to Sycamore House together. He didn't seem to want to be alone that day, so she had taken time to talk to him and listen to what he had to say.

Polly came back to reality and looked for Obiwan. He was sniffing in and around the trees. She whistled and he ran to her. "I feel better about letting you run without a leash," she said to him. "I appreciate you being so obedient." She crouched down and hugged him. "You're a good dog. Let's go on in."

They went upstairs and she checked the time. It was only eleven forty-five, so she sat back down and opened the book again, remembering another conversation she and Thomas had about Poe. She'd asked him which single piece was his favorite.

He'd laughed. "Everyone thinks that *The Raven* is his best piece. It's probably his most popular, but I'm partial to *Annabel Lee*. There is so much love in that poem." He'd paused and his face grew sad. "And so much loss. When I lost my love, I read that poem over and over again. It felt like the angels had stolen her from me. She didn't have a sepulchre by the sea, no place I could go to mourn. The only place I could let it out was in my books."

Polly started. It had to be *Annabel Lee*. She opened the book and began reading the poem. This had to be it. Now what was he doing with it? How did he associate this with the files on the drive? And for that matter, why had he turned this into a puzzle?

Then, she saw it at the bottom corner of the page. Someone, it had to have been Thomas, had drawn an itty bitty heart in pencil. Not enough to cause her to open to that page, but enough to tell her that she was on the right track.

She did a quick search online and found the poem, then copied it into her note program. Then Polly turned back to the folder on her laptop. There were thirty-three files at the top level ... that matched to the thirty-three lines in the poem. She was getting closer. This had to be it. She could feel the excitement building.

Her phone's alarm buzzed at her. What in the world? She checked it and saw that her calendar app was reminding her to meet everyone for lunch in fifteen minutes.

"Dammit." She slammed the laptop lid down, pushed her phone into her back pocket, and strode to the front door. The animals looked up, cat eyes blinking sleepily at her. Obiwan followed her to the door, hopeful to go with her.

"No, you can't go. But why don't you all try to figure out Thomas's puzzle for me, okay?" She scratched Obiwan's head and slipped out the front door, leaving him behind.

Two members of the cleaning crew were hauling large plastic bags down the steps. They smiled at her apologetically. What a horrible job.

She stopped in to see Jeff in his office, "I'm going to Davey's to have lunch with the girls."

He laughed at her. "The girls? Do you know how that sounds?"

"I know, I know ... a bunch of hens. Is everything going okay? Do you need me?"

"Nope. It's all good. Have fun."

The door of the classroom across the hall was closed. She could never remember what group was meeting where, but Jeff kept the place busy. She picked up the pace and cut through the kitchen out to her garage.

The parking lot at Davey's wasn't as busy as usual, and Polly assumed most of the lunch crowd was already back to work. She parked by Lydia's Jeep and looked up when she heard a car roar into the lot. Sylvie pulled up beside her and jumped out.

"Am I late?" she asked. "I got caught behind this fool of a woman. Fifty-two miles an hour. Are you kidding me with this?"

Polly snorted with laughter. "I just got here. You aren't late and besides, is there a schedule I don't know about?"

Sylvie pulled her bag out of the back seat. "I guess not, but I wanted to scream. There is never any traffic on this road and the day I get behind someone who won't even go the speed limit, there are tractors and pickups and ... well, everyone coming at us."

"Maybe you need a drink," Polly said.

"I'd love one, but I have a meeting at three and I don't think this bride's mother would appreciate a drunken chef."

Polly took Sylvie's arm. "How was Jason this morning?"

"He was fine. Not terribly happy with having to go to school, but I didn't give him any option. He knows that if he fakes being sick, he can't work in the barn. That's been a wonderful motivator. I don't know what he'll do when he's really sick."

She looked up at Polly. "I don't know what I'm going to do when either of them are sick. I hadn't thought about that. They're always so healthy. Now that I'm out of town, how will I take care of them?"

"Stop it," Polly scolded. "They'll come over and hang out on my couch with the animals. I can feed them fluids and keep them warm. You never have to worry about that."

Sylvie squeezed Polly's arm, "I don't know what I'd do without you. Who needs a husband when I have a friend like you?"

"Exactly," Polly agreed. "Who needs one of those?" She realized that she missed hanging out with these women. They gave her all sorts of confidence. Sylvie raised two boys on her own. Beryl had kicked one husband out, buried another and loved being single. Andy was dating someone after spending several years alone. She'd loved her husband and then loved being single. It gave her time to do all the things she enjoyed doing.

Lydia was the only one of them who was still happily married and now that her kids were mostly gone, she and Aaron had a good life together. He didn't get in the way of the wild things she enjoyed doing and when she needed him, he was there. For that matter, Lydia took care of him when he needed her, too. They had figured out how to be independent and together all at the same time. Polly wasn't sure how they'd worked it out, but assumed it had something to do with many years of trial and error.

Beryl was waving madly from a table in the dining room. She was nearly out of her seat when Polly saw her and waved back.

"We're with them," she said to the hostess, who smiled and nodded and allowed them to find their own way to the table.

"It's about time," Beryl said. "I thought you were going to be late."

"We're not late," Polly said, "And besides, that late stuff nearly made Sylvie have a heart attack on the way back here. Am I right?" She poked Sylvie, who laughed as she sat down by Andy.

"No, it was the slowpoke that nearly made me have a keel over. I'm not sure why I was so worried about getting here on time, but she had me all worked up."

"What's the special today?" Polly asked.

Andy responded. "It's a steak and pepper salad. It sounds really good. That's what I'm having."

"Gotta watch your weight, eh?" Beryl asked, flicking a bag of crackers at her friend.

"Exactly," Andy said. "I don't want to start looking like you."

"Hey there," Beryl laughed. "You could only pray for a figure like this." Beryl was stick thin. She was one of those women who had made it through her fifties and into her sixties without ever worrying about her weight.

"I hate you," Andy said. "You're the bane of my existence."

"You'd have a boring existence without me, old lady," Beryl snapped. She turned to Polly, "Guess what we did yesterday?"

"I have no idea," Polly looked at Lydia, who shrugged.

"We went to Ames."

"Okay?" Polly pressed.

"We went to Ames because Andy had to take flowers to her daughter's apartment for the winter. Apparently, Amy is really good with these things. But then, guess what else we did?"

"Ummm, you went to a strip club?" Polly asked.

"That would have been better." Beryl turned to Andy. "Why don't you ever think of interesting things like that for us to do."

Andy rolled her eyes and waved her right hand for Beryl to get on with it.

"We went to the Iowa State theater department to check out their costumes for your ball. I think we're on it. We'll be beautiful! But Andy didn't like the corset."

"They're horrible!" Andy said.

"I kind of like it," Polly laughed. "I feel all put together."

"You wouldn't want to stay in it very long. Especially when you're my age," Andy complained.

"Then guess what we did after that?" Beryl pushed forward.

"I have no idea. You picked up men at the local fire station?"

Beryl threw her hands up in the air and said, "Andy, we are never leaving town without her. She has the best ideas for fun."

They laughed.

"What did you do, Beryl?" Polly asked.

"We went to Village Inn," Beryl's voice dropped along with her shoulders. "Village Inn of all places. And then guess what this woman did?"

"Oh, shut up, you." Andy said.

"She ordered from the senior citizens menu. For pete's sake, the senior citizens menu. Can you believe it? I was so embarrassed."

They all laughed except Andy, who blushed profusely. "I didn't want that much to eat and I'd just made a fool of myself trying on dresses that are too young for me."

Lydia grimaced. "You are not that old. Victorian era dresses are made for women of all ages. Get over yourself. Right now."

But Andy continued to protest. "And what's wrong with the senior citizens menu? I might as well take advantage of it."

"It's the principle of the thing," Beryl said. "Once you give in to it, you can never go back. I absolutely refuse to acknowledge the fact that I'm not 42 years old any longer. And as long as my brain thinks that I am, the rest of me intends to go along with it."

Lydia looked at the two of them, shook her head and asked Polly, "Do you have your costume for the ball?"

"Yes I do," Polly said. "I also have a different costume for Halloween. I'm going to have fun."

"What about you, dear?" Lydia asked Sylvie.

"I'm going to be in the kitchen. I'm not wearing a costume."

"We can't allow that to happen, can we, Polly?" Lydia asked.

"You know, we could put together some kitchen help costumes," Polly said. "Something like those British television shows with the cooks and maids? What do you think, Sylvie?"

"But I can't wear a mask if I'm in the kitchen."

"That doesn't matter. We can make this work. Will you do it? And what about Hannah and Rachel?"

"I have a few other kids working that evening too. You're right, it would be fun for all of us to be in costume."

"I'm so glad," Lydia clapped her hands together. She turned back to Polly. "Aaron told me what a mess the middle bedroom was in. Do you need me to help you with that?"

"There was a crew cleaning in there when I left. I thought I'd check it out when they were finished. We need to replace the mattress and rug, but that will be easy. That beautiful desk was smashed, though."

"We can order another one. I have copies of the invoices. Would you like me to go back with you this afternoon so we can get started?"

Lydia had become Polly's personal decorator. She had beautiful taste and wouldn't accept a thing for her time. Someday Polly would find a way to say thank you to her for all she had done.

"That sounds wonderful. Are you dragging these bratty kids back with you, though?" Polly asked, pointing at Beryl and Andy.

"Andy can take Beryl home," Lydia laughed. "Right?"

Andy smiled and nodded and Beryl flared her nostrils. "I can always walk if no one wants to take me."

"We all want you," Lydia reached out and patted her hand. "But plans change and you can be flexible."

"Whatever."

The waitress came back and took their orders. Polly looked around the table at four of her closest friends. They poked at each other, laughed at each other and in the end took care of each other no matter what. She wasn't sure how she'd been so fortunate, but she was glad they were here together.

CHAPTER FOURTEEN

Eventually they ended up back at Sycamore House. Sylvie headed for the kitchen and Lydia followed Polly up to her apartment.

When she'd emptied the storage unit in Story City last summer, everything had come to Polly's garage. A matching pair of tables that her dad had made for her old room was now on either side of her bed and she'd added two standing lamps to the living room. A wing chair and ottoman that had been her father's favorite place to sit were tucked into a corner by the bookcases with a side table holding a lamp and a stack of books, making it one of her favorite spots in the room.

She stopped Lydia and said, "Would you look at my furniture downstairs and tell me if there is a better way to arrange things, and maybe use some different pieces? You have such a wonderful eye for it all."

"I like what you did with the chair in the corner," Lydia said. "That's cozy." She hugged Polly. "I'd love to see what you have and make it work in your space here. You have no idea what it means to me that you trust me to do this."

Polly huffed, "If I didn't have you, I'd have to hire someone who didn't care nearly as much. I know what looks good when I see it, but I have no idea how to get from the initial pieces to the finished room. I can recognize gorgeous furniture, but I'd just plop it down in the most convenient place and be done with it."

"That's what I do, too," Lydia laughed. "I just take a little more time to figure out if convenient and beautiful work together. Will you show me the room across the hall now?"

The mattress and all of the bedding was gone. The room had been scrubbed clean and smelled like disinfectant. Clothing was piled neatly into a box and personal items stacked on top of it. Polly bent over and picked up a framed picture. It a very old picture of Thomas with a young woman standing in front of the ocean. She set it back down in the box. He'd shown it to Polly the night he told her about the girl who stole his heart and whose loss he mourned every day.

She sighed.

"Are you okay?" Lydia asked.

"He had no one to love him," Polly said. "He had friends and acquaintances and fans and toadies, but he didn't have someone who just loved him because he was Thomas." She thought for a moment. "You know, that's what all of his stories were about. His protagonists were always looking for something, trying to find a connection to the world."

"In his murder mysteries?" Lydia asked.

"Yes. His main characters were searching for something more. His most famous character, Eddie Powers, was a former cop. He had seen his wife get murdered and it destroyed him. What was her name ..." Polly mused.

"Wasn't it Annie something?

"That's right? How do you know that?"

"I've been following the casting for the movie. I should probably read the books. It's more interesting now than it was a week ago, that's for sure."

"Eddie and Annie. Edgar and Annabel. Why didn't I see that before?" Polly asked.

"What are you talking about?"

"Thomas was an Edgar Allan Poe fan. He taught classes on him and identified with the author more than I realized."

"Do you think this relates to the puzzle you've been handed?"

"Yes I do, but I'm just not sure what to do with it yet. And every time I get a brilliant thought, something distracts me."

"Maybe you can get to it tonight."

"I have to go to Des Moines for therapy dog training. I don't want to miss that. There isn't another testing session until next spring and I can't wait to get involved at the library with Obiwan."

Lydia was snapping pictures with her phone and pulled a small notepad out of her purse. "Do you mind if I play with the color in here again?" she asked.

"Not at all. I'll order the mattress so it will be here next week. Sal is coming in to surprise Mark and I want her to be able to stay here. My couch isn't all that comfortable." Polly smirked. "And besides, if Henry insists on sleeping on it, there won't be room."

"Henry's sleeping on your couch?"

"He stayed last night after the windows were broken. I have a feeling he'll be back tonight."

"You two are so cute together," Lydia took another picture.

"Cute. Yep. That's what I like to hear." Polly pushed the box out into the hallway and nudged it with her feet to her apartment. She and Natalie needed to decide what to do with Thomas's things.

They went back into her apartment, "Would you like something to drink?" she asked Lydia.

"No, I'm fine."

"Are you sure? I have pumpkin bars?" Polly teased.

Her friend's eyes lit up. "Homemade?"

"Of course! And they're fabulous. This recipe is so moist."

"Then yes, I'd like one and maybe some tea or coffee."

They sat down at the dining room table and Lydia took a bite, then moaned. "That is good. I'd like the recipe please."

"It's easy," Polly said. "I'll email it to you."

"So, dear, do you have any idea who might be vandalizing Sycamore House?"

"I don't. It's someone who knows both me and Henry because the emails call me pretty girl and that's what he calls me."

"Where would they hear that?"

Polly laughed out loud. "Anywhere. He is always saying that to me. He says it when we're out to eat, when we're in the apartment, when we're anywhere. Last week he yelled it down the street at me when we were leaving the diner."

"Who was around?" Lydia asked.

"I don't know," Polly said. "Everyone in town could have been around. I certainly wasn't paying attention."

"Think back, Polly. Shut your eyes and think about the street. Who was walking in and out of the shops? Bellingwood isn't that big. There aren't that many people at any given time."

Polly obeyed and tried to picture Henry walking toward his truck. Who else was there? She rested her head in her hands, her thumbs at her cheekbones, her little fingers braced against her forehead. She looked at the scene again. An older gentleman left the hardware store and stopped to talk to Henry for a moment while she got into her truck. A woman she didn't recognize went into the grocery store and an older couple went into the bank. Mark Ogden's brother-in-law was sweeping the sidewalk in front of his pizza place and an old car backed out of a space.

She opened her eyes and looked at Lydia. "That kind of worked, but it didn't do me any good. I don't know the people I saw and I didn't see that many people."

"When you're ready, you'll figure it out."

"Lydia, I hate to ask, but ... "Polly was hesitant to begin this query. It wasn't fair of her to put her friend on the spot.

"Yes, dear?"

"Has Aaron said anything to you about Thomas's murder? Does he have any leads at all?"

Lydia smiled at her. "He hasn't talked much about it. I know he's frustrated. They're waiting for some evidence to be processed and they've gone through the man's laptop and the disk you gave him. Nothing yet, though."

"I shouldn't have even asked you."

"Don't worry. It has to be frustrating to be on the outside of an investigation when you got caught up in the middle of the murder." Lydia patted Polly's forearm. "I'll tell Aaron you are asking, though. You shouldn't be left out in the cold."

"Thanks. I could call him myself, but I hate the sound of his voice when he realizes it's me on the other end of the call."

Lydia burst out laughing. "He doesn't trust you! He told me after the last call that he's worried the census bureau will check our population every year, just in case you continue to lower it."

"Lydia!" Polly cried.

"It's a joke, dear. Someday you will see the humor in all of this."

"I hate it. Nobody should have this reputation."

"You really don't believe that's your reputation, do you?"

"I see the way people look at me and whisper when I'm in the restaurant or the grocery store."

"Only when something happens. You didn't see any of that behavior two weeks ago, did you?"

Polly hung her head. "No. You're right. I'm being silly."

"You certainly are. Now don't you have to get to Des Moines with Obiwan? I'm probably holding you up."

Polly checked the time. She needed to get moving. "I do need to go. Thank you for coming over. I'll order the mattress tomorrow."

"Don't worry about the room. We'll put it back together and it will be as beautiful as before."

Lydia stood up and Polly followed her to the back steps. "Thank you for taking care of this, Lydia," Polly said. She pulled the woman into a hug. Lydia returned it with an extra squeeze.

"You're going to be fine. Have fun tonight."

Lydia went down the steps and Obiwan looked up at Polly expectantly.

"I know, I know. But, we're going for a ride in a bit." She went back into the dining room and looked at her laptop. Talk about frustrating. She wanted nothing more than to dig into Thomas's files, but it would have to wait.

Polly had changed her clothes and was pulling a jacket on when Jason and Andrew came up the back steps.

"Do you want me to take Obiwan out?" Andrew asked. He loved Polly's animals and she gave him a little money each week for taking care of them. Most of that money was spent on books.

"No, that's fine," she said. "We're heading to Des Moines for our first therapy dog training."

Jason flopped down on her sofa and picked Luke up into his lap. He was rubbing the cat's neck and murmuring at him as well.

"Everything okay, Jason?" she asked.

"Sure. Fine." he said.

"That doesn't sound like it's okay. How was school?"

He wrinkled his nose and looked up, "It was fine. No big deal."

"Okay," she said. "Did you guys see your mom downstairs before you came up?"

"She is making molasses cookies," Andrew said. "Hers are the best."

Polly nodded. "I'm out of here, then. You know where everything is if you need it. I'll see you tomorrow."

Andrew followed her to the steps. "I've never read to Obiwan. Should I do that now that he's in training?"

"It certainly wouldn't hurt," Polly patted his shoulder. "He's a better listener than the cats. You can try it tomorrow."

She went downstairs and took a leash off the hook, clipping it to Obiwan's collar. She hooked it on the door handle to hold him there and went into the kitchen.

"Sylvie?"

"Hi Polly," Sylvie was pulling a tray of cookies out of the oven."

"How did the meeting go?"

"You know brides and their mothers. This mother had decided what she wanted, so we all just agreed and moved on. These poor girls. Such a big deal is made out of one day. They stress because everyone wants something for them. I don't think half of them give a single thought to life after the wedding day. Oh well." She sighed and set the pan on the prep table. "What's up?"

"Did you talk to Jason?"

"Not really. They came in while I was rolling cookies and I guess I didn't pay attention. Is something wrong?"

"I don't know. He didn't want to talk to me. Do you suppose he's still dealing with the fight and the detention?"

Sylvie took a deep breath. "How was Andrew acting?"

"He seemed normal," Polly laughed. "Lots of energy."

"If it was really bad with Jason, we'd see Andrew reacting too. I'll go up and check on him before he heads to the barn." She stopped and thought for a moment. "Maybe I won't. Maybe I'll let a dose of the horses fix his heart and then he'll find a way to tell me what's bothering him." She chuckled. "You know he's getting to that age. I really had hoped we'd get through it unscathed, but every little thing is going to be a big deal for him for a few years."

Polly nodded, "I remember. I didn't do angst like my friends, but it wasn't easy. Between the boys and the girls and the teachers and the ..." This time it was Polly who stopped mid-sentence. "Are they having dances?"

"I don't know," Sylvie said. Her eyes got big. "You don't suppose that's part of this, do you?"

"What if there's a girl, Sylvie?"

"Oh!" Sylvie sighed. She shut her eyes in pain and rolled her head back on her neck. "This isn't supposed to happen," she whimpered. "It's not fair."

Polly giggled. "You should ask Eliseo to see if he can get Jason to talk. We always had dances on Friday nights when I was in junior high. They were horrible, but everybody went to them. Has Jason ever had a girlfriend?"

Sylvie's face twisted into a frown. "I don't want to think about this. He's a cute boy and he's popular and he is always with a bunch of kids, both girls and boys. I'll bet girls are trying to hook up with him and he doesn't know how to respond. I'm a terrible mom, Polly. I ignored this so it wouldn't ever be true."

"You're not a terrible mom. You are so far from that."

"But, I didn't want to pay any attention to this. I wonder why Andrew hasn't teased him about girls."

"Maybe because he's been threatened within an inch of his life by his older brother."

Sylvie slowly nodded. "There are a couple of little girls who say hello to him on Sundays and now that I think about it, those same girls are part of the crowd waiting for him when I drop the kids off at school. I'm really good at ignoring the obvious, aren't I."

"I still think you should talk to Eliseo or Doug or Billy. They are with Jason a lot. Maybe he will let them talk about it."

"But it's not their job. It's my job. He's my son."

Polly put her hand firmly on the prep table. "Sylvie, stop it. He's absolutely your son, but there are a lot of people around here who love him. I keep telling him that sometimes we have to let our friends pick up the slack when we can't do things on our own. You have to trust that these people have your back with your boys. You can't be everything to them all the time."

Sylvie raised her eyebrows. "You know I don't like that answer."

"But am I wrong?"

"I don't have to like it when you're right."

Polly giggled. "Call Eliseo. I'll bet he won't mind talking to Jason while they're working in the barn. Those two are always discussing something. Neither of them would tell you, but it might already be working itself out."

Sylvie took her phone out of her pocket. "You're right. I'm not in this alone." She began scrolling through her contacts. "You know this is strange for me. I spent so many years all alone with those two boys, I'm not used to having this many people in our lives. Sometimes it's nice, but sometimes it is really odd."

Polly hugged her. "Life keeps getting bigger and bigger, doesn't it? You couldn't be all that you are becoming without friends helping and you wouldn't want your boys to spend their entire childhood cooped up in that little apartment. Am I right?"

Sylvie made a shooing motion with her hands. "Get out of here. Of course you're right. I still don't have to like it."

"I love you, Sylvie Donovan," Polly said as she headed for the back door. "Even when you don't like it."

She was giggling as she unhooked Obiwan's leash and led him outside. A quick trip to the grass and then she loaded him up in her truck and headed for Des Moines.

CHAPTER FIFTEEN

That evening, Henry's truck was parked in the second space of her garage when Obiwan and Polly returned. "He's quite the knight in shining armor, isn't he?" she said to her dog as they went in and up the steps.

The training session had been productive and Obiwan impressed Polly with his socialization skills. She figured that the time spent with so many different people and animals at Sycamore House gave him plenty of exposure to outside stimuli.

"Honey, I'm home!" she called out as she hit the first step. She'd texted Henry before leaving Des Moines and he told her that he would have supper ready when she got there. She had actually grumbled a bit at that since she rarely got an opportunity to eat fast food anymore. Sometimes a greasy hamburger was necessary for a girl to keep her sanity.

Henry walked in through her bedroom and met her with a kiss. "Welcome home," he smiled. "Did you have a good time?"

"It was good. I think Obiwan will be fine through this."

"I'm glad. Tell me you didn't stop somewhere and eat."

"I restrained myself," she laughed, "but it wasn't easy. I passed a lot of burger places that called my name. When I remembered that they also had fried cheese nuggets, I had to stop myself from passing out and requiring them to resuscitate me. But I'm here now. What's for dinner?"

"Come in and you can see what I did." He took her jacket and followed her into the dining room. He had thrown a pretty cloth over one end of her table, found candlesticks and her good dishes. The candles were lit, the lights were dimmed and food was on the table ready to be served.

"What have you done?" she asked.

"Have a seat." He pulled a chair out for her, then sat down and began passing food. "I cooked."

"I didn't know you had it in you," she smiled at him. "You really are a catch. How has no one ever managed to hook you?"

"I don't tell all my secrets to just anybody and no one has ever taken enough time to figure them all out."

"You're amazing, Henry Sturtz." She took the first dish filled with mashed potatoes. He'd made a meatloaf and the vegetable dish was roasted zucchini and green beans with parmesan cheese. He pulled a towel off a basket filled with biscuits and then handed her a bowl filled with sliced tomatoes and cucumbers.

"I had to go to Boone for the garden vegetables. There isn't much left in town, but I had fun," he said.

"This is a feast!"

"I needed to redeem myself for all the pizza I keep bringing over here."

"I love pizza, but this is really something. I had no idea." Polly took a taste of the potatoes and moaned, "These have garlic in them. They're good."

"Try the meatloaf." He pointed to her plate.

She took a bite. "Wow. What did you do to this? My meatloaf is never like this."

"I tried something new. I cooked the onions in beer before putting them into the loaf. There's also a spicier pork sausage than I usually use."

"Thank you, Henry," Polly reached out to touch his arm. "This is sweet. And kind of romantic, too." She pointed at the candlesticks. "I'm impressed that you could even find those."

"I just pay attention. I bought the candles. I have no idea where you keep those."

Polly took another bite, and tried to speak around it, "I can't believe you did this for me. I figured it was going to be hamburgers and baked potatoes, which would have been awesome, but this is amazing. Wow, thank you." She picked up his hand and brought it to her lips, kissing it. "Thank you for making me feel special."

"Awww, shucks, it ain't nothin,' ma'am," he laughed.

They finished the meal and then cleaned up together, laughing as they moved around the kitchen. When everything was cleaned and put away, Polly said, "I have a favor to ask."

"What's that?"

"I've been dying to dig into Thomas's computer and now that I think I might have a clue as to how to begin, I've had a million interruptions. Would you mind if I spent some time with that this evening? I'd really like to hear what you think."

"That would be fine. You know I'm not going anywhere, don't you?"

"I assumed," she said, her eyes slitted. "I saw your bag. You know people are going to talk, don't you?"

"Let them talk. We aren't living our lives for their approval, are we?"

She reached out and hugged him, "You are so good for me, Henry. Sometimes I forget just how much."

"Then I'll do my best to remind you."

He walked with her over to the sofa, and sat down, then got back up before she could get settled. "I totally forgot!" he said.

"Forgot what?"

"I have dessert, too." He trotted back to the kitchen.

"You made dessert?" she asked, surprised.

"I didn't say I made dessert," he poked his head out from the freezer door he'd pulled open. "I said I have dessert. I know what my pretty girl likes." He brandished two ice cream sandwiches in front of his face. "Polly want some ice cream?"

"You and I have been together nearly a year and you haven't ever used that phrase with me." She glared at him. "I was doing fine without it."

"So you don't want ice cream?" He moved to open the freezer door again.

"No, I want the ice cream! I'm just not a parrot."

"No, honey, you're not," he laughed. "Not at all. So, tell me something else about Thomas Zeller. What kind of information did you land on that makes you think you can put the puzzle together?

Polly was seated cross-legged in the middle of the sofa, her laptop on her legs. "Would you mind grabbing that book?" she asked, pointing to the Poe collection on a bookshelf.

He handed it to her and sat down on her right since Obiwan had taken the space on her left.

Polly opened to the poem *Annabel Lee* and pointed to the tiny heart that had been sketched in the bottom corner. "I didn't do that. I'm guessing Thomas did one day. I'd pulled this out and he flipped through it, talking about some of the different short stories and poems. I think that's my key."

"Key?"

She turned the laptop toward him. "There are thirty three folders here. I counted," she said when she saw him look at her." Count the lines in Annabel Lee."

"You've already done that. There are thirty-three."

Polly had marked up her book, something she had never thought she would do to a book, but when her mind started working this puzzle out, she needed it to be written down. She had also numbered the words in each line of the poem as well.

"That seems a little obsessive," he laughed.

"But I've been thinking about this and picturing what he has here and it is going to make sense, I promise. He wanted me to have this disk because he knew I'd think about our conversations."

"What kind of conversations?"

"He spent a lot of time talking about his first love. He was so young, Henry. Only eighteen. Would you believe he was in Haight-Ashbury during the Summer of Love in 1967? I've been doing some reading about that. He heard all of those great musicians that summer. He graduated from high school and hitch-hiked down to San Francisco looking for a big life. Even when things started getting really bad, he ended up staying because he didn't have any other place to go.

"Nelly was about four years older. He was living on the street that summer until he met her. She invited him to move into the house where she was living with six other people. They were high all the time, no one cared where they slept or what they were doing. And he remembered that there were people everywhere. Finally the summer was over and a lot of people left, but he and Nelly stayed."

"What were they doing?"

"Getting high mostly. He had the best stories of some of those LSD trips. He tried to tell me that it made Poe come alive for him. When I seemed shocked by that, he laughed and told me that reading Poe while tripping was one of the craziest things he'd ever done. It scared him sometimes because he could see it all happening. Anyway, he said that the next two years were pretty awful in the Haight. Something bad happened. He wouldn't tell me about it, but all of a sudden Nelly was gone and that was the real beginning of his downfall. He managed to get some things written and sold - enough to keep him alive, but most of it was going to drugs and booze. He dried out of the drugs, but couldn't shake the booze."

"I can't imagine living that way, can you?"

"I really can't. But somehow he did."

"How did you know this was a puzzle?"

"One time we talked about ciphers and puzzles, little tidbits authors give to readers without telling them. I wonder how often there are treasures buried in books that readers never uncovered, and the authors went to their graves never telling."

"So what are you going to do with all of this?"

"Maybe you can help me. I'm going to do some serious

counting and associating first of all because I'm not able to figure out ... wait." She looked up. "I'm a moron. Hold up the book for me, would you?"

He did and she glanced back and forth from the book to the computer screen.

"I can't do this without spreading out on the dining room table unless you let me babble at you," she said.

"Babble at me. I'm intrigued."

"Can I tell you a word and then you tell me which line has the first two letters that match my word?"

"What?"

"Look," she said, pointing to the first file. "Window Dressing. That makes no sense, but the word 'with' is the first word of line eleven. That puts it in the second stanza according to the poem." She opened the file. "And there are nine folders in here. How many words are in that line?"

"Nine," Henry said. "Wow. How did you figure that out?"

"I love puzzles. And I've been processing on this for a while. I know that Thomas isn't this haphazard in his thinking. It had to be something. Okay, now I have the words 'In a Small Town.'"

"That's not helpful," Henry said. "There are five lines that start with the word 'in.'"

"Okay, well I have six folders inside."

"Yeah. Three of these have six words - "in the kingdom by the sea."

"Okay, I'll pull that one," she looked at the laptop "and these four over here." She clicked each of them open. "I have one with seven folders ..."

"That's line thirty-two."

"And one with eight folders."

"That's line thirty-three."

"Both of those are in Stanza Five, so I'll put them in here," she said, creating a new folder.

They continued through the process until there were only five folders that didn't make sense as to their placement. The repetition of the line in the poem wasn't going to give her enough to solve it.

There had to be something more.

She wasn't sure how she was going to organize the next layer of folders, but at least she had this sorted and she began to feel like she was getting somewhere. She jammed two folders beginning with 'Of' and with five interior folders in them into the Stanza Five folder, figuring they could reside there until she got a better understanding of the process. That left her with three folders beginning with 'In' and having six words each.

"Ugh," she said. "I was so excited. Now what?"

"Look inside them. Each of these lines of text is just a little bit different. The first one says, 'in a kingdom by the sea,' the second one says 'in this kingdom by the sea,' and the third has a parenthesis after the last word. Maybe he will have given you some kind of a clue."

Polly peered at the folder titles first and separated one away from the other two. "This is easy. It says 'inappropriate.' I'm guessing that is the first one." She put it in the Stanza One folder.

"Oh," she went on, "He really did make it easy for me. This is the third one. 'Invaluable (not finance).' He used the parentheses." She moved the final two folders to the appropriate place and sat back. "Now I have to figure out what he has in all of these things. It seems so random, but maybe now that it's in some type of order it will make more sense."

"We should start at the beginning," Henry said.

"Was there only one ice cream sandwich?" Polly asked him, sticking her lower lip out in a pout.

"I hope not!" He winked and kissed her lip. "That pout seems sad and pathetic." As he walked away, he said, "It seems odd that Thomas put all of this work into creating a puzzle of this information. Surely he didn't do it just for you. How would he know that he needed to do that?"

"I don't think he did do it for me." She put her laptop on the table in front of her and followed him out into the kitchen. He pulled another ice cream sandwich out for each of them and handed one to her.

"He didn't say much, but there were some things that bothered him. A lot. He was scared of something, but no ..." Polly bit her lower lip while she thought. "It wasn't that he was scared, it was more like he knew there was something out there that he was going to have to deal with someday and it was going to be difficult. It was like he wanted to avoid it as long as he could."

"What makes you say that?"

"One day we were talking about kids. He got this real faraway look and said he needed to fix things before he ever found his kid. I asked him if he really thought he might have a child out there and he changed the subject." She hitched herself up onto the counter and looked at Henry. "He knew something."

"Did he ever find Nelly again?"

"He didn't tell me that, but I don't think he ever quit looking for her. I was telling Lydia earlier that the main character in his mysteries is defined by a broken relationship in the past. The detective spends his life looking for something that was lost. In the books, the girl's name was Annie and the detective was Eddie."

Henry nodded, waiting for her to go on.

"You know - Edgar and Annabel?"

"But, Edgar wasn't ever married to an Annabel."

"No, but Thomas loved that poem. And everyone is certain that Annabel Lee is written for Poe's wife who died. It's a little weird that the narrator of the poem sleeps in her sepulcher every night, but Thomas said that losing someone you love that much makes you live in that loss for a long time. He said he drank because he hated going to sleep at night since he dreamed of Nelly and wondered where she'd gone." Polly dropped her head. "You know. That makes sense to me. I dreamt about my mom a lot. In my dreams she was happy and healthy, doing all of the things we'd always done."

"Do you dream about your dad too?"

"I do. Most of the time we're all together. It gets kind of jumbled up with Sylvester and Mary, but sometimes my dreams remind me about how much I miss them."

Henry moved in closer to her, standing between her legs. He

hugged her tight, then backed up.

Polly giggled. "The funny thing is that I still dream about my old boyfriends, too. There was one bad breakup that I had in high school. We just quit talking to each other and after I graduated I never saw him again, but sometimes in my dreams, he shows up out of the blue so we can patch things up and be okay again. Maybe it's just my brain trying to make everyone happy."

"So, Poe wanted to sleep in his dead wife's sepulcher?"

"No, I think he realized that he was spending so much time thinking about her it was like he was already there. Rather than deal with her death, he focused on it until it overtook him. That's what Thomas did too. He focused so much on losing Nelly that the only way to get through it was to make himself totally numb."

Polly reached her right leg out and hooked it around Henry, pulling him back in. She kissed him.

"You taste like chocolate and ice cream," he laughed.

"Good thing you do too. At least I don't taste like garlic." She'd eaten her fair share of garlic mashed potatoes at dinner.

"If you did, so would I." He reached in and kissed her again. She leaned into the kiss, wrapping her arms around his neck. "Whoa woman," he said. "Now you're making me swoon."

"About time!" she exclaimed. "You've spent this last year making me weak in the knees. It's my turn."

She pulled away and laughed, "So do you ever feel like I make you too girly?"

"Where in the world did this come from?" Henry backed up and took the ice cream wrapper from her, depositing both in the trash can.

"Oh, I was just thinking about you cooking for me and telling me you swoon and you were helping me with my project and you're always doing stuff for me. Should I be out tinkering on cars with you or taking you hunting or something?"

Henry laughed until his face got red. "Polly, you come up with the craziest thoughts," he sputtered.

"What?" she asked, jumping down from the counter.

"I love you, Polly, but you have got to quit worrying about

what other people think."

"I'm wondering about what you think!" She swatted his arm.

"No, you are worrying about what other people might think of me or you. We're in our thirties. We get to do what we want without input from other people."

"So that's a 'no' to my question?"

"Do I think you make me too girly?"

"Yes. That question."

"No. I'm still as macho and masculine as I ever was.

"Even when you tell me you swoon from my kiss?"

"Polly, when we are here in your apartment, we can do or say whatever we please. You have got to get past this."

"I probably won't."

"Get past this?"

"Yep. I haven't changed much since you met me, have I?"

"Well, no, but ..."

"No buts about it. I'm probably going to make you nuts forever."

He had begun to walk back to the living room, but spun around on her. "Forever?"

She shrugged. "Unless you decide that I'm too crazy to be around."

"Forever is a long time, pretty girl."

"Okay, then I'm going to make you nuts. Period."

Henry waited for her to catch up, then wrapped an arm around her. "I like the sound of forever, though."

"This first year hasn't been too bad," she said and melted into the kiss he used to stop her from talking anymore.

CHAPTER SIXTEEN

Knitting her brows together in concentration, Polly found it difficult to break away when Jeff came in for the day.

"You're in early," he said, plopping down in the chair.

"Eliseo and I hurried this morning. It was chilly out there. The horses weren't in any hurry to go outside, so we just did a quick cleanup. He's going to make Rachel and Jason work extra hard tonight. I was fine with that," she laughed.

"What's up with your day?"

"I'm ordering a new mattress and then, unless you need me, I was going to huddle up with my laptop and keep working on the information I got from Thomas. Why?"

"No reason. Just keeping an eye on you. Nothing weird happened last night?"

She peered at him over her laptop. "What do you mean? Do you know something?"

"What? No! I was just asking. You still don't have any idea who might be targeting Sycamore House?"

"Trust me, if I had any idea, I'd be all over it. So what's up for you today?"

"Oh, you know. Normal stuff. Meetings and classes and other assorted craziness. We have a wedding tomorrow, so there's a rehearsal and dinner tonight."

"A wedding? We never have weddings here."

"They don't want it in a church, so they're doing it here. It should be interesting. It's a theme wedding."

"What do you mean by that?"

"They're dressing in costume and decorating for it."

"Okay? Why do you sound so tentative?"

"It has the potential for really cool or really weird. I'm betting on really weird and hoping on really cool."

"What's the theme?"

Jeff took a deep breath. "Legend of Zelda."

"I'm sorry, what?" she laughed.

"Yep. It seems that Link has finally found Zelda and they're getting married. The best part is that I think the guy performing the ceremony is the evil guy."

"Ganon?" she asked.

"Yeah. Him," Jeff glanced sideways at her. "How did you know that? You are such a nerd."

"Way too many video games in my life. You have to take lots of pictures. I want to see it," Polly said.

"I'll make sure to drop some in your shared folder so you can be entertained. But I still think it's weird."

"You need more adventure in your life, my boy."

"Maybe I do. When they decide to do a *Sound of Music* or *South Pacific* themed wedding, I'll get really excited."

"Uh huh ... you're a nut."

Jeff stood up to leave her office.

"Jeff?"

"Yes, Polly."

"Just remember: it's dangerous to go alone."

He turned around and rolled his eyes at her. "That's from the video game, isn't it?"

"Maybe." She winked at him. "You aren't very good at this geek stuff, but you'll learn."

"Uh huh." He left her office. She thought about lucky she was to have him. He made the experiences great for their guests. She couldn't imagine doing it without him.

Polly stood and walked over to his door, "Jeff?"

He looked up, "What do you need, Polly?"

"I just wanted to tell you how much I appreciate you. I don't say it enough. Sycamore House would be nothing without you. I couldn't put up with the people you put up with and I could never pull off a Legend of Zelda theme wedding."

"We all have our own strengths. Mine happens to be parties."

"No. Yours is people and parties and organizing and scheduling and everything else you do around here. I just wanted you to know that I should tell you that every day. So, thank you."

He looked a little uncomfortable. "Thanks, Polly."

She winked at him again, "And maybe I'll try to talk Santa out of putting coal in your stocking."

"I'd appreciate that," he laughed.

She went back into her office and grabbed her coffee mug. She needed more caffeine.

Polly took a deep breath and opened the folder she had named 'Annabel Lee.' It was time to dig into the first stanza of the poem and see what Thomas had left for her. Now that there was an order, she hoped the files would begin to make more sense.

She clicked the first folder open. It seemed as if they were PDFs that had been scanned from documents. She opened an image of a Sunday school class attendance record from Springfield, Colorado. The teacher had kept excellent records. There were ten children in her classroom. Polly remembered these attendance charts. Why would Thomas have this?

The next file she opened was Sunday School roster from a year later. The same children, well ... one little girl was gone and another had been added. A different teacher and parent's names were listed. A boy named Auguste McCall had a mother, Camille. That was interesting. Both of those were characters created by Edgar Allan Poe. The other names were fairly mundane.

Another file from the same church was a bulletin. Apparently, little Auguste had gotten himself into a choir and was singing in a Christmas program. Camille was listed as a parent-helper that Sunday. Polly found a copy of a rental agreement from 1969 for an apartment in Springfield. It had been leased to Camille McCall for one year, with six month extensions to follow. A jpeg file made absolutely no sense, so she left it alone.

She opened the next folder. He continued to flesh out a picture of this young woman and her son. There were bills from a doctor ... a pediatrician. She opened the bill from the hospital and found that it was from the child's birth. There was another jpeg in this folder and it too, was odd. Another shot of the sky.

The third folder made her say, "Ah ha," out loud when she opened the birth certificate for Auguste McCall. There was no father listed and the mother was Camille. There was a scan of an invoice for an automobile purchase in the summer of nineteen seventy-three and another jpeg in the folder. It had a head of a woman in the same sky as the other two images.

"Do you think?" she asked herself. She quickly opened the other folders in this stanza and sure enough there was a single jpeg in each of them. She copied them all out into their own folder and looked at them as large icons, then extra large icons. If she took the time to arrange them, they were another puzzle. Soon, she had an image of a young woman and a little boy standing in front of the sign for Springfield, Colorado.

"Oh, Thomas. Was this your Nelly? Is this your son? When did you get this picture?

"Jeff?" Polly called out.

In a moment, he was standing in her door. "Yes, Polly?"

"I'm sorry. I should have gotten up myself. Do you have Photoshop or something on your computer?"

"No, but unless you are doing something intensive, you can probably use a free online tool. What are you trying to do?"

"I need to stitch some jpegs together into one photograph."

"Yeah. You should be able to do that online."

"Thanks. I'm sorry I bothered you."

He grinned at her. "It's no problem, I needed coffee anyway.

Have you even looked up in the last hour?"

"It's been an hour?" she asked.

"Is your mug empty?"

Polly looked down at her coffee mug. "Yes, I guess it is."

"Here, give it to me. Let me get you stimulated."

"Why Jeff, you naughty boy."

"Don't tell my mama. She warned me about girls like you."

"I'll bet she did." Polly handed him the mug, then stood up and stretched. There were people coming into Sycamore House from the parking lot. "What class do we have this morning?"

"Some Halloween crafty thing in the classroom. I don't know what they're making."

"Cool," she said, taking the mug from him. She blew on it and felt the warm steam blow back in her face.

"What are you finding in there?" Jeff asked her.

"I'm not sure yet. Right now there is information on a young woman and her son. It's all from the late sixties into the early seventies. Thomas did a lot of research on them."

"Then don't mind me. You go back to work. I'll just be in my office until the next time you bellow at me."

"Okay, thanks," she said distractedly, then realized what had just happened. He was halfway out the door when she said, "I'm sorry, Jeff. I'd forgotten what it was like to be so focused."

"No problem." He waved at her as he turned the corner into his own office.

"Dork," she muttered to herself and began working on the photograph. She made a few mistakes as she learned her way around the site, but when she had the finished piece, she had to admit it didn't look half bad. She entitled the picture, "Springfield, Colorado" and dropped it into the Stanza One folder.

She'd ignored the other folders once the photograph caught her attention and now she skipped ahead to the last one. There was only one other document in this folder. It was the manuscript for one of Thomas's early novels. It had been years since she read it.

Polly opened the file and began reading to refresh her memory. That was interesting. It was set in a little town in southeast

Colorado. Eddie Powers had been called in by an old friend to investigate the murder of a young woman. The local police had ruled it a suicide, but Powers discovered that a doctor's son had gotten the girl pregnant. The doctor had subsequently poisoned her so that his son would take the football scholarship at Colorado State. The boy devastation at losing her and the discovery of what his father had done, caused him to kill himself. The story didn't have a happy ending and Polly had only read it once, long ago.

She did a quick search for the book and discovered that it had been published in nineteen seventy-six. She continued reading until she looked up in response to a quiet knock on her door.

Jeff was standing there, looking a little sheepish. "Do you know what time it is?"

"No, what?" she asked, then looked at the time on her laptop. "Where did it go?"

"Where did what go."

"The time! It's eleven forty-five! Have I been sitting here for two and a half hours?" She moved her shoulders and her back. They were a little sore.

"Do you want lunch?" he asked. "I was going to call the diner."

"I have food upstairs. Do you want to eat with me? Henry made meatloaf and mashed potatoes last night. I have plenty of leftovers."

"That actually sounds better than what I was going to eat. Sure. Can you take a break now?"

"I'd better," she said, "or I might find myself stuck to that chair."

"What did you find?"

"It took me a while to figure out the photo editing software, and then I found one of Thomas's old manuscripts. I'd only read it once before and I must have gotten caught up in it again."

"Why do you suppose that's on there?"

"I'm not sure yet."

They started out of the office, but then Polly stopped. She turned around and went back in and sat down at her desk.

"What are you doing?"

"I don't feel good about this. There is something on here he didn't want people to know about." She shut her computer down and then snapped the lid closed on her laptop and carried it with her. "I'm just going to be safe."

"Seems a little paranoid," he said.

"Wait until you have a man die at your front door and see if you aren't a little paranoid," she mocked back at him.

"You've got a point."

They went upstairs to her apartment.

"Do you think you'll be able to figure out who murdered Thomas from those files?" he asked as she fumbled for her phone to unlock the apartment door. They both looked up as Grey Linder walked out of one of the spa bathrooms. He was in a robe, his eyes were red. He nodded at the two of them and went on to his room. Polly unlocked her door and gestured for Jeff to go in first. She was about to follow him, when she realized that she hadn't heard Grey's door close. She glanced across the hallway and the door pushed shut.

"He's really strange," she said after she got inside her apartment and had her own door closed.

"Who? Grey Linder?" Jeff asked.

"Yes. Whenever I'm in the hallway, I feel like he's spying on me."

"Talk about paranoid."

"Probably. It's just weird. Do you ever see him downstairs?"

"He comes down in the mornings sometimes to get a thermos of coffee and whatever breakfast food we have on the counter. Sometimes I see him leave in the late afternoon. Should I be paying closer attention?"

"No, I suppose not. I guess I'm just glad that he's not always in that little room. He gives me the creeps."

"Creeps like you're afraid he's going to do something to you?"

"No, creeps like he's just weird enough that I don't want him in my study group because he's always thinking of some random thing that has no context with what we're working on and he insists on talking about it even when no one cares."

Jeff had picked Leia up when she began rubbing on his leg. He was stroking her head and talking quietly to her.

"You should come up more often," Polly said. "They love company."

He followed her into the kitchen. "Can I help with anything?"

"No, you keep snuggling the cat. It's one less animal around my ankles. I'll do this."

She heard a voice from the back steps, "Polly, are you up here?"

"Come on up, Henry," she called. "Jeff and I are about to eat your leftovers."

She heard him come up the steps and soon he was in the living room. "Hi Jeff," Henry said and strode across the room. Jeff set the cat down on the floor and shook his hand.

"Hey, Henry. I hear you cooked last night."

"I did and I'm just in time for leftovers."

"Really?" Polly asked. "You have time today?"

"Jimmy and Sam are working at Frankel's and Leroy and Ben are back at the shop. They're on lunch, so I decided to come over and say hello." He gave her a quick kiss on the cheek, "Hello."

Without asking, he began pulling glasses out of the cupboard and silverware from the drawer, while Polly sliced meatloaf and scooped potatoes and beans onto plates and put them in the microwave.

"Tea?" he asked Jeff.

"Sure, that sounds good."

Henry took the pitcher out of the refrigerator and handed it to Jeff.

When he reopened the refrigerator and grabbed the container with the tomatoes and cucumbers as well as the butter dish, Polly poked him in the side. "You're awfully comfortable here, cowboy," she laughed.

"Do we need anything else?" he asked, then said, "Napkins. Oh, and salt and pepper." He grabbed those from the other end of the counter and handed them across the peninsula to Jeff.

"How you coming on that grub, cookie?" Henry asked, and slapped Polly on the rump.

She jumped at that. "Yours is going to be the last one out if you're not careful and you might lose a few fingers along the way."

"Ahem," Jeff coughed from the dining room. "Should I leave the two of you and go to the Diner by myself?"

"Not if you want to live through the afternoon," Polly threatened, taking the first plate out and handing it to Henry. Soon food was served and they sat down to eat.

"What brings you upstairs for lunch?" Henry asked Jeff.

"I had to dig Polly out of her office. She'd gotten lost in those computer files and I was worried she wouldn't eat."

"You need a keeper," Henry said to her.

"I never do this," she protested. "Leave me alone."

"Did you find anything more?"

Polly explained what she had uncovered. It had left her with more questions than answers, but she also knew that she'd barely skimmed the surface of the files on that flash drive.

"Polly?" Henry asked.

"What?"

"You started a sentence and then just faded away. Where did you go?"

"I wonder what I was saying. I was thinking about Thomas's book. My copy is over here in the bookshelf." She got up and left the table with both men watching her. She'd barely touched her food, but it was the last thing on her mind.

"Here it is. *The Case of Romeo and Juliet.* You know, I should have had Thomas sign my copies of his books. I didn't even think of that when he was here." She opened the front cover and grinned. "But he did. Look! He signed it for me!"

"What does it say?" Jeff asked.

"Polly, you were right. Authors give you more than you realize sometimes. Never forget that."

"That's cryptic," Henry said. "That's all he wrote?"

"Well, he signed his name." She handed the book to him when she got back to the table.

Henry took it and pointed at her plate. "Eat something. I don't want you to fade."

145

CHAPTER SEVENTEEN

"No. I've got this. You two go on so I can get some work done."
Polly shooed both Jeff and Henry out after lunch. She had time
before Aaron and Anita were arriving and wanted to process on
what she had learned this morning. It wasn't nearly enough and
didn't seem to point to a murderer. She wondered if maybe
Thomas hadn't been asking her to find the murderer, but his son.

She filled the dishwasher and smiled as Obiwan followed her
to the back steps. They went outside and she let him wander
through the trees lining the creek. It had turned into a beautiful
fall day. She glanced back at the school and out of the corner of
her eye, saw Grey Linder watching from his room.

That man was creepy. He made her think of the creepy old
man in the creepy old house that every kid ran from in every
small town. It had been a little old lady for her. Whenever she
would walk from school to her friend's house, they passed that
one home where everything was dilapidated. The grass was
uncut, weeds overran the yard and vines crawled up the house.
The only time they ever saw the old woman was when she came
out to get her mail and she was as unkempt as her home.

Now that Polly was older, she wondered what might have happened if someone had just been friends with the poor lady. When she lived in Boston, there was a woman, Gladys Black, who lived next door to her. She was bent over and used a walker and Polly's first encounter with the woman had been at the end of a cane. Gladys yelled at her for making too much noise while she was moving in, but Polly had taken the woman cookies and whenever she saw her in the corner grocery store, carried her bags home for her. It didn't take long for Gladys to invite Polly in for coffee. She would pull out her recipe card collection and tell Polly stories about the different things she had cooked for her husband over the years. There were cards from Gladys' mother and those meant more stories from her childhood. She had also collected salt and pepper shakers and before she died, gave Polly a pair of her favorites, a Snowman and Snow woman Goebbels set. They were tucked away in a Christmas box and Polly couldn't wait to get them out. They always sat on her table through the season.

Polly glanced back up and Grey was gone from the window. Obiwan had done all he needed to do and headed for the horses.

"Obiwan, come." Polly commanded. He stopped, looked at the horses in the pasture and then back to her.

"Come," she repeated. She could almost see him sigh dejectedly as he began trotting toward her.

"You're such a good boy," she told him. He sat down and she bent over to ruffle his head. "You're a good boy. Let's go in."

He followed her back to the apartment and curled up on the bed, knowing she was leaving again. She grabbed her laptop and went out the front door.

Back in her office, Polly continued reading the manuscript of Thomas's first book. There had to be a reason it was on the disk. She scrolled to the end and there wasn't anything that seemed out of place. The story ended and that was that. She scrolled to the end of each chapter and couldn't see that he'd done anything differently with them. It all seemed perfectly normal.

"You are quite engrossed in your work." Polly looked up to see Aaron Merritt standing in her doorway.

"Hi," she said. "I didn't hear you come in."

"I can tell." He sat down in the chair across from her.

"Is Anita with you?"

"She'll be here in a minute. She was right behind me."

Polly sat back and looked at him. He was a huge presence in her office. When he stood, he was over six feet tall. His big barrel chest and immense upper arms and forearms made him seem bigger than he really was. His hair was just beginning to grey and when it did, it would be very attractive, accenting the full head of dark hair that he kept quite short. He didn't go for a military buzz cut, but it was always neatly trimmed to his head.

"Can you tell me anything more about Thomas's murder?" Polly asked him.

"I think we might be able to explain a few things to you. Lydia said that you had done some work on the files he gave you and I'm hoping that between you and Anita, we can understand what we have here."

"Did I hear my name?" The bouncy, young tech came into Polly's office. "I'm sorry it took me so long. Adam desperately needed me to show him how to order pizza online."

"What?" Aaron demanded.

"I'm kidding." She smirked at Polly. "I just ordered it for him." She pulled her laptop out and slipped behind Aaron to the other chair.

"Maybe we should go into the conference room," Polly said. "We can hook the computers up and see things on a bigger screen."

"Wow," Anita said. "Boss, get the name of her supplier. We could use that." She let Aaron stand and walk out first, then followed him.

Polly stopped in Jeff's office, "We're going to be in the conference room. You don't have anything scheduled, do you?"

"No, it's all yours."

They shut the door to the conference room and Aaron pulled the blinds closed before sitting down.

"Secret stuff?" Polly asked.

"It's probably better to be safe than sorry. We still don't know who killed Thomas Zeller."

Polly plugged her laptop into the system and projected her screen on the wall in front of them.

"What have you done here?" Anita asked.

Polly explained how she had sorted things according to the Edgar Allan Poe poem.

"That's awesome, boss. It should really help us."

"I only made it through the first stanza," Polly said. "I got busy stitching the photo together and then I was sidetracked by his manuscript."

"This will make it much easier to work on those photographs," Anita said. "We had bits and pieces all over the place. I printed them out so people could put pieces together, but we didn't know how many photographs and how many pieces we had for each."

"I think that Thomas and Nelly had a son," Polly said.

"Nelly? There is no Nelly in these files."

"That's the girl he met in San Francisco. She left in nineteen sixty-nine. Something bad happened, but he wouldn't tell me what it was."

Anita reached over, clicked into a file, and opened a PDF document, "This is what happened. We're waiting for the rest of the police reports. They don't have everything digitized and we've had to put in a request, but since it was a cop, they haven't shuffled it all the way to the bottom of their cold cases."

"What's a cop?" Polly asked. "What happened?"

"It looks as if Thomas got his hands on part of the police report. His name is on here too, but only as a bystander. And that must be Nelly's name: Eleanor Marie Farber. She was implicated in the murder of a police officer, Bartholomew Andrew Davidson." Anita was pointing to words on the screen.

"Murder? What happened?"

"There are other reports in here," Anita said, clicking another file open. "There were a series of drug raids in the Haight in the summer of 1969. I did some searching on this. After 1967, there were too many people and too many drugs out there and crime was out of control. You can see that Thomas was picked up here," she clicked another file open, "and here, too. He did short stints of time. He wasn't dealing, just possession. He was bailed out by ... " she scrolled down the page. "Yes, both times by Eleanor Farber."

"Which folders did you find these in?" Polly asked.

"Looking at the organization you've given them, they are spread throughout all of the ... what did you call them? Stanzas?" I found them all and just put them together to try to get a picture of what he was researching."

"Did you find information on the woman and her son?" Polly was beginning to get excited. With someone else to talk to about what she had found, things were making more sense. Details were falling into place.

Aaron said very little while the two girls moved back and forth between the files. Finally, he stood up. "I am going to let the two of you keep working. If you find something that I need to know about, call me."

Polly scooted her chair back. "There's nothing else you can tell me about Thomas? You don't have any idea at all who did this?"

Anita reached across and tapped Polly's knee. "There was someone else involved in the killing of that police officer. We are wondering if he might have tracked Thomas here."

"What was his name?" Polly asked.

"There were other people named in the report. Two of them were taken into custody and two of them, Eleanor Farber and Douglas Winters got away. These two," she pointed to mug shots in a file that Thomas had scanned, "both said that Douglas Winters was the one who pulled the trigger. They claimed to have nothing to do with it, they were just in the room when it happened. They also said that Eleanor Farber didn't do anything, but she ran, so it's been an open case on her."

"Those two spent a few years in prison," Aaron said. "Their families hired lawyers who eventually got them off. We don't know where they are now, either."

"So four people were in a room when a police officer was killed and none of them can be found?" Polly asked.

"That's about the gist of it," he said. "We have some prints from the room here, but we haven't found the knife and we haven't come up with any good information from your card key database. The prints don't match the two men who were imprisoned. We're at a standstill unless you come up with something in those files."

"I thought Thomas was asking me to find his son," Polly said. "I didn't realize he had all of this other information on here."

"That may be all that he is trying to do, Polly. Maybe he was trying to clear Eleanor's name. But she would have to come forward for that to happen. They need to ask her questions about what happened that night. There's no statute of limitations on murder. It's not over until it's over."

Polly sighed. "We'd better get to work."

"Don't stay too late," Aaron said to Anita. "I know you." He left the room and shut the door.

She giggled at Polly. "I tend to get involved and forget that it's time to go home."

"Me too. So, what if I start pulling all of the picture pieces together. My online software doesn't stitch them together perfectly, but at least we can see what we have."

"That sounds good. I'm going to tag my files with your stanzas so that I can get things in a better order. We'll meet back here in a little bit?"

"Sure. That sounds good," Polly laughed. They would be sitting at the same table together, but sometimes concentration caused a person to be elsewhere. She opened the folder for the second stanza, copied out each jpeg file, then rearranged them until she had a picture and then did the same thing for each of the other stanzas. The boy continued to age and the woman, though she got older, never lost her innate beauty.

The first picture was the only one with a city sign in it. The others were various attractions. She supposed they probably were related to whatever community the family had lived in.

Anita showed no signs of coming up for air, so when Polly finished the last photograph, she opened the second stanza, hoping to find some names and maybe a city. If Thomas kept to the pattern, the first folder would be school things for the boy. After opening a few PDF files, she realized that the boy's name was now Allan and his mother's name was Rowena Singer. They were living in Tutwiler, Mississippi. Another small town. Allan had started kindergarten in nineteen seventy-four. There was a class picture and he looked to be about the same age as the boy in the first picture she'd uncovered.

She made some notes and moved to the third stanza. The boy was now named Roderick - or Rick. His mother's name was Madeline Clark. They moved to Cardington, Ohio, just before his sixth grade year. There were no school pictures, but the photograph that was located in the second stanza would have been of a boy between the ages of eleven and twelve.

That made sense. Nelly was probably sending these pictures after they moved out of a community. She could only imagine that frustrated Thomas to no end.

The fourth folder began in 1984. Troy and Helen White moved into Davisboro, Georgia, as he began his sophomore year in high school. Polly spent some time looking at the picture Thomas had received after they left Ohio. She could see that the boy was his son. It was in his lips and his eyes. This must have destroyed her friend. Her heart ached for him, but there was nothing she could do now except figure out how to solve this.

"How are you doing?" Anita asked, startling Polly.

"I'm good. How about you?"

"Thomas has a lot of information here, but there's nothing that points to one person and says, 'This is Douglas Winters.' What are you working on?"

"I have the photographs figured out and I'm just trying to get a read on the boy and his mother. It looks like Thomas received a picture from them just after they left a town. I was going to dig into the last stanza. Thomas put education stuff in the first folder of each stanza, so that's where I've been stuck."

"There's a manuscript in each stanza too." Anita said.

Polly thought for a moment. "That's it! He had five novels published before he dried out. I'll bet every one of them is set in one of these little towns that she lived in. He probably spent time there, researching his novel and tracking down information on the two of them. Writing a book would have given him a lot of leeway in a small community. When he was here, people were always talking to him, telling him ..." she slowed down.

"Are you thinking what I'm thinking?" Anita asked.

"He was looking for them here in Bellingwood," Polly responded. "But there's no photograph of them here. What made him come here? The boy would be about forty-four and his mother would be in her late sixties if she was still alive.

"What's in the last folder?"

Polly's heart started to race a little bit and she felt her cheeks get warm. This was exciting. They were getting close to something, she just didn't know what it was yet.

The photo in stanza four was of the boy as a college graduate, standing with his mother. There were records of his high school graduation and then he attended college in Augusta, Georgia. Polly looked at a map. He hadn't gone too far from his mother. She wondered if he had lived at home and commuted. The information was probably there.

She opened the last stanza file and clicked to the first folder. There would probably be no more education information, so she wondered what she would find. The photo was of a young man in a suit, his mother at his side. They were standing in front of a school building. Guy Brothers. He was employed as a fourth-grade teacher in Soda Springs, Idaho. She found employment records until nineteen ninety-four and that was the last of the information. She quickly opened another folder. There was a rental agreement for a condominium to Guy and Lenore Brothers. It ended in nineteen ninety-four as well.

Polly sat back and slumped in her chair.

"What did you find?" Anita asked.

"The information stops in nineteen ninety-four," Polly said, "but this is an outline of their lives."

Anita looked at it. "Do you see what I'm seeing?" she asked.

"Apparently not. What?"

"Look at those names. People always tell you something about themselves."

"Well, the first names are all characters from Poe's writings."

"No. The last names. McCall, Singer, Clark, White, Brothers. Ring a bell?"

Polly was puzzled. She had no idea what Anita was trying to get across to her. "I don't get it."

"Sewing. Those are all names that have to do with sewing. They are patterns, thread, and machines. I'll bet the woman was a seamstress."

"Do you think she is still doing that?"

"It wouldn't surprise me if she is in some form or other. She's probably close to retirement by now, but yes."

"That's a clue!" Polly said.

"It's a little vague, but it is some place to start."

"The son is a teacher and she is a seamstress. If they lived in Bellingwood, that shouldn't be too hard to figure out. We just need to ask the right questions."

"Were those the questions Thomas was asking around town?"

Polly nodded. "He did talk about going to Andrew's band recital with me at the elementary school." She shook her head. "I don't know. I need to think about this some more."

"Well, you've given me enough to work on tomorrow. Have you looked at the time?"

It was six-thirty. Polly couldn't believe she hadn't heard from Henry about supper. When she looked for her phone, she realized that she'd left it upstairs. She was going to be in so much trouble with him. She was surprised that he wasn't already knocking on the door, looking for her.

"I'm sorry I kept you so long," she said.

"It's no big deal. I usually stay late when I'm working on a project. It was nice having someone in the room with me. I'll call you tomorrow if I come up with anything else."

Polly shut down her laptop. "Thanks for letting me get involved with this. I feel a lot better knowing that I might be helping him at least a little bit."

"This is the easy stuff. And you helped me organize things once you told me about the poem. I'm going to go home and read some more of Poe's writings. You never know what else will show up."

They went out into the foyer and there were a few people moving in and out of the auditorium.

"It's a wedding," she said quietly to Anita. "Jeff tells me it is a theme wedding, 'The Legend of Zelda.'"

"Really? That's so cool.

As soon as Anita was out the front door, Polly ran up to her apartment. She quickly turned to the kitchen and saw her phone on the counter and then realized she wasn't alone in the room.

"I'm sorry!" she said. "I got caught up in Thomas's files in the conference room and I left my phone up here!"

Henry was sitting on the sofa holding the television remote.

"I found your phone and your very lonely animals. Obiwan and I have already had a walk. He told me you were getting way too involved. I had to agree with him."

"But you can't believe what we figured out." She flopped down on the sofa beside him and set the laptop on the coffee table. "He had a son. His old girlfriend changed their names every few years and moved to a completely different part of the country. They may have come to Bellingwood. That's why Thomas was here!"

"Whoa," he said. "Slow down."

Polly took a breath and then said, "I'm starving and you and Jeff ate all the leftovers." She stuck her lower lip out. "What are you going to feed me?"

"I had a busy day, too!" he said. "And then I couldn't find you and that stressed me out."

"I'm sorry," she said quietly. "I didn't mean to do that. I'm so sorry."

"It's really okay," he said. "When I couldn't reach you, I called Jeff. He told me what you were doing."

She swatted his arm. "So I'm starving and I want to tell you everything from today. Feed me!"

"I'll drive. You point the way. We can go wherever you want to go. I have plenty of gas, the moon's the limit."

CHAPTER EIGHTEEN

"Oh no! I'm late!" she announced to the animals sitting on her bed while she attempted to hurry into her dress. Nate and Henry had come up with a plot to take her and Joss out for dinner. She knew they wanted nothing more than to drive Nate's car. Women and food were secondary benefits for the evening.

Just as she slipped her right foot into a black two inch heel, she thought about Nate's two-door car. She'd be in the back seat.

"Blast and damn," she said. "I'm late and I'm wearing the wrong clothes."

Polly flung her closet door open and peered at the hanging clothes. "I'm not that girl," she muttered. "I have plenty to wear. I'm not trying to impress anyone. Find something now, Giller."

She quickly landed on a blue and black striped sweater and yanked a pair of black pants off a hanger. A few minutes later, she was dressed. She fluffed her hair and gathered up her phone and a wallet. "Do I need anything else?"

The cats had fallen asleep by her pillow, but Obiwan was still watching intently as she shut her eyes to think. Her dog thumped his tail on the bed and when she reached over to rub his head, turned onto his back. "I don't have time for that," but rubbed his belly anyway. "Now, be good and I'll be back later." She opened the door to the driveway just as Nate's car pulled in.

Joss opened the passenger door and Henry crawled out. "If we sit in the back, we can act like high school kids," he said.

"You aren't sitting up front to talk about cars with Nate?" she asked, astounded.

"Not tonight. It's a date. Remember?"

Polly shook her head. "I'm a little surprised you did."

Joss laughed at them. "Don't let him fool you, Polly. He and Nate took the car out this morning and spent time in the shop. He can probably afford to give you a little attention tonight."

Henry held the seat up while Polly crawled in behind Nate. He sat beside her and winked, then put his arm around her and drew her close to him. She slid across the vinyl on the seat and was practically in his lap before she put her hands out to stop herself.

"Stop that! Seatbelts!" she laughed.

"I think we have a seatbelt right here in the middle for you," he said, waving the ends at her. "You can't get away that easily."

Joss had stepped back into the front seat and pulled the door shut. "You two be good back there. This car might have seen some action in its early days, but it is older than we are. We don't want to give it a heart attack."

Nate hadn't said anything while all of this was going on, but Polly saw his shoulders shake as he quietly chuckled.

"You're awfully quiet," she remarked.

"Just waiting for everyone to get where they belong so we can hit the highway."

"Where are we going to dinner?"

"There's a place I want you to try in Fort Dodge," Nate said. "They have your favorite."

"What's that?"

"You'll just have to wait and see."

Joss turned around and smiled at them. "He won't tell me where we're going, but if it's what I think, we're all really overdressed."

"Then I'm glad I didn't wear the dress I had on first. It would have been embarrassing trying to get in this back seat. And by the way," Polly said as she swatted Nate on the shoulder, "I was afraid I was going to be late. What took you guys so long?"

"It's her fault," he said, nodding at Joss.

"Uh huh. My fault. I'm not the one who walked around the house twice because my wallet and keys were missing. If you had looked where I told you to look, you wouldn't have had to rush."

"If you had picked them up and brought them to me like a good little wife, we wouldn't be having this conversation."

"If you wanted a good little wife, you should have chosen someone else. At least then your mother wouldn't have had to worry about your underwear."

"What?" Polly sputtered.

"When we were first married, his mother was shocked that I bought his underwear. I couldn't believe we were even having the conversation. Mr. Man, here, was wearing really ratty stuff. I'm guessing that she bought it for him when he left for college. He thought it was fine and told me I was weird when I started replacing it with new. She has some strange ideas about what I should and shouldn't do for her little Nate. Sometimes I think she's glad he found a wife and other times I think she's mad because he won't come home and live with her."

"Are you an only child?" Polly asked.

"No, but I'm the youngest," he sounded grumpy.

"By how many years?"

"My twin sisters are fifteen years older. I was a surprise."

"Wow. That was a surprise."

"They both live around mom and have tons of kids to keep her occupied, but she ..."

"She doesn't think anyone can take care of her little boy like she can," Joss finished for him.

"Is your dad still alive?" Polly asked.

"Yes. I told him that he can move out here any time. He threatens to take me up on it when she gets pushy. He golfs a lot."

"Do you golf?" Henry asked.

"Oh, good heavens, no," Nate responded. He glanced around at Henry. "I tipped a golf cart over once with Dad in it. Spilled him out in front of all his buddies. They told him they'd never seen anything quite like that before and the golf pro said he didn't know it was even possible. Dad never took me golfing again."

"Is that what started you with cars?" Henry was laughing.

"No, I dumped Dad when I was in high school. I was in seventh grade when he told me I had to find my own way to pay for a car if I wanted one. Then he offered to help me rebuild an old Buick. All I had to do was work for the parts. By the time I got my license, I had a car. I was the coolest dude in high school."

They drove into a parking lot and Nate stopped. "Here we are," he announced.

"It's an old drive-in," Polly leaned forward in her seat to look out the front window.

"There's a car show here on Friday nights during the summer," Nate shrugged. "But it was a nice drive and we got to know each other better, right? And besides, they have great tenderloins."

"Sure honey," Joss said. "Now get moving and help Polly out of the back seat. You need to redeem yourself."

The food was good and they sat talking at the table.

"Have you heard anything more about Thomas Zeller's killer?" Nate asked. "Everyone has been talking about it all week."

Polly shook her head. "Nothing much." Then she looked up, "But, I haven't told you what we found on his flash drive. I think he had a son and they might live around Bellingwood."

"Really!" Joss said.

Polly explained about the Edgar Allan Poe association and how they discovered that she changed their names over the years.

"I figure there had to be one more name change at least," she said. "I can't find the last set of names anywhere. Can you believe they've managed to recreate themselves that many times? It can't be easy, especially now that everything is computerized."

"The Internet took off in the mid-nineties, so up until that point, records weren't digitized," Joss said. "It would be a lot harder now than it was then."

"And what if he ever decided to have a family? He couldn't make them uproot their lives every five or six years."

"Is the mother still on the hook for the murder?"

"I think it's a matter of her coming forward and explaining things," Polly said. "But she wouldn't know that if she's been hiding all these years."

"Have you read his books?" Joss asked.

"I have them all. They are pretty sad, aren't they?" Polly pushed her plate away and sat back in her chair.

"It's like the detective is living half a life. He lost the best part of himself after his love died." Joss sighed and her eyes grew sad.

"Oh, good heavens, stop with the great tragedy stuff," Nate exclaimed. "It's a fictional character."

"Well, it's still sad. Especially if he wrote that way because he couldn't find his own love," Joss swatted her husband's knee. "And you be nice."

"What makes you think they live near here?" Nate asked Polly.

"When he was writing those early books, they were always located in towns where she had lived. She sent a picture after they moved and then he went looking for traces of her. While he was researching the next book, he was also gathering information on her and her son."

"So he found out their names."

"It was pretty easy. The first names were always characters from one of Poe's literary works and the last name had something to do with sewing. I figure she was a seamstress of some sort. That's probably how she made a living for them."

Nate looked at her, his eyes scrunched together. "How old a fellow do you think he is?"

"He was born in nineteen sixty-nine, so he'd be forty-four."

"And his mother?"

"She's maybe sixty-eight. She was older than Thomas."

"Huh," he said, pursing his lips and wrinkling his forehead. Nate turned to his wife. "Do you know who that sounds like?"

She peered at him over her water glass. "But, the parameters don't fit exactly. I don't know what her first name is, but her last name doesn't have anything to do with sewing and his first name is mundane." Then she looked across the table at Polly. "You met him last summer. Kevin Campbell from Jewell. He was on the committee for the literary competition."

"The guy who wanted us to know how wonderful his student's piece was? That guy?" Polly asked. "He'd be about the right age."

"He's got a wife and a couple of daughters and I think his mother lives with them. She's a lot older, but she made costumes for plays at his school. In fact, she did the costumes for the community theater, too." Nate said.

"But you're right, the names don't work out," Polly slumped her shoulders. "He was kind of odd, too."

"You haven't seen anything," Nate laughed. "You should see him on ..." he spun his head toward his wife. "That's tomorrow night! We should take them. He'll be reading the same thing that he does every year."

"What's tomorrow night?" Henry asked.

"And it's Poe!" Joss exclaimed. "Every year he reads *The Raven*."

"What's tomorrow night?" Polly pressed.

"His Speech teams and Thespians always do a drama night. The One-Act kids perform and then do a couple of spooky things for Halloween. Every year he performs *The Raven* to close the show. It's really terrific."

"Would you go with me?" Polly asked Henry. He nodded yes. "Would you guys take us?" she asked the Mikkels'.

"Of course!" Joss said. " I want to watch it all happen!"

"But I'm still not convinced," Polly said. "His name should be something a little more Victorian than Kevin, don't you think?"

Henry was tapping away at his cell phone. He held it up so she could see it.

"Campbell Lock-Stitch Sewing Machine." Polly took a breath and held it with her hand over her mouth.

She exhaled and said, "Thomas was so close!" Her eyes filled with tears. "He was so close. This breaks my heart."

"We don't even know if it's them," Henry said, taking her hand. "You can't get excited until you know for sure."

"It's them," she said. "It has to be."

"There are a lot of things that need to be just right for it to be them. You can't say anything to anyone about this," he warned.

"What do you mean? Who am I going to tell?"

"What if the person who killed Thomas did it because of this policeman's murder forty some years ago? What if they're still around? What if they don't want Thomas's old girlfriend to come forward and expose them? What if they kill her or kill Kevin and then we find out it wasn't them at all?"

While Henry was talking, Polly's eyes grew bigger. Before she could help herself, she burst out laughing. "Henry Sturtz, you can create a conspiracy theory better than anyone I know."

He raised one eyebrow and wiggled his nose a little. "If you want to tell Aaron, that's fine, but I think you're setting up a perfectly normal family. It's not like Thomas Zeller is unknown. What would happen if his fans got hold of this information and started pounding on their doors to see who it was that broke his heart and made him write sad detective stories?"

"You just won't quit, will you?" she laughed.

He took a deep breath, then chuckled and looked at Nate. "I've been hanging around her too long, haven't I?"

"I don't know, man." Nate raised his eyebrows. "You sound a little crazy. Shall we all cut our palms open and drip blood in the center of the table and make a pact not to talk about this?"

Polly snorted with laughter. "Here's a dull knife, Henry. You go first."

"We shouldn't disrupt someone's life for no reason. Your life already stresses me out. I don't want you responsible for someone else. I'll be exhausted taking care of you all."

"Have you been reading mysteries lately or something?" Polly asked. "Where did you come up with all of that?"

"I read a couple of your Zeller books this week. They're pretty good. Did you know that he signed all of your copies?"

"He did?" Polly was shocked. "I didn't even think to look beyond the first one. That's awesome!"

"They had some odd inscriptions in them, but he signed them."

"What do you mean odd inscriptions?"

"I don't know. Maybe you really have turned me all girly." Henry dropped his head in his hands. "Help me." He reached across the table to Nate. "Save me from what I've become."

Joss looked at him in amazement. "Wow. What's happening?"

"I asked him a couple of days ago if he thought I was turning him girly. He laughed at me then," Polly said, "but apparently he's going to use it when he feels the need to be dramatic."

She pushed at his arm. "You're embarrassing me." She'd never really spent time with Henry around people their own age. He was always with her much older friends in Lydia and Aaron, Beryl and Andy. Otherwise they were around his employees or Doug and Billy who were much younger. He'd gotten comfortable with Nate and Joss and all of a sudden he was playful.

"I'm embarrassing you?" he asked. "So I should sit up straight and be a good boy?"

Polly leaned over and whispered in his ear, "You never cease to amaze me. I'm never going to know exactly who you are, am I?"

Henry put his arm around her back and pulled her close, kissed the tip of her nose and said, "I hope not."

"I'm a little worried about letting the two of you into that comfortable back seat," Joss giggled. "You have to promise to be good on the way home tonight."

"I'll be good if he's good. I promise." Polly sat up straight, pulling away from Henry's arm.

Henry let out a breath and dramatically slumped his shoulders, "I'll be good. But I won't like it."

"Will you really take us to see Kevin Campbell tomorrow night?" Polly chose to ignore his dramatics.

"Sure. What do you think?" Nate asked his wife.

"It sounds great. Do you want to eat before we head over to Jewell?" she said.

"There will be a crew in my building getting ready for Halloween," Polly said, "but I can get out in time for dinner. What if we meet you at Davey's and ride together from there?"

The stars were twinkling and the moon lit all the roads that led from Fort Dodge to Bellingwood as they drove home.

"This is one of the things that I love about being in the country," Polly said quietly. "You can see the night sky."

"It's beautiful tonight," Joss agreed. She leaned into her husband in the front seat.

Henry held Polly's hands and when they pulled into Sycamore House, he asked if she would mind driving him home.

"Of course I can," she said. "What's up?"

"I know you need to walk Obiwan tonight and it's kind of late. I'm not ready to let you do this alone yet."

"I've been doing it by myself the last couple of nights. Nothing has happened," she protested.

"But it's really late tonight. Would you just let me worry about you?"

She wanted to continue protesting, but realized it would do her no good. "Fine. But, after I take you home I will drive back to Sycamore House all by myself and then I will shut the garage door and get upstairs with no problems. Okay?"

"As long as you promise to be careful," he said. "It makes me nervous that there hasn't been any more vandalism."

"Maybe he realized it was useless," she said.

"I'm not taking any chances."

"I know, I know. You can walk with me and Obiwan tonight. I'm not going to fight with you about it."

Nate looked back at them. "You're getting her trained, man. Now's the time to pop the question."

"What question is that?" Polly asked.

"Well, uh ..."

Joss swatted his leg again. "He is an idiot sometimes. I'll take care of him when we get home."

Nate winked at her, "Do you promise? Will we have fun?"

She shook her head and rolled her eyes. "I know, I know. I'm the one who married him."

"And you love me, don't you!" he laughed.

"And I love you." she responded, smiling.

CHAPTER NINETEEN

While she was waiting for the last load to dry, she pulled Thomas Zeller's fifth book down and curled up in the corner of her sofa. Morning chores at the barn had gone quickly. Jason and Rachel were still there, spending time with the horses. It was cold, wet and rainy outside and Polly looked forward to this free time before Lydia and the crew showed up to work on the Haunted Hallway. She pulled a blanket over her legs and patted the top of it. Obiwan lay down and snuggled in as close as he could get.

She opened the flyleaf and read, *"Every chapter told her I loved her. Can you see that?"*

"Yes, Thomas. Now I see that. Your love for her was on every page. I wish you could have found her." Polly had been petting her dog's head, but then she stopped. "That seems like a strange inscription, don't you think?" He looked up at her and yawned, then lay his head back down on her leg. "No really. That's weird. I wonder what he said in the fourth book." Polly flung the blanket over Obiwan's head and watched him back out of the mess. She went back to the shelves and pulled the book down.

"Always look at the first. You'll be glad you did."

"The first what?" Polly asked out loud. She looked back up at the bookshelves and saw that the other three books were gone.

She called Henry.

"Hey pretty girl, what's up?"

"Where are you?" she asked.

"I'm at home. Do you need something?"

"I need the inscriptions from the second and third books."

"Why? Do you think there's another clue?"

"You were right last night. These are odd. Do you have them?"

"I have to go upstairs. What are you doing this morning?"

She heard him walking up the steps and could barely contain herself. Something was going on and she wanted to know what it was. "I've just been cleaning," she said, as patiently as she could. "What about you?"

"Same here. There didn't seem to be much reason to go outside. It's awful out there. Okay, here I am. Which book do you want?"

"Tell me what he says in the third one."

"Okay. It says *'Letters make words. Words make chapters.'* That seems obvious, but why would he tell you that?"

"I don't know yet. Now look at the second book."

She listened as he put the book down and heard pages rustle when he opened the next one.

"There's more to the story than the story itself."

"I think I remember what he said to me in the first book, but could you read it again to me?" she asked.

"Sure, just a second. Here it is, *'Polly, you were right. Authors give you more than you realize sometimes. Never forget that.'*"

She took a deep breath. "There is something in these books and I have to figure out what it is now. He was sending Nelly a message in code in his books. I have to find it!"

"Do you want some help?"

"I'm going to need to see those books," Polly said, and then she stopped. "No, don't worry about it. I have all of the manuscripts on my laptop. I can figure it out from there."

"Why don't I swing by the grocery store and get food for sandwiches. I'll bring the books and we can sit down with them.

Can you wait until I'm there?"

"Don't bother with the grocery store. I have food here. Just hurry. I can't wait very long," she laughed.

"I'm running down the stairs right now." She heard his feet on the steps. "I'm picking up my keys and grabbing my jacket. Just a second." Polly giggled as she realized he had put the phone down to slip his jacket on. "Are you still there?" he asked.

"You're a nut!" she said. "I'm going to let you safely drive over here while I go downstairs and get my last load of laundry. I promise to wait. Just don't drive into anything on your way."

"See you in a few minutes!"

Polly hung up and slipped the phone into her back pocket. She carried the two final books in the series to the dining room table and set them beside the laptop.

"We're going to have company, kiddos," she said to the animals. "You do your best to look good while I get these towels." She went through her bedroom and down the back steps to the dryer. She was folding the last towel into the basket when she heard her garage door open and Henry's truck pull in, so she waited for him.

Henry laughed when he saw her. "I got here as fast as I could. If I'm excited about what you might find, I can only imagine that you are ready to burst."

"A little bit, but I stayed busy." Polly tucked the basket under her left arm and opened the door, motioning for Henry to go up first. He tried to take the laundry from her, but she glowered at him and he went on up. She pulled the door shut and followed him, dropping the basket on her bed.

Henry had become enough of a fixture in her apartment that the cats didn't do anything other than look at him and curl back up. They were snuggled on a blanket Polly had dropped on the chair in the corner by the bookshelves. Obiwan, though, acted as if his long lost best friend had just returned from a year long journey, begging for Henry to give him a little attention.

Henry handed the books to Polly and knelt down. "You know, dog. I've never really had a lot of pets in my life and you make me think I missed out." He stood back up and joined Polly at the table. "He really is a good dog, you know."

"I love him," she said. "I can't imagine life without my animals."

"You know, Eliseo and I were talking about that the other day."

"Talking about what?" Polly looked up from the laptop. "Me?"

"You and your animals. You might need to add some more. You're getting awfully comfortable with what you have."

"You can stop that noise right now. I don't have room up here for any more animals."

"But you do have room at the barn. And if that deal goes through for the pasture land on the other side of the creek, you'll have plenty of room."

"For what? Pigs and cows? That's not going to happen. You two are nuts! I'm getting that land for the horses. I want them to have plenty of pasture land."

"It was just a thought."

"Stop thinking it. You know how I feel about these thoughts you have. When you say them out loud, someone in the universe hears you and the next thing I know they become real."

"You're a strange one, pretty girl."

She shrugged, "Can't help it. You always have a choice."

"Not anymore I don't."

Polly looked him in the eye and saw that he meant it. "I love you too, Henry. Now can we start on this?"

"I've kept you from it too long already, haven't I!" he laughed. "What are we looking for?"

"Let's look at those inscriptions one more time." She pointed and said, "First book?"

"Polly, you were right. Authors give you more than you realize sometimes. Never forget that."

She typed it into a document on her laptop, then shoved the other books at him. "Can you just read them out loud to me?"

"There's more to the story than the story itself."

"Letters make words. Words make chapters."

"Always look at the first. You'll be glad you did."

"Every chapter told her I loved her. Can you see that?"

She read them out loud a couple of times. "What do you think?" she asked Henry.

"Let's start with the first book. Maybe he says something with the chapter titles."

Polly flipped to the first chapter. "Nope. It just says Chapter One. Maybe it's the first word of the chapter. Here, you read them out loud and I'll type them in."

"Never. Eddie. Leaving. Last."

"No, that's not it," Polly stopped him.

Henry reached across to the laptop and pointed at the third inscription. *"Letters. Words. Chapters."*

"That's it!" she said. "Start with Chapter One. The first letter."

He flipped back and said, "N." Then he quickly flipped pages to the second chapter. "E."

"This is taking too long," he said. "Let me get my bearings." He stuck his finger in the table of contents and then flipped to the page for the third chapter. "L." He progressed through the book "L."

"It's 'Y,'" Polly said. "That's the next letter."

"You're right. Now be patient and I'll get these to you as fast as I can." He flipped pages and read the letters to her one by one.

"I. S. T. I. L. L. L. O. V. E. Y. O. U. C. O. M. E. B. A. C. K."

"It really is a code!" Polly cried. She picked up the second book and handed it to him. "Now this one."

They repeated the same process. "I. C. A. N. H. E. L. P. Y. O. U. S. T. O. P. R. U. N. N. I. N. G. L. O. V. E."

Each book contained a plea for Nelly. The third one read, "M. Y. S. O. N. I. S. P. E. R. F. E. C. T. T. H. A. N. K. Y. O. U."

The fourth book's code was sad. "I. A. M. D. E. S. T. R. O. Y. E. D. W. H. A. T. I. S. L. E. F. T."

And the book that was published after the last photograph offered a simple message. "I. L. L. W. A. I. T. F. O. R. E. V. E. R. F. O. R. Y. O. U."

"Do you think there were codes in his latest books?" Henry asked.

"I can look," Polly said. "I'd be really surprised. He didn't write another Eddie Powers book after that one."

She went to the bookshelf and pulled down another stack of books. They opened the first book and she was certain there would be nothing of any interest in these books. Thomas had written them after he sobered up and they were much more of a commercial success than his early stuff, but they didn't have the angst and pain of the Eddie Powers books.

Henry flipped one of them open to the fly leaf. "There's nothing here. Let's just check anyway."

He began flipping through the chapters and reading off letters. "P. L. P. S. I. I. E. W."

"No. There's nothing there. He thought he'd lost her for good after that last photograph." Polly was trying to hold back tears. "She had gotten his son to adulthood and wanted to protect his privacy from then on. That was an awful time for Thomas."

"It would be difficult to pull out of something like that," Henry said. "His heart was broken. How would he rise above that?"

"You know, I think it was his writing that did it for him. He loved telling stories and when he wasn't writing, he was miserable. Somehow he figured it out and realized that the times he was the happiest was when he was putting words on paper."

"It's too bad they weren't together when he was healthy."

"It's tragic, isn't it," Polly said. "I still can't even think about that. I either cry or get really mad, so I'm ignoring it."

Henry reached out and put his hand on top of hers. "I love you, pretty girl. Even when your heart is too big for you."

Polly took a deep breath and sat up, "Enough of that. We should probably eat lunch. Are you going home before you get stuck helping Lydia build a haunted hallway?"

"They're doing that today?" he gasped.

"She wants to get started today."

"Then yes I'm going home before they're here. What are you planning to feed me?"

"I made slop Friday night when you were too busy to come over for supper."

"I had a meeting!"

"At the bar at Davey's. I know what kind of meeting that was," she chuckled. "So, do you want me to heat some of that up?"

"Slop? You really call it slop? What in the world is it?"

"It's spaghetti made with elbow macaroni. We couldn't call it spaghetti, so Dad always called it slop. It's my favorite comfort food and I always make a ton. I even got fancy and put mushrooms, onions and green peppers in it this time."

He sighed, "It sounds great," and then he walked over behind her and squeezed her.

Polly pulled back enough so she could turn around in his arms. She kissed him, "You surprised me with a fabulous dinner and I'm giving you slop. It's not really equitable, but it will have to do."

"Slop," he said. "I can't tell people my girlfriend feeds me slop. At least not here in pig country."

"Then, don't tell anyone. It can be our little secret." She put the ladle in his hand. "You scoop the slop and warm it up. I'll put garlic cheese bread under the broiler. Then it's Italian slop."

"We're being fancy now, are we?"

"Yes we are!"

While they were eating, Polly's phone rang.

"That's Lydia's ring-tone," she said. "I should get this."

"Go ahead. It's always entertaining."

"Hi Lydia," Polly said, answering her phone.

"We're going to be there in just a little bit. Do you want me to bring you some lunch?"

"No. That's sweet, but I'm eating right now. Come on over and I'll see you when you get here."

"Bye, bye, dear. And tell Henry he doesn't have to stay. I have plenty of people coming in this afternoon."

"Uh. Okay. Bye."

Polly put the phone down after making sure she'd hung up and said, "I don't know how she does that."

"What do you mean?" Henry asked.

"She said that you don't have to stay. She has plenty of people."

He started to laugh. "She's scary. My truck is in your garage, so how did she know? You have to ask."

"I will."

"I'm going to get out of here, then. You really don't care?"

"What?" Polly looked up from her plate. She'd been thinking about Lydia. "Not at all! You'll pick me up later?"

He stood up and bent over to kiss her. "I'll be here before five. Don't walk me out. I can find my way. Finish your lunch."

"I love you," she called as he crossed the threshold into her bedroom. She looked down at her plate. She was finished anyway.

"Come on, Obiwan. A quick walk and then I'm going to be gone for a bit." Polly looked at the plates on the table and knew that the animals would probably try to get to the food, so she quickly scraped them clean and put them in the sink.

"Now we can go," she said, touching his head as she walked past him. He followed her and they went outside. The rain had stopped, but the ground was still soggy. Obiwan hit the grass and stopped, then stepped forward again, picking up his paws.

"You've been in worse," she scolded. "Now go." She stepped forward onto the grass and with a lunge, he headed for the trees. Polly let him wander and then called him back. When he got close to her, he shook to dry himself off, spattering water all over her.

"You brat!" she laughed. "You couldn't have done that further away from me?" This time she followed him as he proudly walked inside and then up the stairs to her apartment. Before he got very far, she stopped him by grabbing his collar.

"Oh no you don't." She dug into the basket of towels and pulling out an old one, knelt beside him. "Give me the paw." She tapped his right paw. He licked her face and lifted it so she could dry it. She dried him down and when she released him, he bolted into the living room and jumped on the sofa, rubbing his body along the length of it, back and forth. "I love you, you silly dog."

Polly went down the front steps and was surprised to see a large group of people at work, setting up plywood and braces.

"Hi there!" Lydia came over to greet her. "This is going to be great! We're going to have the kiddos walk in the front door and around this, then they'll come back around by the offices and out the other side of the front door."

Aaron and Billy Endicott were holding up a piece of plywood while Len Specek and Doug Randall nailed braces into place. Andy was following along behind them, straightening the material they had set down on the floor before erecting the walls. Rachel Devins and her mother, Martha, were carrying in large chunks of white styrofoam and Beryl was trailing along with bags hanging off both of her arms.

"What are you carrying?" Polly asked.

"Shh. Don't tell the fuzz. I'm packing Krylon," Beryl said in a stage whisper. "I don't want him to catch me bombing the place."

"Bombing?" Polly asked, puzzled. "That seems over the top."

"Don 'cha know nuttin' girlie? I been practicin' my graffiti slang." Beryl sneered, her upper lip curled in a fake snarl. "Bombing is me bein' an artist and paintin' the wall."

"Umm, you da bomb," Polly replied, her eyes wide. "What can I do to help?" she asked Lydia.

"We're painting styrofoam to look like rocks. They'll sit on top of the braces, so no one trips. Do you want to do some carving?"

"Whatever you need," Polly said. "Just tell me how."

Rachel stopped in front of them. "I can show you. We did this when I was in high school for props. It's easy."

Before she knew it, Polly was carving styrofoam into rocks, both big and small. When she finished with one, Beryl took it outside and spray painted it until she was satisfied. Once the temporary walls were erected, Lydia and Andy brought in the rocks that had dried and set them into place.

"We're painting these old sheer curtains from the thrift store with fluorescent paint. Once the strobe lights and black lights are turned on, this will be insane," Doug explained. "We'll drape them all over these walls and then we're going to make ghosts that go up and down. Their eyes are going to glow."

Andy looked at Lydia, "We are remembering that this is for little kids, right?"

"Yes we are," Lydia said. "It won't hurt anyone to have a little bit of a friendly fright on Halloween. And if they get too scared, we just turn them back around and take them to the front door.

My goodness, it's not like they don't see worse stuff on television."

"Don't get her started," Aaron said. "This woman loves Halloween."

"Kids will want to go through over and over again," Billy spoke up. "I would have. This is going to be awesome."

"I'm just glad the Sheriff is going to be here," Polly muttered. "At least no one can accuse me of torturing their children." She looked at the time.

"I have to go!" she said, jumping up.

"Where are you going?" Lydia asked.

"We're meeting the Mikkels' for dinner and then going over to Jewell for a drama performance."

"That's nice, dear. It should be fun."

Polly started to walk to the steps. "Lydia?"

"Yes dear."

"How did you know Henry was here and that he didn't want to help today? That was spooky."

Lydia just grinned at her. "Oh, Polly. That was easy. Even if he wasn't here, I knew that he would have offered to help if he'd wanted to. When he didn't, I knew he wanted the day off from construction. I was just giving you trouble. I figured you would talk to him at some point, so I set you up. It kind of entertains me to be spooky sometimes. I have to keep the mystique going."

Polly crossed back to her friend and hugged her. "You are an amazing woman and I love you, but you have to stop making me think you're prescient. It makes me nervous."

"You ought to be part of her family. I think our kids were always looking over their shoulders. She knew a lot more than she was supposed to know," Aaron said.

"I still do, cuddlebum," she laughed, taking his arm. "And don't you forget it!"

"Not a chance."

"I'll see you tomorrow," Polly said as she put her foot on the first step. "This is going to be really awesome."

"I'm having a blast," Lydia replied. "Best fun ever!"

CHAPTER TWENTY

Soon, it was time for the last reading of the evening. It had been fun to see parents watch their kids perform. Some parents tensed up, obviously worried about mistakes and when the performance was finished, they visibly relaxed. Others were on the edge of their seat, sometimes mouthing the words along with their kids. Those parents had heard the lines spoken many times as their students worked to memorize their parts. There was a lot of applause and excitement as the evening drew to a close.

Kevin Campbell stood and walked to the microphone and dropped his head. When he raised it, with a low voice that resonated through the room, he began reciting familiar words:

"Once upon a midnight dreary, while I pondered, weak and weary,
Over many a quaint and curious volume of forgotten lore - "

Polly shut her eyes and listened. Henry took her hand, which made her flinch and look up, but then she shut her eyes again so she could savor the experience. The first time he whispered the very familiar words, *"Quoth the Raven 'Nevermore'"* a chill ran across her arms as she anticipated the rest of the story. As the narrator's tale grew more agitated, Kevin Campbell's voice followed suit and when he shrieked his command to the raven to leave, her head shot up and she watched him finish the story.

The room erupted in applause at the final 'nevermore' and his students jumped up to surround him, chattering and congratulating each other on performances well done.

Joss took Polly's other hand, "I may not sleep tonight," she laughed, a bit faintly.

Polly had been holding her breath and with a slight gasp, said, "That was something. No wonder his kids do so well. He really seems to understand how to relate the written word to listeners."

"We should go up to him. I'm sure he'll remember you."

"Let some of the crowd clear out," Polly said. "I still haven't figured out what to say. Can you tell if his mother is here?"

"I don't know," Joss glanced around the room. "It could be anyone. Do you think it would be best to be upfront about this?"

"Sure, but what does that mean? 'Hi Kevin, remember me? Well, I knew your father.' Or," Polly snorted a little, "Kevin," she said in a low voice, "I knew your father."

Henry started chuckling beside her and said, "Stop it. That's a terrible Darth Vader."

"You recognized it," she laughed.

Nate leaned back, stretched his legs out in front of him and put his arm on the back of Joss' seat. Then he leaned over to talk to Henry behind Joss & Polly's backs. "They're going to be here for a while. Do you want to go outside? I'm tired of sitting."

Henry looked at Polly, the question in his eyes.

"Sure." she said. "We'll be fine here."

He took her hand and said quietly, "Are you certain you want to do this tonight? Maybe it's enough that you came over. Aaron would kill you if you messed up a murder investigation."

Polly sat back in her chair and looked back and forth from him to Joss. "I hadn't thought of that." She swatted his leg. "Why did you wait until now to ask me that? I don't know what to do."

"You'd better think quick," Joss said, "He's spotted us and is making his way over here. What are you going to say?"

"I dunno, I dunno, I dunno," Polly breathed. "What do I do?"

But before there was any response, Kevin Campbell was there.

"Hello there!" he said. Polly felt like his voice was ringing through the room. Her mind was desperately trying to get back on track. Henry and Nate both stood and he shook their hands. Joss stood beside Polly and reached out to hug him.

"You are the last people I expected to see here tonight. You made me a little nervous when I saw you in the audience." He smiled at them and Polly peered at his face to see if he was the same man in the last photograph she'd seen. The picture was scanned into the note program on her telephone, but she couldn't very well hold it up beside his face to see if they matched.

She felt Henry's hand on her elbow and stood up, "That was wonderful," she said. "You gave me chills. How long have you been performing that?"

"About fifteen years. When I started teaching high school, I wanted my students to understand what I was talking about when I helped them explore diction and stage presence and telling a story rather than just reading it."

"But why Poe?" she asked.

He laughed. "Kids love the macabre. You'd be surprised at how many of them relate to the darkness of Poe's works. Even the kids whose lives are normal and happy are drawn into his words. Some of them are fascinated by it, others identify with it."

"Have you always liked his work?"

Kevin shrugged. "Believe it or not, my mother started reading Poe to me when I was young. We didn't have very many books in the house, but she had a tattered copy of Poe and another of Shakespeare. Those men taught me how to read."

"Is your mother here tonight?" Polly asked.

Kevin pointed to an older woman seated in the front row. There were two girls standing in front of her. They were too young to have been involved in the performances, but were chatting animatedly with several of the high school kids.

"That's my mother and my daughters. My wife is around here, too. She's probably talking to some of the parents. She's much better with them than I am." He looked around again and pointed to a group of people on the other side of the room. "That's Sonya. The one who can't talk without waving her arms."

Polly knew she couldn't confront him until she'd talked to Aaron Merritt. The Campbells weren't going anywhere, but she would hate it if Kevin's mother took off because she thought she'd been caught after all these years.

"Why did you all come over tonight?" Kevin asked.

"Joss told me about your recitation of *The Raven* and I couldn't miss it. That was pretty impressive."

"Thank you. I'm glad you stopped by. We should have dinner some evening so you can meet my wife and daughters. I'll have Sonya give you a call."

He glanced past them and said, "Excuse me. I do need to speak with someone before they leave. It was nice to see you again and thanks for coming." With that, he walked away.

"Well, I guess that's that," Nate said, matter-of-factly. "It looks as if you don't have to worry about how to tell him. He's not sticking around."

"Just a second," Polly tried to nonchalantly look at the woman Kevin identified as his mother, but couldn't see her face. Her shoulders were hunched and she sat with her hands folded in her lap. Her long grey hair was tied behind her head in a loose pony tail, with tendrils curling around her face.

"It looks as if she spent a lifetime bent over, doesn't it," Polly whispered to Joss.

"Come with me," Joss took Polly's arm. She turned back to her husband. "Go on outside. We'll meet you at the car."

Joss led Polly down to the front and across to the group standing around the seated woman. "Mrs. Campbell?" she said.

Polly recognized the woman immediately. This was Thomas's Nelly. She looked up at them and smiled.

"Mrs. Campbell. I'm Joss Mikkels and this is Polly Giller. We worked with Kevin this summer on the Literary Competition. I just wanted to tell you how much we enjoyed his performance tonight. You have to be so proud of him."

"I am very proud," the woman said. " You worked with him on

the Literary Competition?"

"Yes," Polly said. "In Bellingwood. His student did very well."

Mrs. Campbell's shoulders went rigid and Polly watched as she gripped her hands in her lap, her fingers turning white.

"I remember that," she said. "It was nice of you to say something. If you will excuse me. Ellie?" she stood and took one of the young girls' arms. "Would you take me to the car, please?"

"Sure, Grandma. Come on, Ann. We're going to the car to wait for mom and dad." The other young girl took Mrs. Campbell's other arm and they practically danced up the aisle with the woman. Mrs. Campbell glanced around once at Polly and Joss and then let the girls escort her out into the foyer.

"She knows," Polly said. "We just spooked her."

"I saw that. So it's her?"

"Absolutely. Kevin has changed since his graduation picture, but she hasn't." They started walking toward the back of the room. "I feel terrible," Polly said. "I wish I could tell her how much Thomas loved her and that everything is going to be okay."

They went outside and Polly gave a little wave to Mrs. Campbell and her granddaughters as they sat in the car waiting. Henry and Nate were waiting beside Nate's Impala.

"Is it her?" Henry asked.

"It is. I think we scared her. When I mentioned Bellingwood, the poor woman got nervous."

Nate pursed his lips together, then said. "Well, I suppose that everyone has heard about the famous author being killed at Sycamore House. I wonder if she knew he was this close to her."

"I don't know," Polly glanced back at the car. "I've really messed this up. Aaron is going to have my head if she runs now."

"From the looks of her, she isn't running very far very fast," Nate said, then let out an "Oomph" as his wife poked him in the side. "Well, she's not!"

Henry stepped in and took Polly's hand, "If Aaron is going to kill you, do you think you might as well wade into it all the way?"

She looked into his face and gave him a little smile. "Really?"

He lifted one shoulder and winked, "You've been in trouble

with him before. You're sure that she isn't going to have to face jail time for killing that cop in San Francisco?"

"She didn't do it. The police reports and Thomas's notes all say that she was there before it happened, but had nothing to do with killing him. Maybe she'll need a lawyer, but if she hasn't run for twenty years, don't you think she wants to just be finished?"

He took a deep breath. "I don't know what she wants, but if you want to talk to them and tell them what you've found, now is as good a time as any."

"Come with me?" she asked him.

"I've been in this since the beginning, I want to see it to the end. I'm coming. Do you two mind waiting?" he asked Nate and Joss.

"Oh, I'll just sneak her into my big back seat and see what ..."

There was another oomph and Joss said, "We'll be fine. Go ahead."

Polly saw Kevin and Sonya Campbell coming out of the school and she picked up the pace, running to catch up to him.

"Kevin, can I speak with you a moment?" Polly called out. She could tell that he considered ignoring her, but his wife stopped and waited as they crossed the parking lot.

"Okay," he said. "Sonya, go ahead. I'll be right there." His wife looked back and forth between him and Polly, then walked away.

"What can I do for you, Miss Giller?" he asked.

"I have a very personal question to ask you and before you say anything, you should know that I already have the answer. I'm just looking for confirmation."

He took a deep breath, looked down at the ground and then back up at her. "Yes. I'm Thomas Zeller's son. We've been hiding for nearly forty-five years for something my mother didn't do. I can't believe it's over now."

Polly's heart was in her throat and she reached out and laid her hand on his forearm. "It's not as bad as all that. Thomas was staying at Sycamore House, finishing his last novel. But Kevin, he's been looking for you and your mother your entire life. He has proof that she didn't kill that policeman. In fact, the San Francisco police know she didn't do it. There's no need to run any longer."

She heard a car door open and then shut and looked across as Mrs. Campbell walked slowly across to them. "Kevin? What's this about?" she asked.

"Mother, this is Polly Giller. She knows who we are. Thomas Zeller was staying at her place. She says he was looking for us."

"Of course he was, dear. But, that's all behind us now." She looked at Polly, her eyes clear and full of fire. "I did not kill anyone, no matter what they may say. I suppose it is time to face this, but I had hoped to wait until the girls were a little older."

"How much older do they need to be, mother?" Kevin asked, his strong voice shaking. "And Polly says there is evidence clearing you of the murder."

"I'd like to tell you what I've found," Polly said. "Thomas gave me a flash drive and I'd like to tell you about it."

"Then we'd like to hear about it," the woman responded. "Kevin?"

"Sonya?" he called. His wife walked back to join them.

"Is everything okay?" she asked.

"Sonya, this is Polly Giller. She owns Sycamore House in Bellingwood." His wife's right hand flew to her throat and she looked at her husband. He went on. "She knew Thomas and has something to tell us."

He turned to Polly and Henry. "We've been very honest with my wife. I couldn't live with her and hide the secret. She knows everything. The girls don't know yet, though."

"I understand. Do you want to meet some evening for dinner and we can talk about this?" Polly began to tick off the evenings in her upcoming week. It was busy, but she would find time.

"If your friends aren't in a hurry to get back to Bellingwood, we could invite you to our home this evening," Sonya said. "I doubt that Kevin and Genie want to wait to hear what you have to say."

Nate and Joss had gotten into his car and started it. The night was cooling off and they were probably trying to stay warm. Polly beckoned and Nate drove over, pulling up beside them.

"I know this extends the evening, but the Campbells have invited us to their house. Do you mind?"

Nate chuckled. "We knew you would want to do something with them after the event. We're thoughtful that way, aren't we, wife?" She poked him again, eliciting another oomph. "Of course we don't mind. Get in. We'll follow them."

When they arrived at the Campbell's home, Sonya showed them to a large living room. "I'm going to put some hot water on for tea or cocoa and take a few minutes with the girls. We started explaining this on the drive home, but it's a little much. Make yourself comfortable. Genie and I will be back in a few minutes."

Polly's eyes were immediately drawn to the bookshelves and she asked Kevin, "May I?"

He nodded in affirmation and she looked at the shelves. From the days of only owning a couple of tattered books, he'd certainly enlarged his library. Then she found what she was looking for, the first Eddie Powers mystery. The others were there, but this would illustrate her point. She took it to the sofa and sat beside Henry.

Sonya Campbell came in, carrying a tray with a carafe of hot water and mugs, tea bags and a small pot of cocoa mix. Genie Campbell followed with a plate of cookies and Ellie and Ann trailed behind their grandmother. The girls looked shell shocked and stared at their guests as if they were there to do something terrible to the family. When Genie took a seat in a wing chair, Ellie sat on the floor beside her and Ann pulled the ottoman to the other side, taking positions of support and protection.

Drinks were passed around and Polly felt her stomach grow increasingly tense. The fluttering was beginning to upset her, but she wasn't sure how to begin. Finally, she handed her mug to Henry and said, "I don't know how to start."

"Just tell us what you have to say," Kevin said. "The girls won't understand all of it, but we can talk to them later. Go ahead."

Polly put her hand on the book in her lap and began, "The night Thomas Zeller was killed, he managed to make it to the door of my apartment before he died. He pressed a flash drive into my hand and asked me to 'find him.' At first, I thought that the 'him' was the murderer, but when I finally figured out what was on the drive, I realized it was his son.

"We had talked about those early years in San Francisco. He told me how messed up he had gotten after that and about being an alcoholic and then finally drying out. What he didn't tell me was that he had spent a lifetime looking for you. That information is what I found on the flash drive."

She opened the note app on her phone and pulled up the first picture Thomas had received, then stood up, setting the book on the sofa and walked over to Genie. She knelt down in front of the woman and said. "This is the first picture you sent him, isn't it?"

Genie Campbell nodded.

"He went to Colorado, and found out everything he could about you. He has receipts for automobile work and found the lease for the apartment you rented. While he was there, he researched his first book so he had a reason for being in town."

The woman nodded again, not saying a word.

"Then you sent him a second photograph and he moved to Mississippi and did the same thing. Kevin, he found class pictures of you and more receipts and leases and car purchases. He wrote his second novel while there." Polly showed the picture to Genie and then walked over to Sonya and Kevin, showing it to them.

"Each time you moved and sent a picture, he followed you, trying to anticipate where you might go next. He obviously had no luck, but he wrote the entire Eddie Powers mystery series while he looked for you."

Kevin said, "We followed that series and knew that. Mom figured that as long as we were gone, it wouldn't hurt for him to know where we had been."

"How closely did you read the books?" Polly asked.

Genie Campbell finally spoke. "I read them pretty closely. I wondered if he would send me a message in the dedication or the acknowledgments, but he never wrote those."

"That's because he wrote it in code," Polly said.

Every face in the room was staring at her by this point.

"What?" Genie asked.

"He wrote it in code. He was in my apartment and signed all of my books, trying to give me the hint. Henry and I figured it out this morning. I don't think anyone ever realized what he did."

"Tell me," she said.

Polly scrolled through her notes until she found the list of codes that she and Henry had uncovered, then picked up the book and walked back over to the woman's chair. Ann scooted off the ottoman and gestured for Polly to take it.

"He was writing to you ... and it's Eugenie, isn't it?" Polly asked.

"Yes, how did you know?"

Polly gave a little laugh. "Because he discovered that each time you moved, you changed your names. Your first names were always characters from something Poe had written and your last name always had something to do with a sewing machine. You are a seamstress, right?"

"Right," Genie Campbell nodded. "I thought I was being so clever and here you've found me out."

"I only did it with a lot of help and a little bit of luck. I might not have figured it out if there weren't so many instances of it on that flash drive. I'm not sure if Thomas knew about the pattern for your last name, but he definitely knew about the link to Poe."

"He's the one who taught me about the passion in Poe's writing. His favorite poem was *Annabel Lee*."

"And you taught me," Kevin said.

"I have to ask," Polly said. "Kevin has nothing to do with Poe. What happened to the naming process?"

Kevin Campbell closed his eyes and shook his head. "I chose it as my middle name so that I wouldn't have to be known as Napoleon for the rest of my life. That man had weird taste in men's names. There weren't a lot of options. I've been N. Kevin Campbell since the day we got our new identities."

"Oh!" she laughed, "Well, that explains it. It threw me off."

"Tell me about the code," Genie said.

"He took the first letter of every chapter and spelled out the words he wanted you to read. Henry and I simply went through each chapter and wrote down the first letter and found it."

"Why didn't I put that together?" the woman asked. "We used

to talk about different ways authors could tell their readers things. Even if it was for no other reason than to give them another opportunity to look at the book. It didn't occur to me to think that he might use that, though."

Ellie and Ann had jumped up and gone to the bookshelf. Each had two books and sat down on the floor, flying through the chapters and trying to remember the letters.

"This is what he wanted you to know," Polly said and showed Genie Campbell the note on her phone containing the codes.

"Nelly. I still love you. Come back."

"I can help you. Stop running. Love."

"My son is perfect. Thank you."

"I am destroyed. What is left?"

"I'll wait forever for you."

The woman took the phone from Polly's hand and clutched it to her chest. Tears began streaming down her face. Kevin jumped out of his chair and knelt down in front of his mother. She showed him the note and bent over to rest her head on his. They held on to each other as she cried.

He finally took the phone and held it out to Polly. She put the first Eddie Powers mystery into his hand. "Thank you," he said. "This means the world to us."

"He was still looking for you," Polly said. "I think he came to Bellingwood because he knew you were close. None of that research was on the flash drive, but he was writing a book here and looking for you at the same time. That's why he asked me to find you."

"How did you know?" Kevin asked.

"It was pure luck," Polly responded. "If Nate hadn't mentioned that your mother made costumes for different plays, we wouldn't have put things together. When Joss told me that you read *The Raven* every fall, I wanted it to be you. But I wasn't sure until I saw your mother tonight. She hasn't changed at all."

Polly put her hand on the woman's knee. "You are still the beautiful Nelly that Thomas loved."

The woman began to cry again and this time, Sonya crossed the room with a box of tissues. "I'm sorry you didn't get a chance to talk to him again," she said to her mother-in-law.

"I am, too. I would have liked for him to know Kevin and his granddaughters."

Polly stood up. "We should leave." She pulled a business card out of her wallet. "Call me if you'd like. I would be glad to talk with you about Thomas. His agent is staying at Sycamore House right now, too. She might be able to tell you even more. You are welcome to come over." She paused. "In fact, there is a Black Masque ball on Saturday night. I suspect you have some Victorian costumes. Everyone will be in a mask and it will be a wonderful evening. If you came, I could introduce you to her then."

Genie Campbell looked at her son. "What do you think?"

"It sounds like fun. We'll be there." He stood up and so did the rest of the room. "Thank you telling us. I'll be in touch this week."

Coats were gathered and he walked with them to the front door, stopping Polly as the others went to the car. "My mother needs to talk to someone in law enforcement, doesn't she? Should I get a lawyer for her?"

"I don't know. It couldn't hurt. Sheriff Merritt is running the investigation in Bellingwood and he is a good man. Do you know a lawyer?"

"I have a couple of parents who would help me."

"Then, contact someone and have them get in touch with Aaron. I don't know anything about the process, but I'm sure it's all going to be fine."

Polly was surprised when he hugged her. "Thank you again. I feel like forty years of hiding is about to be over. It will be strange not to worry that someone is going to realize we aren't who we say we are."

"Keep telling her how much Thomas loved her, will you?" Polly asked.

"I will. See you soon." he said as she joined her friends at the car. She gave a little wave, crawled into the back seat with Henry and sighed as Nate backed out of the driveway.

CHAPTER TWENTY-ONE

Mindlessly tapping her fingers on the cell phone in front of her, Polly looked out at the emergence of the Haunted Hallway. They'd gotten quite a bit done yesterday. The wall was draped in burlap and sheer curtains, painted with fluorescent paints. There was fishing line coming down from the ceiling and crates in all the corners, draped with more painted burlap. Sycamore House's main doors had been outlined in strands of orange lights, while pumpkins, gourds and corn stalks were arranged on the front lawn. Halloween had definitely arrived.

She knew she had to call Aaron and tell him what she did again. As nervous as her stomach had been last night, it didn't compare to what was happening to her right now. There was nothing worse than disappointing someone, and for some reason she felt just like she had when she was young and had to face her father after doing something wrong.

Finally she gathered her courage and dialed the phone.

"Good morning, Polly," Aaron said. "I trust that there are no more bodies and you've found out something more on Thomas Zeller's flash drive."

"Hi, Aaron. Well, uh …"

"You're kidding. Another body?"

"Oh no!" she exclaimed.

"Then, what's up this morning. Did you see the wonderful work we did at Sycamore House yesterday?"

"Yes, it's pretty cool. Your wife is amazing."

"She is that. So, what's up?"

"I think I did something bad."

"What do you mean this time, Polly? If I have to arrest you, my wife is never going to let me back into the house."

"Not that kind of bad. Bad, you're going to be mad at me bad. I should have talked to you first, bad."

"In the year that I've known you, you've never really paid much attention to whether or not you should talk to me first. What did you do?"

"I found Nelly and her son and told them that I know who they are." She waited and didn't hear anything. "Aaron?"

"I'm still here. When did you figure out who it was?"

"Well, this weekend and then I knew for certain last night and then I couldn't hold back."

"Of course you couldn't." Polly heard the laughter in his voice.

"How much trouble am I in?" she asked.

He breathed loudly on the other end of the call, "Tell me the whole story and then tell me who it is that you met last night."

Polly took him through the entire weekend's events, from figuring out the code in the books, to Nate Mikkels revealing the possibility of Kevin and Genie Campbell being Thomas's son and former girlfriend, to the drama night and the visit to their home.

"I'm pretty sure they're going to call you," she said before he could speak. "They don't seem like the kind of people who are going to run."

"Polly, they've been running for forty years."

"But that was before he had a wife and children. He's been settled in Jewell for a long time. I told her that Thomas had evidence proving she didn't kill that policeman and she just wants this to be over now. Aaron, she lost the father of her son without ever seeing him again. Don't you think she's had enough?"

"I need to make some calls," he said.

"How much trouble am I in?" she asked again.

"You've interfered with this investigation, Polly."

She felt tears spurt to her eyes. He was going to arrest her. "Okay. You're right. I'm sorry."

"However, you are the one who figured this out, so a little interference isn't enough to get you into trouble. But promise you'll call me before you do anything else?"

"I'll try. I can't guarantee that, though. I never know what's going to happen around here."

Aaron laughed. "Of course you don't. What was I thinking? Let me work on this end and be careful. Can I ask that of you?"

"I'll try," she repeated.

"That's all I can expect."

She relaxed when they ended the call. She would live.

Later that morning, Polly looked up from her computer. She'd spent the time paying bills and making sure things were sorted and filed. But now she smelled something amazing coming from the kitchen and that didn't make sense, because Sylvie was never here on Mondays. She headed for the kitchen, surprised to see Jeff wearing an apron, pulling dishes out of the oven.

"What are you doing in here?" she asked.

"Cooking," he said.

"I didn't know that you cooked. Why are you cooking and what are you making? It smells wonderful!"

He put the casserole dish down on the prep table and peeled back the aluminum foil. "I didn't do this. Sylvie did. We came up with some simple meals that she prepared in advance. All I have to do is get things in the oven. It's easy. Would you like lunch today? If Sylvie cooked, there is enough to feed an army."

"What did she make?"

"We have baked steak," he pulled the tinfoil off a second pan with a flourish. "Mashed potatoes, roasted vegetables and fresh fruit. There are rolls with butter and jam and I just need to take the cottage cheese and apple sauce out of the refrigerator."

"Can I help?" Polly asked.

"Sure," he shrugged. "I didn't want to bother you. We came up with this harebrained idea and I didn't think you needed to feel as if you should do the work."

"If you're going to let me eat it, I can help you serve it," Polly laughed. She walked on into the kitchen and began pulling plates out, then dug around for serving spoons.

"Are they all coming down here?" she asked him. "Do we need to set up a table?"

"No," he responded. "I'm making up a plate for Lila Fletcher. She couldn't ..." he stopped speaking. "Anyway, I'm taking a tray up to her. Grey Linder is coming down and so is Natalie Dormand. The other two men in the addition will be coming for theirs pretty soon."

Jeff opened his phone and swiped it a couple of times, then set it down beside the food. "I have a list," he said, as he put food onto a plate. "Would you hand me two of those small dishes? The cold food can't touch the warm food. Oh and a small plate for the roll?"

Polly smiled at him. "You're a good man."

"Big bonus. That's what I'm looking for. A big bonus."

Polly knew he was kidding. They'd long since worked out his salary package and bonus schedule and he made them happen every quarter. She was certain that Sycamore House wouldn't be quite as successful without Jeff Lindsay running the place.

When he left to take the tray up the steps, she saw Grey Linder coming around the corner, peering back at the set for the Haunted Hallway. He looked worse than he had when he first arrived and Polly wondered just how much alcohol he was consuming.

Grey looked up to see Polly behind the counter and she could have sworn that he faltered in his steps, as if he wasn't sure whether or not he should approach her.

"Hello," she said brightly. "How are you today?" She had no idea why he was acting so strangely, but figured she could assure him that it was safe to be here.

"Fine," he mumbled. "I'm fine."

"I have plenty, how many pieces of steak you would like."

He lifted a single finger and she thought she heard him say "One," so she put it on his plate and handed it to him. That seemed to stymie him, so she helped him finish filling his plate. He continued to take quick glimpses of her and then look back down and she was relieved to see Jeff return to the kitchen.

"Mr. Linder, would you like Mr. Lyndsay to take the tray up to your room?" she asked, nodding rapidly at Jeff.

Jeff didn't wait for the man to answer, but picked the tray up and said, "I'd love to do this for you, sir."

He started to walk away and Grey Linder turned back to Polly, "Did he say anything?" he asked her.

"Did who say anything?" Polly wondered if he was talking about Thomas Zeller, but that had happened over a week ago.

"Zeller. Did he say anything to you?"

"I'm not sure what you mean," she responded. "He didn't say much of anything to me the night he died, if that's what you're asking." She wasn't about to give out any information about Thomas's family. They had stayed hidden for so many years, that until they were ready to out themselves to the world, she wasn't going to let anyone know who they were.

"Mmph," was all she heard as he turned to follow Jeff.

"That was odd," she said to herself, pushing the platters around on the counter in order to align them. She chuckled at herself and pushed the bowl of potatoes back out of line. "You're odd, too, Giller."

Natalie Dormand walked around the corner. Her eyes were bloodshot and there were deep circles under them. She was wearing a dark grey sweater that she continually pulled across her chest as she walked and even as she spoke to Polly.

"Hello," she said, coming into view.

"Hi there! How are you doing?" Polly asked.

"I suppose I'm okay. Thank you for providing a few meals here. I was tired of pizza."

"You really should try some of our restaurants. The Diner has sandwiches and terrific breakfasts and Davey's is also good."

"I'll try to get out sometime."

"Have you been working a lot?"

"After they gave me Thomas's laptop, I've been trying to clear up his life. I was all he had, you know."

"How is his latest novel? Was it complete?"

Natalie looked up from the platter of vegetables. Her brow wrinkled. "His novel?"

"I thought it was pretty much finished. You said you were looking for it. I just assumed you'd found it on the laptop once they got it back to you."

"Oh, that. There is always initial editing that needs to happen."

"He told me he didn't like the editing part of the process."

"He talked to you?" For some reason, Natalie's face had gotten red. She took a small plate and filled it with rolls and butter.

"We had several opportunities. He seemed to want a friend."

"I don't know why you say that. He had me."

Thomas had told Polly very little about the woman. In fact, he'd only called her by name once and that was in passing. Whatever she was to Thomas, he saw the relationship as much less personal than this woman did.

"How long do you plan to stay with us?" Polly asked.

"I have some things I need to clear up. Did Thomas ever talk about his family? I think he was here looking for someone."

This caused Polly to stop. She wasn't sure what to say. So, she asked more questions. "His family? I didn't think he had a family."

The woman looked directly at Polly, her eyes dark and her face grim. "I know you've been investigating his past. You and that girl from the Sheriff's office. I overheard you talking about him. Don't think I didn't know what he was doing here. I knew that every time he wrote an Eddie Powers mystery, he was looking for the woman he loved and her son. You found something, didn't you?"

"You were eavesdropping?" Polly was beginning to worry and she was ready for Jeff to walk back into the kitchen again.

"I came downstairs to get something to drink last Saturday. You figured out his little code. I found it years ago."

"Why didn't you tell him that you knew? Why would you keep that from him?"

"Oh, he needed his little secret. I always figured that if he wanted me to help him find her, he'd ask."

Polly looked up as she heard men's voices. Jeff rounded the corner with their two other guests, who swooped in on the counter with gusto and appreciation. Natalie Dormand took her tray off the counter with enough force that the dishes began to slide. Jeff stepped in and stabilized things for her, then smiled as she glared at him and walked away. He sent Polly a questioning look and she raised her eyes as if to say, "I don't know."

When the kitchen finally cleared out, he asked, "What was up with her? She looks awful and she looked pissed."

Polly realized she hadn't said much to Jeff about what had been going on with Thomas's flash drive. The way things were going, it was probably better to keep him in the dark. It was going to be easier if she simply avoided the question, so she said, "I think she isn't getting a lot of sleep while she works to edit his last novel."

"She looked upset."

"I think she's still pretty upset at losing Thomas. They might have been closer than I realized. Did you get Grey Linder settled in?"

"I tell you what. It worries me when our guests look worse after they've been here for a while than they did when they arrived. It's like he has aged ten years since he got here."

"Do you think he's drinking a lot?"

"I don't know for sure. He wouldn't let me in his room. I'm going to take food back to my office and shut the door unless you want company."

"Don't worry about it. I should go upstairs and spend some time with the animals."

"Okay, I'll clean things up later." He covered the bowls and platters after they both filled their plates and then Polly took hers and went into the back hallway to head for her apartment.

Everything seemed strange today. Maybe it was the spooky stuff in the hallway or the odd interactions she'd had with her guests, but she was ready for something normal and she couldn't think of anything better than a few minutes with her dog and cats.

The washer and dryer were spinning away and she hoped Eliseo knew there was food in the kitchen. She'd text him when she got upstairs. Jeff had more than likely spoken with him, but she couldn't help herself. Right in the middle of typing the text into her phone, it rang. Henry's picture popped up in the screen.

"Hey there, hotstuff," she said. "How are you today?"

"I'm good. Just checking on you. What 'cha up to?"

"About five six, depending on the shoes I'm wearing."

"Smart Alek. What have you been doing today?"

"Paying bills. It was boring. And now I'm getting ready to eat an amazing lunch with my favorite boy." She looked down at the dog.

"I hope that's Obiwan or Luke."

"He's going to be drooling on my feet if I'm not careful."

"Now I really hope that it's Obiwan."

"So do I," she laughed. "So what's up with you?"

"I was worried about your conversation with Aaron. Did you live through it?"

"He was only a little mad at me. I came through relatively unscathed. It's good to have a reputation for being independent. He didn't have high expectations for much else."

Henry didn't respond and she knew he was trying not to laugh.

"Henry?"

"Yes, Polly?"

"This is serious. Don't tell anyone about the Campbells, okay?"

"I haven't. I won't. But why are you telling me that?"

"I got some weird vibes around here today."

"No problem. I don't have anyone I would tell. But last night was a pretty interesting night, even for you."

"You haven't been around the times I've found bodies. Last night was pretty tame."

"Have you ever thought about how strange that is, Polly? You found a long lost son and old girlfriend of a dead author and you think it's tame."

"Welcome to my life since I arrived in Bellingwood."

"Speaking of your life in Bellingwood, I can't believe there haven't been any more vandalism incidents."

"Hush your mouth!" Polly drawled. "I'm happy that I don't have to fix anything or clean anything up. Maybe whoever was doing it got over being mad at me."

"That would really be nice. I hate worrying about you."

Her first reaction was to tell him that she could take care of herself, but she decided to let it go. "I'm glad it's been quiet. I can use the quiet."

"You enjoy your lunch and your quiet. Do you want to do something tonight?"

They'd been out a lot this last week and Polly didn't want to go anywhere. The rest of the week was going to be crazy as they prepared for Halloween and then the Black Masque Ball. She just plain didn't want to.

"No?"

"Does that mean you don't want to do something at all or can you not do something with me around?"

"I can not do something with you around. I really want to watch stupid television or Star Wars or something mindless and eat simple food. Is that okay with you?"

"I'll be there around six thirty. Will the boys be gone by then?"

Sylvie usually picked her kids up by six, even on her latest nights.

"Yep."

"Love you, pretty girl. See you then."

"Love you too."

She set the phone on the table beside her plate and took a bite. Sylvie had outdone herself. Obiwan wagged his tail, as if to tell her that she should share, but she patted the top of his head. "You never get human food, you beggar. I love you very much, but today isn't going to be any different."

CHAPTER TWENTY-TWO

Once she realized there wasn't going to be any more sleep, Polly finally got up and sat on the edge of her bed. She'd been tossing and turning for the last hour. The animals were too close, the blankets were too warm, the pillow was uncomfortable, everything was annoying. Leia had finally taken to the cat tree in protest after being pushed back and forth between Polly's legs.

"Sorry," Polly whispered. "I don't know what my problem is."

The thing was, she did know. There was something about the conversation with Natalie yesterday at lunch that had been bugging her and she couldn't put her finger on it. The jealousy thing was weird, but that wasn't it. Then again, maybe it was.

Polly had never questioned whether or not the woman should have access to Thomas Zeller's laptop. He was paranoid and worldly enough to have password protected it if he hadn't wanted others to have access. She shrugged her shoulders. Maybe she should have called his publisher and asked questions.

Since she'd moved back to Iowa, Polly had found that she lost some of her big city paranoia. No longer did she assume that people were out to get her. She waved at them on the highway and looked up and spoke to them when she was downtown. She still hadn't gotten used to the fact that the locals left their cars running when they had to run into the bank or the post office. It had taken quite a few months, but now was a point of pride that she could walk away from her truck without locking it.

As far as Polly was concerned, if Natalie Dormand said she was the person to take care of Thomas Zeller's things and have access to his laptop, that was the right thing to do. Why would anyone lie about that? But something was still off.

Polly went into the kitchen. Thank goodness Henry wasn't staying here any longer. It would kill her to feel trapped in the bedroom. Living alone and having the freedom to move around without bothering anyone else was a wonderful feeling.

The clock on the microwave told Polly that it was two fifty-two in the morning. "I don't want to be awake at this hour," she said to Obiwan, who had followed her, hoping for something more to eat. Opening cupboard doors and then the refrigerator offered her nothing of any interest, and then she saw a box of cocoa mix.

She filled her favorite mug with water and set it in the microwave, turning the timer on. "Should I put something a little extra in there so I can go back to sleep?" she asked. "If you don't tell anyone, I'll give you a treat."

At that word, he wagged his tail. "You're easy," she said. "You'd tell on me for another treat, wouldn't you!"

When he heard the word again, he walked over to stand in front of the cabinet where the treats were stored. The microwave dinged and Polly took the mug out and set it on the counter. She opened a package of cocoa into it and stirred, waiting for it to cool. When she couldn't wait any longer, she opened a drawer and took out a dish cloth, wrapped it around the mug and started for the living room. A plaintive woof stopped her in her tracks.

"Whoops. I promised, didn't I!" she laughed. A treat on the floor and another in her hand would keep the boy happy.

Television was awful. There weren't even any reruns on that held her interest, so, since a Star Trek:TNG DVD was still in the player, she began watching and then groaned. Season Two. Not her favorite. Oh well. Watching Picard and Riker debate Data's sentience was at least a little entertaining. She took a sip of the cocoa and when Obiwan curled up beside her on the couch, pulled the blanket over both of them and leaned back.

The noise in the background dulled as she shut her eyes and tried to figure out what had bothered her about the conversation at lunch. It didn't take long for Polly's mind to drift away, making no connections at all. The afternoon had been filled with her friends, setting more props into place for the Haunted Hallway.

Henry had come by at six thirty. Polly accused him of watching for Sylvie's car to leave and when he brandished a paper bag, protesting his innocence, she let him off the hook. He'd picked up fried chicken and mashed potatoes from Davey's and they watched mindless television all night long. Henry had finally plucked the remote from Polly's hand after she had been around the dial the third time, stopping for nothing.

"I'm going home," he said. "You should go to bed."

"You're not my mother. I'll go to bed when I want to go to bed!" Polly had whined.

"Did you just whine at me?"

"Maybe." That time she stuck her lower lip out and pouted. "I wish you didn't have to go. I know we don't do anything exciting, but I like having you around."

Henry had tucked the blanket in around her on the sofa. He bent over and kissed her, then put the remote back in her hand. "I like being here, too. But, both of us need sleep tonight. I'm not going to be around much tomorrow. I have a job up in Lehigh and we are on the road early. Text me when you get moving."

"I'll walk out with you."

"Nope. You stay put. Obiwan and I will take a quick walk and then I'll let him back in and lock up."

"You're awfully good to me."

"Remember that the next time you want to yell at me for something stupid I've done, okay?"

Polly had smiled up at him. "I owe you a few of those."

Henry had done just as he said and when Obiwan came back

up the steps he called out, "Good night, pretty girl. I'll talk to you later!"

"Good night."

She had waited long enough for him to get home and then texted him, *"Did you get home safe? No boogey man to bother you?"*

"I just walked in the front door. Good night, Polly. I love you."

"I love you too."

Polly had watched the news, taken the remote around the channels once or twice more and decided to go to bed. Henry was pretty wonderful, putting up with her boring evenings.

The ringing of her phone woke Polly again. She was still on the couch and the cats had curled up around her. She fumbled around looking for the phone, nearly knocking the full cup of cocoa on the floor. Some sloshed out on the table and she whimpered. It was seven thirty and the phone call was Eliseo.

"I'm late! I'm sorry!" she said, jumping up and dislodging the animals. "I'm on the way."

"I was getting a little worried. Do you want me to take care of things down here this morning?"

"No, I'm coming. I need to find my head and I'll be right there. How long have you been here?"

"A little while. We'll wait for you.

Polly quickly got dressed. Calling her dog, she ran full speed to the barn.

Eliseo looked up when she rushed in. "That didn't take long!"

"I'm sorry. I was up in the middle of the night and fell asleep on the couch."

"Did something else happen?"

"No, I think my mind was trying to talk to me, but I couldn't focus enough to hear it." Polly opened the door to Daisy's stall and put her hand on the horse's neck.

"Good morning, girl," she said, feeling the strength of the horse under her fingertips. With one light connection to the horse, Polly stopped thinking about rushing around and stepped in to the stall. She wrapped her arms as far as she could around the horse's neck and hugged her. Daisy nuzzled Polly's hat. "I'm glad you are here, too," Polly said. "I'll be right back with your breakfast."

She stepped back into the alley and into Demi's stall. A quick pat on his shoulder and Polly took off for the feed room. Eliseo was filling buckets and laughed at her when she darted in. "They're good to have around, aren't they?"

"They are. Thanks for waiting for me this morning."

"When I drove in and didn't see any of your lights on, I knew you weren't moving too quickly, so I spent some time cleaning up the shed behind your garage. I didn't want to come down and wake up the horses without you."

"Thank you. I start missing these guys when I don't get down here every day." She headed back to the stalls and after making sure that Demi and Daisy were fed, gave them a few minutes of quiet with their breakfast. She wandered back into the feed room and found Eliseo sliding bales of hay out of the upper loft, so she hefted them into place, building up the stacks. This was work she'd never done with her father on their farm. He hadn't asked her to do much while she was growing up. He kept insisting that it was more important to him that she do well in school and have plenty of time for the activities she chose to participate in.

Mary, on the other hand, kept Polly very busy around the house. She didn't believe in idle time. If Polly wasn't busy with homework or practicing her flute, she was cleaning or doing laundry. Polly hated washing windows and cringed every time she came home from school and saw the bucket and squeegee sitting on the front stoop. But, they did the work together and Polly learned to never be afraid of hard work.

She and Eliseo opened the doors to the outside and let the horses into the pasture, then began the process of mucking out stalls. They worked in silence and her mind drifted back to the conversation she had with Natalie Dormand yesterday. Polly was breaking up a bale of hay in Demi's stall and gasped out loud.

"Is everything okay, Polly?" Eliseo entered the stall with a worried look on his face.

"I just figured out what's been on my mind for the last eighteen hours. I'm sorry to have startled you."

"That's okay. As long as you didn't hurt yourself. What did you figure out?"

"Thomas Zeller wrote another Eddie Powers mystery!"

"Okay?" he seemed puzzled.

"He hasn't written one of those since the early nineties. He wrote one every time he was searching for his son and his old girlfriend. Whenever they left a community, she mailed him a picture and then he went there to find out about her. That's what Natalie Dormand said to me yesterday. She's reading another Eddie Powers mystery. She knows he was close to finding them."

"What does that mean, then?"

"I'm not really sure. I wonder if I can get my hands on the manuscript."

"Can't you just ask her?"

"I don't think she'll let me near it. She seems really offended that he and I had a friendship. I might call Anita down at the Sheriff's office to see if they kept a copy of it somehow."

Eliseo nodded and walked away with the wheelbarrow in order to dump it. Polly began sweeping in the main alley, her mind racing. She rushed through the rest of her chores and when she was finished, ran back to her apartment, waiting rather impatiently for her dog to catch up.

"Come on! Let's go!" Polly called to Obiwan. He rushed up the stairs, wagging his tail. Breakfast was coming.

When she finally got to her office, she quickly waved to Jeff and dropped into her chair. Before the computer came to life, she made the call to Anita,

"Good morning, Polly. What's up?" was Anita's reply.

"You didn't happen to keep an image of Thomas Zeller's computer before you gave it back to Natalie Dormand, did you? And by the way, did you all do any background checks on her?"

"What are you thinking?"

"I want to make sure we handed his life to someone who is who she says she is."

"And the manuscript?"

"If this is another Eddie Powers mystery, there might be a code in it for Genie Campbell. He hasn't written one of those in years and it's a big deal!"

"Let me check and I'll get back to you. It might be later today, though. I have a desk full of work to do here."

"No problem. Thank you for looking into it for me."

"I'll call you later."

"Thanks." Polly sat back in her chair. She could stand it no longer. She got up and ducked into Jeff's office.

"I'm going to my apartment. Call if you need help with lunch."

He looked up, "I don't need you today. Hannah should be here any time. She's going to do some baking for afternoon meetings and handle lunch today."

"Really?" Polly was surprised. Hannah didn't usually work during the week. She and her husband had a little one who demanded a great deal of her time.

"Her mother-in-law told her she would love to take the baby since the older kids are in preschool and school. So, one day a week she is ours."

"That's terrific." Hannah McKenzie was married to one of Polly's friends from high school. They'd met last Christmas and when Hannah ended up helping Sylvie with the Sycamore House Christmas party, the two women discovered they worked well together. Since then, Hannah spent most Saturdays helping Sylvie with wedding receptions and other events.

"Call if you need me." She dodged the Haunted Hallway set and ran up the steps. Thomas Zeller's books were in her bookcase and she wanted to track down his publisher in order to ask some questions. Now that she thought about it, it seemed odd that no one from the publishing company had bothered to come to Bellingwood or even to call her.

Polly found the last book he had written and sat down at her dining room table with her laptop, looking for phone numbers. It took some doing, but she finally ended up speaking to a man whose high-pitched voice had a very affected British accent.

"Jeremy Swanson speaking, how may I assist you today?"

"Mr. Swanson, this is Polly Giller. I am the owner of Sycamore

House in Bellingwood, Iowa, where Thomas Zeller was staying until he died last week. I would like to ask some questions."

"Yes, Miss Giller. I will answer the questions that I am able to answer. Please proceed."

Please proceed? She wanted to giggle, but thought better of it. "Can you tell me if Natalie Dormand is really Thomas Zeller's assistant?"

"Miss Dormand is employed by our firm and has been working exclusively with Mr. Zeller for the last two years."

"She works for you?"

"Yes, Miss Giller, that is exactly what I said."

"Has she contacted you about his new manuscript?"

"I was under the impression that he hadn't finished it. The last I spoke with Mr. Zeller, he intimated that there was quite a bit of work to be done on it before it would be ready for publication."

"Does Natalie Dormand generally do a lot of re-writing for him?"

"That is information I do not have. I am uncertain of the specifics of their relationship."

"Do you know if Thomas had an agent or anyone who might be managing his estate? We've heard from no one regarding his body or personal effects."

"It is my understanding that Miss Dormand has all of that well in hand. I am sure Mr. Zeller had a great many friends here locally and given some time, I could gather information on his local agent and the lawyer he works with. But again, you could also ask these questions of Miss Dormand."

"Does Miss Dormand work out of an office there or was she working directly with Mr. Zeller?"

"I don't understand the reason for these questions, Miss Giller. Miss Dormand does have an office here, but she is not required to be in it. Most of her time is spent working quite closely with Mr. Zeller."

Polly could tell that she wasn't going to get much further with this man.

"Do you carry the publishing rights for the Eddie Powers

mysteries, Mr. Swanson?"

"No, I'm sorry, we do not. We did not purchase those when we took Mr. Zeller on as a client."

"One last question. Do you publish Grey Linder's work?"

"The poet? No, Miss Giller, we do not. The last thing he wrote that was worth any attention was twenty years ago. The man is a washed up hack."

Polly swallowed a snort as the snobby Mr. Swanson's speech pattern flattened out. He spat that last sentence out with more than a little venom.

"How do you know about Mr. Linder?" he asked her.

"He has been working here at Sycamore House as well."

"Don't be taken in by that drunk. He isn't working and I can almost certainly assure you that you will receive no remuneration for his stay there. He will be gone one night and you won't be able to find him."

She was going to have to ask Jeff about that. They'd not yet been stiffed by any of their guests, but she supposed there might be a first time.

Jeremy Swanson interrupted her thoughts. "I must attend a meeting in a short while, so unless you have any other questions ..." he let the sentence hang there.

Polly thought about outwaiting him, but decided to be the better person. "Thank you for your time, Mr. Swanson. If I have any more questions, I will contact you at a later date. I will also let my friend, Sheriff Merritt, who is handling the investigation into Mr. Zeller's death, know that I've spoken with you just in case he has any further questions."

She pressed the button to end the call and snickered to herself. She wasn't sure why that felt so good, but it did.

Another internet search and Polly dialed her phone again.

"Seafold Publishing, this is Ben speaking. How may I help you?"

"Hello, my name is Polly Giller and I would like to speak to someone about Thomas Zeller."

"The only someone available is me and so I guess I'm it. How do you know Tom?" the man asked. He had a deep, resonant voice, exactly the opposite of Jeremy Swanson.

"Mr. Zeller has been staying here in Iowa. I own Sycamore House in Bellingwood and he spent the last month or so with us while finishing his book."

"Did you get to know the old man well before he died?" Ben asked.

"I'd like to think so, but I've been finding out much more about him since he's been gone. I just spoke with Jeremy Swanson ..."

Before she could finish, he let out a hack of laughter, "That fatuous ass. He and his cronies are crooks. I told Thomas as much nearly twenty years ago, but he was looking for big money to build his portfolio in a hurry and they were willing to pay him."

"Do you still have publishing rights for the Eddie Powers mysteries?"

"I sure do. That was part of the deal. Any future Eddie Powers mysteries were to come to me, too. But I guess that isn't going to happen now, is it. I hate the idea that I'm going to have to make a living off of the fact that Thomas is dead, but if I want to keep my father's company open, it's what I'll have to do."

Polly liked this man and before she knew it was spilling everything she knew about the books, the codes, Thomas's search for his long lost love and son and then she said, "I'm pretty sure that he has just written another Eddie Powers mystery, but there's a Natalie Dormand here who has control of his laptop and I don't know what she's going to do with the manuscript. Thomas was out here in Iowa looking for Nelly and his son."

"It's too bad he didn't find them before he died. He spent a lot of time with us during the early years of his search. We scheduled his travel for him and checked up on him regularly when he was working, just to make sure he was taking care of himself. Some of those locations were pretty remote," Ben said. "Do you really think there's another Eddie Powers mystery?"

"I do. And I think there's one more message for Nelly." Polly decided that she wasn't telling anyone about Kevin and Genie. At least not yet. The time wasn't right.

"You don't have another room that I could stay in, do you?" he asked. "I'd like to fly out tomorrow and see what I can do about retrieving that manuscript."

"Let me see what I can do."

They exchanged email addresses and then it occurred to Polly that she'd be in Des Moines for another Therapy Dog Training session. She told Ben about that and gave him the hours she'd be busy. If it worked for her to pick him up, then she would make sure he got to Bellingwood.

"Until tomorrow, then," he said. "Thank you for calling me, Miss Giller."

"It's Polly and I'm sorry, your last name is?"

"Seafold. It's a family business."

"I hope to see you tomorrow, then, Mr. Seafold. Thank you for your time."

They hung up and everything inside her stomach roiled in panic. She didn't know whether she was excited or terrified that she'd completely screwed things up again. If only Anita would call to let her know what was going on.

There was a knock at her front door. Obiwan beat her to the entryway, his tail wagging. "I suppose you know who this is," she said and opened the door.

Jeff was standing there with a tray. "I'm delivering lunch today," he said, handing it to her. "I wanted to make sure you ate something healthy. I brought Mr. Linder's up for him and figured I could just as easily drop yours off, too."

Polly's roiling stomach took another turn at the reminder of Grey Linder's possible failure to pay.

"Jeff?" she started.

"Yes, Polly."

No, she wasn't going to do that now. They could deal with it later and she didn't feel like passing along Jeremy Swanson's negative comments. "Do we have another room available through the weekend?"

"Yes. We have the fourth room over in the addition. Did you invite someone else?"

"It's Thomas Zeller's old publisher. I just got off the phone with him and he wants to come out to see what he can do to help clear the rest of this mess up. He's flying into Des Moines tomorrow sometime. I'll probably bring him back with me after I'm finished with the Pet Therapy session."

"Just so you know, I've had a few media inquiries. I've sent everything to the Sheriff's office in Boone or forwarded it to Natalie Dormand. Thomas Zeller was kind of a big deal."

"Yes he was. Have you talked to her much?"

"Who, Natalie? Not a lot. She stays to herself. In fact, I'm taking lunch to her in a few minutes. Why?"

"No reason. Thank you for this," Polly said, nodding at the tray. "I'll bring things down later."

She watched him go back to the steps, then took the tray in to the dining room table. She barely had time to look at what was there to eat when her phone rang. It was Henry.

"Hey there, pretty girl. You never texted me. Are you up and moving?"

"I'm sorry! I'm sorry!" Polly exclaimed. "I woke up late and haven't been thinking straight since then. How's your day going?"

"I can think of a few ways it could be better, but since you're there and I'm here, it's going well. I can't talk long but I wanted to make sure you were alive."

"I'm alive. I have a lot to tell you, but it will wait." Polly smiled as she said it. Henry's curiosity would kill him.

"That's not fair. What about?"

"It's no big deal. I'll tell you tonight. I love you," she said sweetly.

"You're a brat, but I love you too. I'll talk to you tonight."

They hung up and Polly looked at her lunch. The stew was still steaming and it looked as if Hannah had put their new Panini press to good use today.

CHAPTER TWENTY-THREE

Stopping in front of the airport, Polly looked around. Even though Ben Seafold had arrived while she was in the middle of the training session with Obiwan, he assured her that he could find plenty to occupy himself until she picked him up.

She called his phone and watched a giant of a man reach into his pocket. He answered, "Hello," and looked up as she drove directly in front of him and rolled down the passenger window.

"Ben Seafold?" she asked.

"Then you must be Polly Giller." He had thick, brown curly hair and a full beard and was probably in his late forties or early fifties. He was wearing jeans and a flannel shirt, reminding Polly a little of Paul Bunyan. Hints of grey in his beard shimmered in the light from the truck's cab when he opened the door.

"I am, and this is my dog Obiwan." Polly pulled Obiwan close to her, making room for their guest. Ben dropped his bag behind the seat and after getting himself settled, reached out with one hand to let the dog sniff him.

The next thing Polly knew, Obiwan was draped across the man's lap begging for Ben to scratch him. Ben obliged, rubbing the dog's ears and scratching the nape of his neck.

"I'm sorry about that," she laughed. "He can sit here."

"No, this is fine. I had to leave my Gertrude at home and I miss her when I'm gone."

"What kind of dog is Gertrude?"

"A miniature dachshund."

Polly tried and failed to stifle a snort of laughter. "A miniature dachshund?" The image of the two of them walking together was too much. She pulled out of the airport and headed for the interstate, shaking her head to regain her composure.

"She's my girl. I've had her for six years and she never fails to let me know how glad she is that I rescued her."

Ben Seafold kept his hands on Obiwan. "I got to thinking today," he said. "This trip probably wasn't necessary, but Thomas was such a big part of my life, I couldn't stay away after I talked to you. When I heard he died, I didn't know what to do, so I guess I didn't do anything but stay at home and feel sorry for myself."

"I wish I would have known," Polly said quietly. "I'm so sorry."

"No, no, no, young lady. I'm here now. Maybe I'll take you out for a rousing night on the town and tell you stories of Thomas when he wasn't quite the gentleman you got to know. He taught me all of my vices. Dad wasn't too happy with many of the decisions Thomas made regarding my education into the world, but we all lived through those days and I had the time of my life."

"Did you see much of him in the last few years?"

"He'd come up to the house every October. In fact, he was planning to come see me after he left here. He told me we had things to talk about. He liked to be at my place around Halloween. He'd dress up in a black suit, paste on a fake mustache and part his hair on the side, then we'd spend the weekend haunting some of his favorite clubs. He would recite Poe's creepiest stories and then we'd go home and light a fire, drink hot chocolate and watch slasher movies. I both dreaded and anticipated those trips. After a good solid night of scaring me to death, he'd get up the next day about noon and act like that was a perfectly normal day in his life. Then, he'd beg me to take him to an apple orchard or some mundane attraction and we'd be off, acting like tourists for the rest of the time."

"He really had a thing for Poe," Polly commented.

"I suppose he did. I didn't see it except around Halloween. But, yes, I think that somehow Poe spoke to his soul. Thomas always wanted there to be more to life than the angst Poe expressed, but after so many years, it was as if he gave up on hope and was simply living until it was over. He enjoyed his friends, he loved to write and he liked meeting his fans, but there wasn't anything big and wonderful out there on the horizon for him. He had too much respect for life to do anything other than live it, but he didn't have a lot of ..." Ben paused. "Zest. He didn't have zest."

"Did he have zest when he was younger?"

Ben laughed. "I don't know if it was his alcoholism or what, but when he was up, he was really quite fun. Every time he got one of those pictures in the mail, he cleaned up his act and got excited about looking for Nelly and his son. Then, when the book was finished, he would come back a lost and broken man. He hadn't found them, he didn't know how he was going to start another novel, and each night he drank himself to sleep. Every once in a while Dad talked him into rousing out of his stupor long enough to go on a book tour, but he didn't do many of those, they were too much effort."

"It sounds like those years were rough on him."

"They were rough on all of us that loved him. Dad and I always wondered what he could have done if he'd stayed sober. Actually, even if he had just managed to stay away from that terrible depressed drinking he did, things would have been better. But, it's who he was and honestly, that's what created those great books."

"Did he ever get close to finding Nelly?" Polly asked.

"No, not really. He was always surprised to find out where they'd ended up. They were all over the country, never staying very long. It wasn't that easy to track people down back then and Thomas wouldn't hire a private detective. He figured that Nelly would have left clues for him and if he couldn't find her, he wasn't paying someone else to scare her to death by chasing her down."

"Kind of like the clues he left for her in the book?"

"I can't believe you figured that out. All of those years the books have been in print and no one ever saw that. Thomas never said a word."

"I'm surprised he was able to keep it a secret. He told no one! How does a person do that?"

"There was only one person he wanted to figure it out and I guess she never did or else she would have let him find her."

"What about you," Polly asked, "Do you have a family?"

"Not yet. Dad decided he didn't need a city to build a publishing company. We always told him that he found the most remote location in Vermont and gave the banker some money. Not a lot because they couldn't get anyone to live there except fools. Things have built up a lot in the last thirty years, but it's not a haven for flirtatious women."

They were near Boone and Polly asked, "Have you eaten?"

"Oh, don't worry about me. I had plenty to eat at your little airport in Des Moines. After sitting in airports and on airplanes all day today, I'm looking forward to stretching my legs. I have some manuscripts to read." He chuckled. "Ain't technology grand? I remember toting boxes of manuscripts for Dad. Nowadays, I load them onto a tablet and read until my eyes bleed." Polly heard him chuckle again, "And sometimes it isn't because the tablet is hurting my eyes, but the work is just that awful."

"We're almost to Bellingwood," she said. "There's plenty of room to walk around. I hope you'll like it."

"I'm sure I will. I've done all the talking on this trip. Tell me about your Sycamore House."

She found herself telling her story, of returning to Iowa from Boston to find herself the owner of an old school house that was in desperate need of renovation. As she described meeting her new friends, he laughed in all the right places and encouraged her to keep talking. It seemed like only a few moments had passed and then she was pulling up to the front door.

Obiwan sat back up and his whole body shook with joy when he saw where they were. As soon as Polly was out of the truck, he jumped to the ground and ran to the front door, wagging his tail.

"Someone knows where home is," Ben grabbed his bag from behind the seat and stretched, looking around. "This is a beautiful spot. Really peaceful."

"It's home," Polly said. "Come on in."

She gave him a quick tour of the main level, then took him to the addition. Obiwan followed them to the side door and stopped, expecting Polly to open the door to the outside so he could go to the barn.

"Not yet, bud," she said. "We'll go out later."

"You have a barn," Ben said. "I know that's obvious, but what kind of animals do you have down there?"

"I rescued four Percheron horses last winter. Sometimes timing is everything. I knew I wanted to get a horse or two, so I had this amazing barn-raising event. We didn't even get the barn fully finished before my veterinarian had four horses who needed me."

"Are they okay now?"

Polly pressed the button for the elevator to take them upstairs.

"They are great. They just needed some tender loving care."

They rode up quietly in the elevator. She opened the door to his room and went inside with him, pulling the door closed behind her.

"Natalie Dormand is across the hallway from you. If another room had been available, I wouldn't have put you that close to her. Have you two ever met?"

"We've spoken a few times, but I've never met her. Don't worry. I'll be fine."

Polly emailed the keys to his room and outside doors to Ben. "Feel free to come and go as you please. You might feel a little trapped here without a car, but if you want a ride uptown for anything, just let me know. You can call or text me any time."

"Where's uptown and do they have a diner?"

She smiled. "It's a wonderful diner and it's three blocks that way," Polly pointed toward town. "If you don't mind the walk, it's a nice community. If you do mind the walk, it's still nice."

"I'll be just fine. It looks like you all are ready for Halloween."

"We certainly are. There won't be any readings of Poe's literature and I'm hoping we don't scare the children too much, but the Sheriff's wife is excited about creating some fun for them and we're all going to be part of it." She turned to leave. "Welcome to Bellingwood. I hope we can make your stay worthwhile. Let me know if you need anything."

"Good night, Polly Giller." He held the door as she left. "I look forward to the next few days."

Polly and Obiwan went back down the elevator and out the side door. Obiwan wandered off toward the back of the building and she took out her phone to text Henry.

"I'm back in town and have Ben Seafold safely ensconced in his room. I missed you today."

Within seconds, her phone buzzed with a return text.

"I missed you too. Have you eaten supper yet? Would you like some company?"

She had completely forgotten about supper.

"My truck is out front," she texted, *"Maybe Obiwan and I should come to your house. I can pick up a couple of sandwiches. How about it?"*

Her phone rang this time and she answered it, "What's up?"

"Drive around to your garage. You'll see my truck there. I've been waiting here with the cats for you to return. I figured you hadn't eaten supper and I brought sandwiches."

"You're a nut! We'll be up in a few minutes. Thanks for sitting with the cats."

"They held me down and made me watch an old Superman movie. Don't you have any chick flicks around here?"

"I'm sure I have one or two," she giggled. "I'll be right up."

Obiwan jumped into the truck and Polly drove to her garage.

Doug was out walking along the tree line with Billy's dog, Big Jack. Obiwan took off at a run when he saw them, wagging his tail, jumping in the air and barking at his friend.

"Hi there!" she called out over the sound of two happy dogs.

"Hey." Doug didn't sound like his normal self and Polly walked over to stand with him as they watched the dogs romp around.

"What's up? You don't sound very happy."

"It's no big deal."

"But it's some kind of deal. What's going on?"

He stomped his right foot on the ground beside her and planted himself, then looked up. "I'm tired of being alone."

"Alone? Where's Billy?"

"He's always out with Rachel. They don't even stay to play games anymore."

"Why don't you invite your other friends over?"

"I do. And they come over sometimes, but I feel like I'm the only person without a life around here. And I'm tired of playing online by myself all the time. I should have just stayed in my parent's basement. At least then there was someone to talk to when I came out for dinner."

"They're gone every night?"

"Yeah. They go over to Rachel's house. She has to be there while her mom works. I guess they don't want Caleb to be alone."

Polly took a deep breath and dove in. "Doug, what would you say if I set you up on a date with a cute girl who likes games and geeky stuff?"

"I'd say she doesn't exist."

"But she does and she's into Steampunk and is coming to the Masquerade Ball and I told her about you and she's interested in meeting you."

"Don't be messing with me, Polly. That would be cruel."

"I'm not messing. I promise. Weren't you planning to go to the Ball?"

"I don't know." He scuffed his right foot on the ground. "You're serious about this?"

"I'm totally serious. Her name is Anita Banks and she works for Sheriff Merritt in Boone. You don't have to do anything other than come to the Ball. I'll introduce you and then if it works out, great. If not, that's no big deal."

"You can't tell anyone about this. Promise you won't tell anyone. I mean it, Polly. No one."

"I promise," she said. "Will you be there?"

"I will. But you can't tell anybody. Not even Henry. We aren't talking about this."

"Fine. We aren't talking about it. It's our secret." She jabbed his arm. "See. I'm a really great older sister, aren't I!"

"Did you really set up a date for me? Really?"

"I really did. And it has no strings attached. She's pretty cool."

"Wow." He looked at her. "Wow."

"You should come upstairs to my apartment tonight. Henry's there. He got sandwiches. I'm sure there's plenty of food. We're going to watch a movie."

"Nah, I don't want to interrupt. You guys are probably on a date or something."

"Stop it. If it were a hot date, I wouldn't have invited you. Come on up. Henry's already watched a Superman movie and he's complaining that I don't have enough chick flicks. You need to rescue me."

Doug's eyes lit up. The poor guy really was lonely. The immense apartment that she'd had built over her garage probably was pretty empty with only one person in there. She should have caught on to this earlier.

"Let me take Big Jack up to my place and I'll be there in a few minutes. Is it okay if I come in the back door?"

"Just yell when you open the door and come on up. And I won't say a word," Polly laughed. She called for Obiwan and he followed her in and up the back steps.

Henry was sitting on the sofa when she walked into the room. He jumped up. "I have sandwiches in the refrigerator. Let me get them."

"No, you sit back down." Polly walked to him and kissed him. "We're going to have company. Poor Doug is lonely. Billy and Rachel are spending a lot of time together at her house, so I invited him to come up and watch a movie with us."

He leaned into her ear and whispered, "You are always rescuing someone. I love that about you."

"I love you too."

"You won't believe it, but I was starving when I went to the sub shop, so I bought an extra sandwich."

"Then I'll slice them into chunks and we can share all around. Henry Sturtz, sometimes you are the smartest man on the planet. Thank you for taking care of me and all my friends. Now sit down and I'll get everything out. It's the least I can do."

He followed her to the kitchen, "How was the trip back with that guy?"

"He's such a nice man, Henry. His name is Ben Seafold and he looks like Paul Bunyan. He's huge! But he really liked Thomas and I'm glad he's here. I don't trust that Natalie Dormand for some reason and I think there are a lot of decisions that need to be made that aren't being made."

"Is there any kind of memorial service planned?"

"I don't even know that! You'd think she would have said something to us. But she was so worried about getting to his computer and the manuscript that I don't think she's paying attention to anything else." Then Polly said, "I wouldn't know about any of that though. She's not talking to me or anyone else around here. She hides in her room and comes down for food every once in a while. Weird girl."

"Helloooo!" Doug called from the bottom of the stairway.

"Come on up!" Polly called back. "We're in the kitchen."

Henry took plates down from the shelf and put them on the peninsula.

"I brought chips and some cookies my mom made," Doug said, crossing the room. Obiwan jumped off the couch and followed him, his tail madly wagging. "Thanks for letting me come over. I was ready to go out of my mind and if Mom knew I was lonely, she'd make me come home."

"Then we won't say a word," Henry patted his shoulder. "Come on over and tell me what movie we should watch."

Polly filled the dining room table with food, opened the chips and pulled out two other opened bags from her cupboard. Sodas and a bucket of ice, Doug's cookies and a batch of brownies she'd made over the weekend and the feast was ready.

"What did you find?" she asked. "The food is ready."

"Henry says he's never seen *Lord of the Rings*." Doug said. "Is it too long for tonight?"

"I think we're fine. Turn it on now and if we don't make it all the way through, we'll finish it another night."

Henry sidled up to her, trying to take the plate she'd filled from her hands, but Polly pulled back. "No. I don't know who you are anymore. How can you not have seen this movie? Did you read the books at least?"

He dropped his face to his chest. "No?"

"You haven't read the books or seen the movies? I feel nothing but shame for you!" she laughed, looking at Doug. "I don't even know what to think!"

"It's not my favorite ..." Henry began.

Polly jammed her palm in front of his face. "Don't even. You can redeem yourself tonight by being completely interested in this movie. Any sign that you are bored or falling asleep and I will trickle ice cold water down your face."

"Dude," Doug said. "You are going to love this. I can't believe you've never seen it. Billy and I watch all three of them on Saturdays sometimes."

"More than once or twice?" Henry seemed flabbergasted.

"Of course!" Polly interrupted. "You've seen Star Wars more than once."

"Only because you make me."

"But you haven't complained."

Henry sat down on the sofa. The opening sequence had begun. Polly sat beside him and Doug took a chair.

"Shhh." Doug said. "It's starting. You don't want to miss this."

CHAPTER TWENTY-FOUR

The next morning, Polly was in her office. Anita hadn't called back and she wasn't sure what to do. But with Ben Seafold in town, Polly wanted to get her hands on that manuscript.

"Whatever," she said to herself and dialed the phone.

"Polly!" Anita exclaimed when she answered, "I'm so sorry! I totally forgot to call you back. It's been absolutely crazy down here and things got shuffled around. I'm sorry!"

Polly breathed a sigh of relief. "Has it gotten any better? Because someone is here who should see that laptop if he could."

"We were here until midnight last night, but I think things have calmed down enough that I could get out for lunch today. Do you want me to come up to Bellingwood? Will you feed me if I do?"

"Lunch would be terrific. I'm going to ask Ben to join us. Would you mind coming up to my apartment?"

"That sounds fine. I'll see you after a while."

Ben walked in the front door and Polly watched as he peered at the decorations for the Haunted Hallway. That was happening tonight and Lydia was ready. Candy was already in the large cauldron which would be placed on top of a black lit fog machine.

Polly could hardly wait to see all the effects.

"Good morning," he boomed as he walked into the office. "This is a wonderful place you have here, Polly, and the town is very nice. I had a great breakfast at the diner and a nice brisk walk around town. When are we going to get to work?"

"Come on in," she said. "My friend at the Sheriff's Office is coming for lunch. I thought we'd do that in my apartment so that we don't have to worry about anyone listening to us."

Polly glanced up to see Sylvie walking in.

"I didn't think I'd see you until later," Polly said to her friend.

Sylvie looked at the tall man taking up an immense amount of space in Polly's office and said, "I'm making lunch today. I had an early class and I'm free for the rest of the day."

"Sylvie Donovan, this is Ben Seafold, an old friend of Thomas Zeller's. Ben, this is Sylvie Donovan, our chef."

He reached out to take her hand, shook it and nodded his head. "It's nice to meet you, Miss?" he looked at both of them.

"It's Mrs.," Sylvie smiled, then giggled at Polly, "Well, kind of."

"Mrs. Donovan," he amended. "What wondrous thing will you be cooking today?"

"It was going to be enchiladas, but maybe I'll do something a little more hearty."

"Enchiladas are a favorite of mine. I look forward to eating whatever you put on a plate for me. Now if you will excuse me, I'm going to take a look at those beautiful horses. I spoke with your groundskeeper this morning and he invited me to join him for a ride. Those are the first animals I've seen that are big enough not to cower when they see me coming!"

He strode out of the office and left by the side door.

"Wow," Sylvie said. "That man is impressive."

"Really?" Polly asked. "You giggled. You never giggle."

"Now I'm a little embarrassed. I did do that." Sylvie's eyes snapped at Polly. "Don't you dare tell anybody. Promise me!"

"I won't say a word," Polly zipped her lips shut, thinking she was carrying an awful lot of secrets for her friends. "Not a word. But if you giggle again, I might not be able to control myself."

"I can't make enchiladas. Those are way too common. What am I going to cook? I need to get into the kitchen and see what I have. Why didn't you tell me?"

"You're kidding me, right? He said that was fine. And we have five other guests you've never worried over."

Sylvie hadn't paid any attention to what Polly said. She was distracted as she picked her bag up and wandered out of the office. The Haunted Hallway barrier stopped her and she looked around in confusion, but finally walked to the end of it. Polly hoped she would make it to the kitchen without getting lost.

Ben had certainly grabbed Sylvie's attention. Polly scowled. She didn't need another long distance relationship happening among her friends and she knew nothing about Ben's life.

"Why am I even thinking about this," she muttered just as Jeff stepped into her doorway.

"Thinking about what?" he asked.

"Nothing. I'm being silly. What's up?"

"Are you all set for tonight? Do you have your costume ready?"

Polly hadn't told Jeff what she was wearing this evening and knew he was trying to wriggle information from her.

"I'm good. I have everything that I need."

"Have you talked to Eliseo? Does he need anything?"

"I think he's good too. We're all ready for this."

"Fine." Jeff glared at her. "You're not going to tell me, are you?"

"Nope."

"But, Lydia doesn't have you in the plan for the hallway."

"Hmmm. That's interesting. I wonder what I will be doing then?" She laughed and said, "It's going to be a surprise. That's all I will tell you."

"You're a rat."

"Yes I am and you aren't going to talk me into telling you anything, so stop trying. I seem to remember that you get a great deal of enjoyment out of surprising me every time I turn around. You have to give me this one!"

"Not very happily, I won't. I like planning surprises, not receiving them."

"Well, this will be fun and it won't disrupt you at all. I promise."

After he left, Polly shut down her computer and made sure everything was turned off so the place would be dark tonight.

When she got upstairs, she was surprised to see Luke and Leia wrestling in the middle of the floor. "Do you two do this every morning and I just miss it?" she asked. Leia playfully batted at Luke's head and rolled over on her back. He dove in and they were back at it, ignoring Polly completely.

Obiwan had been curled up on the sofa and jumped off to greet her. "At least you're glad to see me. Will you help me clean?"

He wagged his tail and followed her into the kitchen. "No, there's nothing for you here. I'm just cleaning. Go lay down." Obiwan lay down in the middle of the kitchen floor. "Not there, you dope. I'll trip over you. Go on, get moving." She nudged him with her foot until he stood up. He gave her a forlorn look and went back into the living room.

Polly kept an eye on the clock. She wanted to take Obiwan outside before Ben and Anita showed up. Once the afternoon got started, there wouldn't be much time for him.

Obiwan wasn't ready to come back in when Polly headed for the garage door, but she called and he obeyed. She sent him up the stairs, then headed for the kitchen. Sylvie was pulling pans out of the oven and Polly laughed out loud at her friend.

"You are a crazy woman," she said.

"What?"

"You made your famous fried chicken. I suppose there are mashed potatoes, too."

"Maybe."

"What else did you do?"

"I'm not telling. You'll laugh at me."

"You could have asked me to help. I would have been here."

"It wasn't a big deal. I had everything I needed. Here, is it okay if you do family style upstairs rather than me putting it on individual plates? It's nearly ready to go." Sylvie pointed at a small rubber tub filled with foil covered dishes.

"That's perfect. I'll bring it back down later. Anything else?"

"Just a minute, okay? I have rolls coming out of the oven."

"Homemade rolls, too? Are you asking this man to marry you already?"

Sylvie blushed, "Leave me alone. It's good country food." She took the rolls out of the oven and placed several in a waiting basket. "Now go. Bring things down tomorrow. Rachel will be working in the kitchen. And by the way, I want to talk to you about her sometime. No hurry, though."

"Good talk or bad talk?" Polly asked.

"Oh, good talk. I like her."

"Thank you for this," Polly nodded at the tub as she picked it up. "I'll be sure to tell him you made it especially for him."

"You wouldn't!"

"Bet me!"

Polly hurried to her apartment door before Sylvie could say anything else. As she pulled the door shut behind her, balancing the tub on a step with one hand, she heard her friend growl.

Once upstairs, she took the dishes out and set the table. Sylvie had made a squash and zucchini casserole, green beans with toasted almonds, mashed potatoes, and a tossed salad. Polly put a piece of lettuce in her mouth. Yep, she'd already put her homemade dressing on it.

The first knock at her door was Anita. "I really am sorry I didn't call you back. I'm sure you thought we were avoiding you. I have something interesting to show you, but I promise we weren't hiding it. In fact, I need your help to figure out how to get to it."

"What do you mean?"

"There was another partition on that flash drive. It's encrypted and I'm hoping you can help me figure out what the code is. We've had no luck breaking it. I knew you probably had a better idea about it than me so I didn't try very hard."

"Well, if I don't, Ben Seafold might. He has known Thomas his entire life and his father published the original Eddie Powers mysteries."

"Is that the man I saw coming up from the barn?"

"Probably. He and Eliseo went out for a ride this morning."

Anita set her bag down and looked around the room. "This is really nice. I love all the woodwork in here. It's so soft and warm. And all of these books. Look at this."

She pulled a book down and sat in the chair beside the bookshelves. Obiwan sat at her feet and looked up at her, and then nudged her ankle. She reached down with one hand while flipping through the book with the other, absentmindedly rubbing his head and he scooted closer to give her better access.

Polly watched and smiled. "Anita?" she asked.

The girl looked up from the book. "Oh! I'm sorry! It just sort of drew me in. How rude of me!"

"That's fine. Do you have a dog at home?"

Anita looked down at Obiwan. "At my parents' house. We have two Labs that have the run of the place. Bo and Luke. Why?"

"No reason." Polly chuckled.

There was another knock at the door and Anita hastily put the book back in the shelf. Polly opened the door to Ben Seafold and backed up as he filled the entryway. She wasn't sure whether it was truly his size or his presence. If she paid close attention, he wasn't all that big. He was tall, a few inches over six foot and he was solid, but he seemed to emanate a large character. When Ben was in the room, he was the center of attention.

"Come on in, Ben."

He followed her and stopped to take in the room. "This is lovely." He ran his hand over the wood on the bookshelf that encompassed the television set. "Someone does really nice work." Then he knelt down and ran his finger across the floor. "The floors on this level are wonderful, too. Radiant heat?"

"Yes. It made more sense for these big rooms."

"It does. You've created a beautiful place here, Polly. You should feel very proud of yourself."

"I didn't do the work. A good friend of mine is the contractor ... and the woodworker."

Ben caught sight of Anita in the corner. "Hello," he said.

"Ben Seafold, this is Anita Banks from the Sheriff's Office. She and I have been working together on the flash drive Thomas gave to me. Anita, this is Ben Seafold."

The two met in the middle of the living room and shook hands.

"I'm a privileged man today. I've certainly met my share of lovely women and I get to dine with two of them."

"Dinner is served," Polly said.

Ben regaled them with tales of authors he met as a child. Some were great characters, and his father always had them over to the family home for a meal before signing the final contract. There was the woman who wrote amazing children's books, but lived with 35 cats and two raccoons. He told of a man from Scotland named Jamie McFarlane, who played the flute and got drunk whenever he could, but if there was a parade within one hundred miles, he found his way into it, drunk as a skunk, playing his flute as he danced back and forth across the street. As a boy, Ben had fallen madly in love with a beautiful young woman, who he later found out wrote the most detailed murder mysteries he'd ever read. He couldn't imagine that pretty face was hiding such a sinister mind, but she sold many books for their firm.

The conversation soon turned to Thomas Zeller. Polly said, "I'm dying to know about this other partition. How do we access it?"

"We need a password," Anita responded. "I tried Annabel Lee, but that wasn't it. I tried a couple of other Edgar Allen Poe references, but nothing worked."

"Did you try Polly's name?" Ben asked. "He gave her the drive, telling her that it was for her and no one else. Thomas would have wanted her to be able to open it."

"I didn't think of that." Anita typed Polly's name into the password prompt. Nothing happened.

"What else did the two of you talk about?" Ben asked Polly. "Was there something he focused on when you were together?"

"I don't think so. We talked about everything under the sun. He loved my animals. We talked about the fact that we had probably met when he was in the Boston Public Library doing research for one of his books, and then we talked about some of our favorite places out there. But nothing would have been important enough to either of us to create a password. Let me think." She shut her eyes and set her forehead in the palms of her hands, with her elbows on the table in front of her. As she attempted to process, she was aware that they were staring at her.

"I've got nothing. Did you try any of the names that Nelly and her son used? Maybe the last iteration? Just a second." Polly opened her note program. "Lenore or Guy Brothers?"

Anita nodded. "I did go through all of those names, just in case. They didn't work."

"Try 'Eddie Powers,'" Ben said.

She typed the letters into the prompt and the drive opened. "I can't believe I didn't think of that," Anita sighed. "I feel like an idiot." She pulled the folder to her hard drive and opened it.

"He found them," Polly breathed. "He knew who they were."

"What do you mean?" Ben asked.

"Look at this picture." Polly pointed to one and Anita double-clicked to open it. The picture was of Kevin Campbell and his mother coming out of their home in Jewell. There were more pictures of Kevin's family in and around the community. "He knew they were here." The pictures were all dated the week before Thomas was killed. "That's why he hadn't talked to them yet. There wasn't time."

Another image was a scan of a newspaper clipping about the Drama night at the high school, announcing Kevin Campbell's annual recitation of *The Raven*. The time was circled.

"He was planning to attend this," Anita said. "It's so romantic."

"And so tragic," Ben echoed. "He waited his entire life to find Nelly and now that he was within days of speaking to her, he was killed. Who would do this to him?"

"I have an idea," Polly said. "But I don't know if it's because I don't like her or because I really think she is up to something."

"What do you mean?"

"There is just something really off about Natalie Dormand."

Anita had continued to click through the jpegs on the drive until Polly pointed to the screen. "Stop. Look at that. It's a scan. She sent him a photograph from Jewell. She wanted him to find them." The photograph was of a younger Genie and Kevin Campbell. The girls were toddlers. "It's Little Wall Lake. That's where Dad taught me how to swim." Polly laughed to herself. "That's why he was asking questions about rivers and lakes."

"Here's a scan of an envelope from last year," Anita said. "She must have waited a long time to send it to him. The postmark is from Des Moines."

Then Anita opened a Microsoft Word document. "Here's the manuscript: *The Long Road to You. An Eddie Powers Mystery.* You were right Polly. He was writing another one."

"Do you suppose there is a code in this one, too?"

"We can look. He has the chapters bookmarked. Are you ready?"

Anita clicked through the manuscript, reading off the first letters of each chapter to Polly. "A. L. L. I. H. A. V. E. I. S. Y. O. U. R. S. L. E. T. M. E. L. O. V. E. Y. O. U. A. G. A. I. N."

"Oh that breaks my heart," Polly said.

"There's something else here. It's a Last Will and Testament. Do you suppose Thomas knew he was in trouble?" Anita asked.

"He never said anything, or even acted like something was threatening him. I doubt it. What does it say?"

"He used a lawyer here in Bellingwood. He must have been in a hurry to get this done since he didn't wait to get home. Did he say anything to you about this, Mr. Seafold?"

"No, but he wouldn't have. He was scheduled to come up to Vermont this week for our annual Halloween jaunt. I'm sure he would have told me about it then. I'm sure he would have had plenty to tell me."

"Open it!" Polly waved at Anita's laptop.

Anita skimmed the document and then looked at the photos Thomas had taken of the Campbell family. "He put this into effect two days after he found them. Nearly everything in his estate goes to them. You're mentioned in here, Mr. Seafold, and he left something to Miss Dormand. He also emphasizes that his current publishing contract does not include any of the Eddie Powers mysteries, including this latest story."

Ben nodded. "They won't like that. Thomas Zeller's last book will be a big seller and since he's gone back to the Eddie Powers mysteries, that will draw a lot of readers, new and old alike."

He turned on Anita, "Are you any closer to figuring out who killed him?"

"We have some leads ..." she began.

Ben interrupted her, "That's what they always say when they have no idea who is responsible. I'm going to stir things up. If you think there's something off about Natalie Dormand, she's my first task. I'm going to let her know I'm here." He stood up and began pacing back and forth between the living room and the dining room. The cats looked up from their nap and then put their heads back down. They were wrapped around each other on the sofa. Obiwan had startled awake and his head was bobbing back and forth as he watched the man walk.

"You don't think Genie Campbell could have done this, do you?" Anita asked. "If she saw him taking their picture and followed him back here, he would have let her in with no problem. If she was worried about being exposed, it would be a motive. I should call the Sheriff."

"It wasn't Genie," Polly said. "And I thought they had scheduled a meeting with Aaron."

Anita nodded. "You're right and they did. But, Aaron didn't know that Thomas had found them."

"I don't think Genie did it. She loved Thomas."

"Love does cause people to do awful things, Polly," Ben said. "It's a great motivator for both good and evil."

"Well, I can't believe she would have hurt Thomas. He didn't believe it either or he wouldn't have changed his will," Polly reminded them.

"Polly, would you ask Natalie Dormand to come downstairs to the conference room? It would be quite inappropriate for me to be in her room and I think that it's high time I find out what exactly she is still doing here in Bellingwood. There are too many secrets." He turned to Anita, "Miss Banks, as a representative of the Sheriff's office, I wouldn't mind having you in the same room as well. I intend to force a few revelations from this woman and I want her to know that she can't lie any longer."

Polly checked her watch. It was three thirty. There were only a couple of hours until the Haunted Hallway would be open and she needed at least an hour to prepare. Andrew and Jason would be here soon and she needed to get them settled. She felt guilty for not helping Lydia do any more preparation and had planned to work with them this afternoon to put the finish touches on the set and make sure things were ready to go. But Ben's eyes were flashing. He was intent on moving forward.

"I have a few responsibilities," she said. "I need to make some phone calls in order to let folks know I won't be available until later, if we are going to do this today."

"I'm sorry," Ben sat back down. "I should probably wait until tomorrow when all of this news isn't quite so fresh and I've calmed down. Miss Banks, would you mind copying the contents of that flash drive to this one for me?" He handed her a drive.

Anita looked at Polly, who nodded. They'd seen everything on the drive and if Ben wanted to look over the manuscript and other documents, there was no longer any need to keep them hidden.

"Give him everything," Polly said. "He knew Thomas during those early years. If there is anything we might have missed because we didn't have context for the information, he'll find it."

"You aren't going to do anything that will get me in trouble with my boss, are you?" Anita smiled at Ben as she slid the drive into her laptop.

"I'll keep quiet until you tell me I can talk about it and I promise to stay away from Miss Dormand as long as possible," he assured her. "But can we corner the woman soon?"

Both Anita and Ben looked at the dishes on Polly's dining room table. Before either of them could say anything, Polly stopped them. "I've got this. You go on." She put her hand on Ben's forearm. "We'll be done with the kids tonight by seven thirty and I'm sure we'll be eating together. It's kind of what we do. I'd love for my friends to meet you if you want to join us."

He smiled. "That sounds wonderful. I will come find you."

CHAPTER TWENTY-FIVE

"Oh! There you are! Have you seen everything all lit up?" Andrew Donovan was as excited as a nine year old could be. He ran into the living room from the back steps. "Have you seen it?"

She finished filling the dishwasher and turned it on. "I haven't yet. So it's pretty cool?"

"It's awesome. I can't wait for tonight." Andrew had been given the option of handing out candy or working as a tour guide. He would be dressed as a zombie and had been practicing his lamed zombie walk.

"I can't either," Polly smiled.

"You still aren't going to tell me what you are going to be?" he asked.

"Nope. It's a secret."

"Jason won't tell either. It isn't fair." His half-plea didn't quite make it. Polly knew that he was as excited about the surprises as he was the evening.

"Would you mind taking Obiwan out?" she asked. "I promised him you would, and I need to make sure they don't need help downstairs."

"Sure! Come on Obiwan." Polly followed the two of them down the back steps and went into the kitchen.

"Hey Sylvie," she said when she walked in, hoping to not startle the woman who was stirring something in a large pot on the stove.

"Hi there. How was lunch?"

"It was amazing. Did Ben stop down?"

Sylvie grinned. "He did. I invited him to join us for supper after trick or treating and he said you already did."

"A little crush?"

It didn't take much to make Sylvie blush again. "I don't know what's gotten into me. I never act like this. But don't you dare say anything in front of my boys!" She brandished the ladle, "Or I will beat you."

"I promise. But it's kind of cute."

Sylvie shook the ladle again, "Stop it."

Polly grinned as she walked into the hallway. Her friends were all there.

Lydia looked up when she saw her. "What do you think?" She nudged a piece of netting to one side, adjusting something or other that she saw.

"Can I see it with all of the lighting effects?" Polly asked, "Or should I wait until later."

"Aaron?" Lydia called out. "How are you doing over there? Polly wants to see this in all its glory."

"One minute, love of my life," he responded. "I'm on the floor and it takes me time to get up."

"He's adding fog to the coffin Henry built. That thing is going to glow."

Polly heard grunting and moaning and then he said, "Alright everyone, lights are going off ... turn on your effects."

"Follow me," Lydia whispered.

"Why are we whispering?"

"Because it's haunted, why do you think?"

The first effect switched on - black lights - then Polly saw a strobe light on the other side of the wall. Fog began creeping around the floor and she heard the sound of something heavy being dropped. She whispered to Lydia, "What was that?"

Lydia took her hand and they began walking. The first scene was black material with a black light aimed at it. Hands and a face pressed at the fabric as if they were trying to break through. "What's that?" she asked.

"It's Lycra and that's Andy on the other side. She didn't want to dress up. But it's pretty creepy, isn't it!"

"It's way creepy."

Behind a glass panel, there was an orange glow and as Polly peered at it, the top of a guillotine dropped, making her jump. To her right she saw fog curling around the casket which leaned against the doorway to the lounge. The casket's lid slowly swung open, revealing Rachel inside.

The girl giggled, "I'm going to be a vampire, but I don't have my costume on yet."

There were snakes and spiders on the rocks and up the interior wall. The strobe light effects made them seem as if they were writhing and moving. Lydia pointed to a corner. "Beryl will be there, dressed as a ghastly clown," and above that space was gigantic webbing and a large spider hanging from the ceiling. They rounded the corner and a ghost drifted down, hovering over her head. A fan blew its fabric, creating the illusion of flight.

"Len is in the conference room. The ghost is hanging by fishing line and he can reel it up and down at will," Lydia said. "Aaron will be dressed as Frankenstein and he's going to be located in the doorway to the office. I wanted him to be the last character the kids see. He'll know if they're okay to see him or if he needs to hold back. I trust him."

A skeleton hanging in the corner of the interior wall hovered over a collection of tombstones and rocks. A small gargoyle finished the scene. They turned back toward the front door where a large cauldron hung over a fire. Flickering lights and fog coming from a pile of logs and twigs created the final effect. Lydia said, "I will be here dressed in my full witch regalia. Aaron asked if I was going to have ugly moles on my green face and I informed him that any witch worth her stuff would ensure her face wouldn't be ugly. So what do you think?"

"I think it will be fabulous!" Polly said. "This is perfect. The kids are going to want to go through this a few times. Beryl will probably be the scariest thing they experience, though."

"Hey!" Beryl's voice came around the other side of the partition. "I take exception to that."

"You're an evil clown. How could it be any worse?" Polly laughed. "So you're ready to go here?"

"All we need to do is get everyone into costume. Jeff will turn the speakers on at five forty-five and most of the kids will be walking between six and seven thirty. When are you and Eliseo planning to show up?"

Lydia was the only person who knew what their plans were. Polly couldn't wait. "We'll be back here by six thirty, don't you think? It shouldn't take that long to scare the entire community."

"That sounds wonderful. Is Jason excited?"

"I think so. It's going to take us an hour to get the horses ready and all of us into costume. Mark and Henry should be down at the barn now. I can hardly wait."

Lydia hugged her. "I can't tell you how much fun I've had with this. Thank you for letting me get creepy with your home."

"This is awesome! The town won't know what hit them."

"I love you, Polly," Lydia said. "Have fun tonight and I'll see you when you get back."

"You have fun, too. I might have to do one last walkthrough with everyone in costume, so don't let them break it down until I've seen it, okay?"

"Got it. Now scoot and enjoy your evening."

Polly ran down to the barn and when she opened the door, found it bustling with activity. "What can I do?" she asked.

Eliseo came out of Nan's stall. "I haven't had a chance to drape the wagon yet. Why don't you start on that. The fabric is there on the bench."

Polly gathered up the black muslin. Eliseo had put a pair of scissors and box of tacks on top of it. He thought of everything.

The wagon Henry had restored earlier that summer sat under the overhang. It was painted black with blue trim, and the material would mute the glossy finish. She swooped the muslin along the outer edges of the wagon, tacking it to the top. Then she cut strips and wove them in and out of the spokes of the wheels, fastening the ends. Stepping back, she admired her work.

"Nice job, pretty girl. Eliseo nearly has the horses ready. We should probably get dressed pretty soon."

"Hi there, hot stuff," Polly turned to kiss Henry. "Are you feeling grim tonight?"

Henry had agreed to dress as the Grim Reaper and ride in the back of the wagon with a coffin. "I'm feeling very grim. There are souls to be gathered and it's not a task to be taken lightly. You are the woman I love and you gather bodies as a hobby, so it's up to me to deal with them for you" He kissed her once again. "You make it difficult for a man to feel grim, but I'll give it my best effort. We should go inside."

They went back into the barn. Eliseo beckoned Polly over to Demi's stall. "What do you think?"

They had commissioned a pair of blue and black brocade forehead coverings for the two horses who would be pulling the wagon. It gave Demi an eerie look. Matching blankets would hang over their backs.

"I think they're too beautiful to be pulling a funeral hearse, but that's okay. What about Nan and Nat?"

She followed him to Nan's stall. Eliseo would be costumed as the headless horseman. Nan's head had been wrapped in loose black fabric that looked like leather. With her black cape, she looked like a ringwraith's horse from *Lord of the Rings*.

"Oh my," Polly exclaimed. "How did you do that?"

"It took a little finagling, so I figured that if I was doing one, I'd do two. Nat has the same thing and it will look great with Jason hanging over the horse." Jason was the Headless Horseman's latest victim, hanging like a corpse over Nat's back.

"I never thought I would have so much fun with these horses," Polly said. "I couldn't have done it without you, Eliseo. Thanks for helping make my crazy ideas real."

"You are the only person who could have talked me into this, but the horses have fun playing with us." He checked the time. "We'd better get ready. Do you have everything you need?"

"I'm good. Have you seen Mark?"

"I'm right here, dollface." Mark stopped and looked at Nan. "Okay, that's incredible."

"You look pretty good yourself," Polly said. Mark was dressed all in black, except for the white blouse. A small bowtie at his neck and a black top hat made him the perfect mortician to drive the hearse.

"Well, guys, I'm probably the only one who needs privacy to change my clothes. I'm taking the empty stall over here. Stay out." Polly had ordered her costume online and when the boxes came in, brought them down to the barn so no one else could peek.

The blue and black brocade gown matched the material she'd used for the Demi and Daisy. A five-layered black tulle, floor-length, hooded cape with black roses and leaves sewn into the hem would keep her warm enough. She had talked to Rachel about makeup and put on just enough to give her face an unhealthy pallor. Even though it might not be seen by all, a few drops of red on her chin made her smile. Black slippers on her feet and long black gloves on her hands and forearms finished the look. The only mirror she had was the small one in her makeup case and Polly propped it up on one of the boxes, trying to get a glimpse of the full effect, to no avail.

"It's just going to have to do," she said to herself and opened the door back into the alley of the barn. She stepped out.

"It will do," Henry was standing beside the door and grinned at her.

"Have you been here the whole time?" she asked.

"No, I just wanted to make sure you had all the privacy you needed."

"Like anyone down here would intrude."

He shrugged, "You never know. I'm still not sure if I trust that Mark fella."

Polly spun on him, "You're kidding, right?"

"A little bit." He had his long, black robe on, but had pushed the hood off his head and onto his shoulders. "You're pretty sexy for a soul-less vampire. You might be the only one in town who holds no interest for me on the business end of things. You know what that means, don't you?"

"No, what does that mean?"

"If I can't have your soul, I get the rest of you."

"You can have the rest of me. But later." She checked the time. "We need to get moving."

"Mark and Eliseo are hitching the horses to the wagon and Jason is trying to figure out the best way to drape himself across the horse and look dead."

"We really are having much too much fun with this holiday, aren't we!"

"If I told you that for the last few years I've turned the lights off and hid in my bedroom to avoid having children bother me, would you believe me?"

Polly swatted his arm. "I'd believe you and tell you that you were awful. What was I doing last year?" She stopped and thought. "Oh. That was the night that Joey beat Doug up. Can you believe that was a year ago?"

Polly's ex-boyfriend, Joey Delancy, had come to Bellingwood to talk her into returning to Boston. He had ended up kidnapping her, but before that, had ransacked Sycamore House and beaten Doug until Billy stopped him. The man's delusions had him seeing every male figure, from twenty-year old Doug Randall to Aaron Merritt, as competitors for Polly's heart.

Henry pulled her close. "That's one thing I'm glad is a year behind you."

"Me too." Polly gave him a quick kiss and then said, "We should get moving. It's that time."

They went outside. Jason was holding the reins for both Nat and Nan, who were watching as Eliseo and Mark finished harnessing Demi and Daisy to the wagon. Mark adjusted the blanket on Daisy's back and turned around.

"Well, Polly, you look perfectly delectable. No. Wait. You're supposed to *do* the devouring. I'm sure everyone in Bellingwood will be terrified of the new vampire in town."

Polly gathered her skirts and curtsied. "Thank you. That's exactly what I want. Now, will you help me up?"

Henry climbed up first and gave her a hand, then crawled into the back of the wagon, sitting on the coffin. Mark followed them and sat beside Polly in the front.

"We've been here before, my dear."

"Someday you are going to have to teach me how to do all of this so I'm not relying on you."

"But then I'd never have any fun! I like hanging out with you people. You come up with the craziest things for us to do." He craned his neck. "How are you doing back there, Henry?"

"I'm good. Don't dump me out, okay?"

"Got it, but no promises. I'm not a big fan of death hovering behind me."

They watched Eliseo lift Jason up and over Nat's back. "How does that feel, Jason?" Eliseo asked.

"It's weird. I practiced on a hay bale, but this isn't anything like that." He was lying across a saddle and a rope had been slipped through the cinch so he could hold on. With gloves on his hands, he wrapped the rope so it looked as if he were tied to the horse.

Eliseo slung Nat's lead over his own saddle, lifted himself on to Nan and closed up the top of his costume.

"Well, that's just creepy," Mark muttered.

"That's what we're going for!" Polly laughed.

Mark motioned for Eliseo and Jason to head out and the little procession left the barn. They headed for downtown and then in order to cover as much of the town as possible, split into two groups. The plan was to travel through the residential areas where families and kids were walking and by six twenty or so, head back to Sycamore House and plant themselves in the front parking lot. Henry took his place at the back of the wagon.

Polly tried her hardest to not smile and put her best evil eye on. Every once in a while, she rose out of her seat and pointed at a group of children, causing them to scream and cluster together. She loved seeing the kids watch them pass, pointing and whispering at each other and then giggling in their fright. So far, Halloween was turning out to be a huge success.

They finally headed back toward Sycamore House and stopped at a corner to wait as Eliseo and Jason approached. Children tentatively walked into the street and then ran back to the safety of the sidewalk when they realized that Eliseo had no head and that the horses looked spookier than they should. Nan and Nat walked along as if they carried dead people every day.

Mark pulled into the parking lot and angled Demi and Daisy toward the front door, while Eliseo positioned Nat and Nan on the sidewalk. A large group of children were coming out of the front door and their mouths dropped open when they saw what was in front of them. Mark climbed down and then lifted Polly to the ground. When she pulled her hood back and bared her teeth at the kids, they screamed. Some clutched their parents, others started to laugh. Henry climbed across the seat and strode to the front door, causing everyone to back up. He silently took his place on the other side of the door and stood as a dark sentinel under the front light, his hood completely covering his face.

More cars pulled in and kids piled out, approaching the front door with trepidation. When neither Henry nor Eliseo moved, they continued to step forward. The door creaked open and Polly tried not to giggle as the initial darkness surprised them. Andrew Donovan shuffled out and using his shoulder to do so, beckoned the group inside. Some parents followed, others tried to engage the Grim Reaper. No one knew who he was and Henry remained silent.

Mark climbed back up into the wagon and Polly took her place between the horses, speaking quietly to the two of them and rubbing their noses. She was so proud to be part of this. Her friends had done the work and her horses were the stars of the show. A grin began to break on her lips and she quickly reminded herself that she was supposed to be a scary vampire, so she reached in and kissed Demi and let the smile flood her face.

CHAPTER TWENTY-SIX

Finally, the flow of children slowed to a trickle and Polly said to Eliseo, "I think the horses have earned their keep. We can call this a success."

"Whew! I'll be glad to get rid of this costume," she heard him say, even though she couldn't see his face.

"How are you doing, Jason?"

"Jason isn't here," came the response. "His body fell asleep a long time ago. All you have left is a zombie."

"Are you going to be okay?"

"I'm thirteen. I'm great!" He let go of the rope and slid off Nat's back and then stretched once he stood upright.

"I'll be down after a while to help you get them brushed down and settled," she said.

Mark had driven up behind her. "You have a house full of guests. The three of us can take care of them."

Henry joined them. "The four of us. We'll be done in a flash and these poor horses can go back to their peace and quiet."

Polly kissed him again, "Thank you. All of you. Come on up when you're finished, Sylvie has been cooking up a storm." She watched as four of her favorite men took her horses back to the barn, then turned and went inside. Andrew was there to meet her. He didn't say a word, but took her hand in his. The sun had long since gone down and darkness overtook them. She knew that Andy was behind the Lycra, but jumped when hands pushed out and a face pressed against the fabric. There were strange smells and sounds as the haunted house soundtrack played and fog filled the hallway. When the coffin opened and a vampire surged forward, Polly stepped back. It was all so real. Beryl's clown was hideous. The painted on smile was evil and the costume had as much black as it did red. She cackled a little and moved toward the two of them, causing Polly to pull Andrew behind her. She knew that it was her friend, but in this costume, all she could do was be afraid.

Andrew laughed and pushed them past Beryl, beyond the flowing ghost. Aaron's shadow loomed ahead of Polly and then he stepped out of the darkness, an immense monster bent on destruction. She gave a nervous giggle and was relieved to finally see the candy cauldron, but jumped when Lydia came out of the shadow, the long hair of her black wig sprayed into chaos with bats and bugs as part of the mess. Her long black cloak covered what seemed to be a tattered, torn and filthy wedding dress, covered with more bugs and bats. Lydia had long gloves on her hands, once white, but now torn and dirty as well.

"That was fantastic," Polly breathed.

Andrew dropped out of character and said, "I know! I've been having a blast all night! A lot of kids were scared, but it wasn't so bad. None of them cried, did they?"

Lydia's face changed as she smiled down at him. "No, they didn't cry and Aaron was able to be a monster all night long."

By the time Henry and the others had come back from the barn, there hadn't been any trick or treaters for at least fifteen minutes. Polly shut the outside lights off and turned the interior lights back on. She watched as each person emerged from their respective hideaways and peeled off the outer layers of their costumes.

Sylvie was all smiles when they arrived at the kitchen and

Polly texted Ben to come down and join them.

The meal was simple: chili, with cheese and onions as additional toppings, tossed salad and warm cornbread. Polly hung back to wait for Ben and waved when she saw him round the corner.

"What an interesting group of people," he remarked. "It looks as if you've all come off a movie set."

Polly introduced him to her friends as they went through the line. It didn't take long for him to strike up a conversation with Aaron and they were still talking as they carried their food into the auditorium. Sylvie looked a little disappointed that Ben hadn't taken more than a moment to say hello and thank her for the food.

Polly's heart sank. Even if nothing came of this, at the very least she would like Sylvie to have someone pay a little attention to her. She waited for her friend to fill a tray and the two of them walked into the auditorium. Andrew was holding court with Mark, Andy, Len and Beryl, telling them over and over again about the different reactions the kids had to the evening. Billy, Doug and Rachel were sitting with Eliseo, Jason and Jeff, laughing at something. Lydia and Aaron had taken seats with Henry and Ben. There were two chairs left open at that table.

"Come on," Polly said. "It will be fine."

"I'm being such a junior high girl," Sylvie whispered. "I know better than this."

"Be a junior high girl tonight. Flirt and giggle, enjoy yourself. It won't hurt a thing."

"I might damage my sons," Sylvie laughed. "They've never seen their mother be flirty. I'll be good."

"Whatever. Come on."

"The evening was quite a success," Aaron said. "I'm proud of these women." He hugged his wife to him. "You did a good thing tonight. The kids won't soon forget this experience."

"We're going to make it even better next year," Lydia said. "I have more ideas and I'm going shopping this weekend while things are on sale."

Ben asked, "Is this the first year for this?"

"It is," Aaron responded. "And it looks like I'm going to be Frankenstein's monster for a long time."

Lydia nodded and turned to Ben, "I'm sorry for the loss of your friend."

"It is a real loss. I just hope you can find who did this to him. If there's anything I can do ..."

Aaron glanced at Polly and then back at Ben. "Do you have any influence with his lawyers? We'd like to get a look at his old will to see if there's anything in there that might provide a motive, but they're being lawyers and aren't helpful."

"I'll make a call in the morning," Ben replied. "But surely, your Anita told you we found a will that he executed here in Bellingwood a few weeks ago."

"She did, but the old will might give us some idea of who else was involved in his life."

"Thomas was actually pretty solitary, especially when he started writing. I'm surprised that he made friends with Polly here."

"He made friends with all of us," Lydia said. "We had several wonderful meals with him. He was so interesting."

"Then that had to have been Polly's influence. He was always a bit of a loner, only had a few friends, but when he was working, solitude was the only thing he treasured."

"Our Polly has that effect on people." Lydia reached out and patted Polly's arm. "We adore her and I am so grateful she moved to Bellingwood."

Ben had cleaned his bowl. He picked up his tray. "Excuse me, I'm going to have some more of this wonderful chili. Can I bring anything back with me?"

No one responded and he walked out the door. When Jason saw what was happening, he followed suit and soon others were doing the same. When Ben came back in, he sat down, with a bewildered look on his face.

"Who is that woman?" he asked.

"What woman?" Polly looked at him questioningly.

"She has red hair and is about this tall," he reached his hand above his head. "She was going back up the stairs."

"Oh, that's probably Lila Fletcher. Why?"

"She looks quite familiar. I'm sure I've seen her before, but I can't tell you where."

"Maybe you've seen her picture somewhere. I know she does write. I don't think she's published any novels, but she's probably in your circle somehow," Polly said.

"Maybe, but that doesn't seem like it." He shrugged his shoulders and dug into the fresh bowl of chili. "This is good," he told Sylvie. "You are an amazing cook. Maybe I should steal you and open a restaurant for you in Vermont."

"Polly would never let me leave and those two boys," she pointed at Andrew and Jason, "wouldn't know what to do if they didn't have her in their lives."

"If you ever decide to run away from home, call me first and I'll set you up."

Sylvie giggled, then clapped her hand across her mouth and blushed, looked at Polly. She quietly put her hand back down in her lap and Polly watched her take a deep breath.

Ben turned back to Aaron, "Sheriff, do you think I might get a chance to meet Genie and Kevin Campbell before I leave? I'd like to invite them to visit me so I can tell them more about Thomas and his search for them. It is really a shame that he got so close, but was unable to complete the journey he'd started so long ago."

"I think we can work something out. They are going to have to go to California at some point to deal with paperwork. I've asked them to contact a lawyer."

"Well, I think they can afford a good one now," Polly interrupted.

"They don't know about that yet. We'll keep it under wraps for a few more days, if you don't mind." Aaron looked pointedly at Polly. "Do you think you can do that?"

"Hey! If it weren't for me, you wouldn't know about them and if it weren't for me, Ben wouldn't be here."

She felt Henry chuckling beside her and looked at Aaron's face to see his eyes twinkling in laughter.

"Okay. Whatever. Leave me alone," she grumped.

Eliseo tapped Jason on the shoulder and they stood up, carrying their trays. Soon Len and Andy did the same.

"What are they doing?" Polly asked Lydia.

"We're going to tear this down tonight. Eliseo says he has a place in the storage shed where it can be stored until next year."

"Then I need to change into something a little more practical," Polly gestured at her gown. "This will never do."

It didn't take long before things were stacked neatly in the hallway outside the offices. Sylvie and Beryl had cleaned up the kitchen and finally everyone had driven away. Henry walked upstairs with Polly to her apartment.

"I'm not coming in tonight. I know you have to take Obiwan out, but you should get some sleep. Tomorrow and Saturday are going to be huge days for you."

He kissed her and they held on to each other for a moment. When Polly looked up, she saw Grey Linder peering out the door at her. He quickly shut the door, but she could tell that he looked even worse than he had in the last few days.

"Come inside for a minute, will you?" she asked Henry, unlocking the door.

He followed her inside. "What's up?"

"Grey Linder was watching the apartment and I don't know what's going on with him. I want him to think you're here tonight for a while."

"Are you worried that he's going to hurt you?"

"No, I think I can take him. I'm more worried that he won't show up some morning and I'll find him dead in his bed. I don't need that."

Henry chuckled, then asked, "Are you sure you don't want me to stay tonight? I can go get my things."

"Your truck is out back, right?"

"Yes."

"I just want you to leave that way."

"Polly, his room is in the back. He'll see me leave."

She sighed. "Of course he will. Oh well. Don't worry. I'll be fine. He's been creepy since he's been here and hasn't done anything yet."

"If you're sure."

"I am. But I'm going to walk downstairs with you and Obiwan."

They walked with the dog and once Polly and Obiwan were back in the apartment, Henry left to go home. She watched him drive away, checked the locks and lights in Sycamore House and sat down on the edge of her bed.

"It's a little spooky around here sometimes, but tonight was fun," she told the animals. The cats had already found their place on her bed and Obiwan jumped up to join them. Polly took a few minutes to hang her gown in the closet, running her fingers over the brocade. "Sometimes I think that being able to wear this type of clothing on a regular basis would be wonderful." She pulled off her jeans and t-shirt and dropped a night shirt over her head. "And other times I'm very glad that I get to wear jeans."

Obiwan waited until she settled on her pillow and then curled up behind her. He was snoring before she fell asleep, so she reached around and rubbed his neck. "You're a good boy, now roll over."

CHAPTER TWENTY-SEVEN

Inside the shed, Polly pulled work gloves off her fingers. She and Eliseo had just finished stacking the last of the lumber from the Haunted House set and headed back to the auditorium. Henry and Jeff were hanging lights from the ceiling in the auditorium and the tables were in place. Jeff had purchased six immense gold and silver masks to hang from the ceiling and several large standing masks to be placed strategically around the room.

She was steaming the wrinkles and folds out of dark blue tablecloths when she saw Aaron in the doorway.

"What's up?" She joined him in the hall.

"I know you're busy and I should have called, but could I have a few minutes of your time?"

"Sure." Polly strode across the room to tell Eliseo that she was going to be gone for a while. He nodded and smiled. Polly wondered if he assumed she'd never come back. Something was always interrupting her.

When she went back into the hallway, she was surprised to see Genie and Kevin Campbell there.

"You don't have school today?" she asked him.

"I took the day off," he replied. "My mind has been so distracted this week, I couldn't concentrate on classes. When the Sheriff called to tell me that a friend of my father's wanted to meet us, mom and I decided to do it as quickly as possible."

"Would you all like to come up to my apartment? I can call Ben and ask him to join us there."

Aaron nodded, "That might be best."

"Come on up. I'll put a pot of coffee on."

They followed Polly to her apartment. As had become her habit lately, she glanced back at Grey Linder's room while she unlocked her front door. He was peeking out again. She could have sworn she saw shock on his face before he quietly pressed the door shut.

"Please make yourself comfortable. I'll call Ben and make the coffee. Aaron, could I see you in the kitchen?"

He followed her and filled the coffee pot with water while she dialed Ben's number.

"Good morning, Miss Giller! I've just returned from a wonderful breakfast at your diner and a brisk walk around this lovely town. What do you have for me?"

"I have Genie and Kevin Campbell in my apartment and they would like to meet you. Do you have time?"

"That would be wonderful! I will be right there."

"The door is unlocked. Come on in, you don't need to knock," she said. "I'll see you in a bit."

Then she turned to Aaron and quietly said, "I don't know what is going on with Grey Linder in the back room, but he has been watching everything I do. He peeks through the door and just now I am certain he was shocked when he saw the Campbells."

"I'm not sure what you want me to do, Polly. I have no reason to bother him. Curiosity isn't an offense yet."

"I know, but I think there is something weird about him. Can I talk you into checking on him to make sure he's okay? He's gotten thinner and his face is starting to match his first name. I don't know if he's drinking or dying or what."

Aaron took a deep breath. "I don't suppose a friendly check in would hurt. I will knock on his door."

"Thank you."

He left the apartment and she finished making coffee. "Do either of you like cream or sugar in your coffee?" she asked.

"Yes please," Genie Campbell said. "Can I help you?"

"No, I have it, but thank you," Polly replied.

Ben Seafold walked in the front door and his presence immediately filled the room. Before Polly could make her way to them, he approached the Campbell's with his hand out.

"Hello!" He took Kevin Campbell's hand. "Son, even if I didn't know you were Thomas Zeller's boy, I would have recognized him in you. You have his eyes and my goodness, you have your beautiful mother's cheekbones. You must be Nelly."

"Once upon a time I was Thomas's Nelly, but today I am Genie Campbell," she said, standing to greet him.

"I'm sorry. Miss Polly told me that was your name now. I'm awfully glad to meet the two of you. I only wish Thomas were here to join us. He loved you very much."

"I wish he were here as well," she said. "Until Miss Giller showed us the code in his books, I assumed he no longer cared."

"He never stopped thinking about you or looking for you. Polly, do you have that last set of pictures?"

"Yes!" she said, "I forgot that you hadn't seen them yet." She brought a tray over and set it down on the coffee table in front of them, then went back for her laptop. She quickly logged on and brought up the files they had found the other day. Polly sat on the floor on the other side of the table and showed the Campbells the photographs Thomas had taken of them in Jewell.

"He found us." Genie Campbell breathed through her words. "Why didn't he say something?"

"If I know my friend, he was trying to come up with a good plan to meet you. He wouldn't have wanted to surprise you on the street or make you feel as if he was threatening you."

Polly heard sirens coming through town toward Sycamore House. She jumped up when they stopped outside her home. "What in the world?"

Both she and Ben arrived at her front door at the same time.

Grey Linder's door was open and Aaron was bent over a body on the floor. She ran across the hall to see Aaron doing chest compressions.

"What did you do to him?" she asked.

"He took one look at me and had a heart attack." Aaron nodded around the room. "I think he's been drinking himself into a stupor for quite a while."

"Can I help?"

"Just move out of the way so Sarah can take over for me here."

Polly jumped back when she realized the EMTs were coming across the large open hallway. Sarah smiled at her. "Really, Polly. An elevator, please!"

"I'm going to tell Jeff that we can only put young, healthy people up on this floor. Anyone that looks like they might need you will be in the addition. I promise!"

Aaron stood up and moved into the hall with Polly.

"Did he say anything before he passed out?" Polly asked.

"He did."

She waited a beat and when she realized that he wasn't going to tell her anything more, she pushed at him with her shoulder, "Well what did he say?"

Aaron rolled his eyes at her, "He pointed at your apartment and told me she was innocent. Then, down he went. Thankfully I have the reflexes of a fox and caught him before he hit his head on anything or broke something while falling."

She chuckled, "I'll be sure to tell Lydia that you are her fox. What do you suppose he meant by that?"

"I have an idea or two."

Polly hated it when he withheld information, so she pressed him. "Do you think he killed that policeman in San Francisco?"

"Now don't be putting words in my mouth, Polly Giller. I didn't say that at all."

"Why do you suppose he was here in Bellingwood at the same time as Thomas Zeller? And why didn't Thomas recognize him?"

Aaron glanced down at the man as the EMTs pushed the gurney past them. "Look at him. That was forty-five years ago. I would bet that he looks nothing like his younger self."

"So you do think that's him."

The Sheriff grinned at her. "I don't think anything until I have more information. Now, I'm going to leave you with the Campbells. I have phone calls to make. Some of us are working on a Friday morning," he taunted as he started to walk away.

"Hey," she followed him and took his arm. "This is your fault."

Aaron stopped at the stairway and grinned back at her. "You are an easy target, Polly Giller. I'll talk to you later."

She went back into her apartment and was glad to see that Ben, Kevin and Genie were talking.

"What happened?" Genie asked.

"The man across the hall had a heart attack. Did you ever hear of a man named Grey Linder?"

Ben Seafold turned back to Genie, waiting to see if she recognized the name.

"He's a poet, isn't he?" Kevin asked. "He wrote some dark stuff back in the nineties, but I haven't heard anything about him since then. It wasn't very good, but people bought his book because it fed their angst."

Ben laughed, "I can't believe you remember that, son."

"I was going through a poetry phase of my own and thought I ought to pay attention to my contemporaries."

Polly sat back down on the floor and browsed the internet. When she found what she wanted, she turned it toward Genie Campbell. "Do you recognize him?"

The woman's face lost all of its color and she reached out and grabbed her son's hand.

"What is it mom? That's Grey Linder. Do you know him?"

"That's Douglas Winters," she gasped.

Polly sighed, "I thought so. How did you recognize him when Thomas didn't?"

"Thomas didn't spend any time with Doug. He and I were together before Thomas got to San Francisco and Doug didn't like Thomas very much. Said he was a punk and a hack. I did my best to keep them apart, so I doubt that they spent more than a few hours in the same room."

"How did you end up in the same place with him that day?"

"Thomas and I had a fight that morning. It was all my fault. I had just found out I was pregnant and I wanted him to leave the Haight with me. I was ready to get clean so the baby would have a good life. Thomas was still young and enamored with the Bohemian lifestyle. He wasn't ready to clean up and still needed to sow his wild oats. I didn't have the heart to tell him that I was carrying his baby, so I went to Douglas. He owed me enough money for a bus ticket out of there."

She dropped her head. "Then, we also had a terrible fight. I just couldn't win. He didn't have the money. He told me that all he had to do was get out on the street and sell some of the weed he'd been growing. I was so mad. Then all of a sudden the world erupted. A cop broke down the front door, screaming and waving his gun around. I was already out the back door when I heard the shot. I hadn't gotten two houses away and they were talking about a cop being killed. Everyone knew I was there, so I kept running."

"You didn't run with Douglas Winters?"

"Oh no. I wanted nothing to do with him. I hitched a couple of rides out of town and decided to re-start my life."

Polly looked at Genie and asked, "Do you think he would have killed Thomas?"

The woman was shocked, then said, "I suppose he could have, but I'd be surprised. Douglas wasn't a killer. He had a gun in the house to protect his weed. He kept it in the stupid pocket of that reclining chair he sat in all the time. I think the shooting was purely reflex that day and he's been hiding ever since."

"Well, if he thought Thomas was going to rat him out, would he have killed to save his skin?

Genie thought about it before she spoke. "I don't know anything for sure, but I wonder if he realized that Thomas was looking for me. He wouldn't have killed him before Thomas found me."

Polly excused herself and went out into the hallway and called Aaron.

"I'm tired of hauling people out of Sycamore House, Polly," he laughed.

"Hopefully the last one isn't dead."

There was no response.

"Oh Aaron, tell me he's not dead."

"I'm just messing with you. They're working on him. But he hasn't died yet. What's up?"

"I showed his picture to Genie Campbell and she identified him as Douglas Winters. I thought you might want to know that. And she doesn't think that he killed Thomas Zeller."

"I don't either," Aaron replied. "Grey Linder is frail and was very drunk that night. That kind of drunk doesn't happen in an hour and we didn't find any blood in his room either. Thanks for asking, though. It makes my next phone calls easier."

"Next phone calls?"

"I'm calling San Francisco. With Winters in the hospital and Eleanor Farber, or whatever she calls herself here in Iowa, they might want to send someone out to get this cleaned up. But don't say anything yet, okay?"

"I won't."

"Do you promise?"

"I won't," she growled. "You know I have no problem siccing your wife on you, don't you?"

"That's why I have to get my licks in when I can. I'll talk to you later, Polly. And thanks."

She went back into her apartment and Ben stood up with Genie and Kevin Campbell. "Polly, we're going to get out of your hair. I have a few things of Thomas's that I would like his son to have and they've invited me to their home for the afternoon. I look forward to meeting his granddaughters."

He stepped over and gave her a quick hug. "Thank you for bringing us together. I lost a very good friend when Thomas was killed, but I look forward to getting to know his family better."

Polly walked them to the door. Genie stopped and took her hand. "I had no idea that my life was going to become the center of a strange vortex of events. Thank you for making it easier for us to deal with all of this and thank you for trusting us. I do wish that I'd known long ago that Thomas was looking for me, because I was ready to stop running. What a foolish woman I've been."

"Come on, mother," Kevin said, taking her arm. "No more talk of foolishness. You did the best you could with what you knew. We'll not have any regrets today."

She smiled at him and shrugged, "He doesn't let me get too morose. I'm thankful to have him."

"We'll be here tomorrow night," Kevin said. "My daughters have been helping my wife sew costumes for the Masquerade Ball. I guess one benefit of having a drama department and a family of seamstresses is access to things that most others don't have."

"I look forward to seeing you!" Polly said and watched as they walked down the front steps.

What a morning. She looked at the door to Grey Linder's room. The thought of the filth in there bothered her, but she knew she didn't have permission to go in yet. He was paid up until ... huh. She should ask Jeff about that.

Polly ran down the steps and into the auditorium. The transformation was gorgeous. Jeff and Henry had begun in the center. They had hung a large, glittering chandelier of crystals which reflected the strings of white lights that were strung out in a circle to the walls. Henry was on a ladder with a six foot silver mask, working to affix it to a chain coming down from the ceiling while Jeff stood below him, watching the action.

"Jeff?" she asked as she approached.

"Hi Polly, what do you think?"

"I think it's amazing. But I have a question."

"Sure, what do you want to know?"

"Has Grey Linder paid for his room beyond today?"

He bit his lower lip and then said, "No. In fact he was behind. But I don't suppose he really thought about paying me while he was being rushed out of here on a stretcher."

"So, I could get in there and clean the place up and not be crossing any boundaries?"

"Well, that's kind of an iffy boundary. Why?"

"Because when I looked in there the room was totally trashed. We haven't been in for a while to change sheets and the room is littered with empty bottles of alcohol. I can hardly stand it, knowing that it's that filthy."

"Oh. Well, then, I'd say you have every right to go in. I can't imagine he's going to get back here in time to do pay us. Honestly, if he's in the hospital, I doubt he'll come back at all."

Eliseo had come up behind them while she was talking and said, "Let me bring a trash can. We'll haul the empty bottles out first so I can recycle them. Then, we'll work on the trash."

"Are you okay leaving all of this?" she asked, looking around the room.

"I'm good for now. I'll be up in a few minutes."

"Thanks." Polly went back upstairs and swiped open Grey Linder's room, stepped in and then stepped right back out. The room reeked of sweat and booze and she didn't know what else. The first thing she did was strip the bed. Everything came off and landed in a pile in the hallway. There were quite a few bottles that were nearly empty, so she took those into the bathroom, poured the last little bits down the drain, and rinsed them out.

She heard Eliseo gathering up bottles and went out to find him standing over the trash bin. "How much was this man drinking?" she asked. "It's like he had a huge frat party all by himself."

"It wasn't this bad when he first arrived," Eliseo said. "I cleaned the room several times and there were wine bottles and an empty whiskey bottle every once in a while, but nothing like this."

"When did you quit cleaning?"

"It was just after Thomas Zeller died, so I guess it's been about two weeks. He told me that he didn't want me in the room. I knocked every day and asked for his dirty dishes and if I could change his sheets. I usually got the dishes, but no sheets."

"Poor old guy lost his mind," she muttered and sat down at the desk. It was a beautiful secretary and she pulled the top down to see if he'd stowed anything in there. "Are there any empty boxes downstairs, Eliseo? We're going to have to pack this stuff up."

"I'll take the bottles downstairs and bring some up." He opened the shoe closet and pulled out a couple of suitcases. "I think we can start with these."

"His clothes must be in awful shape. Why don't we wash those as well. I can't send filthy things out of here."

She turned around in the chair and Eliseo glared at her. "You should just buy the man new clothes. This is disgusting."

"Bring me a box and I'll do it," she laughed. "Once hot water hits them, everything will be better."

He left and Polly turned back to the papers in the desk. There was a legal pad with writing on it and none of it made any sense. It was as if the man had written random words, hoping they would turn into something important. She flipped through the pages and found more of the same. He was losing his mind.

There were two more legal pads with the same types of things written on them. Was this what he had been doing for the last month? She couldn't imagine knowing that words were no longer coming out in a coherent manner. Eliseo came back with two boxes and the pair of work gloves she'd been wearing earlier.

"If you're touching his clothes, at least protect yourself," he shuddered, handing them over. "I'm going to open the windows to air the room out. I'll make sure to close them later on."

"Thank you. That's a good idea." Polly opened dresser drawers and found dirty and clean clothing all mixed in together, so she pulled it all out and dumped it in a box. Eliseo had already taken shoes and other things off shelves and dropped them into one of the suitcases. She placed the notepads on top and fished out the man's extra pens, pencils and blank paper, filling the case.

"No computer?" she asked.

"I never saw one. He just sat at the desk and wrote."

"That makes it easier." They opened the drawers and cupboard doors to make sure there was nothing left. "Do you think I need to buy another mattress?" she asked. "This was pretty horrible."

Eliseo didn't respond.

"That does it. I'll call this afternoon and have them deliver one on Monday."

"That's going to get expensive if you have to do it very often."

"I don't generally have old drunks who are losing their mind rent my rooms. This was a lesson I needed to learn." Polly started to pull the door shut and saw something move. There was a robe hanging on the hook. Using just the tip of her finger and her thumb to pick it up, she spied a piece of yellow legal paper in the pocket. "What's this?" She let the robe fall into the box, then gingerly pulled the folded sheet of paper out.

The writing was barely legible, worse than what had been on the pads, but she quietly read what he had written.

"Last Will and Testament.

I soon shall die.
My breaths are numbered
And sleep draws nigh.

I killed the man
My young self shot him
And then I ran.

I am tormented
Lives have I ruined
A man is dead.

The girl named Nell
Who hid her heart from him
Needs me to tell.

She did no wrong
Her innocence true
Her wait too long.

Thomas, now killed
At least 'twas not me
Look close afield.

All that I have
I give to charity
My soul to save."

There were words and letters scratched all over the page as Grey Linder attempted to work out rhymes. If these were his last words, at least they were coherent and he made sure to speak of Genie Campbell's innocence. Polly carried the laundry down to the washing machine. Did he know who the killer was? It read like he was telling them to look at someone close to Thomas.

She put her gloves back on and sorted the clothes, running the first load through on hot, then went back upstairs to her apartment and called Aaron Merritt one more time.

"I'm sorry to bother you, Aaron, but I found a piece of paper in Grey Linder's robe."

"He just died, Polly."

"Wow. Well, this makes it even more important. He wrote a poem as his last will and testament." She read the piece out loud to him.

"Okay," he said. "I need to pick that up. You've certainly cleared Genie Campbell. She shouldn't have run, but his confession tells me that she was innocent. We'll take it from here."

"Thank you, Aaron. I'm washing his clothes now. I don't know what you'll do with them, but at least they will be clean. We've packed the rest of his room, too."

"We'll deal with it. Thanks, Polly."

She sat back on the sofa, not wanting to talk to anyone else. The man's life had dwindled to nothing in his last days. He had ruined so many lives along the way. Polly felt terrible pity for him, dying alone with no one to care, yet she felt sick at what he had done. She pulled her knees up to her chin and sank back into the corner, unsure as to whether or not to cry.

CHAPTER TWENTY-EIGHT

"Too far! Stop!" Sal and Polly were in the bedroom giggling like little girls while dressing for the Masquerade Ball. "You're killing me here," Sal cried, as Polly attempted to cinch the corset.

Sal's plane had come into Des Moines earlier that afternoon and she had driven up to Bellingwood. She told Polly that she didn't want to put anyone out, but after some of their deep conversations, Polly realized that Sal was still afraid Mark wouldn't be happy to see her. The girl wanted the option to make a break for it, if necessary.

Polly, on the other hand, knew that Mark was head over heels for her friend. Even though he didn't know she was showing up for tonight's gala, he was already planning his Christmas so that she would be comfortable while meeting his family. She had promised to come for the holiday week as long as his family didn't think they were meeting his future bride. Sal had never made this type of a commitment to a man in her life. Although she wasn't ready to give up her job and family back in Boston, the fact that she was coming to the middle of Iowa so often told Polly her heart was finding its way to Bellingwood.

"One more time," Polly waited for Sal to take a breath. She quickly pulled the corset into place and laced it together. They were on their fifth attempt and Polly was worried they'd never figure this out before someone wet their pants from laughing so hard. "Are you okay?"

"They did this every day?" Sal asked, spinning around on her left foot to face Polly. "Here. Tug on this. I think you got it this time."

"Are you going to wear the hoop with this dress?" Polly held up her friend's deep, red gown. She'd had it shipped to Bellingwood rather than Boston and it had been hanging in the back of Polly's closet. The red velvet skirt was immense. It was unbelievable that so much material had gone into one dress.

"A corset and a hoop," Sal complained. "And people think my spike heels are uncomfortable. At least I can slip those off under my desk and the rest of my body gets to breathe during the day. This is awful!"

"But you're going to be beautiful."

Sal pranced over to the dresser and pulled out a set of fake vampire fangs. "Beautiful? I was kind of looking for deadly."

"In this dress, you're going to be a bit of a shock. No more deadly this week, though, okay?"

"No more deadly." Sal reached over and touched Polly's arm. "I've been so excited about tonight, I haven't taken the time to talk to you about yesterday. How are you?"

"I'm fine," Polly said. "I know Grey Linder wasn't a friend, or even a particularly friendly person, but what a miserable way for his life to end. To be all alone in a strange place, drunk and waiting to die. He had no friends or anyone who cared about him. At least Genie Campbell figured out how to make a life for herself. And she had a wonderful son that she raised."

"And Thomas Zeller had you there when he died. And he knew that his love was near. He got the opportunity to see that she had a full life."

"It still bothers me that he didn't get a chance to meet her so they could finally voice their love out loud."

Sal sat down on the bed, the corset holding her body upright. She chuckled as she shifted around in it. "You know, Polly, there's no guarantee that they would have even liked each other after all these years. It may have worked out for the best. Sometimes a love that never finds fulfillment is better than discovering it never would have worked."

"I guess that's all she will know. He did love her, though. You know he made sure in his last will that they had everything."

"That has to have made someone pretty angry. Who do you suppose stood to lose everything?"

"I haven't seen the original will yet. Ben Seafold was going to make sure Aaron got it so he would be able to either discover or eliminate money as a motive."

Sal watched Polly shimmy into her petticoat. "I want to wear what you're wearing. You aren't going to work nearly as hard at your costume as I am."

Polly just laughed at her friend. Sal would be glorious tonight. Her pale skin and dark hair were a wonderful complement to the red dress and would accentuate her role as a vampire. Polly always felt like Cinderella's stepsister next to the tall beauty, no matter what she wore.

She'd found a deep, midnight blue gown. The low-cut bodice was velvet, with long sleeves, while the satin skirt flowed with yards of material. Eight inches of lace trimmed the bottom of the dress and the first time Polly tried it on, she'd gone into the front room to spin around and watch the skirt billow around her. There was a large satin bow in the back and she'd found a pretty cameo to wear on a velvet choker around her neck. This was the second time in a week that she'd felt elegant in the dress she wore and hated that these were costumes and not something she would ever wear again. She and Henry needed more opportunities to dress up in Victorian garb.

Polly did a small spin in her bedroom and Sal smiled. "You really are beautiful, Polly."

"Next to you I'm a junior high moppet," Polly complained.

"Don't ever think that and you've gotten even more beautiful since you moved back here. It's that smile of yours that shows up no matter what's going on. You should wear something wild on your lips tonight."

"I'm not wearing bright red lipstick! You can pull it off, I can't."

Sal dug through her travel case. "Then try this one." She handed a tube of lipstick to Polly. "It should be perfect."

Polly took it into the bathroom and read the bottom. Dusty Rose wouldn't be too bad. She applied the lipstick and rubbed her lips together. Sal was right. While she was there, she put on a little more mascara and brushed at the makeup on her eyes. Her mask was on the counter and she pulled it over her head, adjusting the strap. She fluffed her hair into its curls and let it hang loose. She was no Sal Kahane, but she'd do for a simple girl from Iowa.

She looked up when Sal came in, fully dressed, and wearing her mask. Sal smiled and then all of a sudden, her fangs dropped down. While Polly stared, the fangs retracted.

"How did you do that?" she gasped.

Sal handed her the package. "I ordered these a couple of weeks ago and even though I had to spend some time making them fit my mouth this week, I thought they'd be fabulous. Aren't they fabulous?" She dropped them and retracted them a few more times. "Am I deadly yet?"

"You will certainly draw every man's attention and if their wives get nervous, deadly might be in the cards," Polly said. "Sheesh. You're glorious."

"Whatever," Sal waved her off. "So we're on the same page. You don't know me until after Mark has figured out that I'm here. I'm staying away from you, okay?"

"Got it. You're a mysterious guest who came for a Masquerade Ball. Maybe we should make up some crazy story about how you are a wealthy New England financier, in town to open a school that will teach Physicks, with a 'k' because it's steampunky, and Engineering to the young women who aren't allowed at University. You've made your money developing longer lasting wicks for the street lamps." Polly laughed.

"Or I won my great wealth as the first female airship captain and my steam-powered horseless carriage was offloaded from my fantastically opulent airship earlier today and yes, I'm here to look for land and a contractor to build this school. So, who are you?"

"I'm the local school mistress, Miss Pollyanna Percival. My father believed that education was important for all children and he bought this building for me. We have dormitories off to the side for the young people to live on-campus while they learn. It's quite progressive for this newly established state of Iowa."

Sal hugged Polly and they giggled again. Polly loved having her friend around. She held on for a moment. Sal was the one person who had known Polly through the roughest parts of her life and Sal was the one person who had also known Polly's dad and had met Mary and Sylvester Shore. It was so good to have her in town after the emotional ups and downs of the last two weeks.

"Shall we make a grand entrance?" Sal asked, when they finally let go of each other.

"You should go down the back way and slip in, just in case Mark is already here. I need to go through the front doors."

"That sounds great. Don't forget, you're beautiful. Hold that head up high and walk like you own this place."

"You nut," Polly laughed. "You are beautiful too. Thanks for being here."

She waited while Sal walked out and then went down the front steps to the large foyer and into the auditorium. The main lights were dimmed and the white lights streaming from the center of the ceiling gave the room a festive atmosphere.

Jeff looked up when she approached. Two baskets of colorful masks were on the table beside him in case party goers hadn't realized that the invitation was serious.

"Are you ready for a fun evening?" he asked. He was dressed in a long coat with a bright blue vest and black cravat. He had round wire glasses and was holding a gold-tipped cane. His wide rimmed top hat sat on the table beside him.

"You look great," she smiled. "And I'm ready for just about anything."

The string ensemble was playing on stage and Polly smiled to see that they had dressed the part. Rather than formal tuxedos, the men were in brightly colored vests and white shirts with sleeve garters, and the women were wearing extravagant gowns. "Even the orchestra dressed for tonight?"

"Some of them are part of the Iowa Steampunk society. They were looking forward to this," he said. "We actually have a few people from that group who are joining us tonight. The masks are new for them, but the costumes are their own."

"I think Anita Banks is coming in her costume," Polly said. "Have you seen Doug or Billy or anyone else yet?"

Jeff pointed at a table along the far wall. "Your friends are over there. I believe Lydia already has Aaron on the dance floor."

Polly felt a tap on her shoulder and then a deep voice spoke. "Would this beautiful woman offer me the privilege of a dance?"

She spun around and recognized Ben Seafold in a brown tweed coat, carrying an empty pipe in his hand. Polly took a deep breath and drew in the scent of pipe smoke on him. It was a scent she adored. She wasn't sure why, since her father never smoked, but for some reason, the smell made her want to bury her face in his jacket. She restrained herself and said, "Thank you."

He escorted her to the dance floor and she smiled at Aaron and Lydia. Lydia had a huge bustle at the back of her dark green gown. There were quite a few people she didn't immediately recognize because of their masks and she realized how happy she was that so many had gotten into the spirit of the evening.

Sal was lingering around the outskirts, flirting and chatting, trying not to be obvious about looking for Mark.

Sylvie came out of the kitchen, leading a group of kids wearing harlequin masks. Polly was always surprised at her creativity. They had set up a buffet along the south wall and Sylvie had decorated the tables with gears, old clocks, dark amber bottles and skeleton keys. There were even a few pairs of goggles scattered around. She was dressed in a simple white blouse with a long black skirt. A pair of goggles was propped up on top of her head and as busy as she was, no one was going to give her trouble about not having her mask on.

"You're a million miles away, Miss Giller," Ben said to her.

"It's fun to see everyone's costumes and try to figure out who is who with their masks on."

He swept her across the floor toward the orchestra, and they danced a while longer in silence. As the song came to a close, he said, "I probably won't have another opportunity to dance with you this evening, but I want you to know what a gift you've given me this week. Thomas Zeller was my friend and I thought that I'd lost everything when he died. But you found me and allowed me to be here and meet his family. Thank you very much."

Polly smiled up at him, wishing she could hug him, but he had her waist and her right arm, controlling the dance. "I've enjoyed having you here. You are always welcome at Sycamore House."

The room was filling and Polly found it more and more difficult to pick out people she knew. Ben stepped away and approached a table where Kevin and Genie Campbell were sitting. She smiled and waved on her way to the front door.

"Have you seen Henry or Mark yet tonight?" she asked Jeff.

He nodded. "They're both here."

"What?" Polly was surprised. "How long has Mark been here?"

"He came in while you were dancing with Ben."

"What is his costume?"

"Oh, I'm not telling you that. It's part of my job as doorkeeper to keep all of the secrets of our guests."

"Well, that's not fair."

"Fair, shmair, boss-lady. That's half the fun of a masquerade ball, finding your friends when you can't see who they are. By the way, you look beautiful tonight."

Polly gave him a sideways glance, "That won't get you out of trouble with me, buddy."

"I guess I'll have to live with that." He stepped forward to greet a couple entering the auditorium and shot her a smirk while introducing himself.

She waited for him to return. "How about Doug?"

"He's here too. I think he was looking for you. He went thataway." He pointed to where Lydia and Aaron were seated.

Polly went to their table and glanced around, looking for Sal. She was with two young men that looked nothing like Henry or Mark. One of them was dressed in a red vest and black cape.

Aaron stood and pulled out a chair for Polly. "Thank you," she said. "Have you seen Anita yet?"

"I think she's over there in the tight leather," Lydia whispered, "but I can't be sure."

The young girl was standing by herself, dressed in tight brown leather pants with high-heeled boots that came up to her knees. She wore fitted a leather jacket that was covered in pockets, straps and buckles and a white scarf was flung around her neck. On top of her head, she had on an aviator's cap and instead of a mask, she wore goggles.

"Anita?" Polly asked when she got close.

"Polly? I love your gown!"

"Would the lovely Miss Astlebury be interested in meeting her date for the evening? He's sitting with your boss."

Anita peeked around Polly. "He's kind of cute. Does he know that he's meeting me tonight?"

"He's nervous, but he's here and that's a good sign. Come on."

Doug and Aaron both stood when they approached the table. "Doug Randall, I'd like you to meet Anita Banks, aka Claire Astlebury of the East Coast Astleburys," Polly gestured to Anita and said, "I hope you have a wonderful evening tonight."

Anita held her hand out and Aaron Merritt took it before Doug could make sense of the moment. "Mr. Randall," he said, "I expect you to treat my employee with the utmost respect and to remember that you have me to answer to should anything untoward happen to her."

Doug stood there, completely flabbergasted. Anita took her hand back from Aaron and said to Doug, "I'm perfectly delighted to meet you, Mr. Randall. Could I ask you to take me to the punch bowl?" The poor boy hadn't yet made the connection between the reality of the moment and the play-acting that was happening in front of him. He finally nodded and turned away from the table. Anita took his arm and led him away.

Aaron laughed as he sat back down. "That was fun."

"You are awesome," Polly said. "I just hope he remembers to breathe again. My job is done."

Lydia leaned in, "This is fun! Those two are perfect together. Polly, what a great idea. I can't believe I didn't think about it."

"Let's just say I learned everything I know from you and leave it at that. So, where are Beryl and Andy?"

"Len is bringing the two of them. Beryl will make a grand entrance at some point."

Sure enough, Aaron poked Polly and pointed to the front door. She'd recognize Beryl anywhere. Tonight she was dressed like a peacock in a multi-hued gown. It had immense feathers attached to the back that towered over her head. Her mask was blue and green with more feathers attached to it and she held it to her face by its long, golden stem. Andy's white suit with a bustle and Len's long black coat made them look as if they were her chaperone and chauffeur rather than her friends. They followed in her wake as she strode across the room toward Polly, Lydia and Aaron.

Len held a chair for Andy while Aaron scurried around to pull Beryl's chair out. "You're quite a sight," he said.

"I am, aren't I!" she said. "Is the party rockin' without me yet?"

Polly turned toward her, "I don't think it knew what to do without you. It should kick off any time now." The dance floor still had people moving around and she realized that Sal had cornered someone to dance with her.

"Do you have a moment to dance with a poor carpenter?" She stood up and hugged Henry. Like most of the men in the room, he had taken off his hat and set it on the table.

"I didn't know if I'd be able to find you," she said.

"I knew where my pretty girl was. You are beautiful this evening. Let's dance."

Just as he swung her onto the dance floor, Polly heard a commotion. The orchestra stopped playing and the room fell silent. Polly turned to see what was happening and realized that a woman with a gun was standing in front of Genie Campbell. Aaron was slowly walking toward the table, and Kevin was looking at the woman in shock.

She waved the gun wildly around the room, ending up looking at Aaron. "Sit down," she demanded, "or I will shoot you."

She was wearing a mask and a hooded cape that covered most of her face. Aaron sat on the edge of a chair and quietly asked the woman to stay calm. She ignored him and began screaming at Genie and Kevin Campbell. "You can't have any of it. It's all mine. Who in the hell do you think you are coming in at the last minute and taking everything! You can't have it!"

Polly moved quietly and quickly while the woman screamed. Suddenly she realized that it was Natalie Dormand.

Aaron saw what Polly was doing and he set his jaw, moving forward in his chair again.

"I told you to sit down! I'm in no mood. All I want is for these two to leave with me and the rest of you can go back to your damned party."

"Natalie," Polly said quietly. "What are you doing?"

The woman spun around, aiming the gun at Polly. Henry stepped in front of her with his arms out as a shield, but Polly pushed his right arm down and stepped around him, putting her hands out in submission.

"Natalie, this is wrong. You can't hurt them and you can't get away with hurting all of us."

Aaron stood up again and was moving across the room when Natalie saw him. She aimed at Polly and said, "If you do not sit down, I will kill someone. Polly is close enough that I don't even have to aim. Sit the hell down!"

He sat back down, his eyes pleading with Polly.

"Natalie. I thought we were friends," Polly said. "You came out here to take care of Thomas's things. What has happened? Why didn't you come talk to me?"

"We were never friends. You didn't like me and you didn't tell me the truth about any of this. I had to find it out on my own. Did you think I was stupid? I knew you sent for that old man to steal the manuscript from me. I knew that Thomas was in Iowa looking for his long lost love and I knew he found her because he finished the damned book. I knew he was going to give it away and I'd never see a penny of it. But if they die, that new will he wrote won't mean a thing."

"How did you know about the will?" Polly asked. "We just found out about it this week."

"People talk. The old man called someone on Friday and he didn't have his door shut. I heard it all. Your silly friend from the Sheriff's office called her boss on her cell phone to tell him what you found. They all ignored me, but I heard everything and I'm not going to lose out on those years with Thomas Zeller just because he re-found his youth. Now stand up," she waved the gun at Kevin and Genie, gesturing for them to stand.

All of a sudden another woman, dressed in leather pants, practically flew across a table beside Polly. She pushed Natalie Dormand's gun hand into the air and then twisted it behind the woman, put a knee into her back and dropped Natalie to the floor. She kneeled on her and looked up at Polly. "Is that the Sheriff over there?" she asked.

Aaron was already moving toward them and with a handkerchief he drew out of his pocket, picked up the gun, checked the safety and emptied it. The woman stood up and yanking Natalie Dormand's arms behind her, brought her to a standing position. The two walked Natalie out into the hall and Polly followed close behind.

When they got out of the room, the woman drew off her mask and hat and revealed herself to be Lila Fletcher, the guest in the front room.

"Who are you?" Polly asked. "I know you're an author, but what in the world?"

"I am an author," she smiled. "But I was supposed to be guarding Thomas. He'd had some threats and asked me if I would join him. We both thought that this would be a nice quiet place for him to finish the manuscript and didn't expect anything to happen here. I had my suspicions about Miss Dormand, but since she wasn't here, and he kept in touch with her while she was out east, I set it aside."

"Why didn't you tell us who you were when he was killed?" Polly asked.

"I didn't want to tip my hand. I hoped that the killer would show him or herself and I was certain when Natalie Dormand showed up that it was her. But then she stayed and I didn't know what to think. There was no sign that she'd been here when he died, so I thought I'd been completely wrong."

Aaron hung up his phone and turned back to them. "There is a sign that she was here for the murder. We found the knife that killed Thomas in Stratford. She'd bagged up her bloody clothing and tossed it into a dumpster behind the gas station. But the bag split open and the owner spotted it. It won't take long for us to match her fingerprints to it."

"Why did you do it?" Polly asked Natalie. "Why? As long as he was alive, you had a wonderful job."

"He was leaving us and going back to Seafold Publishing. He wanted to write more of those inane Eddie Powers books," Natalie said. "Since I had turned over all of my other clients to work with him, I'd have nothing. I came out here to beg him to stay. I cornered him when he was out for a walk and he took me up to his room to talk." She turned to Lila. "He knocked on your door, but you were gone. It's your fault I killed him, you know."

"How is it my fault?" Lila asked.

"He told me there was a woman he wanted me to meet. I was furious! He wasn't supposed to have another woman. We went to his room and I knew then that I was had to just be done with him. Hell, I knew I was going to kill him before I got here because I made sure that knife was sharp. When I confronted him about another woman in his life, he told me that I didn't know what I was talking about. Oh, I knew. I knew. He was leaving me and I'd have nothing. I just started stabbing him. Then I took my shoes off and ran out the front door. No one even knew I was here."

"Grey Linder knew you were here," Polly said quietly. "But he didn't realize it because he was so drunk."

A crowd had gathered around them, listening to the tale and the orchestra had started playing again in the auditorium. Genie and Kevin Campbell were in the doorway, in shock. Kevin's wife had her arm around Genie's waist and was holding his hand with her other hand.

Polly heard sirens approach and soon, two deputies came in. After handcuffing Natalie Dormand, they took her out the door to their car.

Aaron said Lydia. "I'm sorry. I need to leave. Can you get a ride home?"

"Of course you need to go. But I got one dance from you tonight and that's all that counts. Len will take me home. You go do your job." She reached up and kissed him, then patted his arm as he turned to leave.

Before he got too far, he glared at Polly. "What did you think you were doing in there?" he asked.

"I was trying to get her to talk to me so that maybe she would calm down and realize how crazy her actions were."

"She murdered Thomas Zeller and then threatened people, including myself, and you thought you could calm her down? Polly Giller you are going to be the death of me!" He stalked out the front door, leaving her standing there with her mouth open.

Lydia came up and said, "Don't worry. He was scared tonight. He's not really that angry with you."

"But she wasn't going to let him get near her and I thought maybe I could talk her into giving me the gun. I had no idea that Lila was his bodyguard," Polly protested. "If I'd known that I probably would have ..."

"You wouldn't have done anything differently," Henry sighed. He had taken his mask off and his face was bleak. "You terrified me again, Polly. I thought you were going to die."

"She wasn't going to kill me," Polly said, then she repeated it, "She wasn't going to kill me." She felt her knees buckle and Henry caught her. "Oh crap, Henry. She could have killed me. She could have killed you. What were you doing stepping in front of me?"

Lydia grinned. "Darling, that was the most chivalrous thing this town has seen in years. People will be talking about Henry's heroic behavior tonight for days to come. Now you get back inside and sit down."

Lila Fletcher took one of Polly's arms, while Henry practically carried her with his arm around her waist. They sat her down at the nearest table and within moments Sylvie was there with a glass of water. "Are you okay? You scared me. What were you thinking?"

Polly looked up and discovered that everyone was staring at her. Sal had removed her mask and was standing beside Mark. All of her friends were there, some looking at her with concern, others in amazement.

She stood up. "I'm fine, everyone. Please. You came here to have a good time. We've had a little bit of extra entertainment this evening, but I believe it is all over now. Sylvie cooked a wonderful dinner for you, the music is beautiful, the room is decorated and you all look fabulous."

As some of them turned away, she said, "Oh, and in this story I'm the heroine and Henry is my hero. That's the way it will be told, okay?" She laughed and pulled Henry to her for a kiss and the room applauded.

"You are my hero, Henry Sturtz," she said out loud and then whispered into his ear, "and don't you ever do something that stupid again!"

He kissed her lips and refused to release her until he felt her melt, then he pulled her close. "I will always step in front of a bullet for you, so if you never want that to happen again, you have to be smarter than you were this evening."

"No guarantees," Polly grinned.

"Then you will always have to worry about how I'm going to protect you."

He tugged her in to him, squeezing her as tightly as he could.

"I can't breathe," she gasped.

"I don't care. I don't want to let you go."

"Just a little bit so I can breathe, please."

He released her and she saw Genie and Kevin Campbell standing there with Ben Seafold.

"I'm sorry I missed all of the excitement, Polly." Ben said. "I hear you two are heroes."

"Where did you go?" she asked.

"I'd gotten a call from Miss Dormand asking me to meet her in my room. She told me she wanted to discuss coming to work for me since she had experience with Thomas and his books. I had no idea that she was just getting me away from the Campbells."

Genie Campbell stepped forward, "Meeting you has certainly given my heart a workout, Polly, but I wouldn't change any of it."

Kevin interrupted. "I might change the whole having-a-gun-waved-in-my-face thing."

"Now that it's all over, you'll come up with a wonderful story to tell about the evening," his wife laughed, swatting him in the arm. "I don't think I've ever been so frightened. Thank you for stepping in, Miss Giller. Even if all you did was distract her, you were wonderful. And Miss Fletcher, you have some amazing moves! It was like something out of a movie!"

"I wasn't nearly as frightened as the rest of you. The Sheriff was too far away to see that the safety was on. The poor girl had no idea. We were safe, but rather than give her a chance to do anything stupid, while Polly was attempting to talk her down, I decided I could make a bit of a scene and bring the whole thing to an end. I'm glad it worked out for all of you. Thomas told me that he had found you and it made him very happy to see that your family had grown. He was planning to contact you soon, but was still trying to figure out how to tell you that everything was okay."

Lydia interrupted, "Miss Fletcher? My husband would like to speak with you." She handed the woman her telephone and Lila walked away.

She returned and handed the phone back to Lydia. "I need to go down to Boone. I will only be here for a few more days, Polly. Thank you for your hospitality."

Ben grinned as he watched her leave. "That's how I know her! She's been around before as a body guard. I've seen her at Literary Conventions. Whaddya know. She's kind of hot stuff!"

He escorted the Campbells back to their table and Polly sat down again.

Sal dropped into a chair beside her. "How ya doin' Giller?"

"I'm exhausted. Adrenaline wiped me out," Polly said. "I see you found your dashing veterinarian."

Sal grinned and lowered her fangs, then retracted them. "I surprised him. He didn't know it was me until you were in the hallway. Everyone was taking off their masks and his eyes nearly popped out of his head. It was perfect. I'm going home with him tonight. I think I'm going to test these babies out." She snapped the fangs down and back up again.

"You're twisted," Polly said. "Have fun!"

Henry took Sal's seat when she left to go back to Mark. "Can I get you something to eat or drink?"

"I should be taking care of you! You're the one who got up on his white charger for me tonight."

"What if we just sit here for a while and let the party happen around us." He scooted his chair closer to hers and pulled her into his arms. "I think I want to hold onto you a little more."

"I like that. We can eat tomorrow." She looked around the room. People were talking to each other and eating at their tables. Some were dancing and every once in a while someone would sneak a quick peek at her.

"Does it seem odd to you that my friends take an evening like this in stride?" she asked. "One minute they're dancing and having a good time, and in the next minute a lunatic is waving a gun around the room. Once the craziness dies down, they all go back to eating and dancing, just like it never happened."

"I'm afraid they might be getting used to you living in Bellingwood. If they're going to be friends with you, anything could happen."

"Are you used to it? Because I'm sure not."

"I don't know if that's what I'd call it, but I'm doing my best not to be surprised at what happens when you're in the room."

Polly kissed him again. "I love you, Henry Sturtz. Thank you for being my hero."

THANK YOU FOR READING!

I'm so glad you enjoy these stories about Polly Giller and her friends. There are many ways to stay in touch with Diane and the Bellingwood community.

You can find more details about Sycamore House and Bellingwood at the website: http://nammynools.com/

Join the Bellingwood Facebook page:
https://www.facebook.com/pollygiller
for news about upcoming books, conversations while I'm writing and you're reading, and a continued look at life in a small town.

Diane Greenwood Muir's Amazon Author Page is a great place to watch for new releases.

Follow Diane on Twitter at twitter.com/nammynools for regular updates and notifications.

Recipes and decorating ideas found in the books can often be found on Pinterest at: *http://pinterest.com/nammynools/*

And, if you are looking for Sycamore House swag, check out Polly's CafePress store: *http://www.cafepress.com/sycamorehouse*

ROOM AT THE INN

A Bellingwood Christmas Story
by Diane Greenwood Muir

Bellingwood - #5.5

CHAPTER ONE

Brushing her hand down the skirt of her dress, Polly stood in the doorway. She smiled at the man she loved as he took her arm and they walked down the aisle of the church. The excitement in the room was palpable. There had been so much work done in preparation for the wedding and the day was finally here.

She had spent the day with her friends, Lydia, Beryl, Andy, and Joss Mikkels, decorating the auditorium. Sylvie Donovan and Hannah McKenzie had conscripted young Rachel Devins to help in the kitchen as they prepared the evening meal. The day had been busy and Polly felt like she hadn't stopped moving until this moment. Henry Sturtz, her contractor, friend, and the man she had fallen in love with, stopped at a pew, took her hand, squeezed it and waited for her to step in and sit down.

Polly smiled at Lydia and Beryl as she sat beside them. Henry winked and returned to his duties as usher.

"The church is beautiful, don't you think?" Lydia whispered.

Two arrangements of white carnations and red roses sat on the altar. Deep green holly branches wrapped around the vases; their red berries glistening in the flickering candle light. Ribbons of gold wove through the arrangements, creating a festive look. The church had been decorated with candles in the windows, wreaths draped in gold, red, and white on the walls, and garland entwined with little white lights wrapped around the communion rails. The large Advent wreath was in front of the organ on a golden pedestal and an immense Christmas tree stood in a corner with colorful lights circling its branches.

"What a wonderful time of the year to get married," Polly said. "The church is already beautifully decorated!"

Sylvie Donovan and her two sons, Jason and Andrew, moved into the pew behind them, joined by Eliseo Aquila and Jeff Lindsay. The music changed and Henry slipped in to sit with her.

Andy Saner's four grandchildren came down the aisle carrying brass candle lighters. Two split off to light candles in the windows, while the others lit candles at the altar. The overhead lights dimmed, bringing a warm glow to the room. Rev. Boehm and Len Specek came down the aisle followed by two of Andy's children, Melanie and John.

Polly felt tears threaten and her throat constrict as she tried not to cry. The organist played a triumphant fanfare, the congregation stood, and turned to watch Bill Saner escort his beautiful mother down the aisle. She was dressed in a simple, ivory dress with gold accents. It was belted at the waist and a short jacket with gold buttons finished her elegant look. Andy smiled at Len who beamed back at her. He couldn't take his eyes off her, as if he was surprised this moment was really here.

Andy had shown up in a panic the morning after Len proposed. She was carrying a brand new notebook, ready to attack and organize. They didn't want to wait long and she loved the idea of a Christmas wedding. Polly knew that if anyone could pull off a wedding in a little more than a month, it would be Andy Saner. They sat down with Jeff. Holiday weddings were popular and Christmas parties filled the calendar, but Jeff had pointed to a Friday evening in the middle of December.

He'd just laughed and said, "Andy, your future husband asked me to hold this date last April."

She'd gasped, "Why did he wait so long to ask me?" When she thought about, she said, "Because he wanted to make sure."

Len Specek and Andy had known each other in high school, but then went on to live separate lives. His first wife had died two years ago and his daughter, Ellen, worked as an IT Specialist for the State Department at the American Consulate in Barcelona, Spain. She came home for three weeks each year to spend Christmas with her father and this year that included a wedding.

Polly felt Henry tug on her arm. She quickly sat down beside him when she realized the congregation was no longer standing. She'd been paying attention to Ellen Specek, who was seated alone in the front pew, her hands clasped in her lap. Every once in a while, Ellen lifted a perfect white handkerchief to her eyes. Polly nudged Beryl and pointed. Beryl nodded, then tugged on Lydia's arm to get her in on the story. Lydia patted her friend's knee and returned her attention to the pageant in front of them.

Andy's son, Bill, shook Len's hand, then placed his mother's on top of it. He kissed her on the check, and stepped back to sit with his family. Henry drew Polly close, put his left arm around her shoulders and reached across with his right hand to hold hers.

When they exchanged rings, Polly stole a glance at Lydia. The woman had a fresh package of tissues in her purse, knowing she would cry through the ceremony. What Polly didn't expect was to see Beryl's face scrunched up and teary. She reached over to squeeze Beryl's hand, then grinned when her friend lifted her upper lip in a snarl.

Rev. Boehm pronounced the couple man and wife, delivered the benediction, and invited them to kiss. Amidst laughter and clapping and a traditional wedding recessional, Len and Andy Specek led the wedding party back down the aisle.

Andrew leaned forward in the pew, "I'm supposed to go back with you, Polly," he whispered when Sylvie, Eliseo and Jason left.

"That's great," Polly said.

Andy and Len came back down the aisle and spent a few moments talking with their children, then greeted their friends and made sure everyone knew there would be time for conversation and hugs at the reception.

Most of the crowd waited in the large foyer. Len helped Andy into a beautiful white, faux fur, full length coat and after pulling on his own coat, took her arm and escorted her out of the church.

Eliseo was seated in the sleigh that Henry and Polly had refurbished. Jason stood beside it, dressed in a long waist-coat and top hat. Andy took Jason's hand and stepped in. Len followed and Jason climbed up to sit beside Eliseo. Polly looked at the boy beside the man. She took out her phone and snapped a few pictures, emailing one to Sylvie. Len reached under the seat for a furry blanket and laid it across their knees.

Eliseo signaled to the horses and they moved off. He and Jason had driven around town earlier to find the prettiest Christmas lights for a sleigh ride.

"Wait here with Andrew," Henry said. "I'll bring the truck up."

"We can walk with you," Polly protested. "The parking lot isn't that big."

Henry stood in front of her, "Can't I ask you to do one thing without an argument? I want to do something nice for you."

She dropped her head and chuckled. "Fine. We'll wait. But, we're going to laugh behind your back."

He walked away, shaking his head and Andrew looked up at her. "Why are we laughing at him?"

"Because every once in a while he has to remind me that I should let him do nice things for me."

"He does nice things all the time, doesn't he?" Andrew was perplexed.

Polly put her arm around the little boy's shoulders and realized that he, too, was growing taller. "Yes, Andrew, he does. But sometimes I'm not very gracious about it."

"Will you let me ride in the sleigh when there is snow?" he asked, setting aside the conversation. Polly smiled. Sometimes the most important thing was a sleigh ride in the snow.

"I can hardly wait until we have snow on the ground. Do you see how much fun Demi and Daisy are having with the sleigh today? Just imagine how great it will be when they can pull and it glides across the ground. We'll all take rides then."

"Jason looked pretty cool in that hat and coat."

"Yes, he did." Henry's truck pulled up. "Here he is, let's go."

They approached Sycamore House. Jeff had strung white Christmas lights around the old schoolhouse and strategically placed small Christmas trees in some of the windows. Their lights twinkled and the streets lamps glowed in the darkness. The arch in the garden was wrapped in colorful lights while luminarias lined the driveways and sidewalks. The white fence around the pasture was draped in swooping greenery wrapped with light.

Henry drove into her driveway and parked. "This looks really nice," he said when they entered the auditorium.

Gold tablecloths and colorful Christmas balls nestled into greenery decorated the tables. Small cakes were placed at the center of each table on a stand. Each was a different flavor and covered with a simple butter cream icing. Andy and Len's friends and family mingled around the tables, reading the different cake types and settling when they found one they liked.

Ellen Specek came in the main doors by herself and looked around the room, trying to orient herself.

"She looks a little lost," Polly said to Henry. "I can't let her stand there by herself."

"Go rescue her," he laughed. "You're good at that."

Polly swatted him and made her way across the room.

"Hi, Ellen! We haven't met yet, but I'm Polly Giller."

The girl looked up at Polly's voice with gratitude in her eyes. "You own this place, don't you?"

"I do," Polly nodded. "Come with me. I think they have you over here at Andy and Len's table."

"Thank you. I thought I would know more people, but it's been so long since I've lived here, I'm having trouble putting names and faces together."

"I have the same problem, but I don't know enough people yet. How long have you been gone?"

"Since I graduated from high school." Ellen thought about it. "I went to California for college, and then ended up in Spain five years ago. I think the only time I'm ever home is at Christmas. Well … and mom's funeral, but that was only for a week."

"I know what that's like," Polly commiserated. "I left Iowa to go to college in Boston. After Dad died, I didn't even come back for Christmas. Everything changed in the years I was gone."

"Or maybe you changed," Ellen replied. "I feel like everything has stayed the same, but I don't fit in any longer. All of their lives kept going on without me. It's difficult trying to poke a hole back into the fabric of the community to make myself fit in again."

"Maybe that's it. It's been easy for me to get involved in Bellingwood, though."

"And you find dead bodies!" Ellen said. "I've never heard of such a thing. Dad started emailing me about your adventures last spring. No wonder you've managed to get involved. People keep waiting for what new thing you'll uncover."

Polly looked at her in shock. "I don't mean to do any of that!"

"I think that's why people like you so much," Ellen said. "They love watching you be surprised by everything. Dad thinks the world of you."

The decibel level in the room had risen as more and more people found seats. All of a sudden, a hush fell as Len and Andy appeared in the doorway. The light from the foyer encircled the two. Andy's face was flushed red from the chill of the evening and Len Specek grinned as he took her hand and stepped into the room. Applause erupted, following the couple to their seats. Polly quietly moved away and watched Andy sit down beside Ellen.

Polly and Henry sat with Joss and Nate Mikkels. Beryl plopped down beside Polly and let out a whoosh, "This place is too, too, tonight," she said, dramatically.

"Too, too what?" Nate innocently asked.

"Too much! Too elegant, too friendly, too Christmassy, too happy. Too, too, too!!

"What's up with you?" Polly asked. "I think it's lovely."

"Of course it's lovely. Everything Andy touches is lovely. But, it's too much."

Then it hit Polly. The last month and a half had sped by. From the day that Len proposed to Andy, she had been fully focused on pulling this wedding off and engaged everyone in her busyness. Beryl, Lydia and Andy had spent weekends traveling to Chicago and Kansas City, Omaha and Minneapolis looking for the perfect dress. No one was more surprised than Andy when they found it in a shop in Des Moines.

It was over for Beryl. Andy had a life with Len to get started and Beryl was afraid of losing all that time with her best friend.

Polly squeezed Beryl's hand again. "You're right. It is over the top. What was Andy thinking? We should have done this in the barn with the horses. That makes so much more sense!"

"Shut up, you brat." Beryl laughed. "Tomorrow I step back into my studio and I'm not coming out until my work is finished."

Dinner was soon served and the new couple made their way around the auditorium, stopping at each table.

Andy was nearly at their table when Bill Saner stood and said, "Excuse me. Please?" He waited for the crowd to grow quiet. "Mom would like me to tell you that in lieu of a single large wedding cake, there are cakes at each table. I hope you have been able to find a flavor you can enjoy. If not, feel free to wander around and steal from someone else."

The crowd chuckled and people craned their necks to see what might be at other tables around them.

"Before you dig into the cake, though, I'd like to ask you to open the bottles of sparkling grape juice at your tables. It's time to drink a toast to the union of Andy and Len Specek."

Nate pulled the bottle from its icy bed and with a little effort, unwrapped, then unscrewed the top. Plastic champagne flutes were passed around and filled.

Bill waited until most everyone had a drink in their hands, then said. "I spend my days alone in the fields, so I'm not much of a public speaker. When Len asked me to do this, I asked my wife to find something that says what I feel. The toast she found speaks of how parents are happy when their children find love. Today, *we* are happy that our parents have found another opportunity to love and to live. So, from John, Melanie, myself and Ellen: When parents find love, their children find joy. Here's to your joy and ours from this day forward."

"Hear, hear!" rang through the room and glasses were lifted to Andy and Len. Within seconds, silverware began tapping the water glasses on the tables. Len bowed to the crowd and dipped his new wife, kissing her deeply. The flush Polly had seen when they entered the room returned to Andy's face. They walked away from Polly's table, only to have it happen again. Not to be outdone, Andy reached up, placed both her hands on Len's cheeks and pulled him down for another kiss.

"Now stop," she said to the room. "Enjoy your cake."

"I'll be right back," Polly said to her friends at the table. She walked to the head table and sat down in Andy's seat next to Ellen. "I know your dad is leaving for a week. Do you want to have lunch with me at the diner?" She nodded back to the table where Joss and Nate were cutting cake. "I'd love for you to meet Joss Mikkels. She's the librarian. I think you'd enjoy getting to know her, too."

"Are you sure?" Ellen asked. "I know you're always busy. I don't want to be in your way."

Polly shrugged. "Jeff Lyndsay and Sylvie Donovan do most of the planning. I just go where they tell me to go and show up when they tell me to show up. I have time. Are you committed to this cake?" Polly pointed to the center of the table. "Come over to our table and meet my friends."

Ellen picked up her purse and leaned over to say something to John Saner, who was sitting on her other side. He nodded and smiled, then turned back to help his daughter cut a slice of cake.

"What do you have at your table?" Ellen asked.

"Maybe spice cake. I didn't pay much attention," Polly laughed. When they returned to the table, dishes had been cleared and cake was sitting at her place. "Everyone, this is Len's daughter, Ellen."

Beryl jumped up and pointed to her chair. "I've warmed this up for you and haven't touched my cake yet. I'm going to go poke at Lydia a little and see if I can't get her to let me hold her grandbaby." In a stage whisper, she said, "Not that I like holding babies or anything, but it terrifies Lydia when I ask. She's afraid I'm either going to drop them or corrupt them."

Ellen sat between Joss and Polly. "She's such a character. Dad has told me a lot of funny stories this last year."

"Have you seen her studio?" Henry asked. "Your father did most of the work during the remodel."

"He told me about that, but I haven't seen it yet."

"Did he build things while you were growing up?" Polly asked.

"That might be why he is having so much trouble giving up the house. He and Mom re-designed a lot of it. She came up with the plan and he built it for her. I keep telling him it will make some young couple very happy." She sighed. "I don't know how he's ever going to sell that house. It's not fair to Andy, though."

"I wouldn't worry too much about Andy," Polly said. "They'll figure it out together."

It was ten o'clock before the auditorium was finally empty. They kicked Len and Andy out, insisting that they should go home and relax before their honeymoon.

Henry walked out with Polly. "Let me walk with you and Obiwan tonight. I'm not ready to go home."

"I'd like that," she responded. "Will you be warm enough?"

"My heavy coat is in the truck. We'll grab it on the way out."

Polly changed into jeans and a sweatshirt, then pulled on heavy socks and boots. Her coat was hanging over the newel post of the banister upstairs and she slipped it on as she took Obiwan down the back steps, meeting Henry at the back door.

"You look more comfortable," he laughed.

"I love dressing up, but this is better!"

They stopped at his truck for the coat and she took her gloves out and put them on.

"It's gotten cold tonight," he said.

"Do you have gloves?"

"I'll be fine."

"Take my hand, you nut. We won't be out long."

CHAPTER TWO

A familiar voice interrupted Polly while she worked in Demi's stall.

"Polly, are you in here?"

She stuck her head out. So did everyone else. Saturday mornings Jason and Rachel joined them to clean stalls and spend time with the horses.

"Hi, Mark, what are you doing here?" she asked. Mark Ogden walked in and got the attention of every horse in the place. They loved him. Even though he was the one who spent time poking and prodding, checking teeth and feet and sometimes giving them shots, these horses all liked their veterinarian. They were loose inside the barn while their stalls were being cleaned, since Eliseo didn't like to let them out into the pasture until the sun had warmed the air a little. Before Mark could get to Polly, he was surrounded by four very large Percherons, all asking for attention.

"Hi there," he laughed. "I need to speak with Polly. Will you let me through?" He spent time quietly speaking to each of them, rubbing their foreheads and scratching their shoulders before he stepped through the gauntlet.

"I should probably make an appointment with you from now on. The welcoming committee is a little intimidating," he laughed.

"It's your fault. If you were meaner to them, they'd ignore you," she said. "So, what brings you over this morning?"

"I have a huge favor. I mean, a *huge* favor."

"When is she coming into town?" Polly asked.

"What? She?" Mark's confusion gave way to laughter. "Oh no, not her. She's coming on Saturday, but that's not the huge favor."

He was desperately trying to maintain a long-distance relationship with Polly's friend, Sal, from Boston. So far, things were going well. She'd been to Bellingwood twice, the last time for Sycamore House's first annual Halloween Masquerade Ball. Polly already knew that Sal was coming for Christmas. They had reserved a room upstairs for her.

"What is it then?" Polly asked.

"I might need Eliseo's permission, too," he continued. Polly wanted to smack him. She hated it when people wouldn't just come out and tell her what was going on.

She sighed, "Eliseo? Mark has a favor he wants to ask of us. Could you come here, please?"

Eliseo came out of Nan's stall. "Good morning, man," he shook Mark's hand. "I see you got the four horse greeting today!"

"They do warm up a room, don't they?"

"What is the favor?" Polly asked, "Don't keep me waiting."

"I have a friend down in Malvern. He rescues donkeys."

Polly took in a short breath. "Donkeys? There's a rescue just for donkeys? In Iowa? I've heard of a lot of things, but that's a new one for me. He rescues donkeys?"

"You'd be surprised," Mark said. "He'll take in other equines, but it's mainly a donkey rescue."

She shook her head. "I think I've heard everything now. What does this have to do with me?"

"Well ..." he started.

"Oh no. You want me to take a donkey, don't you. I barely know what I'm doing with horses and now you want me to take in a donkey?"

Eliseo grinned, watching the two of them. He said nothing, but waited while she worked it out.

"You have extra stalls here," Mark spoke quickly. "And they're great with horses and they love being around kids and they're absolutely beautiful animals."

"Wait. They? There is more than one?"

"Yes," he said hesitantly. "One doesn't go anywhere without the other. You'll love their names, too. Someone else had a flair for the literary and named them Tom and Huck."

Polly put her hand on the neck of the horse that was closest to her. She looked up and saw that it was Daisy.

"He wants me to bring donkeys into the barn, kids. Donkeys. What am I going to do with donkeys?"

"You don't have to do anything with them, Polly. You get to do whatever you'd like."

"Why do you need me to take in a couple of donkeys?"

"The rescue just got another call and they have to pick up four more. They've had Tom and Huck for a while. They're in great shape. You don't have to do anything to bring them back to health, they just need a good home."

She sat down. "Donkeys? It never crossed my mind. Eliseo?"

Eliseo smiled. "Donkeys would be great. We've got the space and they'll be good with the horses."

"From what my buddy tells me," Mark said, "these guys are really friendly. They were raised by a family with kids and then they had to move from their acreage south of Omaha to St. Louis. I think you'll fall in love with them. What do you say?"

"When will they get here?"

"Ummm, this afternoon?"

"This afternoon! I don't have time to get things ready for this afternoon. What were you thinking?" Polly felt her face flush as her temper rose.

"He has to make room." Mark was really apologetic now. "The others are coming in today. I told him I would drive down to get them. I just knew you wouldn't say no. Even if it's only temporary, I had to help him out, Polly."

Eliseo stepped forward. "All we have to do right now is get them a safe place to live. There's an extra stall right there. They only need one. They'll stay together. Right, Mark?"

"Uh huh."

"We have plenty of bedding. Jason and I can set up their stall this morning."

"But, you have that big wedding this afternoon. The place is going to be packed with people," she continued to protest.

Mark sat down beside her. "Are you going to say no to this or are you just freaking out?"

Polly couldn't help herself, she backhanded his arm. "You know I won't say no, damn it. Of course. We have room. If you two say they'll be okay with the horses, then I guess there isn't any reason to stop this. But, geez, give a girl some notice, will you?"

Mark laughed. "If I'd known, I'd have told you earlier, but he called me last night and I knew you were busy with the wedding. I'm heading out now. Do you want to ride along?"

Polly felt trapped, "No? Does that make me a bad donkey mom?"

"No, Polly," he laughed again. "It doesn't. I didn't think you'd be able to make the trip. I'll be back this afternoon."

"You're really getting donkeys?" Jason asked. "I saw some at the county fair. They were pulling carts with kids on them. That would be so cool."

"I saw those, too," Rachel said. "It *was* cool. All the kids in town will want to be here."

Polly bent over, her elbows on her knees, her head in her hands. "I don't believe this. What's next? Llamas, alpacas and goats? I'm going to have a zoo before I know it!"

Eliseo led Nan back to her stall, shut her in and then took Daisy into hers, "Jason, will you and Rachel make sure the horses are where they belong? We need to get the empty stall ready." They had managed to fill the last two stalls in the barn. One of them had been turned into a wash rack and the other was used for storing the muck rakes and anything else that came into the barn.

Mark left after patting Polly on her back and chuckling. She followed Eliseo and picked up two of the muck rakes.

"You're really sure about this?" she asked.

"I am. Donkeys are generally pretty calm. They'll be good for everyone around here."

"Are you talking about me?"

Eliseo laughed out loud. "I wouldn't do that! Not even for a minute!"

"Hah. I'm having trouble believing you, but it seems fair to leave this alone," she said.

"Donkeys are smart and lovable. The horses will be fine with them. The only one who might have a problem is Obiwan. They're not necessarily fond of dogs since they are so close to wolves, and donkeys see those as predators that must be dealt with, but your dog is pretty friendly and very calm. We'll take some time introducing them and before you know it, they will all be friends."

"You know, Eliseo," Polly said, "when Mark talked me into rescuing these horses, I was so naive. I didn't think there was any reason I couldn't handle all of the work. Then you showed up ... "

"... and I showed you exactly how much work they took?"

"No, you showed me what they were missing and you made it easy for me to love them and enjoy them. Now you're letting Mark talk me into two more animals down here."

"Four more," Eliseo quietly laughed.

"Wait. What?"

"We talked about a couple of barn cats."

Polly stopped in the middle of the alley. "Cats? Down here? Won't they be cold and lonely?"

"They'll be fine. There is plenty of hay for them to curl up in and stay warm and they'll love the donkeys. We're seeing more mice. The barn could use a couple of cats and I'm pretty sure your pampered kitties wouldn't like it very much."

"I'm going to have a problem not taking them up to my apartment," she said.

"These will be my cats, Polly," he said as sternly as possible. "They live down here."

"You're mean."

"Whatever it takes." Eliseo hauled the last wheelbarrow into the alley while Jason and Rachel finished sweeping the room out. Then Polly and Eliseo hauled in pine shavings for bedding.

"This is going to be so awesome," Jason said. "Andrew might even like the donkeys since they're not as big as the horses. If there are cats down here, he'll really like that."

"I'm surprised you want him down here," Rachel said. "I like not having Caleb around all the time. He drives me nuts."

"Andrew's cool." Jason just shrugged.

When they finished, Polly and Rachel went back up to the main building. Eliseo and Jason left for Boone to pick up a few things to make the donkeys' homecoming more fun.

Rachel ran through the kitchen, waving at Sylvie as she went past. "I'll be right back. I just need to shower and change."

Sylvie watched the girl pass through. "I guess it's convenient for her to be dating Billy, but I wonder what her mother thinks."

"I'm not asking," Polly said. "I can't think about it. Eliseo took your son for a quick trip to Boone. Is there anything I can do to help you out here while he's gone?"

"He already has the tables set up in the auditorium. We're in good shape until the family gets here. Rachel and Hannah will be here and I have servers hired for the reception. I think it's all good! So, what are they doing in Boone?"

"Oh Sylvie, we're getting donkeys."

Sylvie was walking toward the sink with a stack of pans and stopped, then slowly turned to face Polly, "You're getting what?"

"Donkeys. You heard me. Donkeys. A pair of them. Mark is heading down to Malvern to pick them up right now."

"Why are you getting donkeys?"

"Because they need a home and apparently they'd be great with the horses and Eliseo thinks it is a great idea. Even Jason and Rachel are excited."

"But you aren't?"

"I have no idea. I wasn't prepared for four Percherons, but I didn't have time to think about it. I'm not prepared for this either, and since Mark didn't give me any time to think about it, I'm getting two donkeys - Tom and Huck."

"It's never boring around here, that's for sure," Sylvie laughed and set the pans down in the sink.

"Oh. Mark and Eliseo also decided we needed barn cats. It's going to be a regular zoo out there."

"Barn cats make sense. Jason said that when it got cold, the mice showed up in force. I make him clean the mouse traps at home and he hates it."

"You're a mean mom."

"You bet I am. So, what are you going to name the cats?"

"Eliseo told me I couldn't bring them inside ... that they were his cats, so I'm going to let him name the things."

Sylvie laughed at her. "You might as well give up, Polly. We all know you aren't really upset about this. You just need some time to absorb it."

Polly lifted her upper lip into a semblance of a snarl, "I hate that you know me so well. It's not fair."

"You'll fall in love with those donkeys as fast as you did the horses and before you know it you'll have a thousand ways they're involved here at Sycamore House."

"I suppose." She breathed out, then said, "Lydia's church is starting the Live Nativity tomorrow night in the garden."

"That's my church, too," Sylvie smiled.

"Well, Roy Davidson is one of the shepherds and he's bringing two of his sheep with him. What if Tom or Huck play Mary's donkey? Both of them could hang out, for that matter. Would Jason want to be part of this? I should call Lydia and ask."

"Jason would love it. I can't imagine we'll be able to pry him away from the barn tonight."

"He thought Andrew might like the donkeys better than the horses because they are so much smaller."

"He's probably right. Andrew has been in no hurry to be at the barn with his brother."

"I'll take him down later this evening after Mark and Eliseo get them settled in," Polly told her.

Rachel walked in. "Did Polly tell you about our new donkeys?"

Polly grinned. It certainly didn't take long for people to become part of the Sycamore House family. Rachel had begun dating Billy Endicott earlier this summer. Although she still preferred dressing in black with wild streaks of color through her hair and wore her piercings and tattoos with pride, she had become much more comfortable with Polly and the rest of the staff at Sycamore House. She no longer hid behind Billy when they were in a group of people, and managed to engage in conversation even when he wasn't around. Polly attributed much of the transformation to Eliseo and the horses. When Billy had asked if she could spend time helping at the barn, Eliseo instinctively knew what the girl needed. He wasn't put off by her outer appearance or her inner fears, he just introduced her to the horses and some hard work and let the girl find her own way.

Sylvie and Rachel were laying chicken out on pans while Polly watched. She shook herself from her reverie and headed out.

"I'm going to call Lydia about tomorrow night. You can send Jason up when he gets here. Is Andrew already up there?"

Sylvie nodded and went back to dipping chicken and Polly went upstairs. When she entered the living room, she saw Andrew draped backwards over the couch, his head on the floor.

"What in the world are you doing?" she asked.

"I was playing with the cats. They thought I was funny."

She slowly nodded. "I'd have to agree with them. Are you comfortable?"

"Yeah. This is an interesting way to look at the world. Can you imagine what it would be like to live upside down all the time? What if you were the only person who walked upside down and everything else was right side up? Would teachers let you read your books upside down or would they make you learn how to read upside down." He stumbled and said, "You know what I mean. I heard an old man say that he was left-handed and his teachers made him learn how to write with his right hand. What if it was an upside down world for you?"

"Maybe if there were a lot of people who were upside down, the rules would change, but since only one person was, don't you think that person would have to adapt?"

Andrew moved around until he was sitting upright on the sofa. "Whoa," he said. "That made my head spin." He rolled his head around on his shoulders, smiling. "Cool! So, we only have one person in a wheelchair at school and there are ramps on the stairways for her. It shouldn't matter whether there is only one person who walks around upside down, should it?"

Polly could tell this conversation was going to get philosophical really quickly and she wasn't sure she was prepared for it. "You're right. No matter what a person needs, they should be able to have access to it. You're absolutely right."

"That's what I thought," he agreed and flipped himself over so he was upside down again.

Polly was just about to call Lydia when her phone rang in her hand. She was so startled, she nearly dropped it.

"Hello?" she answered.

"Hello Polly, this is Aaron Merritt."

"I didn't call you. There are no dead bodies." Andrew turned himself right side up and swayed a little as the dizziness left him.

"You're right," Aaron said, "but I could use your help."

"What do you need?"

"There's a young couple whose car broke down out here by the old motel on the highway. They've got a baby and need a place to stay tonight. I wondered if you had room."

"Of course I have room. Bring them over!"

"We have access to funds for situations like this. We'll cover it. I wasn't asking you to do this for free."

"Oh, come on, Aaron. This is Sycamore House. If we can't help someone who needs it, what use are we? Are you with them now? Do you need me to come get them?"

"No, that's fine. They're warming up in my car. We'll be there soon."

"Come in the front door. I'll put them upstairs across from me. Have they had anything to eat?"

"I don't know. I can deal with that before bringing them over."

"No you don't. Just bring them."

"Thank you, Polly. I appreciate it."

"Andrew," she said, turning to the boy on the sofa. "We're about to have guests. Would you mind helping me get a room ready across the hall?"

"Okay." He jumped up and ran to the front door. "What do we need to do?"

"We're going to put sheets on the bed and then make sure that the bathroom is stocked."

"Is it somebody poor?" he asked.

"Their car broke down and they need a place to stay. I think it's wonderful that Aaron thought to ask me. If I could fill this place with people who need it, I would do that every night."

"Do we have homeless people in Bellingwood?" he asked.

"I'm sure we do," she said. "But you don't see them on the streets like you do in the cities. They live in their cars or live with different people. We have poor people in Bellingwood, just like in every other town."

"I'm glad these people don't have to live in their car. It would be really cold right now."

"Me too, Andrew. Me too."

She pulled a set of sheets out of the cupboard in the hallway and with Andrew's help, they quickly finished.

They were leaving when she heard Aaron's footsteps on the stairway. He carried two black garbage bags and was followed by a man carrying a brightly colored diaper bag and two dilapidated suitcases. The young woman with him carried a baby in a car seat.

Polly smiled in greeting and walked over to meet them. "I'm glad you're here," she said. "We have a room all ready for you."

"Thank you," the man responded.

Aaron strode across the floor to the open door, while they all followed. He placed the bags on the floor in front of the bed and said, "Polly, I'd like you to meet Maria and Jose Rivera. This is their little boy, Salvador."

Polly shook the man's hand and bent over a little to look at the child. He had a beautiful smile and jet black hair. "Maria?" she asked and the woman looked up at her.

"Have you had anything to eat today? My friend Andrew and I were about to make lunch. Would you join us?"

The woman peered at her and then looked at her husband, who spoke rapidly in Spanish. She turned back to Polly and shook her head and said, "No, thank you."

Polly looked helplessly at Aaron.

In the moment it took the two of them to acknowledge they weren't sure what to do next, it was Andrew who spoke up. "Polly always makes too much food for me. She thinks I should eat more so that I grow up faster. It's just over there in her apartment. Won't you come? Please? She's a good cook."

Jose Rivera looked at the young boy and smiled, then spoke to his wife again. She smiled as well and he said, "Thank you. You are kind."

"Let me show you the bathroom," Polly said and reached out to touch his wife.

"Cuarto de baño," he said to her, nodding at Polly.

She followed Polly after placing the baby's car seat on the bed. When Polly opened the door and turned the light on, the woman's eyes grew big. Polly showed her how to turn on the spa bathtub and the shower and then pointed to the towels. She opened a cabinet door to show her where there was soap and shampoo, bubble bath and several bottles of lotion. They had re-stocked the drawer with toothbrushes and razors, ensuring that anything needed might be available.

"Para nosotros?" the woman asked, pointing to herself and gesturing to the other room.

Polly had limited knowledge of the language, but assumed that she was asking if they should use these things, so she nodded yes and smiled.

"Thank you," Maria said again. "Thank you."

They went back into the room and Polly said, "I will send Andrew," nodding at him "when lunch is ready. I hope you are comfortable here."

Jose spoke to his wife in Spanish again and she gave Polly a quick hug. "Thank you."

Aaron pulled the door shut as they left and walked with Polly over to her apartment.

"You aren't going to have to do something horrible like deport them, are you?" she asked.

"Polly. How many times have I told you that I don't try to hurt people who need help?"

"I know, but are you?"

"As a matter of fact, they're quite legal. When he got out of the car to meet me, the first thing he did was show me their papers. They are traveling out west for work."

"Okay then." She looked back across the hall. "If I keep providing rooms for young families, I'm going to have to invest in a crib," Polly laughed. "Maybe Lydia will lend me your travel crib again." It was just last Christmas when Polly had two small children and a baby stay with her while their parents were being investigated for transporting drugs. Fortunately, it had all worked out, but Lydia had arrived in the nick of time with toys for the children and a travel crib Polly could put in her bedroom. That had been about more than Polly wanted to handle when it came to infants, but as long as the mother was around, she was glad to bring anyone into her home.

CHAPTER THREE

Rapping at the front door caught the attention of both Polly and Andrew. Lydia entered just as they finished setting the table.

"I have the travel crib. You can keep it here at Sycamore House," Lydia said.

"Don't you need it for all the babies in your life?" Polly asked.

"You know what, dear? If someone needs something once, I'm glad to lend it and take it home. If they need it a second time, I figure that God is telling me to give it to them. We'll be fine until I get another one. Sycamore House needs this more than I do." She walked into the dining room, "Can I help with anything?"

"Andrew's been a lot of help already. We're nearly there. Would you like to join us? I have plenty of food."

"No, I won't bother you. Thank you so much for helping Aaron out today, though. This is above and beyond."

"Nonsense. I have everything I need. Why wouldn't I help?"

Lydia hugged her, "Well, thank you." She began to walk toward the front door.

"Oh, I was going to call you before all of this happened," Polly's voice stopped her.

"What's up?"

"I'm getting donkeys."

"Donkeys?" Lydia laughed.

"Yes, donkeys. They'll be here in a few hours. Mark thinks I need two more animals in the barn. At least they have been in a good home, so they'll be healthy. But anyway, if they're good boys, what do you think about dressing Jason up and having him out at the live Nativity tomorrow with them?"

"It would be terrific. There is plenty of room. We're building a large shelter to protect everyone from the wind and cold. We've got lots of hay bales. We can spare a couple for two donkeys."

"Well, if you need more, I have a loft full. We just filled it."

"The answer is yes. Whatever happens will be great."

"Thank you. I won't know for sure until they arrive. I don't even know if Jason will want to do it."

"If he doesn't, I will," Andrew piped up.

"Got it," Polly said. "We'll work it out one way or another."

Lydia headed back to the front door. "The crib is just outside. Call if you need anything else!"

Polly heard her talking to someone in the hallway and Jason came in to the apartment. "We got blankets and Eliseo stopped at the grocery store for a big bag of carrots. Donkeys like treats."

"That's great. Are you here for lunch?" she asked.

"Can I? Mom is really busy downstairs."

"Sure. We're going to have company today. There's a young couple across the hall with their son."

"Their car broke down and they don't have anywhere to go," Andrew interjected. "And they speak Spanish!"

"I know some kids from school who speak Spanish. Sometimes when Eliseo gets mad he speaks a *lot* of Spanish," Jason said.

Polly chuckled. She had never seen Eliseo get mad. It was nice to know that he was normal and had let Jason see that side of him. "Jason, would you get another plate out for yourself and Andrew would you mind going over to get the Riveras?"

Andrew took off and Jason set a place for himself while Polly put food on the table. She'd made spaghetti and pulled a pan of garlic cheese bread out from under the broiler. The bag of shredded cabbage had turned into a bowl of coleslaw and she took a container of chocolate chip cookies out of the freezer. Since Andrew and Jason had come into her life, there were always homemade cookies or bars somewhere in the kitchen. They were generally fresh, but she'd run out of time in the last few days and relied on a previously baked storehouse of treats.

"I asked him how to say 'my brother' in Spanish," Andrew announced when he came back through the door. He pointed to Jason and then said to Maria and Jose, "mi hermano, Jason."

Jose Rivera crossed the room to shake Jason's hand and then stepped back, gesturing for his wife to join them. She was carrying the car seat and Polly pushed a stool up beside one of the chairs.

"Please, have a seat," Polly said. She put the food on the table and sat down to join them. Everything went quiet as the young couple took hands and bowed their heads.

He spoke softly in Spanish, then said "Amen. We are so blessed by your gifts today."

"Polly? Polly?" Henry's voice came from the back stairs.

"Excuse me," she said. "Go ahead and eat. I'll be right back." She ran into the bedroom and stopped Henry. "Hi there. What are you doing here? I thought you had to be in Des Moines all day."

"Not enough people showed up to make it last all day, so I'm back. What's up?"

"Have you eaten?"

"Not yet. I thought I'd beg you for food."

"We have guests."

"Guests? That never happens."

"I know. Aaron found a young couple stranded at the old motel. Their car broke down and he asked if they could stay here at Sycamore House. I don't think they have much at all."

"Do you have enough food for me?" Henry grinned at her.

"You know me. What do you think?"

"I think you have enough to feed two armies. Come on and introduce me to your guests."

She took his arm and they went back into the dining room.

"Jose and Maria Rivera, this is my boyfriend, Henry Sturtz." It sounded strange to call him her boyfriend. He was so much more, but there was no better description for their relationship.

Jose stood to shake Henry's hand and stepped back to give up his seat.

"No, no," Henry said. "I'll be fine over here by Andrew. Just let me get a plate and some silverware."

"I've got it, Henry," Polly assured him. "Sit down." She handed him what he needed, then said, "I'm going to slice more bread and put it in the oven. You all keep eating. I'll catch up in a minute."

It was funny how she relaxed when Henry sat down. He spoke to Jose about his car trouble. She put the bread in the broiler, set the timer and sat back down. Maria was stroking her son's head, reaching over to kiss his cheek every once in a while.

Andrew could hardly take it, "Polly's getting donkeys!"

"She's what?" Henry set the fork filled with spaghetti back on his plate. "You're what?"

"I'm getting donkeys. Two of them. Tom and Huck."

The timer on the oven dinged and she jumped up. "Mark and Eliseo think it's a good idea. Mark is also bringing a couple of cats over to live in the barn. They think that's a good idea, too!"

"What are you going to do with donkeys?" Henry asked.

Polly touched the bread, yanked her hand back, and picked up a pair of tongs. "I don't know. I guess I'll take care of them. Eliseo says I will fall in love with them. Do I look like I have time to fall in love with more animals? Don't I have enough?"

"Where are the donkeys coming from?"

"Mark has a friend who runs a donkey rescue in Malvern. He says they need someone to adopt these guys right now to make room. He thought of me." She set the basket back on the table. "Don't let him talk me into building another barn, okay? I don't want to even think about the next animal he'll want me to rescue."

Jose and Maria were smiling at them. He was whispering to his wife, obviously translating as the conversation progressed.

"Donkeys," Polly said and rolled her eyes.

"Burro," Jose responded, the r's rolling off his tongue.

"Of course! Burros," she repeated. "I know that word."

Henry sat forward. "When are the donkeys showing up?"

"This afternoon," Polly giggled. "We've cleaned out a space for them and Eliseo is in charge of introducing them to the horses."

"I go away for one single morning and you get yourself in trouble. It's not safe to leave you alone!"

"Hey. At least it isn't ..." she stopped and looked at her guests. "At least it isn't something worse."

Jason and Andrew watched them bicker. Jason wasn't quite as entertained as Andrew, who tried to keep from laughing. His eyes grew worried as he looked back and forth between them.

"We're only teasing, Jason. It's fine," Polly said, reaching out to touch his forearm.

"Are you sure? Because maybe Mark should have talked to Henry before he did this," the boy said.

Henry gulped and the grin on his face nearly reached his ears.

Polly licked her lips and shot daggers at him with her eyes. "No, Jason. Mark doesn't have to talk to Henry. Sycamore House decisions are mine to make. If they involve animals, I include Eliseo. If they involve things in the kitchen, your mom helps me. Jeff consults on business decisions and Henry knows about construction. I always hope that all of my friends give me good advice, but it really is okay for Mark to have talked to me."

"Okay. I just didn't want Henry to be mad about this. They are going to be so awesome."

"I'm not mad, Jason," Henry said. "Not at all. I'm just surprised and to be honest, Polly surprises me all the time, so I should be used to it." Henry patted Jason on the back and turned to Jose.

"There will be burros. Maybe they can get you to California!" Both men laughed and went back to talking about the car.

When the meal was finished, Polly began clear the table and Maria stood to help her.

"No," Polly said gently. "Sit with your baby. Andrew and Jason will help." Both of the boys jumped up, gathering their plates. Before long, the dishwasher was full and the table was empty.

"We will go now," Jose said. "Thank you. It was very good."

Maria nodded her agreement and repeated the two words she was comfortable saying, "Thank you."

"I have a travel crib for you to use. It's right outside the door." Polly went out and saw the crib there and a large stack of baby blankets. "I'm sure I remember how to set this up."

"No, no. I can do this," Jose protested. "This is too much."

"It's fine. A friend offered this for you to use while you are here. We want Salvador to be comfortable, too."

A tear escaped Maria's eye. "Thank you," she said again. She spoke to her husband and he translated, "You are much too kind."

Polly smiled and watched them cross the hall to their room, then turned and went back into her apartment.

"Do you want to take a ride with me?" Henry asked. "I'm going to meet Nate out at the old motel and look at their car. I called Aaron and he hasn't gotten a tow truck there yet."

"Sure! Jason, will you call if Mark shows up before I'm back?"

"Okay. We're going to play games," he responded

Andrew stepped in front of her. "I'll take Obiwan outside first. I'll bet you forgot him, didn't you, Polly." He and Jason made a little money each week helping Polly with her animals. Sylvie had protested at first, but Polly insisted. Having the boys there to ensure Obiwan got outside in the afternoon, and the cats had someone to play with, made it easier for Polly to stay busy with everything else she had happening at Sycamore House.

"Maybe a little, but I always know you'll take care of him. We'll see you later." She grabbed her coat off the tree in the entryway and ran to catch up with Henry.

He waited until they got in the truck, then leaned over and kissed her. "You are quite the one for rescuing people and animals. Now others call you to take care of their problems."

"What do you mean?"

"Mark calls when he needs you to adopt some donkeys ..."

Before he could go any further, she chuckled, "and a couple of cats for the barn."

"Of course," he said. "You obviously need more cats. And Aaron calls when he needs a place for a homeless couple to stay."

"Would you have me do something differently?" she asked.

"Nope. I guess I'm just stating the obvious. Will it always be like this?"

"What do you think?"

"I think you are the most interesting and compassionate person I know and I will never know what to expect when I'm with you."

"Good answer." She reached over and patted his knee.

He drove to the old motel and they saw the car sitting there.

"While we wait for Nate to show up, do you mind if we drive around the property?"

"Sure. That's fine."

He drove through the parking lot to the road and pointed to the land behind the motel. "This is where I'm building that lodge for the winery that's opening next fall." Four friends from the area around Bellingwood were opening Secret Woods Winery and had hired Henry as General Contractor. The news had the entire community buzzing and they couldn't wait for it to be open.

"It's a shame this old eyesore is here," Polly remarked.

"I know. That's one of the reasons I wanted you to come with me. I've been thinking about it and wondered if you'd be interested in another investment. We could buy this old place for a song and renovate it. Maybe call it Sycamore Inn. With the winery opening, there's a better probability of tourists coming in who will want a place to stay and you're always saying that you don't have enough room for your friends. You told me that Jeff is filling up the rooms at Sycamore House. What do you think?"

"Aren't you going to be too busy with the lodge for this?"

"We can do interior work during the winter and then figure out what we want to do to the exterior later. I'll have time."

"How many rooms are here?"

"There are twenty. But, I was thinking we could knock out some walls and make a few extra-large suites, and then leave a few as smaller rooms."

"We'd do this together?"

"I think it's a good idea."

She took a moment to consider it. "You're right. It's a good idea. But I want to talk to my financial advisor and we need to figure out what the investment really is."

"I'll start all of that on Monday if you want to do this with me."

Polly took his hand. "If I was going to do it, the only person I'd want with me is you. Drive all the way around so I can see what the whole place looks like."

Henry drove back the way they had come, then turned to go around the back side of the old hotel. It had been built in a U-shape with eight rooms facing the highway, six on the base of the U and six more on the back side. There was a small building which had held an apartment for the owners, the front desk and a small patio in the center of the U. It was separate from the other structure.

"What's that in the middle?" Polly asked.

"I think it was a swimming pool, but the city filled it in."

"I don't want to be responsible for something like that."

"We could create a garden, maybe plant a sycamore tree."

"I'm going to sound like a nerd, but this is really neat."

"This place has been falling apart for years. It hasn't been in use since the late seventies. They've had trouble with transients so I don't know what it's like inside. It's probably a horrible mess."

Polly began to feel the same excitement as when she decided to renovate Sycamore House. She and Henry had so much fun planning and working through the process. He figured out a way to make all of her craziest ideas become reality and she was starting to imagine the possibilities for this building. This was going to be huge, though. It changed everything about what she thought she was doing in Bellingwood. When this was ready, it would mean she ... and Henry ... would be business owners.

Sycamore House was more an extension of herself than a separate business. Owning a hotel would change all of that. Was she ready to run a hotel? What would Jeff think? He had the hospitality background. Would he think she was nuts?

"Are you in there?" Henry asked.

"I'm thinking. Do you mind if I get out and wander around? You go talk to Nate about the car while I explore."

"Don't you dare go inside any of those rooms. I don't want to worry about you hurting yourself or running into an animal or even a person. Promise?"

Polly crossed her heart. "I promise. But I am going to look in windows. I want to get a feel for it."

Before he could say anything else, she unbuckled her seatbelt, leaned across the cab of the truck and kissed him. "I'll be careful." She jumped out of the truck and closed the door, then waited while he drove off. She had forgotten her gloves, so she jammed her hands in her coat pockets and walked the inside of the complex. Peering in the window of the first room, she was struck at how big it was. All of the original furniture was still there. It was hideous stuff, from the nineteen fifties at least. The curtains were still hanging, a horrible brown, orange and green print.

The dirt pile in the old swimming pool had never been flattened and she wondered if Henry really knew what he was getting into. Polly desperately wanted to get into the caretaker's house. She walked up a set of rickety steps in the back, praying that they wouldn't give way, and looked in the window. Ancient appliances were still in place. The linoleum covered table looked like one she remembered from some friend's homes when she grew up. She gingerly went back down the steps, knowing that if she hurt herself, Henry wouldn't let her hear the end of it.

There was a counter in the front room and two round tables. An old sofa faced a fireplace. Metal patio furniture was barely bolted to the cement in front of the main window. The bolts were rusty and when she pushed on the table, it creaked and moaned. There was no reason this place couldn't be renovated into something quaint and wonderful.

She laughed out loud. "You great, big brat, Henry Sturtz. You give me trouble about rescuing the world and now you ask me to rescue a building. I'm going to make this one hurt!"

Polly rounded the corner and saw Henry and Nate Mikkels standing over the engine talking to each other. The hood was up and they were both rubbing their hands for warmth as they talked.

"What did you find?" she called out.

"Nate says he can fix it. We need to get some parts on Monday. Are you okay with them staying for a couple of nights?"

"It's fine with me if they aren't in a terrible hurry to move on. How are you going to get it over there?"

"Aaron has a truck coming to tow it to Nate's garage. I'll take you home and talk to Jose about what we're doing."

"Are you rescuing a car, Henry Sturtz?" Polly asked.

Nate looked back and forth between the two of them, with a slight smile.

"I guess I am," Henry laughed. He shook Nate's hand. "I'll talk to you later, brother. Thanks for helping out with this."

"I'm glad to do it. I have all the equipment and the tools. I might as well use them for good. See you later, Polly."

Nate drove away and Polly hopped up into Henry's truck. When he turned it on and the heat surged through the air, she rubbed her hands in front of the vent.

"So, what do you think of the place?" Henry asked.

"It has potential, but it's going to take a lot of work. Are you sure you want to rescue this hotel?" she taunted.

"That's two!" he laughed. "I need to be careful about what I say to you, don't I!"

"Yes you do," she patted his leg. "If we can make this work, I think it will be fun. Are you ready to be my partner?" Polly batted her eyes at him.

He removed his gloves and took her cold hand in his warm hands. "I think the idea of being your partner sounds like the greatest adventure in the world."

"Wow. I was just talking about real estate," she said quietly.

"So am I. For now. Any partnership with you will be an adventure."

CHAPTER FOUR

"Eliseo hasn't called to tell me the donkeys are here yet. Do you mind if we stop at the Antique Shoppe before going back to Sycamore House?" Polly asked.

"What are you looking for?"

"This summer when Sal was here, she fell in love with a little dresser. I wouldn't let her buy it because I couldn't figure out how she was going to get it back to Boston. Since she is driving out for Christmas, I want her to have it."

Henry turned to go downtown and in a few minutes, he parked in front of the shop. "You go on in. I need to get something at the hardware store."

The bell hanging on the front door clanged when she opened it and went inside. It smelled like an antique store and she smiled at the man behind the counter. It had been over six months since Sal had seen the dresser and Polly wasn't even sure it would still be here. She walked to where she had last seen it and of course, it was gone. Her heart dropped. She turned around and around, just to make sure it really wasn't there.

Antique Christmas decorations were scattered throughout the

store and Polly stopped to look at an old Santa Claus. She remembered seeing one like it in pictures from her Dad's childhood. The Santa was filled with sawdust and she looked for the Rudolph that was part of the set. Santa had also stood beside a red sleigh. Absentmindedly, she picked him up and carried him with her as she perused the rest of the shop.

"Could I help you find something?" She was startled by the owner coming up behind her.

"I was in here several months ago with a friend and there was a lovely little dresser back there," she pointed. "Has it been sold?"

"Oh no. I moved it over here." He led her the front of the store. If she hadn't been so focused on getting to the back, she would have seen it. "I've had it for quite a while, so I lowered the price."

"I'll take it!" she said. "And I'll take this Santa Claus, too. My father had one like it when he was a child. The pictures show it with a red sleigh and a Rudolph. You don't have those, do you?"

"I might have a sleigh, but no Rudolph."

"That's fine," she said. "I'll just take Santa."

She ran her hand over the dresser top. She couldn't wait to give it to Sal. Last year, Christmas gifts had been the last thing on her mind. Polly had been so focused on getting the business of Sycamore House going, she hadn't had time to think about it.

Everything felt different now. This year there were so many people in her life and Christmas was a perfect opportunity to tell them how much they meant to her.

The bell on the door clanged again and Henry walked in. "Hello, Simon," he said. "Did she find what she was looking for?"

"It's right here," the man replied. "She's buying one of my favorite pieces."

"You say that about everything. It's a wonder you make any money. We all know the only reason you have a shop is because your wife won't let you keep all of these things in your house."

"You be quiet, young man. Now, are you going to carry this for her or will you make me do the heavy lifting?"

Henry chuckled, "If you take the drawers, Polly, I will carry this to my truck."

The store owner pulled the three small drawers out and Polly took two. She tucked the Santa under her arm and followed Henry to his truck. They loaded it and when she turned around to thank the owner, he was coming back with a red sleigh in his hand.

"You need this for Santa Claus. Take it."

"You don't have to do this," she protested.

"It's Christmas. Santa needs his sleigh."

"Thank you very much." She took the sleigh and then reached out to shake his hand. "Merry Christmas!"

"He's a nice old man," she said to Henry when the truck doors were shut. "He didn't need to give this to me."

"He was flirting with you, Polly. And if I'm not being too cynical, don't you think you'll buy more from him?"

"Of course I will!" Then she laughed, "Oh. Of course I will. That was as shrewd as it was nice."

"He's been in this business a long time. It was a very nice thing that he did, and he ensured that you would be a customer for life."

When they got back to Sycamore House, Henry carried the dresser into the garage, tucking it up against the wall. Polly slid the bottom drawer in and then the middle drawer while Henry grabbed the last one from the bed of his truck. He handed it to her and when she attempted to slide it in, met with some resistance.

"I must have these in the wrong order." She shifted them around and when attempting to put a drawer in the top slot, met resistance again. "Or there's something wrong with this."

Polly pulled the drawer out and looked inside. She couldn't see anything along the sides, but there was something hanging down from the top of the piece. She reached in and tugged on it, feeling it finally give way with a little effort.

"What do you have there?" Henry asked.

"It's a package. There's no address on it or anything, but it was stuck to the top of the dresser."

"Maybe it's advertising from the company who built this."

"That's probably it," she said and slid the final drawer into place. She grinned to herself as she placed the package on top of the dresser and began to walk toward the door to go inside.

"Aren't you going to open it?" he asked.

"You're probably right. It's nothing. It will be fine. I'll just make sure it goes with Sal, too." She did her best not to laugh out loud as she put her hand on the door handle.

"You don't fool me," Henry said, picking up the package and following her inside. "You are as curious as I am about this."

"I don't know what you mean. You gave me a perfectly plausible explanation and since I think you're the smartest man in the world, it must be true."

Henry reached out to take her arm and she pulled away, running for her apartment door. He chased her up the steps, as she ran up and through the bedroom, coming to a lurching stop in her living room. Sylvie and her boys were hovering over Maria Rivera and her child while the baby wailed.

"What's wrong?" Polly asked.

"He won't stop crying," Andrew said. "He started after you left and they've done everything. I went down and got Mom."

"He's got a fever, Polly," Sylvie said. "I think it's pretty high. Do you have a thermometer in your bathroom?"

"I think so, but if he's sick, we should get him to someone who can help. I don't know anybody in town, do you?"

Sylvie nodded. "You bet I do. Doctor Mason knows my boys very well. Let me call his office."

Polly dashed into her bathroom to find the thermometer. She was never sick and didn't know if she could even put her hands on it. And then, there it was, still in the original packaging.

Cracking the plastic wrapping open as she went back into the living room, she handed it to Sylvie, who knelt beside Maria. The baby squalled and finally Sylvie stood back up. "It's over one hundred and one degrees. He needs to see a doctor."

She stepped back and pulled out her phone, then walked into the entryway to talk. When she returned, she said to Jose, "You and Maria need to take the baby to a doctor. Polly can get you there and he's waiting for you."

He spoke to his wife and if they could, her eyes filled with more fear than before. "We have nothing to pay," he stammered.

"It's not important. The baby needs a doctor. Today. Polly, warm up your truck." When Sylvie began giving orders, Polly knew things would happen. Jose Rivera's lack of funds and Maria's lack of English couldn't stop that train from rolling forward.

"My truck is already warm," Henry interrupted. "And there is more room in it. I can take them. Polly, will you go with us?"

"Sure," she said, setting the package on the table.

Andrew and Jose left the living room and returned with coats and blankets. It took a few minutes to get the car seat buckled in, but soon everyone was loaded and Henry pulled out of the driveway. Polly was grateful that the medical building was just a couple of blocks away. Between the baby's coughing and crying, she wondered if she would ever be prepared to have children.

Henry pulled up to the front door and after they were out of the truck, drove off to a parking place. The receptionist smiled in greeting as Polly stepped to her desk. "Is this the family that Sylvie Donovan called about?" she asked.

"Yes. I'm Polly Giller."

"Oh, I know who you are," the woman laughed. "My kids loved your Halloween Haunted House. They talked about it for days! I need to get some information from the family, though."

Polly beckoned to Jose, who was helping his wife and son get comfortable in one of the waiting room chairs and he joined them at the desk. She backed away to give him room to tell their story and stood beside Henry when he came inside.

"I'm going to be a terrible mother," she whispered. "This freaks me out. The crying, the noise, the worry, the doctor. I don't like it."

He put his arm around her waist and hugged her tight. "I'm not a big fan either. Any parent who does this several times over and manages to raise their children to adulthood should get a medal."

"Doctor Mason will see you now," the receptionist said. Jose took the child from his wife and the three of them followed her through a door to the back.

When she returned to her desk, Polly stepped forward again. "I know they can't afford this, so I want to cover the cost. And let me take care of any medication they need, too."

The woman waved her off. "Doctor Mason is glad to see people who need him. He won't charge for the office visit. I'll bet this is pneumonia and he'll give them advice and antibiotics. But we'll talk to you before worrying them with any costs."

"Thank you," Polly said.

"Aaron didn't expect you to do all of this for them," Henry told her when she sat down beside him.

"You're right, but what else could I do? They need help."

"And that's why I love you. It doesn't occur to you to ignore someone who needs help. You just step in and deal with it."

"Kind of like you and Nate fixing their car?"

"I guess. Kind of like that."

She picked up a magazine and idly thumbed through it. After several minutes the door opened again and she saw an older man hold it while Jose and Maria walked through.

Henry jumped up and said, "I'm going to make sure the truck is warm. I'll be out front in just a minute," and left the office.

The doctor stopped at the front desk and his receptionist nodded toward Polly. He walked over to her and handed her a slip of paper. "The baby will be fine, but just in case he starts to wheeze or need some help, I've prescribed a nebulizer. The pharmacy has what you need." He touched her shoulder. "Thank you for bringing them in and make sure they stay warm. They shouldn't travel for a few days so the little boy's lungs can heal up." Then he leaned in and said quietly, "I don't believe the heater in their car is working, if I understood him correctly."

Polly nodded and took the prescription from him. "Thank you for everything."

"It's my pleasure." He turned back to Jose and Maria. "Be sure to give him his medication regularly for the next ten days. If he isn't better by Monday, come back and see me."

"Thank you," Maria said, looking down at her shoes. Her husband shook the doctor's hand and repeated the words.

Polly saw Henry's truck pull up and touched Maria's elbow,

then pointed. The woman smiled at her and held the baby out to Jose so she could put her coat on. After another short trip to Sycamore House, Henry pulled into the garage and Polly shut the door behind them. They got everyone upstairs and the Riveras went back to their room. Maria had dark circles under her eyes and Polly hoped she would sleep. Henry stopped Jose long enough to tell him that he and a friend would fix the car.

The poor man just kept shaking his head and then shaking Henry's hand. He finally left to join his wife and son.

"I noticed you didn't tell him you were going to try to fix the car, you told him you would."

Henry laughed at her, "I learned a lesson from your Star Wars Trek movies. 'Do or do not. There is no try."

"Star Wars. You know better," she grumbled at him.

He kissed her on the cheek. "Yes, I do. I also know that saying it wrong makes you crazy. Nate told me there would be no problem getting it running, and I'm confident in his assessment. We'll pick up parts on Monday and it will be good as new."

"Speaking of that. The doctor said he thought Jose was telling him the heater didn't work in the car. Can you check that out?"

"I'll tell Nate. I can't imagine driving across the Midwest in December without a working heater. How did they stay warm?"

"I have no idea," she said. "And don't be in too much of a hurry to fix it. They need to stay here for a few days to make sure that little Salvador gets better."

"Got it. Now, if I head over to Nate's, are you going to be okay by yourself around here? Your day has kind of exploded."

Polly looked around the apartment. Andrew and Jason were nowhere to be seen and she wondered if they were at the barn."

"I'm going to be fine. I'll bet my donkeys are here."

"You go play with your livestock and I'm going to go play with something a little less warm-blooded." He kissed her again and headed for the back steps.

"Wait. Henry?"

"Do you miss me already?"

"Of course I do, but could you stop by the pharmacy and pick this up? Doctor Mason said we didn't need it unless Salvador had a problem, but I'd rather be safe. Do you mind?"

He took the slip of paper from her, "Of course I don't mind. I'll be back tonight." He gave her a quick kiss and left.

Polly turned around to look at Obiwan on the sofa and gave him a pitiful smile. "I'd love to take you down to the barn but until those donkeys get settled in, I think we'll wait. Tonight they will get used to being in the same place as four big horses."

He knew she was talking to him and wagged his tail, then jumped off the sofa. She knelt down and hugged him. "Sorry about this. Another time."

She slipped out the front door, not daring to look behind her at his soulful eyes. That dog could make her feel guilty every single time she left him in the apartment. She glanced across the hall and heard intermittent coughing, but at least little Salvador had stopped crying.

CHAPTER FIVE

Seeing Mark's truck and a horse trailer parked at the barn, Polly put on a little burst of speed. Now that she'd had time to think about it, she was excited about new animals in her life. The doors to the barn were closed since it was pretty chilly out. When she went inside, she was greeted by a rather large reception.

Both Andrew and Jason had come down to greet the newcomers and Eliseo and Mark were standing beside Demi in the alley with the two new residents.

Andrew started to run toward her, then glanced up at Eliseo and instead, walked quietly over to join her. He whispered, "Aren't they great? They don't scare me at all." He took her hand, "Come on, you have to meet them!"

Polly let him lead her to the donkeys and Mark slipped two small carrots into her hand as she passed him.

Demi nosed her in the back as she approached the donkeys and bent down in front of them.

"Hi guys. Welcome to Sycamore House," she said. She put a carrot in each hand and held them out in front of the animals. They each nibbled the carrot from her hand and sniffed at her.

"You two are pretty adorable." She turned around to Mark and asked, "Which is which?"

"The light brown is Tom and the dark brown is Huck."

"I can remember that," she said as Andrew stroked Huck's back.

"He feels different than a horse," Andrew said.

"Their coat is different," Mark assured him. "In fact, they don't like rain and snow very much, so they'll be glad to have a nice dry home to hang out in this winter."

Polly stood up, "How are they doing with the horses?" She felt something in her hand and realized that Tom had pushed his head under it, so she stroked him between his long ears.

"So far we've only introduced Demi to them. He's the easiest going of them all. He's perfectly fine, as you can see."

The donkeys didn't react to Demi's nosing and sniffing. The horse pushed Tom a little with his head and Tom simply moved away with the shove and then came back under Polly's hand.

"Once they get more comfortable, they will own the barn," Eliseo said. "We won't be able to keep them out of anything they want to get into and I suspect they'll feel comfortable going in and out of the horses' stalls. We've walked with them past the other three horses several times, letting everyone smell each other. No one has had a bad reaction, so I'm confident this will be fine."

Polly sat down on a bench and Tom followed her. "He's kind of like a big dog!" she laughed.

"They like a lot of attention. If you are here and not doing anything, they want you to be playing with them or touching them. These two were part of a family who treated them more like pets than anything. They'll take any love you can give them."

"What do you think, Andrew? Are you ready to spend some time hanging out with the donkeys?"

"Can I read down here?"

"Of course you can," she said.

"The donkeys like being outside, even in the winter," Eliseo said. "But, if you come down with some apple slices or carrots, they'll be right in to play with you."

Tom and Huck knew they were the center of attention and walked back and forth between everyone.

Eliseo led Demi back to his stall. "I need to go up to the main building and make sure things are in place for the reception. Sylvie hasn't called to tell me I'm needed, but I want to check." He shook Mark's hand, "Thanks for bringing these fellas home today."

Mark grinned, "I didn't give you much of a choice, but I knew they'd be happy here. And don't worry, Polly. They're in great health. My friends down in Malvern made sure everything was good to go before they left today. They are up to date on all of their shots and Marnie will get their health history into your file."

He started to walk out with Eliseo and Polly panicked. "Wait. Both of you are leaving? What are we supposed to do with them?"

The two men turned around. Mark was grinning and Eliseo simply shook his head. Mark said, "You aren't supposed to *do* anything. They've been fed and their bedding is in the stall. They won't want to be penned up, so we've shut the door to the feed room. They'll be fine on their own."

"But they just got here!" She hugged Tom's neck to her chest. "How can I just leave them alone?"

"Polly. They have each other and a new place to explore. You can stay as long as you'd like, but they don't need you."

"But ..." Polly looked at Jason and Andrew for help and then laughed. She was arguing with two men who knew what they were doing and looking for support from two boys, one of whom had spent the last nine months avoiding the barn like a plague.

"Fine," she said. "But we're staying for a while. I don't want them to be scared on their first day here."

"They're already scared. Everything is different for them," Mark said patiently. "Just give them time to get used to the place. They have a lot to learn about living at Sycamore House. They smell those four immense horses everywhere. But they are smart and just need time to figure it all out."

"I can't make this any easier on them, can I?" she asked quietly.

"You already have," Eliseo said. "They need time. They aren't running away from you or the kids and they aren't showing any outward signs of stress. You'd see it in their ears or their tails. You need to be the one who is okay right now."

"Got it," Polly said. "I'm okay. I'm okay."

The men left and she was there with two young boys and two strange donkeys. The horses poked their heads over the stall doors to see what the excitement was about, but had all gone back to what they were doing before people showed up in their space.

Tom and Huck spent time sniffing the three humans, then wandered off to explore. Tom stopped in front of Nan's stall and she came forward and leaned her head down to sniff at him. She bared her teeth and he stood his ground. Polly was glad there was a wooden door separating them while they got used to each other. Pretty soon, the donkey wandered off in search of another adventure. Huck followed him into the stall they used to bathe the horses. There were quite a few smells in there, as evidenced by the animals sniffing all around the walls and floor.

"They don't play like Obiwan, do they?" Andrew asked.

"No, they seem to be pretty independent."

Jason hadn't said much.

"What do you think, Jason?" she asked.

"They're really different than horses. I thought they'd be exactly like them, just smaller. I like their ears. They're all soft and fuzzy."

Andrew followed the donkeys from a safe distance, watching them explore their surroundings. He finally sat down beside Polly. "Eliseo told me I have to be calm and quiet and not startle them. I try not to get really excited, but they're fun!"

Both donkeys wandered back out as Jason sat down on Polly's other side. They waited patiently for the animals to join them and before long, they were all laughing and snuggling Tom and Huck.

Polly looked up when Eliseo returned.

"It looks like you have been making friends," he said. "How are things going?"

"Do you think I could ride Tom or Huck someday?" Andrew asked Eliseo.

The older man grinned, "Of course you can!"

Andrew said to Polly, "At least if I fall, it's close to the ground."

"You're right!" she laughed. "Do you think you'd like that?"

He nodded and pulled Tom's neck close to his face. "I think he likes me."

She smiled at Eliseo and he winked, the damaged skin on his face pulling along his cheekbone. She rarely saw his burns. Every once in a while, he did something to remind her how badly he'd been hurt, but most of the time he was simply Eliseo.

"Jason and I are going to do evening chores," he said. "Andrew, if you want to stick around, I can show you what we will do for the donkeys. I'd love to have you help us."

"Can I, Polly?" he asked.

"Sure! What should I do?" she asked Eliseo.

"You aren't dressed for this," he said. "We'll take care of things tonight. You have guests upstairs. That should keep you busy."

"Thanks." He was right. She wanted to make sure they had supper. Maybe Sylvie would have leftovers from the reception. Or maybe they'd really like a pizza. She'd check with Sylvie first.

A quick glance into the kitchen when Polly returned to the main building told her that they were much too busy to deal with any special requests, so she went on up to her apartment.

She flopped down on the sofa and was soon surrounded by her three inside animals. Obiwan immediately began to sniff her, trying to identify the new animal scents on her clothing. Luke and Leia gave perfunctory attention to her clothes and then settled back to sleep. Polly glimpsed the package from the dresser on her coffee table and after pushing Obiwan out of the way, sat up and flipped it over. There wasn't anything on it, a simple sealed envelope, about the size of a large greeting card. The glue on the seal easily gave way and she gently pulled the contents out.

It was an old Christmas card. The front said, *To a sweet little girl at Christmas*, and had an adorable drawing of a little cherub dressed for winter. She was singing from a caroling book held in her little mittened hands. Polly opened the card and found several photographs of a happy family. In one, two older brothers were proudly holding their new baby sister and the parents were seated on either side of them. In another, the children were a little older and dressed to play outside in the snow. The little girl was bundled from head to toe and her brothers were standing on either side of her, holding her hands. Another photograph was obviously a professional shot done of the three children, followed by a family photograph of all of them. In addition to the photographs, there was a handwritten letter, neatly folded.

Polly looked at the inside of the Christmas card and found written there, in a shaky hand:

"Dear Marian, You may never remember your mommy and daddy, but they loved you very much. There isn't much left to give you so that you will have any memories of your life with them, but I have enclosed what I could. I hope you treasure these memories as much as they treasured you. Your mommy didn't live for very many days after the accident, but I helped her write one last letter to you. Always know that you were loved. Beatrice Hogan."

"Wow," Polly said out loud. "I wonder what happened!"

She unfolded the letter and skimmed through it, her eyes filling with tears as she came to the end.

"My dear Marian Jeanine,

There are so many things I would have told you as you grew up, things that any mother would tell her daughter. I can only hope and pray that you have someone wonderful who will watch over you and love you for the rest of your life.

For the few short years I have known you, you were the light in our family. Your brothers, Doug and Paul, were quite a bit older than you and were very proud to show you off whenever they could. Doug would have been your hero. He was always helping people and he loved to pick you up when you fell down. If you cried, his heart broke and he ran to fix whatever you needed him to fix. Paul would have been your entertainment. When you laughed, our hearts soared, so he did everything he could to make that laugh happen. Those two boys left this life much too soon and the world is a darker place without them.

Your daddy and I loved each other more than even seems fair and he adored you. When he tossed you in the air, you screamed with delight, begging for more. You knew when he was coming home from work and waited under the coat tree to surprise him. Every evening, he would hang up his hat and his coat and wait for you to jump up and giggle, then he would swing you up into his arms and call out, 'Why is no one minding the animals in this place? Another one has escaped their cage.' Even though he was wearing a suit, he would fall to the ground with you and roll around, making sounds like a lion or an elephant, just to hear you squeal.

Your name comes from two amazing women. Your daddy's mother was named Jeanine and she was very old when he was born. He was her only child and though I didn't ever get to meet her, he loved her. My mother's name was Marian. We lived in England. I met your daddy when he was a handsome soldier in the war. We fell in love and when the war was over, he came back to find me. He made me very happy every day of our lives together. It was difficult to leave my home and family, but I knew that I could never be happy without your daddy by my side.

Each day, Mrs. Hogan brings you in so that I can see your shining face. I know she hopes that I will live because you need me and if I could, I would do just that, but the accident hurt me too much. You must know that your family would have done anything we could to be with you. She has promised to give you the few photographs I was able to save and to make sure this letter goes with them. There is nothing left but you and that is enough. You are special, you are unique, you are loved and when you think about the family who brought you into this world, I hope that you will always know that they were happy because you were part of their lives.

We will wait for you in heaven, but please don't hurry to see us. Live a wonderfully, full life. Be happy while you grow up, I pray you marry a good man and have a house full of children who make every day a joy for you, just as you did for us.

I love you more today than I did yesterday and not as much as I will tomorrow.

Mommy"

Polly sat back on her sofa and pulled the dog close to her, then sobbed into his soft neck. "That's the saddest thing I've ever read," she whispered. "It breaks my heart."

She finally wiped her eyes with the collar of her shirt and stood up, announcing. "I need to make dinner. Everybody likes pizza, don't they? Or sandwiches." It always made her chuckle when the animals watched as she talked to them. If they ever responded, she was certain she'd be found in a dead faint on the floor. "Don't ever learn to talk," she wagged her finger at them. "I don't want you to tell my secrets to anyone!" Just the thought of the stories those animals could tell made Polly clutch her chest dramatically.

Polly wondered what Henry was doing for the evening, so she texted him. *"What's up for supper? How long will you be at Nate's?"*

"I'm driving to your house right now. Do you want me to pick something up? What about the Riveras?"

"Come on over. I was thinking pizza. I can feed Andrew and Jason and the Riveras and you and me with a couple of those."

"I'll be there in a minute."

Polly thought about it and sent one more text, *"Do you two want to come over for pizza in about a half hour?"*

Doug Randall immediately responded with *"Yes! What should we bring?"*

"No worries. I've got it," she sent back.

Life was much more fun with a people around and the more she fed this evening, the more varieties of pizza she could explain. She called Pizzazz downtown and placed her order, then texted Jason to let him know there would be food for all of them, Eliseo included, when they were finished. There. That should do it.

She gathered up the photos, card and letter and set them on the bookshelf in a corner so they would be out of the way, and went to the kitchen to rummage around for paper plates and cups. Once everything was on the peninsula, she ran across the hall to the room where the Riveras were staying and softly knocked.

Jose opened the door and stepped outside.

"I'm having a little party in my apartment tonight. We're eating pizza. Would you and Maria please come over? I'd like you to meet Eliseo Aquila. He works here and sometimes I feel badly that I don't speak Spanish. Eliseo does and it might make things a little easier for you two while you're here."

"We're okay," he protested. "You've done too much. As soon as the car is fixed, we'll go away."

"Please come over," Polly repeated. "I want you to meet Eliseo. Please?" She knew it sounded as if she were begging, but she didn't care. There was no way she could have a family living under her roof and not make sure they were well taken care of.

"Maria is sleeping." He looked at the watch on his hand.

"I'll send Andrew over in about forty-five minutes. If she's still sleeping, maybe you could come for a while." Polly wasn't letting him get out of this evening if she could help it.

He finally nodded. "Forty-five minutes," he said.

"Good. I'm glad." Polly went back to her apartment and found Henry sitting on the chair by her bookshelves reading the letter.

When he looked up at her, his eyes were glistening. "Do you think she ever got this?"

"I don't know," Polly said. "I was going to ask what you thought."

"Had it been opened before you got to it?"

"I don't think so. How do we even start looking for her?"

He shrugged. "I suppose we go back to see Simon on Monday and find out where he got the dresser. Then we begin asking questions. I have to think that people would remember an accident which killed a family and left a little girl alone."

"Marian would probably be about Lydia's age. Maybe she knows something." Polly leaned against the bookshelf. "We're going to have an apartment full of people tonight. I've invited Doug and Billy, told Jason and Andrew to come up and bring Eliseo and I just invited the Riveras. Let's put this away until tomorrow."

Henry folded up the letter and put everything back together and slipped it into the envelope. "That's so sad. Wouldn't it be wonderful if we could tell someone how much she was loved?"

"Yes, it really would be," Polly leaned over and kissed his forehead. "Being loved is a pretty amazing thing."

CHAPTER SIX

"Come on, let's go!" Obiwan was sleeping in a sunbeam and Polly was ready to head outside. He stood up and stretched, then waited while she put the leash on. They walked to the corner garden where a group of people were gathered. The churches in town were working together this afternoon to build the structure for the Living Nativity. She found Lydia standing off to one side, watching as hay bales were stacked around the wooden walls to add insulation as well as stability.

"Hi, dear," Lydia said. "What do you think?"

"This is so cool. It will be beautiful!"

"We've been advertising in the area. Hopefully that will bring traffic." Lydia nodded back toward Sycamore House. "And with your Christmas lights and decorations, this corner will be lovely."

"We have an event every night this week, so it will be nice for people to make this part of their celebrations."

"Office parties?" Lydia asked.

"Some of those and some different groups are hosting parties. There's a wedding on Friday night and another on Saturday."

"I'm sorry you aren't having your big Christmas party this year.

That was quite a celebration."

"Jeff filled the calendar and I have plenty of opportunities for parties throughout the year. After Halloween, we needed a break."

"That's smart. So, what do you think about Jason and the donkeys? We are creating a little home for them right here. They can come and go as they please and Jason can be in the shelter.

"I wouldn't be surprised if both boys will be here. You aren't expecting them every night, are you?"

"No. Our church is here tonight and the kids know everyone. We'll be here again next Sunday, so they can do it again."

" Oh, Lydia, those donkeys are adorable! I'm in love with them already. They were so happy to see me this morning."

"How are the horses getting along with them?"

"Nan isn't sure about it yet, but the others seem to be taking it in stride. I'll take Obiwan down sometime when we don't have so much work to do. I want him to be comfortable with them, too."

"It will all come in time. Excuse me, just a minute," Lydia stepped into a cluster of people and pointed to the back of the structure, speaking quietly to them. Then she returned to Polly's side. "I should get busy."

Polly stopped her by touching her arm, "I found something yesterday in an old dresser that I bought down at the Antique Shoppe. It's a Christmas card with pictures and a letter that a mother wrote to her daughter. The family died and this daughter ... I don't know. Would you come upstairs when you're finished to look at it and tell me if you have any idea who it might be? I don't think the letter ever made it to the person who was meant to have it and I'd love to find her."

Lydia scrunched her eyes in thought and said, "Of course I'll come up. It will be good to get warm. Do you have coffee?"

"I'll make it! Come on up whenever. I'm taking Obiwan for a walk right now. We both need the exercise. It's supposed to get cold tomorrow and he likes being out in that more than I do.."

"I'll see you in a bit," Lydia said.

Polly crossed the road into the parking lot by the swimming pool and then ducked onto the trail that followed the wooded area behind it. There was snow beside the trail and Obiwan took his time sniffing it, looking for something interesting to mark. When they returned to Sycamore House, lights were being strung up on the outside of the nativity structure and two men were unloading the manger. Old horse blankets were covering hay bales and she laughed as she saw women holding heating pads. She wondered if they planned to heat the manger with those.

She and Obiwan ran back upstairs and she quickly put a pot of coffee on, then straightened up the living room. The pizza party had gone longer than she expected last night, with everyone having a good time. Jose and Maria finally relaxed when they realized that there was someone else who could understand them and help them integrate into the group. Eliseo talked more than she'd ever seen, trying to draw the two newcomers out. Rachel came upstairs when she was finished in the kitchen and not long after, Sylvie joined them before taking the boys home.

Sylvie had checked the baby and smiled when she saw that Salvador was sleeping and quiet. After they left, the party continued. When Jose and Maria finally took their baby back to their room and Eliseo hadn't made a move to leave, Doug mentioned watching a movie. Before she knew it, they were watching *Christmas Vacation* with everyone reciting lines.

Billy went to get his dog, Big Jack, for a last run that evening and Doug had offered to take Obiwan along, leaving her and Henry and Eliseo to clean up. They'd worked quickly and Henry took the pizza boxes and a bag of trash downstairs for her. Eliseo finally seemed to be part of the family. He'd sacrificed his Sunday morning to play with them. Since she knew he'd be in the auditorium cleaning this morning, Polly had helped get the horses and donkeys ready for the day, then followed him in and insisted he let her help clean up. They'd worked steadily, gathering trash and the few leftover plates and silverware off the tables, then wiped everything down. While Eliseo put the majority of the tables away, Polly had vacuumed.

Jose Rivera had come down while they were working and helped Eliseo rearrange the tables for the evening's holiday party.

Polly couldn't imagine being stuck in a single room all the time and was glad he felt he could move around freely. He took over the vacuuming and Eliseo had given her a nod to let him, so she'd gone into the kitchen to see if Sylvie had leftovers for lunch.

Not only were there leftovers, but on one of the containers, Sylvie had written a note: "Polly. Serve this for lunch."

She opened it and found sliced roast beef and ham. She loved that woman. A bag on the prep table also had Polly's name on it and in it was a package of buns and two bags of potato chips.

Polly went back into the auditorium and said, "Sylvie has lunch for us. It's just sandwiches and chips. Jose, you and Maria can eat wherever you'd like, but please help yourself."

Eliseo and Jose spoke to each other in rapid Spanish and she sighed, then walked away. Pretty soon Eliseo showed up at the kitchen window. "We'll eat here, if that's okay, Polly. He's going to get Maria and Salvador."

"Are they going to be all right with this?" she asked.

"It's difficult for him to accept your hospitality. He's a proud man and has had some trouble. They were living in Chicago with his family, but are heading to southern California where her family lives. I don't know if they have enough money to make it across the country. But I told him that you were generous and a good person and that if I could learn to accept it, he could, especially when there was a baby involved."

"I don't want him to feel bad," Polly said. "What can I do?"

"We could use the help this week. Let him work with me."

Polly breathed a huge sigh of relief, "Yes! That's perfect. You figure out what you need from him and please, let me find a way to give him some cash at the end of this to help them keep going. I don't want him to be working here simply for room and board."

"I'll do that and I will speak with Sylvie. Her Christmas break has started, so she won't be in school, but I suspect she might be able to use Maria in the kitchen, too."

He stepped back, his face blushing.

"Can I leave you to this?" she asked, pointing at the food on the counter. Eliseo nodded and Polly went upstairs.

The last day and a half had been busy and Polly was ready to settle in. Henry was coming that evening and she wanted to beg him to help her go through the stacks of boxes in her garage to look for her family's Christmas decorations. The Santa Claus Polly had picked up at the Antique Shoppe was in the middle of the dining room table, but that was it.

There was a knock at her front door and Polly waited a heartbeat. Lydia opened the door and called out, "Can I come in?"

"I'm here!" Polly said. "Come on in. I have fresh coffee."

"It was getting chilly out there. I'm glad they have some heaters for those poor folk who will be sitting outside tonight."

Polly poured two cups of coffee and handed one to Lydia. "It's over here. Let's get comfortable."

After they sat down in the living room, Polly handed the envelope to Lydia, who looked at the pictures, read the card and then, the letter. Lydia's eyes were swimming with tears and Polly pushed a box of tissues toward her. "I know. It destroyed me, too. Henry even got teary-eyed last night when he read it."

"He didn't have any idea who this might be? His family has lived in the area for a long time."

"He didn't say anything. He thought maybe Simon at the Antique Shoppe might remember where he got the dresser, but I figured if anyone might know something, it would be you."

"I don't remember this, but it probably happened before I was born. I can ask some of the older ladies that I know. Someone is going to remember an accident that killed four people. Especially when two of them were little boys and there was a baby girl who lived through it. We have to find out what happened to her."

"I'll ask Henry to call his mom. Maybe she'll remember something, too," Polly said.

"You should bring all of this to the women's meeting Tuesday morning. It's our Christmas party." Lydia laughed at the horrified look on Polly's face. "It's not that bad. Okay, maybe you wouldn't have quite as much fun as we do, but still, you might be able to get some good information. These women have been around a long time and they know everyone's history in all the surrounding counties. Trust me, they're better than the CIA and the FBI together when it comes to holding on to secrets."

"That doesn't make me feel any better about showing up, you know," Polly chuckled.

"You already know some of them. I always invite Beryl, but she knows better than to come. I dragged her to something years ago and she had one of the meanest old biddies in the group backed into a corner in the kitchen after the woman had torn into some poor young woman for using the wrong dishtowels to dry dishes. It was the young woman's first time in the kitchen and the rest of us should have paid more attention. Old Mabel was a terrorist and we generally kept her occupied, but somehow she escaped us and before anyone knew what had happened, Beryl was on the offense. Looking back, it was pretty hilarious, but I thought I was going to have to call for the cavalry to separate them."

"Still not helping."

"Oh, after Mabel died, there were a few more ladies who wanted to run the kitchen with an iron fist, but that's calmed down a lot over the years. However, they would be one of your best resources for tracking this Marian Jeanine down."

"If I don't get information from nearly anyone else, I'll call."

"There is a program at ten and then luncheon begins at eleven. If you give a presentation, they'll mull it over during the meal and I can guarantee you'll have an answer before we leave."

"I'll think about it. You aren't giving up on this, are you?"

"If you tell me you'll come, I'll invite Beryl."

"You are really sick and twisted, aren't you!" Polly laughed.

"Aaron says it's my best attribute. Being dull, boring and sugary sweet all the time isn't much fun."

"Well, I love you this way. You always surprise me."

"That's what my sweet baboo says and I like being able to surprise him after thirty years of marriage." Lydia looked through the photos once more. "So, you'll come on Tuesday?"

Polly grimaced, "I'm not going to get out of it, am I."

"Not if I can help it."

"You're kind of mean."

"And manipulative. Don't forget manipulative. Whenever Beryl thinks I've backed her into a corner, that's what she calls me. Just because I'm always thinking and planning and involving and organizing, she gets huffy."

"You're one of the smartest people I know," Polly reached over and hugged her friend, "and I'll bet that brain of yours never turns off when it's looking for the best way to make something happen."

"See. You get it," Lydia laughed. "My kids and Aaron finally figured out that if they pay attention to what I'm saying, it will be the easiest way to do something."

"What you're telling me is that I'll get my answers on Tuesday."

"That's exactly right, dear! And you'll meet people and get a good lunch."

Andrew and Jason showed up after Lydia left that afternoon, since their mother was in the kitchen. Both boys were carrying a small bag and when Polly asked what they had, Andrew proudly pulled out a brown robe.

"Mrs. Randall had a bunch of old costumes that Doug wore and she let us have them. We're going to be donkey herders!"

"You are! That's wonderful," Polly said. "Which donkey are you going to herd?"

"Tom likes me better, so I'm going to hold his leash."

"His lead, you're going to hold his lead," Jason scolded.

"Whatever. Just because you ride horses, you think you know everything."

Jason walked into the kitchen mumbling, "I know *that*, runt." Then he spoke a little louder. "Can I get something to drink?"

"Sure. There's juice and milk and cold water in there."

"Do you want anything?"

"No, I'm good," she said, watching Andrew play with the two cats. Obiwan lay on the floor beside them, doing his best to ignore the activity.

Andrew jumped up, "Should I take Obiwan out for a walk?"

"You can any time you want to. He always likes going outside with you." Andrew bolted for the back stairs and called Obiwan to follow him.

"He's weird," Jason muttered and sat down on the couch with a glass of milk.

"He's your brother," she laughed.

"Polly?"

"Yes, Jason?" Polly had her back to him as she walked into the kitchen. His glass of milk had given her a craving for a cookie. There was still at least one more container in the freezer.

"Now that I'm thirteen, I want to make sure Mom has something nice for Christmas. Not some little kid gift that we make at school, but something important."

Polly spun around. He was staring into his glass.

"What are you thinking about?"

"I don't know," he said. "That's why I'm talking to you."

She refilled her coffee mug and took it and the cookies back to the living room, then sat down beside him. "Do you want to get her perfume or something for the house? What kind of money do you want to spend?"

"I've saved twenty dollars and Andrew gave me ten dollars. We want this to be special."

Then it hit Polly, "Why don't I meet you downtown tomorrow after school. I saw some jewelry at the Antique Shoppe and I bet you could find something that would be perfect for her."

He dug around in his pockets and handed her a wad of cash. "Would you keep this? I don't want to take it to school and lose it. It's the whole thing."

"I'll be glad to hold it for you."

"Thank you. Mom always makes sure we have a good Christmas, but I've never been able to put a present under the tree for her. Starting this year that changes," he declared. "It's about time she had something nice."

He put his empty glass down on the coffee table with a flourish and Polly held herself back from hugging him. The little boy who still had traces of a milk moustache was doing all he could to grow up and be a man.

CHAPTER SEVEN

Unless the world ended, Polly needed to leave soon. She wasn't sure why she dreaded going to this meeting, but the thought of it sent shivers down her back. Lydia told her to be there at ten forty-five. Polly's presentation would be just before lunch.

She'd met Jason and Andrew at the Antique Shoppe yesterday afternoon. Before they arrived, she had a conversation with the owner, Simon Gardner, about the dresser. He told her that it had been in the store for at least five years and thought maybe it had come from an estate auction.

The boys had entered the store with wide eyes. Jason was on a mission to buy a necklace for his mother, while Andrew's idea of the perfect gift was an immense, gaudy, blue glass vase. Polly led them to the jewelry counter, where Simon patiently set out pieces for them to hold. Jason's eyes lit up over a lapis and rhinestone necklace with matching earrings, but was crushed to see it marked at fifty dollars. He pushed it aside until Simon stopped him.

"Young man," the man had said. "This is the Antique Shoppe. You make me an offer. None of these prices are set in stone."

Jason had looked up at Polly. She bent over and whispered,

"Don't offer him all you have. Start low. Let him meet you."

The boy stood a little straighter, looked at Simon in the eyes and said, "I can give you twenty dollars."

Simon clutched his heart, "You're killing me. I can't go that low! I'll sell them to you for forty dollars."

Jason looked at Polly again and she pointed her finger up and he said, "Maybe twenty-five dollars for the set."

"No," Simon said. "You'd take out all my profit. I need to make a little bit of money. It's Christmas!"

One more glance at Polly and she winked at him. Jason stood a little taller and said. "The very highest I can go is thirty dollars and that has to include sales tax, because that's all I've got."

The man sighed as dramatically as he could and after exhaling loudly, said, "For someone who didn't know how to make a bargain, you did very well, young man. This is quite a deal you've made. I hope that it makes a wonderful gift for someone special."

Andrew's eyes were as big as saucers. He'd watched the entire transaction take place with his mouth open. "It's for our mom. This is the first time we've ever bought a present for her. We work at Sycamore House and Polly pays us to take care of her animals."

"Your mother must be pretty special to have sons who are willing to spend thirty dollars on her. Let me get two nice boxes for these. Do you want me to wrap them?"

Jason shook his head, "No thank you. We will do that."

"I'll be right back," Leaving the jewelry on the counter, Simon walked toward the back of the store.

"I was so nervous," Jason said. "I didn't know I could do that."

"You can always bargain in a place like this. It doesn't work in regular stores, but when it comes to antiques, most shop owners are willing to strike a deal. Mr. Gardner must have been ready to sell that jewelry today. You did very well."

"Do you have the money?" he asked.

Polly handed him the cash. When Simon Gardner returned, he wrote out a receipt for the transaction, boxed up the jewelry into two plain white jewelry boxes, and placed them in a bag.

"Thank you, boys. Stop in again to take a look at our toys. I'm always willing to negotiate!" he had said as they left the store.

When they returned to Sycamore House, the boys had taken the necklace and earrings in and out of the boxes several more times. They'd stayed through supper and late into the evening since Sylvie was cooking for another holiday party. Both boys helped in the barn with evening chores. The donkeys were happy to see their new friends and Eliseo continued to teach Andrew how to lead Tom. Polly had been glad to finally see them go home though, ready to simply sit on her sofa and read a book.

Now, she sat at her desk, watching the clock. Finally, she couldn't take it any longer, grabbed her keys and cut through the kitchen for the garage. She was just going to sit in the background until she had to talk. Her heart felt like it was crawling into her throat as she pulled in. Without giving it much more thought, she made sure she had the package and walked across the parking lot.

They were meeting in the basement of the church and she was greeted by noise and background Christmas music. She found a chair at an empty table and quickly sat down.

"Now it is time for our poinsettia giveaway," the woman standing at the front of the room said. "Each person should take a slip of paper with a number on it from the bowl at your table."

Rustling was heard around the room as the bowls were passed.

"All of the numbers should be taken. If you don't have eight people at your table, someone will have to take two." She waited while the ladies at the tables sorted themselves out. "I am going to choose a number between one and eight and that person will take home the poinsettia from their table. Are you ready?"

The women each held up their numbers and waited. "It's number four! If you have the number four, then you get to take the poinsettia with you when you leave. You can thank the Men's Club for their gift to our party today."

"We aren't finished yet," she continued. "There are other door prizes. The first is a beautiful nativity scene, hand painted by Amber Grossman. Have you finished your Christmas shopping?"

There was muttering and laughter around the room. "If you are buying presents for at least three children under the age of eighteen, stand up." Nearly everyone in the room stood. "Now, if you are buying for at least five children under the age of eighteen, stay standing, the rest can be seated." Many were still standing and as she increased the number of children, more people sat down until the woman who was purchasing gifts for twenty-three children under that age was standing and blushing.

"Lily Biggerstaff, you have a lot of grandchildren in your life. Congratulations! You deserve this nativity set."

"It might end up being one of the gifts," the woman laughed.

"We usually have a door prize for the oldest and the youngest person in attendance, but last year I got into trouble for embarrassing our ladies about their age," the emcee announced.

A few women grumbled, "I'm proud of how old I am," someone said, while others quietly clapped.

"So rather than have you admit your age, I am going to present this gift," she held up a wrapped package, "to the youngest guest with us today, Miss Laney Griffith, who is here with her grandmother. Since her grandmother brought the little cherub, she will receive the adult gift." She waited while the packages were handed to the winners and then said, "Now, Lydia Merritt has asked for a few moments. When she spoke with me about this, I heartily agreed. I think you'll like the end to today's program. Lydia?" She stepped aside as Lydia came forward.

"Good morning, ladies!" Lydia said, and the entire room loudly responded, "Good morning, Lydia!"

She smiled at them and began. "I've asked Polly Giller to join us. She has a little mystery and I told her that you might be able to help her solve it. You will love the story and if you can, you will want to help. Polly, could you come up here?"

As Polly walked toward the front, Lydia said, "I think you all know who Polly is. She purchased the old schoolhouse last year and has transformed that corner of Bellingwood into something beautiful. Many of you helped with the garden this summer and others of you have enjoyed receptions with your daughters and granddaughters in Sycamore House's auditorium. We're glad you've joined us, Polly." Lydia said and began to clap. The women joined her while Polly stood there feeling terribly embarrassed.

"I'm not sure how to begin," Polly said. "I purchased an old dresser at the Antique Shoppe and discovered a package stuck to the inside top of the dresser. In that package was an old Christmas card, some photographs and a letter. I'd like to pass the card and the photographs around while I read the letter to you."

She handed the pictures and card to Lydia, who passed them to several tables in front. The women looked at the photographs while Polly read the letter out loud to them.

"My dear Marian Jeanine," she began and when she finished, her voice cracked with emotion. Most of the women watched her while others peered at the photographs before passing them on.

"The nurse's name was Beatrice Hogan, but I don't know anything about little Marian Jeanine. I'd love to get these pictures and her mother's final letter to her, but I need help."

Lydia stepped up beside her. "I told her that many of you might remember this. We figure it has to have been in the mid to late nineteen fifties. The mother was a war bride and the brothers were several years older. What terrible accident happened that killed a family, leaving the baby alive with only a few mementos?"

Several of the older women got up and moved to other tables, talking among themselves. Soon, one of them spoke up.

"They weren't from Bellingwood. This happened over around Pilot Mound."

Another joined in, "It was in all the papers. It was nineteen fifty-six. I remember because my Amy was three years old, too. The same age as the little girl. Their house exploded. I don't remember the details. But, the little girl was still in the car when it happened. It was at Christmas. They had just gotten home from the store and were unloading groceries. The poor boys were both in the house. The father was at the door and the mother hadn't quite gotten there. If she had been carrying the girl instead of groceries, all of them would be gone."

"But what happened to the little girl?" another woman asked.

"What was their name?" Lydia asked.

A woman that Polly knew quite well, Adele Mansfield, spoke

up. "It was Detweiler. Norman and Julie Detweiler."

"How did you remember that?" one of the women asked.

"My brother was a volunteer fireman. He stopped after that experience. It was the worst thing he'd ever seen. The house was gone by the time they got there. The little girl was screaming when they found her. She was walking around in the cold and trying to wake her mother up. That poor woman didn't live very long. The burns were too awful."

"Do you know where she ended up?" Polly asked.

"There wasn't any family. Maybe friends took her."

"That doesn't make any sense," Lydia interjected. "Why wouldn't this nurse have given them the card and letter so Marian could have it later on?"

"Maybe they didn't tell her she was adopted," a woman said snidely. "Maybe they wanted her to think they were her family."

"But she was three. She would have remembered an explosion that big. How would she ever forget her first family?"

"I don't know. Don't you have enough information now? Can't we have lunch? It's ready," the woman said. "I have things to do this afternoon. If the rest of you want to help with this, go ahead, but some of us don't know anything about it and we don't care."

"You're right," Lydia said calmly. "We should eat. And besides, Reverend Boehm has just walked in to bless the meal." She looked up at the pastor who was standing in the back of the room and he simply raised his hands while the women bowed their heads.

"Thank you, dear Lord, for this gathering and for the food we are about to share. May it bless our bodies and may our fellowship bless our hearts and may our words bless your ears, O God. In Jesus' name we pray. Amen."

The woman who had led the meeting stood and said, "We will start with the left side of the room. Enjoy your meal, ladies and thanks for coming! Merry Christmas!"

She turned to Polly, "I'm sorry. But I think you have a small contingent who would like you to spend more time with them."

"Thank you," Polly replied.

Lydia said, "Bite your tongue, dear. Ignore the mean lady."

"How are you so nice?"

"Years and years of practice. Now come with me. Your old friend Adele has some people you should meet."

Polly had met Adele Mansfield at a slumber party Lydia threw when Polly first came to town. Adele held a special place in Polly's heart because her sister had known Mary Shore, the woman who stepped in to care for Polly after her mother died.

Adele stood and hugged Polly. "We love this little mystery of yours. Now, did we collect all the photographs?" Polly flipped through them and glancing around the tables, saw one more. The table was empty of people, so she stepped over and picked it up.

"We have them all now," she said.

"Sit with us. You'd think they'd let us old ladies go first, but some of those younger gals are oh, so busy."

The other ladies at the table laughed out loud and introduced themselves. Polly tried desperately to ensure that she had faces and names together, but it was all a blur. There were six women with Adele and they began chattering about the explosion and the stories that had cropped up during that time.

Polly asked, "Does anyone know Beatrice Hogan?"

"She was probably a nurse in Boone. That's where they would have taken her. I recall she was dying and everybody knew it. There were stories about how she wouldn't leave because she didn't want to be far from her daughter," one of the women said.

"Do you suppose that was Beatrice Livengood? She was a nurse down there," another woman said. "She married Manny Livengood. She died about five years ago."

"That's when Simon Gardner said he got the dresser," Polly encouraged them.

"Then that's who it was. They had a heck of a time cleaning out her house. She saved every scrap of paper."

"Which is probably why that package got jammed into the top of the dresser," Polly said. "I wonder if she just forgot it, or it got lost and she thought it was gone."

"That makes sense," Adele nodded. "Now, if the little girl did go to live with family friends, they probably kept her name the same. Pilot Mound is only ten miles west of here. Isn't Nina Black from there? She'd know about this. Let me make a call."

Adele dug around in her purse and pulled out a very nice smart phone. Polly looked at it in surprise and the woman laughed. "My grandkids think I'm cool because I have this. I hate to admit how long it took me to figure out how to use it. But at least we can video chat with it and I can see their little faces."

"I think you're cool!" Polly said. "You figured that out on your own?"

"Well, I might be old, but I'm not stupid," the woman retorted.

"No, I mean, that's awesome. Oh, I'm messing this up. Most of the time kids complain about how their parents don't know anything about technology and they have to program their DVD players for them and help with their computers."

"Not me," Adele said. "If I own a gadget, I will learn how to use it. I'm not ready to fade away and let my children feed me pudding. I'm going to step out and make this call."

The other women stood to get in line for food and Lydia turned to Polly, "I told you this group could help."

"Should we get some food?" Polly asked. "It looks wonderful."

The two of them were in line when Adele slipped in behind her and whispered. "I have the information you're looking for. Nina Black remembered everything. Your Marian Jeanine lives with her husband just five miles east of here on a farm. Her last name is now Maxwell. I even have her phone number."

Polly stopped mid-scoop over a macaroni salad. "You found her? Just like that?"

"I told you!" Lydia laughed.

"Should we tell the group?" Polly asked.

"No, not yet. If you tell these women, someone will be on Marian Maxwell's doorstep before you get back to Sycamore House. We'll let them stew about it. They'll know soon enough."

It was all Polly could do to sit quietly and eat. She sat beside Adele and reached over to squeeze her hand. "Thank you," she whispered. "Thank you!"

CHAPTER EIGHT

Escaping as soon as she could, Polly headed back to Sycamore House. She dialed Henry's phone as she went upstairs.

"Hey, pretty girl, what's up?"

"We found her. She lives five miles west of here."

"You found her? That's amazing! Does she know she's found?"

"No, not yet. Lydia was right, though. That woman's group has information on everyone!"

He laughed. "It's a little frightening, isn't it? So, what's next?"

"I have no idea."

"Well, what do you want to do?"

"My stomach is all tied up in knots. Where are you?"

"Polly, I've got good news, too. I just left Ed Greeves' office. He's getting the details together on that motel for us."

"Really? Wow! Can you come over?"

"I'm on my way."

"I'm taking the dog outside. I'll meet you out back in a few minutes," Polly said and hung up.

Obiwan was waiting for her when she went into her apartment and they ran down the back steps. He wandered to the tree line while she paced back and forth waiting for Henry. The truck finally rounded the corner onto the highway and she watched as he turned in the lane, parked in front of her garage and got out.

She kissed him, "Can you believe it! This is so much fun!"

"Which part?" he asked and bent over to rub Obiwan's head. The dog had run back when he saw that it was Henry.

"All of it! Come upstairs so we can warm up."

"So, how was your morning with the church ladies?" he asked.

"Interesting. But I got a name and number. What should I do?"

"You should call her. Maybe invite her over to dinner."

"I could do that. When should I do it? I don't want to wait."

"Call her. Tell her who you are and why you're calling, then invite her over. She'll tell you when they're available."

Polly dropped to the sofa and sat there, staring at her phone. "What if she doesn't care?"

"Stop it. Now you're just making things up. Call her."

"Okay, here I go." Polly dialed the number that Adele had given her and a man answered.

"Hello, Maxwell residence," he said.

"May I speak with Mrs. Maxwell?"

"Just a minute." She heard him call out in the background. "Mother? Phone for you." Then he returned to the call, "She'll be right here. She's in the basement." A clunking sound told Polly the phone had been set down on a table.

As she listened, she heard a woman's voice, "Who is it, Sam?"

"I don't know. She asked for you," the man responded.

"Hello, this is Marian."

"Marian, this is Polly Giller. I own Sycamore House over in Bellingwood."

"Yes, I've heard about you. You restored that old school house. We were planning to drive over tonight to see the Living Nativity and look at lights. How can I help you?"

Polly took a deep breath. "If you are coming to Bellingwood tonight, could I invite you to my home for dinner? I would like to talk with you about something."

There was silence on the other end of the call, then, "What in the world could you possibly want with me?"

"Mrs. Maxwell, I found a package in an old dresser that I bought at the Antique Shoppe downtown. I think it might be pictures of you as a child. There's a Christmas card from Beatrice Hogan and in it is a letter she helped your mother write to you."

"Oh my," the woman said and Polly heard her drop into a chair, then the man's voice say, "Mother, are you okay? Marian?"

"I'm fine," the woman said quietly. "You have pictures of my family?" There was a catch in her voice.

"I think so. I certainly hope that I have the right family."

"Beatrice Hogan was my mother's nurse before she died. I heard from her several times through the years. She never said anything about pictures or a letter, though." The woman chuckled, "But then, she might have thought she'd already given them to my parents. I visited her once or twice and she wasn't all that tidy."

"This was jammed in the top of the dresser like it had been on the top of a stack and gotten stuck when the drawer was opened."

"After all these years," Marian Maxwell said quietly.

"Would you and your husband like to come for dinner?"

"Let me ask. Sam, would you mind going out to dinner tonight in Bellingwood? The gal who owns Sycamore House has some pictures and a letter that might be from my mother."

The quality of tone was lost as she obviously put her hand over the phone's mouthpiece and then she returned. "We would love to come. What time would you like us to be there?"

"Will six thirty work for you?" Polly asked.

"We'll be there. Should we just come in the front door?"

"That will be fine. A young boy named Jason will be downstairs to greet you and show you to my apartment." It had just hit Polly that Sylvie worked tonight and she was responsible for Jason and Andrew. They would love being part of this.

"We'll see you tonight. Thank you, Miss Giller."

"It's Polly and I look forward to meeting you."

They hung up and Polly squealed.

Henry laughed at her and said, "I don't know if I've ever heard that sound come from you."

"We have to get moving! I know Dad had an artificial tree downstairs and I want to get some Christmas decorations up."

"You're decorating for Christmas now? What about dinner?"

"I have no idea." She took off at a dead run for the back door, leaving a room full of startled animals and Henry behind her. Doug and Billy were coming into the garage to go to their apartment as she ran to where she had stacked her boxes.

"What's up, Polly?" Doug asked.

"I have to find my Dad's Christmas decorations. I've got five hours to decorate the apartment and get dinner on the table." The boys followed her and began to help her sort through the boxes.

"Why are you here and not working?" she asked

"It's really slow right now. We don't have much until after the New Year. We forgot about this part of the job," Billy said.

"Then you should definitely come and have supper with us. It's going to be fun. I found the woman who belongs to those pictures." Polly pushed a stack of boxes aside and handed a table lamp to Billy, who set it down on top of more boxes.

"Where is that tree?" she growled.

"Hello boys," Henry said, entering the fray. "Did you offer to help or did she beg?"

"We offered. She said we could come to dinner," Doug replied, moving more boxes. "Polly, you have a lot of books."

"Yeah, yeah, yeah. There's a tree in here somewhere."

"I found it!" Billy popped up from behind a tall stack of boxes. "It's a tall box. Dude, I'm gonna need help." He started lifting it over his head and both Doug and Henry ran to take it from him.

"Are there any more Christmas boxes?" Polly asked.

"Here's one," he responded. "And a box of ornaments."

Polly pulled her wallet out of her back pocket and handed a twenty dollar bill to Doug. "Would you go downtown and buy me, like, five boxes of white lights?" She pulled another twenty out. "Make it six or seven boxes. Thank you! Billy, can you help us haul these up to the apartment?"

Both boys looked at Henry and he shrugged. Doug left and they carried boxes up the steps to Polly's apartment. She pointed to the corner where her favorite chair sat. "Don't you think the tree would be pretty right there?"

Henry and Billy nodded and she giggled, "Do I have to beg you two to put it up? I need to start dinner and figure out where I'm going to seat everyone. And I have to call Lydia and Adele."

They both stood there and Polly cried, "Please help me!"

Henry opened the top flap of the box with the Christmas tree in it and began pulling green branches out. "How old is this tree?"

"I don't know," she laughed. "The ends are painted the same color as the hole on the trunk. I used to put it together every year." Polly stepped close to him and kissed him on the cheek, "Thank you for helping even if you think I'm crazy."

She stepped close to Billy and he bent backwards at the waist. "What?" she asked, "You don't want me to kiss you?"

"No ma'am," he slyly said. "My girlfriend would kill me."

"You just ma'am'ed me." Polly chuckled.

"On purpose, too," he said and bent over into the box to pull out more branches. Polly gave him a push when she saw that he was nearly off balance and he toppled into the box, knocking it over to the floor. Billy scrambled to get back up and Henry backed away from the two of them. "You're mean, Polly Giller," Billy said.

"I am and I'm a little amped up right now, so it's even worse," she laughed and walked toward the kitchen.

Henry and Billy built the tree from the ground up while she opened cupboards and looked in the refrigerator. "I'll be back. If Doug gets here before me, would you string lights on the tree?" She ran out the front door and down to the kitchen. Sylvie and Rachel were preparing dinner for a party that night. The two looked up when she ran in.

"What's going on, Polly?" Sylvie asked.

"I invited way too many people over to my apartment tonight for dinner and while I have plenty of chicken, I wondered if you had an extra ten pounds of potatoes down here."

Sylvie chuckled and looked to Rachel. "Only at Sycamore House, would she think there was an extra ten pounds of potatoes. Yes, Polly. I do."

"I'll make sure to replace them by tomorrow."

"No, don't worry. I'll stop at the store before I come over. Do you need anything else?"

"I just need to get these boiling for mashed potatoes."

"No you don't," Sylvie said. "We're making loads of mashed potatoes for tonight. Maria is coming down to help when the boys get here. Andrew is babysitting little Salvador. Send Jason down before dinner starts and I'll have the potatoes ready for you."

"Really? Thank you!" Polly hugged her and ran back out and up the stairs, slowing when she got to her front door and took a deep breath, then walked inside. The tree was nearly finished.

"Do you want to put the top on?" Henry asked.

"That's okay. It looks great though."

By six o'clock, the tree was decorated, lights and garland were hung and two tables were set with her mother's china, crystal and silver. Andrew was across the hall with Salvador and Jason was downstairs waiting for the guests. Henry, Doug and Billy had gone home to dress for the evening and Polly was changing clothes. She still couldn't believe she had managed to pull off a dinner party and decorated her apartment in less than six hours. How did people ever make things happen without friends!

The first knock at the door was Lydia. Aaron followed her in, holding a pie carrier. When Polly had called early that afternoon, Lydia had offered to make pie. At that point, refusing would have been suicide.

"Are we the first ones here?" Lydia asked. She looked around, "Your place is gorgeous! You did all this today?"

"Yes and I'm glad to see you. I'm really nervous about tonight. I couldn't leave anyone out, but I think there are too many people. Doug and Billy helped me today and I need to feed them. Jason and Andrew will be here and you and Adele and how could I not invite Henry?"

"Don't worry, dear. When she gets here, take her aside and show her the package. Let her have some time alone with it and if she needs to leave, she can sneak out the back. We'll celebrate no matter what. You've done a wonderful thing today. Stop fretting."

Aaron held up the pies and said, "Kitchen?"

"Oh, I'm sorry, Aaron. I'll take that. Thank you, Lydia."

"Lydia?" he exclaimed. "I'll have you know that I was the one who …"

His wife interrupted him, "The one who did what?"

He grinned and passed the carrier to Polly. "The one who says thank you to my beautiful wife for being so gracious and the one who carried them up here. That's all."

Another knock on the door and a woman's voice tentatively called out, "Hello?"

Polly set the carrier down on the peninsula and ran back to the door. She didn't recognize the couple standing there and asked, "Mr. and Mrs. Maxwell?"

"The nice boy downstairs told us how to find you. Sycamore House is quite lovely," Marian Maxwell said.

"Come on in. Let me take your coats." Polly waited as they removed their coats and she hung them over the coat tree. "I have to apologize. There will be a large group here tonight. People kept helping and I kept inviting them to join us."

Marian Maxwell smiled and said, "It's Christmas. But I hope all of those cars out front aren't for this party."

"No," Polly laughed. "There's a corporate party in the auditorium. Please come in. Before everyone gets here, I'd like to show you what I found."

She led them to the sofa and placed the envelope onto Marian's lap. Sam Maxwell set his large, callused hand on top of his wife's and squeezed it. She gently opened the envelope.

"I'm sorry it isn't as pristine as the day I found it," Polly said. "Several people have read this as I've been looking for you."

There were no words from either of them as she pulled the card out, opened it and thumbed through the pictures. They read the note in the card and she looked at the photographs again.

"I couldn't remember what they looked like," she said quietly. "My two big brothers. I couldn't remember them. Look Sam. These are my brothers."

She ran her finger across the family photograph, stopping to rub the image of her mother and then her father. "I remember that night. People didn't think I would. I was asleep in the car and mommy didn't want to wake me up. We'd been out shopping all day and stopped at the grocery store. Daddy stayed in the car with me when mommy went into the store. I pretended to sleep because I didn't want to walk any more. Then I did fall asleep and woke up when the world exploded. That's all I remember."

"The letter is from your mother," Polly said. "If you want to go into the bedroom to read it, I understand."

Marian looked into her husband's eyes and he shrugged. She opened the letter and her lips moved as she read through it. Sam followed along and his arm reached around her shoulders as Polly watched her eyes fill with tears.

"Oh Sam," Marian said and slumped into him.

Polly turned around and the apartment was empty. She assumed Lydia had corralled them elsewhere. When she turned back, Marian Maxwell was brushing the tears from her eyes.

"I didn't know anything about my past. The Garrisons were wonderful to me, but they didn't have any information about my family. It is so good to know who I was named after. My son gave his little girls my names as their middle names. Now I can tell him that they are from two other women in my family."

"I'm so sorry that I have a house full of people tonight," Polly said. "If you want to go home, we will all understand."

"No!" Marian said. "I would love to meet your friends. This is a celebration! You've given me an amazing gift this Christmas. It's been over fifty-five years and I want to share this."

She looked around, "Where did they go?"

Polly smiled. "They are probably in the hallway. Lydia Merritt is a genius at knowing when not to be in the way. Let me get them." She went to the front door and found everyone milling around. Lydia had baby Salvador in her arms and smiled.

"How are things in there?"

"Things are great," Polly responded. "Come on in and meet the Maxwells. They are looking forward to celebrating tonight."

CHAPTER NINE - EPILOGUE

Room at the inn. Polly thought about how fortunate she was to be able to offer space for the Living Nativity and for animals who needed a home and for a young family whose car had broken down. This was the last night of the Living Nativity. Sycamore House was finally quiet. Polly had driven Jeff to Des Moines earlier in the day so he could catch a flight to Ohio for Christmas with his family. Her friend, Sal, was at Mark Ogden's house decorating for the onslaught of his family from Minnesota. She promised Polly they would spend time together, but Polly wasn't holding out much hope and that was fine.

Jose, Maria and Salvador were still here. The baby was healthy and laughing. Nate and Henry had gotten the car working again and it was parked out front. Jose and Maria had been a huge help to Eliseo and Sylvie throughout the busy week and decided that they would stay until after Christmas. Polly and Eliseo worked out a fair salary for them and she'd let him be the one to pay Jose.

Yesterday morning, when everyone had been down at the barn, Mark showed up with a crate. He opened it and introduced Hansel and Gretel. Hansel, the male cat, was pure black and beautifully sleek. The female, Gretel, was a gorgeous dark calico. They made their way around the barn, cautiously sniffing until they found Tom and Huck's stall. The donkeys were already out in the pasture and both cats climbed through the straw until they found a place to curl up. It had nearly killed Andrew to stay away, but Polly asked him to be quiet so he wouldn't scare them.

According to Mark, the cats had come from another barn and were more comfortable being here than inside. As long as there was food, water and shelter, they would be content and happy. Polly had already added a large bag of cat food to the feed room.

While they worked, they tried to ignore the cats, hoping they would get comfortable enough to explore the barn. Andrew was sitting on a bench when Tom came back in looking for some affection. Before they knew it, a black cat was standing beside Andrew. He tentatively reached out his hand and the cat brushed his face on him. Tom got closer to the cat and Andrew grew still. The moment passed, the donkey pushed his head against Andrew's leg, and the cat jumped down.

One year ago, Polly had a dog and two cats. Now there were more animals in her life than she knew what to do with. Eliseo could never leave. Jason had come out of Nat's stall to watch Andrew with the donkey and the cat and she heard him laughing quietly as he went back in to finish mucking it out. One year ago, these boys lived in a small apartment with their mother. Today they lived in the same apartment, but because of the family's involvement at Sycamore House, they had room to play and grow. Both of them had grown up a lot since she first met them.

This morning everyone was there again. Weekends were fun at the barn. Jason and Andrew didn't have to be in school and they all spent time with the animals. Hansel and Gretel had apparently found their way around the entirety of the barn overnight. When Eliseo opened the doors, he found them curled up in Demi's stall tucked in for warmth.

Jason and Andrew were bringing the donkeys up for the Living Nativity one last time. They had already donned their costumes and were down with Eliseo. Polly put the finishing touches on dinner. She had invited all her friends, and everyone but Jeff would be there before they began their family Christmas celebrations. Dinner would be simple. Sandwiches and appetizers, salads and plenty of crackers, chips, and cheese.

Andy and Len were back from their honeymoon and were bringing his daughter, Ellen. Beryl had come out of seclusion, announcing she was finished for a month. She needed a vacation. Billy and Rachel were coming and Doug had finally gotten up the nerve to ask Anita Banks for a date. He was bringing her and texted Polly that she had to be nice because he was really nervous. Polly had made Sylvie promise to take a long afternoon nap and stay away from the kitchen this evening. The Merritts were coming, Sal and Mark would be in attendance, and Nate and Joss Mikkels said they wouldn't miss it. The party would be a grand way to celebrate friends, both old and new.

Polly dimmed the overhead lights, allowing the strands of white Christmas lights to stand out. She lit candles in the kitchen and turned on the flickering electric candles in her windows. The coffee was brewed, cider was bubbling, hot water was ready for cocoa and the egg nog poured into a punch bowl. She was ready.

Cars slowly passed the Nativity outside and some pulled into the parking lot. People walked over to spend a few moments considering a night long ago, when the world changed forever. Each night the tableau had been filled with different participants and each night Polly spent time watching as they prepared themselves to represent that very holy family, the shepherds and wise men, who were the first to greet the Savior. Those moments were filled with reverence, even amidst the craziness of donkeys and sheep, attempts to keep warm and the bright lights of cars flashing over them as the twenty-first century clashed with images from two thousand years ago.

She looked out the window and watched as the scene played out one more time. Lydia's Jeep pulled into the lot and Beryl glanced up to the window and waved at Polly.

Polly propped her front door open. Footsteps coming up her back stairs, along with Obiwan's wagging tail, told her that Henry had arrived. She met him at the top of the steps and when he kissed her, she allowed the moment to take her breath away. She was going to savor every moment this evening with her friends. She hadn't felt this much love since she'd been home with her father, Mary, and Sylvester. That had been too many years ago.

"Halloooo," Lydia called.

Polly pulled back from Henry and said, "I'm glad you're here. Did you have a good day?"

"I think the house is finally ready for Mom and Dad."

"What time will they be in tomorrow?"

"Knowing Dad, they'll get in tonight, but they really aren't supposed to be home until tomorrow afternoon."

Polly had spent time with him yesterday scrubbing down bathrooms, washing curtains and re-making the beds. When she'd left, the house had been sparkling, but Henry told her this morning that he was still cleaning and decorating. She supposed it would be difficult having your mother return to her old home. His mother couldn't be that much trouble, though. Polly tried not to be nervous about meeting them and then shook her head. Now wasn't the time to think about that. She had guests.

They went into the living room and saw that Andy, Len and Ellen, Joss and Nate and Sylvie were also there.

"Merry Christmas!" resounded through the room as everyone greeted each other. Billy, Rachel, Doug and Anita all showed up, then Eliseo came in with Jose, Maria and Salvador. Eliseo was carrying the baby and laughing at something Jose had said. Mark and Sal were the last to arrive and Polly smiled and shook her head when they walked in holding hands. Sal's laughter was contagious and soon they were mingling with everyone.

Polly turned on Christmas music. She was glad to not have the pressure of a large Christmas party this year.

"I'm glad you are all here tonight," she said. "You are my family and I couldn't imagine not spending Christmas with you. One of the best parts of family is that it grows. Andy and Len are back and I am thankful he is part of my family. Welcome home."

She reached over and took Henry's hand. "This last week

Henry and I have been working on a new business deal and we are going to begin a partnership ... "

Before she could finish her sentence, there were gasps and smatterings of applause around the room. "No, not that," she scolded. "A business partnership. We are purchasing the old hotel out by the new winery. Sycamore Inn will open next summer or fall. Bellingwood needs a hotel and I can hardly wait to begin work on this. I've spoken with both Eliseo and Rachel. Rachel will begin working for us full-time just after the New Year. She will help in the kitchen and be responsible for the guest rooms here at Sycamore House, leaving Eliseo more time to be outside. This spring he is going to plant a rather large vegetable garden out back and we will start having a monthly Farmer's Market here in the spring. It is going to be an exciting year and I look forward to our continued growth. I wish Jeff were here to celebrate with us this evening since he has been such a big part of everything."

"To Sycamore House!" Beryl said, lifting a glass of eggnog.

"To Sycamore House!" came the response from the others.

"Thank you all for being part of my life this last year," Polly said.

Sal stepped forward and hugged her. "I'm proud of you," she said. "I knew you had this inside you. Your dad would be proud."

She moved back giving way to Joss and Nate. Joss hugged her as well and then whispered into her ear, "Our lives are getting bigger next year, too. We've finally decided to do something about adopting and everything is in place. We weren't going to say anything until we were approved, but it's starting!"

Polly looked up at Nate with excitement. "I'm so happy for you two. Did you know?" she turned to Henry.

"Know what?" he asked.

"They're adopting a child!"

"Congratulations, man," Henry clapped his friend on the back. "Before you know it, you'll own a minivan instead of the Impala."

"Bet me," Nate laughed. "That was the first conversation I got out of the way. No minivans allowed."

"He's not kidding. He made me promise that we wouldn't ever

park a minivan in our garage," Joss said. "I can agree to that."

Polly hugged her, "I really am excited for you. This is going to be a great year!"

When she had finally spoken to everyone and they were milling around the food buffet, she stepped back into Henry's arm. "You know, it's hard for me to believe all that has happened this year."

"It's been a good year."

"I barreled through, hoping I wasn't making some huge mistake. But when I kept meeting all of these wonderful people, I knew it wasn't a mistake. Can you imagine what next year is going to be like? I'm going to need a bigger place just to have all of my friends in the same room at once."

"Pretty girl, I love watching you make friends. Nothing stops you when you decide someone is going to be part of your life."

"I'm glad you are part of my life."

"Me too. We've had a lot of fun so far."

"And we're going to have more fun next year!"

They had backed away from the main party and were standing next to the Christmas tree. Polly reached over and took a small package off one of the branches and handed it to Henry. "This is for you," she said.

He took it. "I thought we were exchanging gifts on Wednesday with my family."

"I know, but I want you to have this now."

Henry opened the box and kissed Polly on the nose. "You're a nut," he said.

The engraved pen and pencil set read, "Sturtz & Giller, Partners, Bellingwood, Iowa."

"I had one made for myself, too. We're official now."

"I like being official with you," he laughed and kissed her on the lips. "Merry Christmas."

"Merry Christmas, Henry Sturtz. I love you."

Made in the USA
Columbia, SC
09 May 2020